B.J. .... best-
selli.................. .... er as
an award-winning newsp...... ....ist and author of
thirty-seven published sh.............. .....ves in Montana
.... her husband, Park.........
.... n not writing, she ....
.... act her at bjdaniel ....
.... anielsauthor.

.... s Fossen, a *USA TODAY* bestselling author, has
.... ver seventy-five novels, with millions of copies
.... r books in print worldwide. She's received a
.... sellers' Best Award and an RT Reviewers' Choice
.... Book Award. She was also a finalist for a prestigious
.... ® Award. You can contact the author through her
.... te at www.dcloresfossen.com.

Also by B.J. Daniels

Cowboy's Redemption
Dark Horse
Dead Ringer
Rough Rider
Renegade's Pride
Outlaw's Honor
Hero's Return
Rancher's Dream

Also by Delores Fossen

Cowboy Above the Law
Always a Lawman
Gunfire on the Ranch
Lawman from Her Past
Roughshod Justice
Grayson
Dade
Nate
Kade
Gage

Discover more at millsandboon.co.uk

HARD RUSTLER

B.J. DANIELS

FINGER ON
THE TRIGGER

DELORES FOSSEN

MILLS & BOON

First Published in Great Britain 2018
by Mills & Boon, an imprint of HarperCollins*Publishers*
1 London Bridge Street, London, SE1 9GF

Hard Rustler © 2018 Barbara Heinlein
Finger on the Trigger © 2018 Delores Fossen

ISBN: 978-0-263-26591-0

0918

MIX
Paper from
responsible sources
FSC® C007454

This book is produced from independently certified FSC™ paper to ensure responsible forest management.

For more information visit: www.harpercollins.co.uk/green

Printed and bound in Spain
by CPI, Barcelona

HARD RUSTLER

B.J. DANIELS

This book is for Julie Simundson Nagy, a true fan, who has been a bright spot in so many of my days. Writing is such a solitary endeavor with lots of stress. I will see Julie and she will remind me that I'm not alone in this. Her smile and enthusiasm keep me grounded. Thank you, Julie!

Chapter One

As her sports car topped the rise, Annabelle Clementine looked out at the rugged country spread before her and felt her heart drop. She'd never thought she'd see so many miles of wild winter Montana landscape ever again. At least, she'd hoped not.

How could she have forgotten the remoteness? The vastness? The isolation? There wasn't a town in sight. Or a ranch house. Or another living soul.

She glanced down at her gas gauge. It hovered at empty. She'd tried to get gas at the last station, but her credit card wouldn't work and she'd gone through almost all of her cash. She'd put in what fuel she could with the change she was able scrape up, but it had barely moved the gauge. If she ran out of gas before she reached Whitehorse…well, it would just be her luck, wouldn't it?

She let the expensive silver sports car coast down the mountain toward the deep gorge of the Missouri River, thankful that most of the snow was high in the mountains and not on the highway. She didn't know what she would have done if the roads had been icy since she hadn't seen a snow tire since she'd left Montana.

The motor coughed. She looked down at the gauge. The engine had to be running on fumes. What was she going to do? It was still miles to Whitehorse. Tears burned her eyes, but she refused to cry. Yes, things were bad. Really bad. But—

She was almost to the river bottom when she saw it. At a wide spot where the river wound on its way through Montana east to the Mississippi, a pickup and horse trailer were pulled off to the side of the highway. Her pulse jumped at just the thought of another human being—let alone the possibility of getting some fuel. If she could just get to Whitehorse...

But as she descended the mountain, she didn't see anyone around the pickup or horse trailer. What if the rig had been left beside the road and the driver was nowhere to be found? Maybe there would be a gas can in the back of the pickup or—*Have you stooped so low that now you would steal gas?*

Fortunately, she wasn't forced to answer that. She spotted a cowboy standing on the far side of the truck. Her instant of relief was quickly doused as she looked around and realized how alone the two of them were, out here in the middle of nowhere.

Don't be silly. What are the chances the cowboy is a serial killer, rapist, kidnapper, ax murderer...? The motor sputtered as if taking its last gasp as she slowed. It wasn't as if she had a choice. She hadn't seen another car for over an hour. For miles she'd driven through open country dotted occasionally with cows but no people. And she knew there was nothing but rugged country the rest of the way north to Whitehorse.

If there had been any other way to get where she was headed, she would have taken it. But her options had been limited for some time now.

And today, it seemed, her options had come down to this cowboy and possible serial killer rapist kidnapper ax murderer.

She let the car glide into the spot next to where the cowboy had pulled off the highway. *I'll just bum a little fuel and be on my way. Nothing to worry about.* Just the thought made her laugh. Her life was one big worry right now, she fretted, as she took in the rangy-looking cowboy standing by his truck.

"What's the worst that could happen?" She groaned. *Taking risks is what got you into this mess.* Like she had to be reminded.

The engine let out a final cough and died. Committed now, she had no choice as she braked next to the horse trailer. Turning off the key in the ignition, she checked her makeup and hair in the mirror. *You're Annabelle Clementine. You can do this.* The woman who stared back at her from the mirror looked skeptical at best.

Bucking up her courage, she stepped out of the car, careful not to let her last pair of expensive heels get muddy. "Excuse me?" she called, determined also not to get too far away from her open car door. "I'm afraid I have a small problem and really could use some help."

She was ready to make a hasty retreat back into the car, if need be. Not that she would be going far if things went south. But at least she could lock herself in. She instantly regretted the fact that she'd bought a canvas-topped convertible, which had been perfect in Southern California.

The cowboy had his back to her and hadn't looked up from where he'd been digging around in the back of his pickup bed.

"Excuse me?" she tried again. He had to have heard her. But so far, he hadn't acknowledged her presence in any way.

Forced to move away from the car, she took in the cowboy as she approached and wasn't impressed with what she saw. But then again, she'd grown up with cowboys so she'd never understood the fascination. Admittedly, this one was tall, broad shouldered, slim hipped, long legged and not bad from the backside.

Unfortunately, everything else about him looked worn and dirty, from his jeans, boots and canvas jacket to the Stetson on the too-long dark hair curling at the nape of his red neck.

At her approach, he gave her a quick glance over his shoulder. She could see little of his face. He wore mirrored sunglasses against the winter glare, his hat pulled low. Under the dark shadow of his Stetson, she glimpsed several week's growth of beard, making him look even more craggy and unkempt. No designer stubble on this cowboy.

Either he'd been on the range for days or this was as good as it got with him.

You're not marrying him. You're just bumming fuel. "Hello?" she said louder and with more attitude as he went back to what he was doing.

"There a problem?" he drawled in a low, lazy tone as he finally finished and turned, seemingly reluctantly, to give her his attention. She saw that he'd been feeding his dog in the back of the pickup. The dog—little more than a puppy—was a furry mutt with one blue eye and one brown one circled by a patch of black. He didn't look much better than his owner.

She shifted her gaze back to the cowboy who was looking at her car as if he'd never seen one like it before. *Probably doesn't get off the ranch much.*

He slowly slid his gaze back to her with a nonchalance that made her grind her teeth.

"Yes, there is a problem." She'd thought she'd already told him that.

He lifted the brim of his hat, dropped his sunglasses down to look over them for a moment. She caught a glimpse of brown eyes as he surveyed her, making her feel nearly naked under the black cashmere sweater and slacks she was wearing, before he lifted his sunglasses again.

"I'm afraid I forgot to buy gas at the last station," she said, wanting to get this over with as quickly as possible—even if it did make her look like a fool. She had worse problems. "I was wondering if you might have some gas that I could borrow? Just enough to get me into town?"

"Borrow?" He chuckled at that. "And town being?"

She hated to even admit where she was headed. "Whitehorse."

"That's another hour up the road."

As if she didn't know that. "My car used more gas than I thought it would." She gave a nervous laugh, hating that she had to resort to acting as if she didn't have a brain. Back when she was making money, fuel was never an issue. She hadn't realized how much a lot of things cost—until she couldn't pay for them anymore.

He nodded, glancing toward the river as if considering her request. "I suppose I could siphon some out of one of my tanks." He didn't sound thrilled about it. Nor had he moved.

"I would appreciate that so much." She glanced at her watch.

"Got some place to be, do you?"

"I have an appointment."

"In Whitehorse?" From under the brim of his hat and behind the mirrored sunglasses, he studied her a few moments more before he sighed. "Best pull up next to my pickup while I grab a hose."

She feared the car wouldn't start, let alone move. But there must have been just enough fumes left for her to pull up before it died again. She shut off the engine, staying in the car to pop the gas compartment open and watch him move slow as molasses. He acted as if he had all day. *He* probably did.

Patience had never been one of her strong suits. She tapped a toe as she heard him talking to his dog, mumbling so she couldn't make out a word. As if she didn't know he was giving the dog an earful about her.

The dog, still in the pickup bed, wagged its tail enthusiastically at whatever the cowboy said. Whatever he was saying, he certainly found it amusing from that hint of a grin under the beard. Annabelle consoled herself with the thought that the mutt was probably the closest thing the cowboy could get to a female companion.

After a good five to ten minutes, he finished. She hadn't thought past getting enough gas to get to Whitehorse. Now her stomach clenched at a thought. Not only should she offer him money, but he also might demand it. And since she had no money and doubted he took credit cards—even ones that weren't frozen for lack of payment...

She watched him walk to his pickup to put the hose away and knew what she had to do. It was the coward's way out. But she told herself that she had no choice. She'd been telling herself that for months now. Not that it made her feel any better as she quickly started her car and threw it into reverse.

Whirring down the passenger side window, she called out, "Thank you so much. If you're ever in Whitehorse..." With that she took off, torn between guilt and glee over seeing that he'd given her almost a full tank of gas.

When she dared look back, she saw him standing by his pickup shaking his head as he watched her leave. She thought of that glimpse of golden brown. Even shaded under the brim of his old Stetson, those eyes... They'd almost seemed...familiar.

Chapter Two

Dawson Rogers swore as he pulled off his worn Stetson. Raking a hand through his hair, he watched the silver sports car take off like a bat out of hell.

"Annabelle Clementine." He said the name like a curse. For years, he'd only seen her staring back at him from glossy women's magazine ads. He'd been just fine knowing there was no chance that he'd ever lay eyes on her in the flesh again. She'd been real clear about never setting foot in this state again when she'd left all those years ago.

So what was she doing headed for Whitehorse?

That his heart was still pounding only made him more furious with himself. When he'd heard her voice behind him…he couldn't believe it. He'd thought for sure that his worn-out, dog-weary body was playing tricks on him. He'd frozen in place, counting to ten and then ten again, afraid to turn around for fear he'd be wrong—or worse—right.

Now he swore, remembering his reaction to just the sound of her voice. Could he be a bigger fool?

And yet that voice had brought it all back. The ache in his belly, the stompin' she'd done on his heart. Worse, the hope that set a fire inside him at just the sound of it. In that instant, he'd wanted it to be her more than he'd wanted his next breath. After everything she'd done to him, he'd actually felt a spike of joy at the thought of seeing her again.

And still he hadn't turned around, because he'd known once he did, the disappointment would be as painful as the last time he'd seen her.

Turning, he'd seen her standing there and thought, *Damn, the woman is even more beautiful than when she'd hightailed it out of here.*

He'd been shocked—and still was. Annie. In the flesh. That she hadn't changed except to become more gorgeous had left him shaken. A dust devil of emotions whirled inside him as he watched her drive away.

"What is she doing back here?" he demanded as the pup came over to the side of the pickup bed to lick his hand.

Sadie wagged her tail in response. "What am I doing asking you?" He ruffled the dog's fur. Still, he found himself squinting after the sports car as it climbed the mountain on the other side of the river and disappeared around a curve. "What's a woman who said she'd never set foot in Whitehorse doing back here? If I hadn't seen her with my own eyes…"

For just a moment there, earlier, before she'd asked for gas, he'd thought…

Hell, he didn't want to think about what he'd thought as he shoved his hat back on. "Let's get on home," he said to the pup as he reminded himself that Annabelle Clementine's coming back had nothing to do with him.

He told himself that he shouldn't have been surprised that she hadn't changed. Still, it galled him. Her clothes might be more expensive and she drove a much fancier car, but she was still the same girl who'd looked down her nose at him—and Whitehorse—all those years ago.

It nagged at him. What could have brought her back? He shook his head, telling himself it was obviously none of his business. Best thing he could do was to forget about her—something he'd been working on for some time now.

After two weeks in hunting camp, he recalled that before he'd seen her, all he'd wanted was to get home, have a hot shower and climb into a warm, soft bed. If he hadn't stopped beside the road to take a leak, let Sadie out and give the pup a snack...well, he might not have seen her at all.

The only thing that didn't surprise him, he told himself as he lifted Sadie into the pickup's front seat and climbed behind the wheel, was that the woman hadn't given him the time of day. Hell, he couldn't even be sure she remembered him. After all, it had been... How many years *had* it been? He wondered with a frown as he started the truck engine.

Thirteen. He let out a low whistle. Sadie's ears perked up, but she lay back down and closed her eyes for the ride home.

And it wasn't like Annie had ever given him a thought since she'd been gone, he reminded himself. She'd made it perfectly clear that they had no future before she'd left right after high school to find fame and fortune.

Dawson pointed the pickup toward Whitehorse, all the time trying to imagine what could have brought her back. Certainly not her grandmother's funeral. Only her two sisters had made it back for that. Of course, they'd attended the funeral and left right away, but at least they'd shown up. He shook his head, thinking that he'd expected better of the girl he'd fallen in love with all those years ago. Given how much her grandmother had doted on her...

But he reminded himself that he'd *always* been wrong about the woman. He could no more predict what Annabelle was going to do than predict the Montana weather. He thought of that young fool cowboy who'd saved every dime he made that year to promise her something that would make her stay. He growled under his breath at the memory.

Well, he wasn't that young fool anymore. Which was

why he was going to give her a wide berth as long as she was in town. Not that he suspected it would be for long. Knowing her, she would be hightailing it back to California as fast as she could. Back to her fancy life in the spotlight.

"Which is just fine with us, huh, Sadie," he said to his pup. "Don't need the likes of her around here messing with our minds." Sadie barked in answer and curled closer to him, making him laugh. "This was before your time," he said to the dog, "But that woman was once nothing but walking heartache for this cowboy. Fortunately, I'm not that man anymore."

His words sounded hollow, even to him. He felt his face flush at how much gas he'd given her and mentally kicked himself. He should have left her beside the road to fend for herself. But then, he'd never been able to say no to her—even when he should have known that a girl like her wanted something better than a cowboy like him.

ANNABELLE PUT THE cowboy and his dog behind her as she drove north. She was determined that nothing would get in her way. Once she did what she'd come for, she was out of here. Another one of those limited options.

She took the back way into the small Western town. The first settlement of Whitehorse had been nearer the Missouri River. But when the railroad came through, the town migrated north, taking the name with it. Old Town Whitehorse, as it was now known, was little more than a ghost town to the south.

Not that Whitehorse proper was a thriving metropolis. The whole town was only ten blocks square. Nothing but a siding along the railroad tracks more than a hundred years ago, it had become a small rural town like a lot of small rural Montana towns.

Why her grandmother had settled here was still a

mystery, but when Annabelle's parents had been killed, Grandma Frannie had taken Annabelle and her two sisters in without hesitation. Annabelle had grown up here, dreaming of a life she envisioned far from this dusty old Western town.

As she drove down the tree-lined street with the large houses that backed onto the Milk River, images of her childhood flickered like the winter sun coming through the leafless cottonwood trees. From as far back as she could remember, she'd grown up with one thing in mind: getting out of this town and making something of her life.

That sick feeling she'd become acquainted with over the past few months now settled in her stomach. Right now, she couldn't face even thinking about how she'd messed up. Sitting up a little straighter behind the wheel of the car, she assured herself that everything was going to be fine.

She would just take care of business and put all the unpleasantness behind her. As she tried to look for a silver lining in all this, she noticed that she still had plenty of gas. It should last her for what little time she would be here, thanks to that cowboy. She shoved away the guilt. If she ever saw him again…

Down the block, she spotted the house. Her foot came off the gas pedal, the car slowing as she felt a rush of déjà vu. The house hadn't changed—just like she doubted the town had—and for a moment it was as if she'd never left. So much had happened to her, she'd expected this part of her past would have changed, somehow.

Instead, it looked so much the same, she almost expected Frannie to come out on the porch as Annabelle pulled up in front of the large, two-story house and shut off the engine. The key to the front door was in her pocket, but she wasn't ready to go inside. Not yet. Glancing at her watch, she saw that she'd gotten here early. There was no sign of the Realtor. Taking a breath, she let it out and tried to relax as she studied the house.

The white siding could use an overall paint job and the emerald trim needed a touch-up. But if she closed her eyes, she could picture herself and her sisters, the three Clementine girls, on that wide porch drinking Grandma Frannie's lemonade and giggling like the schoolgirls they'd been.

She hadn't realized that she'd closed her eyes until she felt them burn with tears. Her guilt was like one of her grandmother's knitting needles to her heart. Yes, she should have made it to Frannie's funeral. She'd had her reasons, and they hadn't all been out of embarrassment for the way her life had turned out.

Her grandmother would have understood because Annabelle had always been the favorite. At least, that's what she told herself.

"You're so much like me, Annabelle Clementine, that sometimes I swear you'll be the death of me." Then Grandma Frannie's expression would soften and she'd press a cool palm to Annabelle's cheek. "So much like me. It's like seeing myself at your age."

"That's why I'm your favorite," she'd say, and her grandmother would shake her head and laugh before telling her to run along outside.

But it had to have been true. Otherwise, why would Frannie have left her the only thing she had of any value— this house. And left it only to her instead of to all three sisters?

A tap on the passenger-side window startled her. Her eyes flew open, but it took a moment to chase away the bittersweet memories along with the guilt and the tears.

REALTOR MARY SUE Linton glanced at the silver sports car and shook her head. Leave it to Annabelle to show up in something like that. She shouldn't have been surprised since this was the Annabelle Clementine she'd known since grade school.

She had been surprised, though, when her former classmate had called and asked Mary Sue to represent her in the sale. Not surprised. Shocked. The two of them had never been friends, traveling in a completely different circle of friends, even as small as the classes had been. The truth was that Annabelle hadn't uttered two words to her throughout four years of high school. Did people still say stuck-up?

Blonde and blue-eyed, with a figure that Mary Sue would have killed for, Annabelle was The Girl Most Likely to Become Famous. At least, that's what it had said in their senior class yearbook. Everyone knew Annabelle was going to be somebody. Annabelle had said it enough times.

But, then again, she'd also said that she would never come back to Whitehorse. And here she was.

Still, why come all this way to sell her grandmother's house? Mary Sue had told her on the phone that she could deal with everything but the paperwork and save her the trip. She had expected Annabelle to jump at it. Instead, the woman had insisted on coming back to "handle" things.

"If you don't trust me to get you the best price…" Mary Sue had started to say, "you can kiss my—"

But Annabelle had interrupted with, "It's *my* grandmother's house."

Right. Just like it had been *her* grandmother's funeral. Everyone in town had turned out. Annabelle's two sisters had flown in and out. No Annabelle, though. So was Mary Sue supposed to believe the house had sentimental value to this woman? Not likely.

After tapping on the sports car window, she bent down and looked in. One glance and it was clear that her former classmate had aged well. She looked better than she had in high school. Mary Sue felt that old stab of jealousy.

She started to tap again, but to her surprise, Annabelle appeared to be furtively wiping away tears. Shocked at such a sign of emotion, Mary Sue was taken aback. Maybe she was wrong about Annabelle. Maybe she did have a heart. Maybe she did care about her grandmother. Maybe she even cared about this house and Whitehorse and the people she'd once snubbed.

The thought almost made her laugh though as her former classmate climbed out of the convertible sports car saying, "Okay, let's get this over with so I can get out of this one-horse town."

DAWSON UNLOADED THE horse trailer, parked it and went into the ranch house he'd built himself. He'd worked hard the past thirteen years and now had a place he was proud of on the family ranch. The oldest son of two, he'd had to take over helping his mother run the ranch after his father had died. He'd worked hard and was proud of what he'd been able to accomplish. Annabelle wasn't the only one who'd done well over the years, he told himself with no small amount of defensiveness.

"Got a chip on your shoulder, do you?" he grumbled with a curse. He'd been thinking about her again. All the way to town he'd been trying to exorcize her from his thoughts with little luck. Before she'd left town, she'd made him feel as if he was never going to amount to anything. It still stuck in his craw.

He kept seeing her sitting in her car while he refueled it. She hadn't even had the good grace to look at him— not to mention acknowledge that she'd once known him. Known him damned well, too.

Dawson gave that memory an angry shove away. When

Annabelle Clementine had left town in a cloud of dust years ago, she'd said she was never looking back. Well, today proved that, didn't it?

Worked up over his run-in with her, he told himself he just needed a hot shower and clean clothes. But as he caught his reflection in the bathroom mirror, he came to a startled stop and had to laugh. He wouldn't even recognize himself after two weeks in a hunting camp in the Missouri Breaks.

He stared at his grizzled face and filthy, camp-worn clothes, seeing what she'd seen today. Even if she had recognized him, seeing him like that would only have confirmed what she'd thought of him all those years ago. He looked like a man who wasn't going anywhere.

Stripping down, he turned on the shower and stepped in. The warm water felt like heaven as he began to suds up in a fury. He just wanted that woman out of his hair—and his head. But his thoughts went straight as an arrow to that image of her standing beside the river. Her long blond hair gleaming in the sunlight and that black outfit hugging every unforgettable curve he'd once known so well. Growling, he turned the water to cold.

Out of the shower and toweling himself off, he looked at his reflection in the mirror again. Was it really possible that she hadn't known him? He reached for his razor, telling himself it didn't matter. With a curse, he acknowledged that he'd been lying to himself for years about his feelings for her—ever since that day he'd rescued her from his tree house when she was five.

And he'd rescued her again today, he thought with a curse. He just never learned.

ANNABELLE TOOK THE key from her pocket and opened her grandmother's front door, Mary Sue Linton at her elbow. Taking a deep breath, she stepped inside, bracing herself for more painful memories. Instead, shock stopped her cold just inside the door.

"You can't sell the house like this," Mary Sue said, stating the obvious next to her. "I thought you said your sisters cleaned everything out?"

"They said they took what they wanted." She couldn't believe what she was seeing. Her grandmother hadn't been a packrat, she'd been a hoarder. The house was crammed full of…stuff. She could barely see the floor. The rooms appeared to be filled with furniture, knickknacks, stacks of newspapers and magazines, bags of clothing and clutter. The house looked more like a crowded old antique shop than a home. Unfortunately it didn't take a trained eye to see that all of this wasn't even junkshop worthy.

"What am I supposed to do with all of this?" she demanded. "I can't very well have a garage sale this time of year. If there was anything in all this mess worth selling." It was late November. Christmas was only weeks away.

Mary Sue shrugged. "You could hire someone to help you pack it all up. Unfortunately, the local charity shop can't take most of this. If there are things you want to save—"

"No."

"I was going to say that you could put them into a storage shed."

Annabelle was shaking her head, overwhelmed as they worked their way along the paths through the house.

"Otherwise, I could give you some names of people who might be able to help you at least haul it out to the dump."

"Great. How long is that going to take? I need to get this house on the market right away." She followed the narrow trails, going from room to room, Mary Sue on her heels, until she reached what had once been a bedroom but now looked more like a storage room where a bomb had gone off.

"This is no normal hoarding," Mary Sue said. "It looks like someone ransacked this room."

Annabelle agreed it did appear that someone had torn into all the boxes and dumped the contents on the floor. Her grandmother before she died? Her sisters when they'd come back for the funeral?

"Look at the window," Mary Sue said in a hoarse whisper as she grabbed Annabelle's arm, her fingernails digging into tender flesh.

"Ouch." She jerked free and kicked aside some of the mess to move to the window, which was now half open, the screen torn. "The lock is broken."

Behind her, Mary Sue let out a shudder. "Someone broke in."

That was the way it appeared, although she couldn't imagine in her wildest dreams why they would want to. She closed the window and turned to find Mary Sue hugging herself.

"Whoever broke in isn't here anymore," she tried to assure the Realtor. "Let's look upstairs. Maybe it's better." Unfortunately, the upstairs wasn't any better; both bedrooms were stacked full of clutter, including her grandmother's old room.

Back downstairs, she took another look at the front downstairs bedroom. It wasn't quite as full as the others. She checked the closet, found what must be her grandmother's clothing and assumed that, as Frannie got older, she'd moved downstairs.

"Could this be anymore outdated?" Mary Sue called from the kitchen.

"I think I can clean out one of the downstairs bedrooms so at least I'll have a place I can stay," Annabelle said as

she joined her in the kitchen. The front bedroom downstairs had been hers growing up.

Mary Sue didn't seem to hear her. Instead, she was
frowning at the clipboard she had in her hands.

"What?" Annabelle demanded. "Don't tell me there is
another problem."

"No, not exactly. But it is strange. This is a layout of the
house I got from the records department at the courthouse,"
she said, indicating the sheet on her clipboard. "That wall
shouldn't be there."

"What?"

"This shows an alcove."

"An alcove? Maybe it's back there behind all the junk
and you just can't see it."

Mary Sue's frown deepened. "Do you remember an alcove from when you were growing up here?"

She was supposed to remember an alcove? Seriously?
"No. The plans for the house must be outdated."

"Not according to the courthouse. Your grandmother
bought this house when she was in her twenties so she
had it for…"

"She was seventy-six when she died, so she had it for
more than fifty years." Annabelle hadn't realized how long
Frannie had lived in Whitehorse until she'd seen it in the
obituary that one of her sisters had sent her. It hadn't been
out of kindness that Chloe had mailed it to her. Her older
sister had never been that subtle. Both Chloe and Tessa
Jane—TJ—had tried to make her feel guilty about their
grandmother leaving her the house—let alone Annabelle
missing the funeral.

"Frannie owned this house almost from the time it
was built," Mary Sue was saying. "So if anyone made
the changes, it had to have been your grandmother. Why
would she wall up an alcove? I wonder what's behind it?"

"Okay, you're giving me the creeps now," Annabelle said. "Clearly, you have the plans for the wrong house. Aren't there a bunch of houses along this street with similar floor plans?"

Mary Sue nodded, but didn't look convinced. "I can check at the courthouse again I guess. But you have to admit, if the plans are right, then it is more than a little odd to wall up the alcove, let alone—"

"You're letting your imagination run away with you. You *knew* my grandmother."

With a lift of one eyebrow, Mary Sue said, "She said her husband died before she moved to Whitehorse, but what if—"

"Seriously? You think my grandfather's body is stuffed in there?"

"Ever seen the play *Arsenic and Old Lace*?"

"Frannie Clementine was one of the most kind and generous people in town. She wouldn't hurt a fly." Standing just over five feet, Frannie had been a tiny, sweet-tempered woman who loved kids, garage sales and cooking. She attended church every Sunday, come rain or shine or snow.

Annabelle could tell that Mary Sue was enjoying trying to scare her. Was it any wonder that they hadn't been friends in high school?

"Just sayin'," the Realtor said, clearly trying to hide a grin. "Did you know that since her death right before Halloween last month, kids are saying that this house is haunted?"

"That's ridiculous. Just because she died in this house…" Annabelle tried to hide the shudder that moved through her at the thought. If one of her neighbors, old Inez Gilbert, hadn't come over to check on Frannie, she would have been lost in all this mess for weeks. That thought did nothing to improve the situation.

"On Halloween some kids saw what they said was a ghost moving around in the house. They said it looked like an old woman dressed in all white and—"

"Stop," Annabelle snapped, having had enough. The house was creepy as it was with all the memories, not to mention being filled to overflowing with collected junk. She really didn't need this. "It was probably Inez from next door. The woman is a horrible busybody and always has been."

If Mary Sue thought she could scare her, then she didn't know what scary was. Unfortunately, Annabelle did. It was losing a dream job and a fabulous lifestyle, and being forced to do things she'd told herself she would never do, like return to this town and all the memories that came with it.

"The house isn't haunted. There never was an alcove—"

Mary Sue tapped her clipboard. "But the plans—"

"The alcove isn't here now so that's all I care about. I need to get packing and you need to get this house sold. Just get me the names of people who will help clean it out."

Right now, though, she needed a breath of fresh air and Whitehorse had plenty of that. She stepped out onto the front porch, letting the door close behind her. She'd known this wouldn't be easy, but it was turning out to be more difficult than she could have imagined. The memories, the stories, the stupid missing alcove, not to mention all that junk. She definitely had more pressing things to worry about than a bunch of local kids thinking the house was haunted.

The clock was ticking, she thought, looking at her car, the last vestige of her former life other than the clothes on her back. She had to get this house sold.

Mary Sue gritted her teeth. Annabelle annoyed her to no end. "Hasn't changed a bit," she muttered. "Get me this, do this for me." She looked around the house, her gaze going to the kitchen and the missing alcove. "I hope there is a body walled up in there—and a vindictive ghost who hates blondes." That would serve Annabelle right.

She felt guilty, but only a little, for trying to scare her former classmate. But she was still puzzling over the missing alcove as she stepped out onto the porch. Her mother had been a Realtor. Maybe she'd ask her if she knew anything about the old Clementine house, as it was known around town. It sat along with a half dozen others on a street locally and affectionately known as Millionaire's Row. The houses were large, a lot of them the same basic floor plan.

Mary Sue moved to the end of the porch to look back at the rock wall that marked the property line. On the other side of the wall was the Milk River. Between the house and the river, though, were large trees and an expanse of grass broken only by some cracked sidewalk that ended at an old garage that had seen better days.

"That should come down," she said of the dilapidated structure and marked it on her sheet on her clipboard. Through the trees, she could make out only a portion of the neighboring house's eaves in the distance. These really were beautiful old houses along this street, so private because of the old-growth trees and the huge lots. Not exactly Millionaire's Row now, but definitely prime real estate in this town.

"So where can I reach you?" Mary Sue asked, turning to Annabelle who appeared distracted. Not that she could blame her. The supermodel had quite a job before her.

"You have my cell number and you know where to find me. I'll be staying here."

"In the house?" Mary Sue couldn't help her surprise.

Annabelle turned to look at her. "Why *wouldn't* I stay here?"

"No reason, except…" She remembered all the clutter and the fact that Frannie had died here. Not that unusual for a woman her age, but still, add to that the walled-up alcove… Mary Sue shivered.

While she had been trying to scare Annabelle earlier, she had to admit that the house had an odd feel to it. Maybe it was just her, but there was something… Or maybe she had managed to scare herself more than she had Annabelle and all because of that discrepancy in the floor plan—and the fact that someone had broken into the house and might come back.

She mentioned this to Annabelle who only waved away the idea. "It was probably kids. You know how teenagers are, an empty house, ghost story dares…"

Mary Sue didn't know, but she had a feeling that Annabelle was all too aware of how kids like *that* acted because she'd been one. "I just thought you'd want to stay at the hotel, since that's where your sisters stayed when they came home for the funeral."

Annabelle made an angry sound under her breath. "*They didn't stay here?* No wonder they didn't take much—let alone tell me how full this house was. I thought they were here going through things. From what I can see, they didn't take anything. You were the one who let them into the house with the key I sent you, right?"

Mary Sue sighed, wondering if Annabelle was going to blame her. "Yes, but I didn't come inside. The house was left to you. I was the one who was responsible for opening the door and making sure it was locked when they left. That was all. I wouldn't have felt comfortable going in the house without you."

"So did they take *anything*?"

"Not as far as I could tell." She shrugged. "I let them in, they went into the house, but only for a short period of time, they sat on the porch steps for a little while and then they left and I locked up. From what I saw, they took a few framed photographs, but I think that was about all."

Annabelle looked as if she was going to blow a gasket. "I should have known they wouldn't be of any help. That's just great. Well, they're not getting anything now. Not that there is anything worth keeping in there. From what I've seen, most of the stuff is on the way to the dump just as soon as I can get it loaded up. I'll need help right away. Did you make those calls yet?"

Mary Sue tried not to bristle. "You do realize that tomorrow is Thanksgiving, right?" she asked. "And the day after that is Black Friday, when a lot of people in town will be shopping, either locally or driving the three hours to Billings." Billings was the largest city in Montana and two hundred miles to the south. Mary Sue was planning to go down to shop with a couple of friends, spending the night at a hotel and making a trip out of it.

"Your point?"

"It's going to be hard to find anyone to help this time of year," she said, and added quickly before Annabelle could argue. "But let me make a few quick calls." She hurriedly stepped off the porch and walked down the cracked driveway toward her car, phone in hand. Even though it was now close to freezing outside, she didn't want to go back into the house. Nor did she want Annabelle to hear her phone conversations. When she told people who they would be working for, she expected them to balk.

A few minutes later, she returned to the porch where Annabelle was pacing. The model looked cold, but no wonder, since she was inappropriately dressed for Montana weather. Mary Sue guessed that she wasn't anxious to go back inside the house, either. "I found a couple of men who are willing to help for thirty dollars an hour."

"Thirty dollars an hour? I'm not asking them to remodel

the house." Annabelle looked through the window with a shake of the head as if calculating how many hours work was in there. "Forget it," she said with a sigh. "I'll do the packing myself. Where can I find some boxes?"

"Behind the town recycling center. But you aren't going to be able to get very many into that car of yours. Are you sure you don't want—"

"I'll figure it out."

"Okay, but once you get everything boxed up, you're going to need a truck to take it either to the dump or a storage unit, if you decide to keep some of it."

"Got it. I'll deal with all that once it's boxed up."

"I have plans, otherwise..." Otherwise what? Did she really feel guilty about not offering to help? If Annabelle was too cheap to hire help, that was her problem.

With a wave of her hand, her former classmate dismissed her.

"All right, then let me know when the house is ready to go on the market," Mary Sue said, not about to mention that the place would need to be cleaned. A nice coat of fresh paint in the rooms would also help. But she didn't feel that Annabelle was up to hearing more bad news right now and Mary Sue wasn't up to giving it.

Anyway, she was anxious to talk to her mother. As she walked to her car, her clipboard in hand, she tried to convince herself that she'd gotten the wrong floor plan from the courthouse.

Except she knew better. She prided herself on being thorough. Frannie had walled up the alcove. But why? And what was in the closed-up space?

"Shouldn't you be asleep?" the assisted-living nurse asked from his doorway.

Bernard "Bernie the Hawk" McDougal gave her the

smile that had worked on women since he was a boy. Even at eighty-nine, the old mobster still could make a woman blush with no more than a wink and a grin. There might be snow on the roof, but it was still plenty hot down in the furnace.

"Just finishing up here," he told her from his desk and waited until she moved on before he picked up the scissors again.

He pulled the newspaper clipping toward him, still shocked that he'd discovered it online while surfing for obits of women of a certain age. The moment he'd seen this one, he'd printed it out, but the resolution wasn't good so he'd called the newspaper where it had run—the *Milk River Courier*—and had the paper overnighted to him.

It had arrived this afternoon while he was napping. When he'd awakened, he'd seen the envelope waiting for him on his desk and quickly torn into it. Inside he'd found the complete edition of that week's Whitehorse, Montana, newspaper—all four pages of it.

Now he studied the face in the obituary mug shot. The photo didn't do her justice. The one he'd seen on the internet had been much more flattering.

But no photo of his Baby Doll could hold a candle to the woman in the flesh—especially back when she was young. She'd been a blonde beauty. Tiny and gorgeous, she'd been exquisite. The kind of woman who stopped traffic and turned heads. She'd certainly turned his, he thought with a curse. And the things she'd put him through from the first time he'd laid eyes on her.

That was something else about her that had attracted her to him. She wasn't intimidated by him or any of his goons. Oh, that woman had a mouth on her. She could cut a man down to size as if her tongue was a switchblade.

He chuckled to himself. He'd wanted her and would

have married her, but she wasn't having any of that. She liked being mysterious. Hell, he'd never known her real name. That first night at the party, he'd seen right away that she and her friend had crashed his little get-together on the posh rooftop of his favorite New York City restaurant. He'd thought about booting the two of them, but there was something about her.

She'd flirted with him but refused to tell him who she was, as if she thought he'd call her daddy to have her picked up and taken home. A few minutes with her and that was the last thing he planned to do.

"Okay, you want to play it coy? You'll just be my Baby Doll, then," he'd said, knowing even then that he had to have her.

"Baby Doll? I like that," she'd said, coming off older than she was. She hadn't been more than seventeen. Jailbait. Like that had stopped him. He had a reputation for going after whatever he wanted—and getting it. But then, so did Baby Doll as it turned out.

Opening the scissors, he began to slice the paper around her mug shot. Bernie couldn't stand sloppiness. He liked things done a certain way. It had saved his life more than once and kept him from being behind bars.

Now he found himself looking into her eyes, remembering. This was her. There was no doubt about it. He'd thought he found her before, but this time… He wished he had been able to find a photograph of her when she was younger but there was nothing on the internet. Francesca Marie Clementine had kept a low profile. Another reason he was convinced that this woman was his Baby Doll.

Oh, those blue eyes. The memories of her in his arms. Just being with her had felt like living on the edge, she'd been that kind of woman. She kept his blood revved up. He'd known he could never get enough of her. He'd asked her to marry him more times than he liked to remember. He shook his head. While he'd only known her a short while, he'd thought he could trust her with his life, his secrets—and his loot. His first mistake.

That was the problem, wasn't it? he thought as he clipped the photo free from the newspaper. He'd trusted a woman who hadn't even trusted him enough to tell him her real name.

"Come on, Baby Doll, tell me your name," he used to tease her. "We can't get married until I know exactly who you are."

"Oh, you know who I am." She'd smiled that coy smile of hers and said, "I'm Bernie McDougal's Baby Doll. That's enough. For now." Her look had been a promise of a lot more to come and he'd been a goner. Oh, the swanky parties they'd attended, the fur coats and fancy dresses he'd clothed her in, the expensive champagne they'd guzzled, the money they'd burned through. Nothing was too good for his Baby Doll.

His stomach roiled at the memory. She'd blindsided him from the beginning, he thought, able to admit it now, more than fifty years later. He'd thought she was young and naïve. He'd never seen it coming.

The obit was short, but it did provide some useful information, such as where she'd been all these years—and that she was survived by her three granddaughters, Annabelle Clementine, Tessa Jane Clementine (TJ St. Clair) and Chloe Clementine. No husband. That didn't surprise him.

He'd had to look up the town on the internet. Whitehorse, Montana. It surprised him that she'd disappeared to some wide spot out West. He'd always thought of her living it up in Paris or London, or even New York City where it had all begun. It was why he'd looked for her in the faces of every woman he'd passed all these years.

But Baby Doll had always been full of surprises, hadn't she? He still couldn't believe that she'd evaded him. He'd had his men looking for her as well as his associates. He'd put a price on her pretty head. And still nothing. It was as if she'd stepped off the face of the earth.

But he'd finally found her. The problem was, it seemed too late. She was dead. Which meant that she'd probably taken their secret to the grave. It filled him with regret. He would have loved to look into her eyes one last time before he killed her.

He took her photo, stuck a pin between her eyes and put it up on the bulletin board next to his desk. As he started to throw the rest of the newspaper away, his gaze lit on the name *Clementine* again.

It appeared to be a real estate ad. Moving the paper where he could see the ad, he saw that it read *Clementine Place*. His breath came out on a laugh. Of course. She'd owned a house and now it was for sale. A house where she'd kept her secrets. He told himself not to get his hopes up, and yet he was reaching for his phone since it was still early out in Montana.

Francesca's house was for sale? Why hadn't he thought of that? There were some things she wouldn't have been able to take with her. That is, if she'd still had them when she'd died. She could have gone through everything a long time ago. Probably had. But there was only one way to find out.

He dialed the number of the Realtor who was selling the house. The newspaper was a week old. The house could have sold by now.

A woman named Mary Sue Linton answered on the third ring.

"I'm calling about a house you have for sale," he said. "I believe it's called Clementine Place?"

"That's right. It just went on the market. What can I tell you about it?"

He had the photo of the house in front of him. But he couldn't imagine Baby Doll living somewhere like that. It was too common after the penthouse they'd shared. It all came down to that one question that had niggled at him all these years. Why? Why take off like she had—let alone end up where she had? Which led to his second big question. What had she done with what she'd stolen from him?

"I'd like to send someone to look at it in the next few days," he said. "Is that possible?"

"It's not quite ready to show."

Really? "I don't care what kind of shape it's in."

"One of the relatives is in the process of cleaning everything out. I'm afraid Frannie was a...collector." Yes, she'd collected a few things from him before she'd left. "But the house will be pristine in a few weeks if you'd like to see it then."

Frannie? "You say a relative is cleaning it out?"

"Her granddaughter, Annabelle."

His old heart thumped hard against his ribs. What if she'd already thrown it out? She had to be stopped. "Then I'll check back with you."

"That would be ideal."

He hung up and made a call. "I need to see you. *Now.*"

Oh, Baby Doll, he said to himself as he disconnected. The woman had thought she'd outfoxed him. Soon she would be turning over in her grave. As for her granddaughter, she could be joining Frannie very soon.

Chapter Three

Dawson hadn't driven by the old Clementine place in years.
After he'd cleaned up, he'd driven into town since there was
still some daylight left in the winter day and his brother
had called wanting to hear about his hunting trip. He'd told
himself he wasn't going near Annabelle's grandmother's
house, but it was as if his pickup had a mind of its own.

There was a time that this neighborhood had been his
second home. That was back when his best friend lived
two doors down from Frannie Clementine's house. Back
when he and his best friend had built a tree house only to
find five-year-old Annabelle in it and unable to get down.

With a bark of a laugh, he reminded himself that she
hadn't been filled with gratitude that time he'd saved her,
either.

He slowed his pickup, surprised how long it had been
since he'd driven through this neighborhood. His best
friend had moved away years ago and once Annabelle
left…

The house, on so-called Millionaire's Row on the west
side of town, sat on a huge lot surrounded by massive trees.
Behind it, the water of the Milk River curved slowly past.
An old single-car garage stood off to the side, looking like
it needed to be torn down.

He pulled up on the opposite side of the street. There

was a For Sale sign in the yard, which shouldn't have come as a surprise. Mystery solved. Of course that was what had brought Annabelle back. She was planning to get rid of the house—the only thing still tethering her to Whitehorse now that her grandmother was gone.

Pulling under the protective boughs of a huge evergreen, he left the engine running and took in the home. He was wondering what Annabelle could get for the place when he saw a woman in a bandanna, a gaudy sweatshirt and a pair of baggy jeans come out. She carried a large box out the front door to the side of the porch closest to the driveway. Even from a distance, he could tell that the woman was covered in dust and dirt. So Annabelle had hired help. That, too, shouldn't have surprised him, although he didn't recognize the woman.

As she set the box at the open end of the porch, she stood to stretch, as if her back bothered her. A lock of blond hair escaped from beneath the bandanna. With a shock, he realized what he was seeing. *Annabelle?*

The sight of the supermodel looking like a janitor made him laugh and shake his head in disbelief. He was tempted to take a photo with his cell phone. But he could just imagine how horrified she would be if he did. He had barely recognized her, and not just because he suspected Annabelle had never done a day's manual labor in her life. Surely she wasn't packing up the entire house by herself.

But as he looked around, he saw that the only vehicle near the place was the silver sports car. Nor did anyone else emerge from the house carrying boxes as he sat watching, truck engine running. Why hadn't she hired help? It was so unlike her.

A thought struck him like a swift kick to the shin. She'd said she'd forgotten to get gas, but what if… The idea was so preposterous that he laughed out loud as he put his pickup into gear to drive away. Whatever Annabelle was up to, it had nothin' to do with him. He didn't even know why he'd driven by.

His cell phone rang, making him jump. He really wasn't good at this cloak-and-dagger stuff. He hit the brakes and quickly answered as he watched Annabelle put down another box, stretch and go back inside. As she glanced in his direction, he slowly let out the clutch and eased the pickup down the street, making sure he kept his head turned. The last thing he wanted was for her to think that he had any interest in her.

"You on your way?" his brother asked without preamble.

He'd lost track of time. "I am. Be right there." He disconnected, hoping his brother's invitation was only about having a beer. The way news traveled around this county, by now everyone could know that Annabelle Clementine was back in town—his brother Luke included. And that was a subject he didn't want to discuss.

Luke was already sitting on a bar stool at the Mint when he walked in. Seeing him coming, Luke ordered him a Moose Drool and patted the stool next to him. "Some pretty nice weather for November, huh?"

"Uh-huh," Dawson said, groaning inside. Luke was grinning like a jackass and it had nothing to do with the weather.

"Annabelle Clementine is back in town," his brother blurted, as if unable to hold it in a second longer.

"Who?" Dawson asked innocently and took a sip of the beer the bartender set in front of him. Luke was as subtle as a horseshoe to the head. At least he'd been smart enough to know that Dawson would need a beer.

"Who?" Luke echoed. "Annabelle Clementine, or as you used to call her... Annie. You aren't going to tell me that you've forgotten about the woman who—" His brother

stopped and gave him a you-had-me-there-for-a-minute grin. "So, you already heard?" He sounded disappointed.

"Actually, I saw her."

"*No kiddin'?* She still gorgeous? She say why she's back?"

Dawson ran his thumb around the top of his beer bottle for a moment. Something stopped him from telling his brother about siphoning gas out of his pickup to practically fill her fancy sports car. "Saw her packing up at her grandmother's house. She's got the place for sale." He took a sip of his beer.

"You just happened to be in that neighborhood, did you?" Luke couldn't seem to get that goofy grin off his face. "She say how long she's staying?"

"I said I *saw* her. Didn't say I made a point of talking to her. So I wouldn't know, but I think it's a pretty good assumption that she'll be hightailing it out of town just as quickly as she can," he said without looking at his brother.

"Why didn't you talk to her?" Luke asked.

"Why would I?"

"After all these years, I would think you'd be curious. Maybe it isn't just her grandmother's house that brought her back. Maybe—"

"It's just her grandmother's house."

"You can't know that. Maybe—"

"So, what's the plan for tomorrow?" Dawson asked, hoping to change the subject. Thinking about Annabelle gave him a headache. Talking about her was even worse. It had been years since he'd called her Annie, let alone allowed himself to even say the word. Annie was the woman he fell in love with. Annabelle was...well, she was a supermodel he didn't know, didn't want to know.

"Tomorrow?" Luke asked, as if confused by the quick change of subject.

"Thanksgiving Day."

"Don't remind me." Luke took a drink of his beer, clearly upset that this was all he was going to get. He sighed. "I haven't gotten my deer yet. But you know Mom. Said not to be late. She's invited some of the neighbors."

Dawson nodded, smiling to himself at the thought of their mother. There was no one quite like Wilhelmina "Willie" Rogers. She'd managed to raise both of her sons on her own after their father died when they were boys— and run the ranch, as well. When it came to anyone who needed a hot meal, Willie was always ready to rustle something up. His mother equated love with food. She spent half her time making casseroles for anyone who'd fallen on hard times or families who'd had an illness. Anyone in town die? The family would have a dish on their doorstep within the hour.

"Mom said we both better be there," Luke said. "She already read me the riot act about going deer hunting beforehand. Speaking of hunting, how'd you do down in the Breaks? Get anything worth bringing home and stringin' up?"

Dawson shook his head. "I saw one big buck, but didn't get a shot." The truth was, he loved hiking around looking for deer and elk, but when he still had plenty of meat in the freezer, he wasn't much for killing anything. He wasn't a trophy hunter.

Two weeks in hunting camp with some buddies, though, was a tradition he wasn't apt to miss. He liked sleeping out under the stars, working his way through rugged country during the day, eating food cooked over a camp stove and sitting around the fire later, listening to his friends' outrageous stories before climbing into his bedroll. He always slept like the dead at hunting camp.

Not that he wasn't glad to get home to a hot shower and his own bed.

"Any idea how much the old Clementine place might go for?" Luke asked.

"Haven't given it any thought."

"Still, you have to admit it's strange that Annabelle wouldn't let Mary Sue handle it so she didn't have to come back here," Luke said. His brother was dating Mary Sue's younger sister, Sally. "Unless the house wasn't the only reason she's back," he said, clearly baiting him. "Kinda makes you wonder, doesn't it?"

"What makes me wonder is what *your* interest in all this is," Dawson said and looked over at his brother.

"Actually, I find your apparent so-called *lack* of interest more fascinating. You don't think I didn't know how you felt about her? Now she's back. You aren't even going to stop by her place and talk to her?" Luke shook his head. "My big brother, as it turns out, is a coward."

"It's not going to work," Dawson said and drained the rest of his beer.

"The brother I knew would have given his left arm for that woman," Luke said. "He wouldn't pass up a possible second chance to be with her. You telling me you don't still feel somethin'?"

Dawson shook his head as he stood. "I'm not tellin' you anything. I'll let my walkin' out of here speak for itself. Thanks for the beer."

Luke sighed. "Fine, have it your way, you stubborn jack-ass. But you're going to be sorry."

"I've been sorry before. Tell Mom I'll stop by early to-morrow to see if she needs any help."

"You always have to be the good son, don't you? I'm going deer huntin'. Save me a place at the table just in case I get something and run late." The door closed on his last words.

Even as Dawson started his pickup, he knew he was going to do it. And it made him madder than hell. He turned down the street. It wasn't late, but it was already dark this time of year. Deep shadows hunkered in the trees. The temperature had dropped.

As he drove by her house, he saw that the light was on. There were more boxes stacked up under the porch roof. He turned out his headlights as he stopped across the street again. Several large pines blocked most of the house, but he would get glimpses of her inside working.

There was still no sign of anyone helping her. "What's going on, Annie?" he asked in the dark cab of his truck. If she didn't get out of town before the next snowstorm, she probably wouldn't be able to in that impractical car of hers. He doubted she had snow tires on it since she'd been living in California. Not that they would help much. A car like that would get high-centered on the first snow-drift across the highway. Hell, she'd be lucky if she could get out of her driveway.

Dawson reminded himself that it wasn't his problem. And yet he couldn't help thinking about what his brother had said back at the bar. Unfortunately, he'd already been a fool when it came to her. He liked to think he was too smart to do it again as he watched her pass in front of the large picture window. She looked exhausted. How many hours had she been packing up her grandmother's things by herself?

But even from this distance, he could see the determination in her expression, in the way she moved. There had never been a more stubborn woman, he thought, as he turned on his headlights again and headed for the ranch.

ANNABELLE HURT ALL OVER. She closed another box on more of her grandmother's chipped and cracked knickknacks, but realized she was too tired to take it out to the porch. For hours, she'd been boxing up her grandmother's junk. Now she looked around the room with growing discouragement. She'd thought she was making progress, but she hadn't even made a dent in all this…stuff.

Earlier she'd removed what she could from the front bedroom. Her grandmother had been using the one in the back of the house opposite the shared bathroom. Apparently, she'd turned the bedroom Annabelle had chosen into an extra wardrobe. An array of ugly, gaudy sweatshirts was hanging in the closet. Each was bedazzled with anything shiny you could tack onto it. Where did the woman find these horrific things? A lot of them were seasonal, with Santas, elves, Christmas lights, overdecorated wreaths, even an Easter egg one that was so bright it could put an eye out.

Not wanting to ruin the last of the good clothes that she hadn't sold to pay for the trip north, she'd changed into one of the less garish ones, a sweatshirt with a bejeweled clown face, along with a pair of her grandmother's pull-on jeans that she had to tie around her waist so they'd stay up, a pair of sneakers and socks with lacy tops. They'd do to work in.

After she'd decluttered the bedroom, she cleaned. She'd discovered some laundered sheets and made the bed so it would be ready for tonight. Then she'd gone down to the recycling building in town and loaded as many boxes as she could into her car by putting smaller ones into larger ones and holding some out the window as she drove.

Back at the house, she'd started dumping the worst of the junk into boxes and carrying them out to the porch.

Now she just wanted to sit down. *You were so right,*

Mary Sue. I really could have used some help. But not at thirty dollars an hour. And no one was going to work for her with only the promise of getting paid *after* the house sold.

She wandered into the kitchen, one of the only rooms that had chairs that weren't covered with junk. As full as the place was, she couldn't help but be thankful to her grandmother. Frannie had never had a lot of money, but in the will she'd made sure that the taxes and utilities were paid six months in advance.

Clearly, she'd known what a job it was going to be to clean out this house and sell it.

Brushing an errant lock of hair back from her dirty face, Annabelle wondered if her grandmother had also somehow figured that she was going to need financial help. Six months was generous. Frannie had to have known that Annabelle wouldn't be staying that long. But it definitely allowed her time to get the house sold.

She glanced around the kitchen, tempted to fill another box with the ceramic knickknacks that crowded the windowsill. Her grandmother had saved *everything*. Was it an old lady thing? Or had her grandmother lost her mind before the end? She couldn't understand how the woman had been able to live here with junk piled waist high throughout the house. It seemed at odds with the woman who'd raised Annabelle most of her life.

But it was also odd that her grandmother had willed the house to her and not her sisters. It still bothered her. "Why, Grandma Frannie? Why leave the house to just me?" she asked the knickknacks. Several frogs looked back at her with big, dusty eyes. Maybe TJ was right. Frannie had left the house to the granddaughter she thought would need the most help.

At the time, Annabelle had been furious at such an insinuation. Now she wondered if her grandmother hadn't been the only one who'd expected her to fail. Maybe everyone had seen it coming but Annabelle herself.

For whatever the reason, this house was now hers and unless she got it sold and soon… She shook her head, stood and reached for the ceramic bric-a-brac.

Her stomach rumbled. She hadn't even thought about food—until this moment. For years she'd had to watch her weight. She still wasn't used to being able to eat anything she wanted. Now she could give in to her hunger. It was a new feeling. One that signaled more than anything that she would never be modeling again. Too bad she couldn't afford to eat.

She pushed that thought away. Looking down at the hideous clothes she was wearing, she told herself that she couldn't go to the grocery store, even in Whitehorse, in this outfit—even if she had any cash. She stood for a moment, feeling lost and close to tears. As she put one of the ceramic creatures into the box she was loading, she spied a container that her grandmother had used for her grocery money.

She was reminded of the time Grandma Frannie had caught her red-handed with her fingers in it and felt a stab of remorse for even having thought about taking the money, let alone getting caught. But mostly what she felt was regret that she hadn't come back to see the grandmother who'd loved her so much.

That day, her hand literally in the cookie jar, Annabelle had fished around for an excuse. Her grandmother had stopped her and said, "If you're going to steal, then own it. Same with getting caught," her grandmother had said. "Lying and sniveling makes you look weak."

With a sigh, she now lifted the lid of the container, telling herself it would be empty. Reaching inside, her fingers brushed something. She pulled out a handful of crinkled-up twenties and began to cry.

"Grandma," she said, her voice breaking. She swallowed the lump in her throat and wiped at her tears. Frannie had known she was going to need money. She *was* the one her grandmother had known would fail. As much as that hurt, her heart filled to bursting with love for her grandmother, who was still looking out for her after all these years. Because someone needed to, that was for sure.

There were enough bills to keep her from going hungry for a while. She said a whispered thank-you to her grandmother and glanced at her watch. Did she really have the energy to shower and change to go to the grocery store to get something to eat?

The answer was a resounding no. If she sneaked in and out of the only grocery store in town quickly, hopefully she wouldn't see anyone she knew.

ROBERT "ROB" MCDOUGAL saw that it was his uncle calling and ignored the call. The old mobster probably just wanted to bitch about the way-too-expensive assisted-living facility where he'd been the past four years.

Since Rob was paying almost twenty grand a month to keep him in the resort-like place, he didn't have much sympathy. It was a deal his old man had made with the "family."

Rob wasn't stupid enough to renege on the agreement, since that would get him killed. But he didn't have to listen to the old man's constant complaining. Nor was he in the mood to indulge his uncle.

But when his phone rang once again and he saw that it was Bernie calling yet another time, he finally listened to the original message his uncle had left.

"I have a job for you. A real one. Get your butt out here. This is urgent family business."

Urgent family business? Rob groaned. What now? He didn't bother to call his uncle back. He simply texted that he was on his way to Golden Years Retirement Living and Spa.

The moment he walked into his uncle's room, the old codger patted the arm of his wheelchair and said, "Let's take a walk."

In his uncle's generation that might have meant he was about to die. But he didn't think Bernie had a gun on him or a garrote or even a butter knife from the kitchen. But you never knew.

"What's this about?" Rob asked impatiently as he pushed the old man's wheelchair out to the canal after getting a special pass at the main desk to do so. It was hot as hell, even though it was late at night, but it often was this far south. Florida. He hated it. He missed the change of seasons up north. But as long as Bernie was alive... And the old codger didn't seem to be aging in the least.

"Isn't this far enough?" Rob asked, swatting at a mosquito as he kept an eye out for alligators. Each year down here alligators attacked ten people on average. They snatched pets from the sides of pools, grabbed little kids and even ate a few adults, twenty-three since 1948, he'd read. Walking along the canal always made him nervous.

His uncle finally signaled they could stop. Looking around he checked to make sure they were alone. They were. Rob was losing patience. His shirt was soaked with sweat and sticking to his back. He swatted at another bug flying around his head and swore under his breath.

"The Marco Polo Heist," Bernie said.

Rob felt his stomach twist. He'd grown up without a father because of that heist. Everything had gone perfectly until an off-duty guard had shown up. His father and one of the other thieves had been killed. Only one of the thieves had gotten away clean—Bernie. The cops had known Bernie was involved but they'd never been able to prove it.

Bernie had walked away with the loot—which was never recovered since, according to his uncle, it had been stolen right out from under his nose. It had been the only black stain on the mobster's otherwise glowing criminal career—and something that remained stuck in the old man's craw.

"I have a lead on the goods," his uncle said.

After more than fifty years and a lot of blind alleys and wild-goose chases? Rob stared at him. "It just came to you?"

Bernie cuffed him in the back. "Don't be a damned fool. I know you think I'm getting senile, but I'm as sharp as a shank."

Right, Rob thought as he watched the old man dig a newspaper clipping out of his pocket.

"That's her," his uncle said, handing him the black-and-white photo. "Francesca Clementine." When Rob had no reaction, he added impatiently, "Baby Doll."

The notorious Baby Doll. Rob wanted to laugh. He'd had to hear about her all of his adult life. The moll who'd broken Bernie's heart and stolen a king's fortune from him.

"That's her?" He couldn't help being skeptical. They'd been here before.

His uncle nodded and handed him the obit. He read it, trying not to roll his eyes. "Whitehorse, Montana?" He couldn't be serious.

Bernie smiled. "Her house is coming up for sale."

"You want me to buy the house?"

"Hell, no. Too obvious. We don't want to call attention to any of this. The Feds are still watching me." Rob doubted this but said nothing. "There are too many people still looking for the loot, you know what I'm saying?"

Just like they were still looking for Jimmy Hoffa.

"You need to leave right away," Bernie said, keeping his voice down, apparently afraid the Feds were listening from the mangroves beyond the canal. They'd had to come all the way out here by the canal with the wild alligators because his uncle was convinced that his room was bugged. "I think you can handle this alone. Better that way."

Rob nodded, telling himself he wasn't going to Montana on some wild-goose chase.

"I'm depending on you," Bernie said and grabbed his hand to squeeze it hard "I trust you, Robby."

"Rob," he corrected for the millionth time. Nor had he been chosen because his uncle trusted him. There was no one else who would do it. He had been appointed his uncle's babysitter. Not that the family didn't still fear Bernie. The old man had his connections. It was why Rob came when his uncle called, eventually. But Montana?

The doctor had said Bernie didn't have more than a year to live. But that was four years ago. Tough as old pigskin and meaner than a junkyard dog, the old man had defied modern science with just stubborn determination alone, Rob thought.

"I'm honored that you would trust me to take care of this," he said.

His uncle chuckled and met his eye. "Honored. And smart. You know what will happen to you if you don't come back with my goods."

His goods. Arrogant bastard. "Let's say this dame is your... Baby Doll."

"Don't call her a dame, okay?"

"What if she still didn't have any of it when she died?" Rob asked for the sake of argument. "What if she's been selling it off? After all, it's been over fifty years."

Bernie shook his head. "I would have heard if any of

it had turned up. She took all of it, the cash, the jewels, the gold. I'm betting she still had it when she died. Just to show me," he said, admiration in his tone. "She willed the house to one of her granddaughters, someone named Annabelle Clementine. The Realtor made it sound like I should know who she was."

Rob shrugged. "Never heard of her."

"Apparently she's getting the house ready to sell. Take care of her and soon. She might throw out something not realizing what it is. Just don't call attention to yourself or her. I shouldn't have to spell it out for you."

"No," Rob said. But he hadn't done any wet work in years. He didn't want to start again. "Tomorrow is Thanksgiving—"

His uncle shot him a look of disbelief and the rest of the words in Rob's mouth dried up. "When you find my loot you'll want to take off with the whole lot, but you won't. You know why?"

He shook his head even though they'd had this discussion before, since his uncle never got tired of telling him.

"Because there's a curse on the loot, but nothing like the curse that would be on you. Take me back to my room and then get on a plane. You can't waste any time. If that house sells before you get there…or the granddaughter finds the goods…"

Rob nodded since there was nothing else he could do.

"There's one more thing," Bernie said. "I doubt I'm the only one to recognize Baby Doll. Nor am I the only one who's been looking all these years." Rob doubted that was the case but kept his trap shut. "Which means you won't be alone even if the Feds aren't wise to her. There's the insurance company guy who had to pay out all those years ago, not to mention the museum curator who swore he'd get his priceless jewels back and see me in prison."

Rob didn't bother to mention that both of those guys were probably dead by now.

"So watch your back," his uncle said. "If they recognized Baby Doll like I did... You know our photos were all over the society pages. Me and Baby Doll at the swankiest parties. She was some woman."

DAWSON KICKED AROUND his house, unable to settle more than a few minutes in any one place. He'd cleaned the kitchen after making himself some dinner, washed his hunting clothing, unpacked all his gear and even put clean sheets on his bed.

He'd been looking forward to that bed all the way from the hunting camp, but even though he was bone-weary tired, he knew he wouldn't be able to sleep. Sadie didn't have that problem. She was curled up on her bed in front of the fireplace, snoring softly.

At a hard knock on his door, he started. His first thought was Annabelle. She'd come to thank him for the gas and apologize for not saying something earlier. His heart began to pound until he reminded himself how unlikely that was. He told himself it better not be Luke with more news about Annabelle. He thought about not answering the door, but the knock was so insistent...

He opened the door and blinked when he saw that it was his neighbor from the adjoining county. "Cull?"

"Sorry to bother you so late," the cowboy and horse rancher said. "I was riding fence earlier and you've got some barbed wire down that I thought I better warn you about. I did what I could, but I'm worried you're going to have cattle out on the county road if you can't get it fixed soon."

"Thanks for the heads-up." He liked Cull McGraw. He liked all the McGraws, actually, and was glad to have them as neighbors. Anyone else might not have bothered to tell him until his cattle were running wild. "You want to come in? I think there's a couple of beers in the fridge." Suddenly he didn't want to be alone.

"Thanks, but I need to get on home," Cull said, and he realized his neighbor was probably anxious to get home to his wife. "Maybe some other time."

He closed the door and turned back to his empty house. Empty. Funny, but he'd never thought of it that way until… He swore. Until Annabelle's return. Cursing himself, he began to turn out lights. After making sure the screen was on the fireplace, he headed for bed.

Behind him, he heard the soft patter of four feet as Sadie decided to join him. He told himself the pup was all he needed for company as he heard her lie down on the floor at the foot of his bed.

But the moment he was between the cool sheets, his thoughts spun back to Annabelle, his first love, his first lover. What was he going to have to do to get her out of his system?

Chapter Four

Whitehorse, Montana. Rob swore as he sat for a moment in the dark in the parking lot of the expensive nursing home. Unfortunately, this wasn't the first time Bernie had been convinced he'd found Baby Doll. Before, it had been some old woman in Maine. Then one in California. Another in Maryland. Oh, and that one in Tennessee.

Now Whitehorse, Montana? He'd gone on too many wild-goose chases, all of them dead ends. None of the women had been Baby Doll. None of them had had the loot. All they had in common was that they were six feet under now.

He pulled the photocopied snapshot and obit from his pocket and looked at them again. Francesca Clementine? At least he wouldn't have to kill this one—she was already dead. But the granddaughter wasn't, he reminded himself.

He debated not going and telling the old man that he had and that Francesca Clementine wasn't his Baby Doll. It would break the old man's heart, but it wasn't the first time. After all, what were the chances that this Francesca Clementine had even been to New York City, let alone had a love affair with a mobster and stolen a king's ransom in already stolen loot? Less than nil.

So why waste his time? Just give it a few days and then report back to Bernie… It was a gamble, though. He suspected the old man had Alzheimer's or dementia and his brain was more pickled than his aunt's canned beets.

But that didn't mean Bernie wasn't dangerous. He still could make Rob's life a living hell. That's if he didn't just cut bait and have Rob killed.

He considered what to do. The old man was crazy. If he found out that Rob hadn't gone to Montana…

Swearing, he pulled out his cell phone and called the airport for a ticket to the closest airport—Billings, Montana, some three hours away from Whitehorse.

This, he thought, was going to be the worst wildgoose chase ever. Montana in the winter. For the granddaughter's sake, he hoped the old man had gotten it wrong again and he could prove it quickly.

ANNABELLE'S PLAN, WHEN she left California had been to sneak back into town, if at all possible. She'd thought she could sell her grandmother's house and be gone before anyone noticed. Now, as she drove the few blocks to the grocery, she realized how foolish that had been.

Whitehorse was so small that it didn't even have a stoplight. The closest big-box store was three hours away—and that was when the roads weren't icy or under construction. To say that the small rural town was in the middle of nowhere was an understatement. Sometimes in the winter the highways out of town would close because of a blizzard and they'd be trapped until the plows could get through.

That was one of Annabelle's worries. That she would get snowed in here before she could sell her grandmother's house and she ran completely out of money. Meanwhile, she just hoped she didn't see anyone she knew. But the way she was dressed, she hardly recognized herself, she thought, as she straightened the bandanna she'd decided to leave covering her blond hair.

Parking at the side of the grocery store, she turned off the engine and sat for a moment. Only a few people came and went. It was late and the store would close soon. She saw a few older people who could have been familiar but they didn't pay her any mind. A couple of teenaged boys eyed her car, but didn't give her a second glance.

Her stomach growling, she finally climbed out, locked her car and headed inside. Whitehorse was the kind of place where everyone returned the grocery carts. No one would dream of leaving theirs outside for fear someone would see them and they'd be the talk of the town.

Once inside the store, everyone was always very polite. There was no cart bumping, no angry looks, let alone words. This was Whitehorse. People here were beyond civilized.

Fortunately, the first aisle she went down was empty of people. She considered what she needed. Some time ago, on one of those rare occasions when she'd had too much to drink and was feeling nostalgic, she'd called home. Her grandmother had told her that the biggest news in town was that the grocery store had expanded to include a deli.

But the store still seemed small, the aisles narrow, and at one corner of the store, she swore the floor dropped a good three inches toward the back wall. Now that she was here, she felt overwhelmed. She'd never cooked, even though her grandmother had encouraged her to learn.

"You might be hungry someday," Frannie had said, making Annabelle realize that her grandmother had apparently seen this all coming.

Her sister TJ loved to cook. Chloe loved to bake. Annabelle had realized early on that there was no need for her to learn either skill if someone else cooked and baked. Even at a young age, she'd believed she would never have to cook for herself—not with the life she had planned—and that had been the case. For a while.

Faced with fending for herself in the kitchen now, she didn't know where to begin. Her grandmother had gone down to the senior center for her meals. Food-wise, the cupboards were bare.

Catching a whiff of something that smelled already cooked, she followed her nose and was delighted to find the new deli. She peered through the glass, her mouth watering, even though the deli was a far cry from the grocery stores she was used to.

"I'll take some of that," she said pointing at the breaded chicken. "And some of that," she said of chopped salad. Not having to worry about calories anymore, she feared she wouldn't be able to stop once she started eating real food again. She pointed out a few more things and happily put the containers in her cart.

"I should get something for breakfast," she said to herself spying the pastries. Lemon-filled donuts. Cream-cheese-laced rolls. Maple sticks. She hadn't faced such tough decisions in years.

"Annabelle?"

The voice behind her made her freeze in mid-drool. The years seemed to disappear and she was a tongue-tied, knobby-kneed teen again.

As she turned, Wilhelmina Rogers said, "If it isn't my favorite almost daughter-in-law." Dawson's mother threw her arms around her, hugging her as if she hadn't seen her in years. She hadn't.

Almost daughter-in-law. "Willie." It was all she could get out. Willie's reaction to seeing her again was surprising. Shocking, actually. Annabelle had just assumed that Willie would hate her after what she did to Dawson. The woman's greeting made her feel…loved and forgiven and guilty. Tears filled her eyes as she was enveloped by the long and lean ranchwoman's strong arms.

"Let me look at you," Willie said as she held Annabelle at arm's length and gave her the once-over. "You look good enough to eat, although I'm going to have to fatten you up before I do," she said with a hearty laugh. She instantly sobered. "Seriously, it is so good to see you."

All Annabelle could do was nod and fight tears. She'd always loved Dawson's mom. Maybe if things had been different… Who was she kidding? Maybe if *she'd* been different. Maybe if she'd wanted something different. But back then, staying in Whitehorse hadn't been an option. It would have felt like settling. It would have felt as if she wasn't good enough to leave and make it. Like she would have failed without even trying. Did she really feel all that different, even now?

"I expect to see you at my house tomorrow at 11:45 a.m. on the dot," Willie ordered.

"Tomorrow?" Annabelle parroted, feeling off-balance and confused.

"Thanksgiving! Don't even bother arguing. You don't show up, I'll send one of my ranch hands to get you. I mean it. You're coming." Willie patted Annabelle's arm. "I'm so glad you're back. You remember the way out to the ranch, don't you?"

She nodded, choked up. The last thing she wanted to do was have Thanksgiving at the ranch with her ex-al-most-fiancé.

"Luke said something about them going huntin' so I'll need your help," Willie said, as if to let her know Dawson probably wouldn't be there. Apparently thinking it was all settled, Willie breezed off with a cart overflowing with food. She'd made it sound as if Annabelle showing up for Thanksgiving was doing *her* the favor. That was Willie.

But just the thought of one of Willie's meals made her stomach rumble. Also, she had no doubt that the woman would do exactly what she said she would, send a hired hand after her. So Annabelle knew she had no choice. She'd be back on the Rogers Ranch tomorrow for Thanksgiving—just like old times.

Except Dawson would be hunting with his brother instead of sitting next to her.

What had she just agreed to? Reaching into the bakery display, she grabbed a package of assorted donuts, one each of all her favorites. Now if she could just get out of this store without anyone else recognizing her.

MARY SUE HAD tried a half dozen times to reach her mother. When Carla answered, she recalled that her mother had gone shopping in Havre for the day.

"I just saw all your messages," her mother said. "What was so important that I had to call you the moment I got home?"

In the background she could hear that her mother was putting away groceries. "The old Clementine place. Have you ever been inside it?"

"No, why? I heard it's a mess and that Frannie collected everything under the sun. Is it in terrible shape inside?"

"Full to the brim, but there is something odd. On the plans from the county office, it shows that there was once an alcove off the kitchen."

"So, what is there now?" her mother asked as she worked.

"A wall."

Carla stopped putting away her groceries. "A wall?"

"It's as if there never was an alcove."

She heard her mother sit down heavily. "Why would someone close off an alcove?"

"That's what I want to know."

"You sure the planning office didn't give you the wrong house?"

"I'm sure. I even went back down there this afternoon and double-checked. There was definitely an alcove there about three wide by six feet long and eight foot high." Just large enough to hide a body. Or more bodies, if you stacked them, she thought, but didn't say.

"That is definitely odd," her mother agreed. "It shouldn't hurt the sale of the house, though. Annabelle is going to leave the wall, isn't she?"

"I got that impression. Still, it's kind of spooky, don't you think?"

"Oh, Mary Sue," her mother said, clearly hefting herself to her feet again. "Stop watching those zombie shows all the time. Why don't you come over and help me bake the pies? I'm dead on my feet."

Why not? "Do you need me to bring anything?"

Her mother had grown quiet, as if thinking about the question Mary Sue had asked her. But when she spoke it had nothing to do with Thanksgiving pies.

"You know, it didn't come out until she died, but Frannie never married."

"But I thought her husband died before she moved to Whitehorse?"

"But there'd been a man in her life, her son's father. So who was he?"

"Don't know. As far as I heard, Frannie never even dated, although Inez told me that she saw a man over there one time. Never saw him again."

Mary Sue was more interested in why Frannie had closed up that alcove. "Maybe she killed the man and walled him up in the alcove."

"Oh, Mary Sue, Frannie wouldn't hurt a fly."

"That's what Annabelle said." But Mary Sue couldn't help but wonder what—or who—might be behind that wall. People often surprised you, especially the innocent-looking ones, she'd found.

Chapter Five

Annabelle felt sick as she pulled into her driveway. She glanced over at the box of donuts on the passenger seat next to her. The box was almost empty. She hadn't even waited until she got home before she'd started in on them. Seeing Willie had upset her. It had brought back too many memories of Dawson. Too many memories in general.

She couldn't take her eyes off the remaining donuts, especially the last lemon-filled one. It had been years since she'd had a donut. Now that she had…

Hurriedly she slammed the lid closed on the ones that were left. Had she really thought she could sneak into town, sell the house, take care of her problems and slip out in the dead of night before anyone learned the truth?

"I'm such a fool," she said as she grabbed the donut box and the bag of food she'd ended up buying and exited her car. Earlier, she hadn't bothered locking the front door of the house and was glad now. Juggling everything, she managed to open the door and get inside without dropping the donut box.

Kicking the door closed behind her, she moved through the dark house toward the kitchen. Moonlight fingered its way through the open blinds, painting the floor and walls with bands of light and dark. She was fumbling for the kitchen light switch when she thought she heard something.

Suddenly the hair stood up on the back of her neck. She felt her eyes widen in alarm as her gaze slowly shifted to the far side of the kitchen and that stupid wall that wasn't supposed to be there. Enough moonlight came through the window over the sink to throw a ghostly white haze over the dated kitchen.

But it was the dark spot that held her gaze. She stared at *the wall* as her heart began to hammer in her chest. There appeared to be a stain on the lower half of it. Dark like… blood, she could hear Mary Sue say, as if something had leaked through from the other side.

That was impossible after all these years. But still… Annabelle took a step back and bumped into the counter making her drop one of the bags of groceries and let out a stifled scream. The bag with the milk, orange juice and coffee hit the floor with a loud crash.

Still her eyes were on the spot with the stain. It had to be just a trick of the moonlight. Just a strange shadow. She groped for the light switch, anxious to prove that that was all it was.

She managed to put down the rest of the groceries and the donut box on the counter, all the time keeping an eye on the stain as if she thought it might grow. Or worse, begin to seep out onto the faded linoleum floor.

Pulling out her cell phone, she dialed her sister Chloe as she kept looking for the overhead light switch. "Why didn't you and TJ stay at the house?" she demanded the moment her sister answered.

"Annabelle? Are you drunk? What time is it?" Chloe sounded as if she'd been asleep.

She glanced at the clock. It was only ten. But ten in Montana was midnight back East. "You heard me. Why didn't you stay in Grandmother's house?"

"So it's Grandmother's house now? I thought it was

yours? You're the one who inherited it, as you are fond of telling us."

"You're not answering my question." She moved cautiously along the counter until she reached the wall with the light switch—right where she now remembered it being. She snapped it on, blinded for a moment by the sudden light that filled the kitchen. The spot on the wall disappeared. Disappeared as if it had never been there at all.

Her relief made her go weak, even as she felt foolish. Of course it had been just a trick of the light and dark. A shadow. What had made her think blood? Mary Sue. She shivered, though, since she still had a wall where an alcove had once been.

"We didn't want to stay in the house." Her sister sounded defensive.

"Why?"

"Why do you care?" Chloe demanded. "We don't talk for months and this is what you have to say to me?"

"Was there something in the house that…unnerved you?" Annabelle forced herself to ask. Forced herself to admit that the house spooked her. She wanted to throttle Mary Sue for telling her about the missing alcove, about old ladies who killed people and buried them who knew where, about school kids avoiding the place on Halloween night after her grandmother had died because they saw her ghost in the window.

"What's going on, Annabelle?"

She shook her head, exhausted, dirty and donut sick. She hadn't called her sisters when she'd gotten in trouble because they'd had a fight over the house and weren't talking. But she also hadn't wanted to admit that her career was over and she was flat broke. So there hadn't been anyone close to her to confide in, since her circle of so-called friends already knew and had disappeared. Disappeared like the stain on the wall, leaving her scared and alone.

"It's nothing. Everything is fine," she said, remembering her sisters' reactions when they'd gotten the news about their grandmother's will. She was still hurt and angry about the snotty things they'd said—even if they'd been true.

"So, you've sold the house."

"Not yet, but soon. I'm sorry I bothered you." She disconnected and stood staring at the wall. Why would her grandmother close off the alcove? What if there had never been an alcove?

She swore that if Mary Sue showed up tomorrow and admitted she'd had the wrong set of house plans, Annabelle would throttle her.

Chapter Six

"Did he get on a plane?" Bernie said into the phone as he pushed out of the wheelchair to the window.

"He did. I'm babysitting his cat."

"He has a cat?" Bernie realized how little he knew about his nephew, and yet he felt good about this errand he'd sent Robby on. This time he wasn't wrong. This time the woman really was Baby Doll. It surprised him that, more than getting back what she'd taken from him, he wanted to know why. Why she left him. Had it always only been about the money for her?

Bernie shook his gray head. He knew in his heart that couldn't be true. He'd loved her. Baby Doll had to have loved him. Robby had to find proof. Bernie couldn't die in peace until he knew.

"If you hear anything, let me know. I'm like on another planet in this place." As he disconnected, he happened to look down at his wastebasket. It hadn't been emptied, but the newspaper, the one from Whitehorse, Montana, was gone.

He was positive that he'd put it in the trash. But maybe he'd only thought about it. Getting old annoyed the devil out of him. His memory...it played tricks on him. He glanced around the room, sure the newspaper had to be here. Who would take the paper—with holes in it where he'd carefully, almost surgically removed sections?

His heart began to pound. The paper wasn't here. Realization settled in like crowbar to his gut. Someone had taken it from his wastebasket. He glanced toward the hall, thinking of his pretty, nice nurse. He shook his head. It hadn't been her. But he hadn't been paying close attention lately to new employees, new patients and their visitors, strangers on the property.

Damned if he wasn't getting old. He'd let his guard down, a mistake he would never have made when he was younger.

His legs suddenly felt weak. He moved to the wheelchair and dropped into it. His pulse thundered in his ears as he looked out toward the canal. Past it, he saw a boat moving slowly down the canal with two men in it and swore. Feds.

ANNABELLE WOKE AT daylight after a night of tossing and turning. The old bed sagged and groaned under her as she flung her feet over the side. Her head hurt and her stomach didn't feel all that great, either. But then again, that could have been the donuts.

After seeing what looked like a bloodstain on the wall in the kitchen and calling her sister, half in hysterics, she'd lost her appetite and gone straight to bed. Had she really eaten almost all of the donuts? Just the thought made her nauseous.

As she opened the bedroom door and padded across the hall to the bathroom, she couldn't shake off the weird dreams she'd had during the night. They seemed to float in and fade out like a weak radio station.

She shivered as she sat down on the cold toilet seat. One dream was more real than any of the other bits and pieces that kept coming back to her. Grandma Frannie had been standing at the end of her bed last night, looking so real and alive that Annabelle had been terrified. Worse, her grandmother had spoken to her.

I know you wonder why I left the house only to you. I'm sorry, but you're the only one can handle it. You're the one most like me. Your sisters can't deal with the truth about what's behind that wall.

Now Annabelle laughed with a shake of her head. It was obvious where that dream had come from. Mary Sue and all those crazy things she'd been saying.

Finishing her business, she padded back to the bedroom and pulled on the same dirty clothes as yesterday. She didn't see much reason to look for more ugly clothes to wear to clean out this place.

As she padded barefoot across the bedroom floor, one of the boards creaked loudly, reminding her of all the moaning and groaning the house had done last night. She didn't remember it being this bad when she was young. Or maybe that, too, had been part of the dream.

She took another step and felt the floorboard under her give a little. Looking down, she saw that the board appeared to be loose. Leaning closer, she made out a scratch mark at the end where it looked as if someone had used a screwdriver on it. To pry it up?

Kneeling down, she tried to work it free with her fingers. It moved enough that she had no doubt it would come loose—with a little help. In the kitchen she didn't locate a screwdriver, but she did find a butter knife.

Back in the bedroom, she knelt on the floor again and pried at the end where she'd noticed the scratches in the wood. The board popped up, bringing with it an old-house smell. She hesitated. There could be all kinds of creepy-crawly things under there.

Still, she carefully lifted the floorboard, aware of the

spiderwebs stuck to it. Setting it aside, she cautiously peered down into the space below. Under the floorboards was another board. While the space was dusty and filled with cobwebs, she thought she saw something pushed back out of sight. Grimacing, she reached down and pulled out a battered metal box.

With a cleaning rag she'd been using yesterday, she removed the spiderwebs and dust on the box. Sitting down she pulled it between her legs and tried to open it. Locked.

She picked up the butter knife and had just gone to work on the lock when she heard the doorbell ring. As she looked out, she saw an old man standing out there. He wore a baseball cap on his short white hair. His coat was red-and-black checked wool, and he appeared to be wearing a dress shirt under it.

He rang the bell again. She thought about staying where she was behind the corner of the curtains until he went away, but he seemed determined as he rang the bell yet another time. He glanced toward her car and seemed ready to keep ringing until someone answered.

With a groan, Annabelle got to her feet. She stuck the box into one of the dresser drawers and went to the front door, patting at her hair as she went. Whatever the man was selling, she wasn't buying.

"Yes?" she asked briskly as she flung open the door. "I'm sorry but I'm really busy and—"

"You must be Annabelle," the man said as he smiled and leaned on his cane. She hadn't seen the cane from the window. Nor had she been able to see his face clearly. He looked to be in his late seventies or early eighties, though fit.

"You're just as your grandmother described you," he was saying.

It was worse than she'd originally thought. He wasn't

just some random passerby. The slacks and dress shoes should have been a dead giveaway. Men in Whitehorse wore dressy boots and jeans to everything from a wedding to a funeral.

This man must be the pastor from the church her grandmother attended. Or a well-meaning member of the congregation who wanted to invite her to Sunday services.

"I'm sensing that your grandmother didn't tell you about me," the man said. "Where are my manners? I'm Lawrence Clarkston. Your grandmother's...boyfriend."

"Boyfriend?"

The man laughed. "Male companion?"

"You and grandmother..." She didn't know what to say. Frannie had a beau? After all these years? Clearly, he wasn't from around here. Something about the man made her nervous. He kept trying to see past her into the house. "I should get back to work."

"I can see that you're busy." He glanced over her shoulder again. "Packing up her things, huh? Looks like quite a job. I'd be happy to help. If I could just come in for a minute—"

"Thanks, but I have it."

"If you're sure," he said. "I'll come some other time." The man turned back toward the street, leaning heavily on his cane as he headed for a dark car parked at the curb, making her wonder how many secrets her grandmother had kept from her.

DAWSON TOOK OFF his Stetson to shoo the last of the cows back onto Rogers Ranch property before going to work on the fence. The sun was barely up, just hitting the tops of the Little Rockies. The November air was cold enough that he wished he were in front of his kitchen woodstove having another cup of coffee.

But he'd been awake for hours after a long night of toss-ing and turning. He didn't need to search for a reason for his unrest. Annabelle Clementine. That she'd haunted his dreams only made him more angry with himself. He'd thought he'd put that woman out of his life for good and now she showed up back in town?

He cursed under his breath as he pulled his chain saw from the bed of his truck and cranked it up. A tree had fallen and taken out a portion of his barbed-wire fence. He made short work of cutting up the tree and tossing the firewood into the back of the pickup. Sadie watched from inside the cab, barking at the cows that came over to see what was going on.

As he was loading the chain saw, his brother drove up. For a moment, he thought Luke had come to help. But then he noticed that Luke wasn't alone. His girlfriend, Sally, was with him, and his brother was clad in hunter orange and winter boots.

He wondered how much hunting Luke would get done with Sally along. No wonder his brother hadn't gotten his deer yet.

Dawson leaned against the side of his pickup as Luke approached, telling himself to keep that thought to himself. "I wondered what you were doing up so early," he said as his brother pulled alongside and whirred down his window.

"Mom said you were mending fence." Luke quickly lost interest, his gaze going to the Little Rockies. "Heard about a big buck that was seen on up the road. We thought we'd check it out." His baby brother's gaze finally lit on him again. "You look like hell. Rough night?" There was humor in his brother's tone as if enjoying the moment. Not that Luke wanted him to lose sleep over Annabelle Clem-entine's return. But Luke wouldn't mind seeing proof that his big brother cared more than he'd said he did.

"Just worried the cattle would get out with the fence down," Dawson said noncommittally. He might look like hell, but he wasn't about to admit who had kept him awake most of the night. "Some of us put work ahead of…" he shot Sally a look "…hunting."

"Uh-huh," Luke said, not taking the bait.

"I need to get this finished." Dawson pushed off the side of his pickup. "Good luck finding that big buck."

Had he really thought he could make his brother feel guilty enough to help him? Luke drove off toward the Little Rockies with a honk of his horn, a wave of his hand and a shouted, "Save me some turkey."

CLOSING THE FRONT door as Lawrence Clarkston left, Annabelle went back into the house and immediately resumed filling boxes. Her grandmother had a boyfriend? In all the years she'd lived with her grandmother, Frannie had steered clear of men, saying that her husband had been the love of her life. That there was no other man for her.

And then along comes Lawrence Clarkston? Annabelle tried to figure out why he'd made her nervous. Because he wasn't Frannie's type, she thought, frowning, as she carried the full box of junk out to the porch. But, then again, who *was* Frannie's type?

It wasn't until later, when Dawson's mother called to tell her again that she was depending on her to show up at the house at eleven forty-five, that Annabelle quit working and went into the bedroom to start getting ready.

As she entered, she saw the gaping hole where she'd removed the floorboard and now quickly replaced it. All she needed to do was step into that hole and break her leg. Seeing the hole, she remembered the metal box. The surprise of meeting Frannie's boyfriend had caused her to forget all about it.

She took the box out of the drawer and, butter knife in hand, went to work on the lock. As she worked, she thought of Willie's call. She really couldn't be late. She hadn't planned on going out to the Rogers Ranch for Thanksgiving. Yesterday, even as she was nodding agreement, she was thinking of an excuse for when she would call her today to get out of it.

Now, though, she realized she had little choice but to show up. She knew the woman well enough to know that Willie didn't make idle threats. She would send someone after Annabelle. And what was the harm with Dawson and his brother out hunting? It wasn't like Willie was playing matchmaker, hoping to get her and Dawson back together.

Also, she remembered other Thanksgivings she'd shared at the Rogers Ranch. Willie put on a feast. Just the thought made her stomach growl. But she doubted Willie needed her help. She'd always admired Dawson's mom and had felt close to her. Maybe Willie felt the same. Why else would the woman forgive her for hurting her oldest son and invite her to Thanksgiving dinner?

The lock finally gave on the metal box. Putting down the butter knife, Annabelle carefully and slowly pried open the lid. Who had hidden this under the floorboards? The first people who owned the house? Or her grandmother? But if it had been Frannie, why hide a locked box under the floorboards?

The hinges groaned as the lid rose. An even mustier scent than the house rose from the metal box. She'd been worried about what she would find and was a little disappointed to see that the box was only filled with old photos and some yellowed newspaper clippings.

She picked up a few of the black-and-white photos, thumbed through them and realized that she didn't recognize any of the faces. Who knew how long they'd been under the house? She doubted they were even Frannie's, given the way the people in the photos were dressed. Either way, Annabelle didn't have time to go through them right now.

Hearing the coffeemaker shut off, she carried the box into the kitchen and absently put it on the table out of the way while she poured herself a cup of strong coffee before taking a shower and getting ready.

It had been years since she'd driven out to the Rogers Ranch, not that she could ever forget how to get there. It would feel strange being there, though. At least Dawson wouldn't be around, although she feared it was only a matter of time before he'd hear she was back. Or worse, that she'd run into him.

She couldn't help but wonder how much he'd changed in the past thirteen years. He could be bald with a potbelly. The thought made her laugh. She wondered if she would even recognize him.

WALKING INTO THE large ranch house on Thanksgiving Day, Dawson saw that the table was set for at least a dozen people. He shook his head, smiling. His mother. Around the holidays, she took in every stray who crossed her path.

"Nothing like offering people a decent meal," Willie would say. "It's a small thing, opening your kitchen to those who can use it." Every year, his mother found those who could use it and filled every seat, and then some, at their huge ranch-house table.

He followed the aroma of turkey and dressing, passing a dozen pies on the sideboard. How many people had she invited? He found Willie in the kitchen laughing with one of the neighbor ladies. His mother was in her element in this kitchen, her face glowing, her eyes bright.

"Well, look who's here!" Willie announced when she

saw him and hurried over to give him a kiss on the cheek. She was a tall, lean woman with a warm face that was tanned year-round and seemed backlit with sunshine. Her smile had warmed more hearts than even he could imagine.

She'd had dozens of offers to remarry since Dawson's father had died, but she'd laughed them off, saying the last thing she needed was a husband. He often worried that she had turned down some good ones because she hadn't wanted to install a stepfather for her sons.

His mother motioned to the other women in the kitchen. "You know Kay from down the road," she said, indicating a gray-haired woman in her seventies. "And Patricia." The fiftysomething spinster who belonged to his mother's church nodded at him. Whitehorse, as small as it was, had a half dozen churches—and as many bars.

He smiled. "Yes, Mother, I've known Kay since I was two. Hello, Mrs. Welch. And I've known Patricia for only half my life."

His mother laughed. "And I guess I don't have to introduce you to this woman," she said as Annabelle Clementine came out of the pantry holding a huge bowl of cranberry relish. "I believe you've known her since you were…ten."

"Seven," he corrected as his gaze met Annabelle's. She looked as startled as he was to see *her*. Had she thought he wouldn't be here? "She was five."

She wore the black outfit that he'd seen her in by the river just the day before. She looked sexy as hell, but then, she'd looked good even in the sweatshirt and baggy jeans she'd been cleaning in yesterday.

"Seven," his mother repeated. "My mistake. Just put that on the table," she said to Annabelle. "Dawson, you can take this out." She reached into the refrigerator and handed him several plates with sticks of butter on them.

He shot her a Mother-how-could-you? look.

She gave him an impatient look back. "I was delighted to learn that Annabelle was back in town. I'm just happy she could join us for Thanksgiving dinner." His mother cocked her head and narrowed her eyes as if to say, *You'd better be polite, or else*, and then shooed him out to the dining room. No son of Wilhelmina Rogers would dream of being impolite to a guest at her house.

He followed Annabelle out to the dining room and out of earshot of his mother. "What are you doing here?" he asked under his breath.

"What are *you* doing here? I thought you'd be hunting."

"I was. Until *yesterday*." He waited for her to say something about their meeting on the highway. When she didn't, he added, "Which was a good thing or you could still be sitting beside the road in your fancy silver sports car without a drop of gas."

Her eyes widened in alarm and her cheeks flushed. "That was...*you*?"

He let out a bitter laugh. "How easily she forgets."

Chapter Seven

Those golden-brown eyes. She felt a shiver. How could she not have recognized him? She hadn't gotten a good look at him, not that she'd been trying. The cowboy had looked so…scruffy, so filthy, so rough.

She groaned inwardly and lied, since she would have run out of gas not a half mile up the road if he hadn't helped her. "I wouldn't have stopped if I'd known it was you."

"Thanks."

"No, what I meant was…"

"Don't worry, I got the message." His gaze locked with hers. "Just like I got it thirteen years ago."

"Dawson—" She stopped. Just saying his name was a painful reminder of the intimacy they'd shared—and she'd thrown away. "I never—"

"Please don't."

No matter what she said, there was no way she could take it all back. She looked into those warm brown eyes, now so familiar in that handsome face. He was clean-shaven today, accentuating the razor edge of his unyielding jaw. Dawson looked damned good. The Western shirt he wore stretched over the taut muscles of his wide shoulders. She didn't need to see his abs to know they would be rock hard and still tanned from a summer spent bare chested on the ranch.

She swallowed, remembering the feel of his body against hers. "I'm sorry. I should have at least offered to pay you something for the gas."

"Seriously?" He looked even more disappointed in her. "Girl, you've been livin' in the big city for too long," he said with a shake of his head. "Out here in this part of Montana we help each other without expecting anything in return. I thought maybe you might have remembered that from growing up here, but then again, you couldn't wait to get out of here, could you? What was it you said to me? Unlike me, you were going to make something of yourself."

She felt her cheeks flame again. "Daw—"

"Don't bother. You were real clear when you left town. You didn't stutter," he said and turned on his boot heel to stride off, all long legs and attitude.

She watched him go, swamped with a wave of regret that she hadn't expected. For years she'd told herself that she hadn't left behind anything in Whitehorse. She hadn't even come back for her grandmother's funeral. What kind of woman was she?

"I understand that you need to spread your wings, Annabelle," Grandma Frannie had said the day she'd packed to leave. "There's nothing for you here. You need space to find what it is you're looking for. I was just like you when I was your age. I wanted to take a big bite out of the world. I craved it so much, it was eating me up inside. Fame, fortune, whatever it is, I know if anyone can find it, it will be you. I just hope it's everything you expect it to be."

"But I hate to leave you."

"Don't be ridiculous. It's time for this little bird to fly the nest." She'd hugged Annabelle. "I have great hopes for you no matter what happens."

"That's because I'm your favorite."

Frannie had laughed. "You're the one, all right," she'd

said with a wink. "You're the one I'm depending on in the end."

Annabelle realized now that Patricia had come into the dining room and said something to her. "I'm sorry. My mind was a million miles away."

"I gathered that," the woman said. "I was saying that I hadn't realized you and Dawson had a history. Willie was just telling me that she always thought you'd be her daughter-in-law."

There was that pain again. She'd left this life behind without a backward glance and yet... She thought of the tree house two doors down from her grandmother's and the first time she'd laid eyes on Dawson. Being the way she'd always been, she had climbed up the ladder to the tree house even though she could read the sign: Do Not Enter. She'd been reading since she was three.

Earlier, she'd sneaked away from her sisters. They'd been told not to let her leave the yard, but they often got to playing with their dolls and not paying any attention to her.

Once up in the tree house, she hadn't been able to get down. She'd been five. "Precocious for your age," is what Frannie always said. "A brat," is what her older sisters contended.

Seven-year-old Dawson had come along and seen her up there. "Get down from there right now!" he'd ordered. "The sign says—"

"I know what the sign says," she'd said, surprised by how scared she was about being this high off the ground. Her words had come out in a stutter.

"What's your name?" he'd asked as he started up the ladder.

She'd watched him, feeling sick to her stomach and wishing she hadn't looked down. She tried to say her name but it came out "Anna."

"All right, Annie, you just have to trust me, okay?" He had been almost to her by then. He was nice, nothing like those boys her sisters made goggle eyes over.

Instinctively, she had trusted him. She'd let him help her down from the tree house, saving her. Just like he'd saved her on the highway yesterday.

"We used to play together as kids, that's all," she said to Pamela now, feeling the pinch of the lie. Dawson had always been there for her when she'd needed him. But while his feet had been firmly planted in this county's soil, hers had itched to kick the dust off her shoes and put this town in her rearview mirror. Too bad it hadn't turned out quite like she'd planned it.

"You look like a woman who could use a drink," said a male voice behind her. She turned to see Dawson's best friend, Jason Reynolds. "Welcome back to Whitehorse."

She felt a surge of relief. "I can't tell you how great it is to see a friendly face." Jason had always been nice to her and was one of the few people who had seemed to understand her need to leave Whitehorse—and Dawson.

He laughed now and hugged her. "I heard you were back, but I didn't believe it."

"Just long enough to sell my grandmother's house."

"Oh," he said and glanced toward the kitchen where Dawson was leaning against the counter scowling. "That explains a lot, then. What do you say when we're done here today we meet at the Mint Bar?"

She hesitated, but only for a moment. "One drink. I have a lot of work to do, but you're on."

DAWSON DID HIS best to be civil during the meal, but having Annabelle there just like old times had ruined his appetite. His mother had acted as if his high school girlfriend was part of the family.

"Jason flirted with her the entire meal," Dawson snapped after he and his brother had helped take dishes to the kitchen. Their mother had shooed them out to the family room where there was a game on the television. Jason had left right after the meal, saying he had to stop by the nursing home to see his grandmother. Annabelle had cut out shortly after that when their mother wouldn't let her help with the dishes.

His brother now grinned from the couch. His girlfriend, Sally, was having Thanksgiving with her own family. Willie and an assortment of guests were in the kitchen, finishing up. "It's your own fault. You're the one who gave Jason your seat next to Annabelle. Looked like the two of them were having a fine time."

Dawson growled under his breath. He hadn't missed a moment of it. "It wasn't my idea, having her over for Thanksgiving. It was Mother's. All I need is Willie playing matchmaker."

Luke laughed. "Well, if it makes you feel any better, Mom wasn't all that happy that Jason and Annabelle hit it off at dinner."

Dawson got to his feet, unable to sit another moment.

"Oh, come on. What's the harm if Jason flirted with her? Like you said, she isn't staying. So lighten up. Anyway, once she gets her grandmother's house sold, she'll be gone."

"Just not soon enough."

"I thought you were over her?" Luke said. "That you didn't care she was back. That—where are you headed?"

"I need a stiff drink."

"I think Mom's got some brandy that she uses for her fruitcakes. I know where she hides it."

Dawson shook his head. "I need to get out of here. Want to go to the Mint?"

THE MOMENT HE and his brother walked in, Dawson spotted Annabelle and almost turned back around and left. He would have if his brother hadn't stopped him.

"You can't keep dodging her," Luke argued. "You two are going to see each other. If you really don't care, then what's the big deal?"

He knew he was being manipulated, but he wanted a drink more than he wanted to argue with his brother. The band was finishing up a cheating song. Just the sight of Annabelle there with Jason… He was moving toward the bar when Jason saw him and called him over to their table.

"Everything all right?" his friend asked. Dawson ordered a shot of whiskey and a beer from the waitress who appeared.

"Why wouldn't everything be all right?" he snapped as he looked at Annabelle. She was pretending interest in the couples out on the dance floor.

"Your mama outdid herself on that Thanksgiving dinner," Jason said, as if ignoring the tension at the table.

"You should know. You've been showing up there every year since we were kids."

His friend smiled. "Got up on the wrong side of the bed, did you?"

Dawson glared at him, feeling like a jackass. Jason was his best friend and part of the Rogers family. The waitress brought his drinks. He picked up the shot of whiskey, downed it and chased it with some of the beer. As the band wrapped up their song and broke into a slow one, he turned to Annabelle.

"Let's dance," he said and reached for her hand.

She hesitated, but he caught her fingers and pulled her up from her seat and out on the dance floor. "Dawson, what are you doing?" she demanded once they were away from the table.

"Dancing." He leaned closer, caught a whiff of her perfume and felt his head spin. Did she still wear his favorite? Or had she just put it on for the dinner, thinking he'd be there? Or had she known Jason would be there? Hadn't she said she thought Dawson would be out hunting?

He hated being jealous, but he couldn't seem to help himself. "Don't you think you at least owe me a dance?"

"For the gas?"

He shook his head as they began to move to the music. "One dance for breaking my heart. It's a cheap deal at twice the price."

ANNABELLE COULD HEAR the hurt in his voice, the anger and something she couldn't put her finger on. They hadn't spoken at dinner after that short discussion in the dining room before the turkey was served. But she'd felt him watching her throughout the meal.

"I broke your heart?" she asked, wondering if that was true. He'd been furious, that much she'd known. And hurt. But he hadn't even bothered to stop by the day she'd left. Nor had she heard from him since.

"What do you think?" He locked eyes with her.

She felt them drilling into her. Surprisingly, as angry as he was, it felt intimate. She swallowed and looked away, thinking he'd given up pretty easily when she'd said she was leaving town. "If that's true, I'm sorry."

"Don't be. You proved that leaving was your best choice. If you'd stayed here and married me…well, as you said, you weren't cut out to be a Montana ranchwoman. Clearly you made the right choice."

Her smile hurt her. "I didn't think I had a choice back then. It felt like leaving was something I had to do."

"And look how it turned out."

"Yes." She glanced away, her eyes burning with tears. Yes, look how it had turned out. "It hasn't been easy."

"But then, no one is stronger or more determined than you are."

He made that sound like a compliment. She looked into his handsome face. Those warm brown eyes had always been her downfall. "Whether you believe it or not, it wasn't easy to leave you."

Dawson laughed. "Oh, you didn't seem to have that much trouble doing it." He brushed a lock of her hair back from her forehead. His fingertips felt hot against her sensitive skin. She trembled even though it was warm on the dance floor. Dawson's hand on her waist seemed to burn the tender flesh under her blouse.

She looked into those eyes and remembered all of it—from their first kiss to the last time they'd made love. Leaving him was the hardest thing she'd ever done. She hadn't wanted him to make it easy. Had she wanted him to fight for her? To beg her to stay? Well, he hadn't. He'd let her go and walked away.

Not that she would have stayed, she told herself. But they would never know, would they? "Dawson." The slow country song was coming to an end. His gaze shifted to her lips and she knew he was going to kiss her. The ache at her center intensified as he brushed his mouth over hers. "Dawson," she breathed.

His arms tightened around her and she was drawn into his rock-hard body. Her lips parted as his mouth took possession of hers.

Had the song not died away, she could have stayed right there in his arms, captured in the elixir of that kiss. But the music stopped and so did the kiss. She looked at the handsome cowboy and felt the full weight of the lie she was living. If he only knew how she'd traded him for a life she'd thought she wanted more than her next breath only to fail so miserably—

She stepped out of his arms, saw the hurt and experienced a loss like none she had ever felt before. She couldn't hurt this man again. But walking away from him broke her heart one more time. She'd compared every man she'd met in the past thirteen years to Dawson—and they'd all come up lacking.

She tore herself away and headed for the door. She was almost there when someone grabbed her arm. She turned, thinking it would be Dawson. It was Jason.

"Dawson just left by the back way," he said, drawing her back to the table. "One drink," he reminded her. "It will give Dawson a chance to make a clean getaway and I think he needs that right now."

Annabelle felt unsteady on her feet as she let him lead her back to the table. The last thing she wanted was a drink. But she couldn't bear running into Dawson in the parking lot. Tears burned her eyes. She touched the tip of her tongue to her lower lip. Her mouth still tingled from his kiss. She bit down on her lip and tried not to cry.

"I should never have come back here," she said, picking up the drink Jason pushed in front of her as they sat down.

"It will get easier," he told her.

She shook her head. "I'm not staying that long. Once I get that house cleaned out…" The magnitude of what she still had to do overwhelmed her. The band was taking a break but had punched in some songs on the jukebox.

"I can't let you hurt Dawson again," Jason said, taking her by surprise. "He was a mess for a long time after you left. I'm not sure he's tough enough to go through that again."

She realized that he'd seen her and Dawson kissing. "He's the one who made me dance with him and the kiss…"

She was going to say it was all Dawson, but that would have been another lie.

"It's taken him years to get over you. You hurt him bad," Jason said, not unkindly. "He spent months saving up for that engagement ring."

Wanting to disappear under the table, she took a gulp of her drink. It tasted bitter on her tongue and it felt as if she was trying to wash away the memory of the kiss. Another lie. She wanted to take that kiss to her grave.

"I'm only telling you this because he's my friend and so are you," Jason was saying. "I really thought you'd come back. You know, that day you left, I thought you'd realize what you were giving up. But then I saw your photograph on a billboard down in Denver a year later. I said, 'Wow, I used to know that girl.' You really showed Dawson. Hell, you showed everyone in town."

She felt like crying. "I didn't show anyone anything," she said under her breath. "Don't worry. I'm leaving just as soon as I can. In the meantime, I will stay as far away from Dawson as possible, and I'm sure he feels the same way." She pushed the remainder of the drink away. Alcohol was the last thing she needed. "I have to go. Thank you. For the drink. For…" She reached for his hand and squeezed it. "For the advice." For telling her that she'd broken Dawson's heart and warning her not to do it again?

"I don't want to see you hurt, either," Jason said. "Dawson is never leaving Montana. He's a cowboy. He'd die in California."

She nodded. "I know." Why hadn't she just let Mary Sue sell the house and send her the money? Why had she come back here?

DAWSON LEFT THE BAR, needing fresh air and distance. He should never have danced with Annabelle—let alone kissed her. He was mentally kicking himself for that impulsive moment of weakness when he noticed her fancy sports car. What called his attention to the vehicle was the man hooking it to a wrecker.

As he walked closer, he realized he didn't recognize the towing company. Nor had there seemed to be anything wrong with Annabelle's car. Other than running out of gas. That couldn't be the problem, since he'd given her almost a full tank.

"Hey," he said as he approached. "Why are you towing that car?"

"Stay out of it," the man said. "Just doing my job. I don't want any trouble. I have the paperwork right here." He reached into his jacket pocket and pulled out some folded sheets of paper.

Paperwork? "I know the woman who owns that car. I want to see those," Dawson said.

The man sighed, but stepped to him, unfolded the papers and handed them to him.

Reading under the streetlight, Dawson couldn't believe what he was seeing. *Her car was being repossessed for lack of payment?* He looked toward the bar, then at the wrecker operator. "There must be some mistake. Do you know who Annabelle Clementine is?"

"No mistake. She's a deadbeat like any other deadbeat."

He bristled at the man's words. "Look…" He glanced at the name on the paperwork: Chet's Retrieval Service. "Look, Chet. Come on, give the lady a break."

Chet gave Dawson an impatient look. "She's been given all kinds of breaks and now I had to come all this way to get the car. She's used up all her breaks."

"What does she owe?"

Chet kept hooking up the car.

"Just give me the amount." He withdrew a loose check from his wallet. "You have a pen?"

The wrecker operator stopped to look at him for a long moment, then sighed and took the papers from his hand, thumbed through them to a page and pointed at a figure at the bottom.

The amount took Dawson's breath away. How could she have gotten so far behind in her car payments? What had she been thinking, buying such an expensive car to begin with if she couldn't afford it?

The wrecker operator grinned, seeing Dawson's surprise. "Still want to bail her out?"

"Yes." He ground his teeth as he wrote the check for the full amount and handed to it him. "Unhook it."

The wrecker operator looked at the check. "I'm staying in town at the motel and cashing this first thing in the morning. If this bounces—"

"It isn't going to bounce," Dawson said indignantly. "Unhook it."

"I'll be going to your bank as soon as it opens in the morning. Don't make me have to look for this car again."

"I'll transfer the funds tonight online to my checking account. Don't worry. The owner of this car isn't going anywhere, anyway." He doubted she could afford money for gas to leave town right now. Things were beginning to make sense. Like the reason she was so anxious to get her grandmother's house sold. Why she was packing it up by herself, instead of hiring help. Why he'd seen her in the same outfit twice.

"But we keep this between us," Dawson added.

Chet gave him a pitying look as if he was the biggest sucker he'd ever met. "It's your money." The man folded the check, pocketed it and began to unhook Annabelle's car.

From behind him he heard a door slam, then a plaintive wail. "Wait!"

Dawson groaned as he turned to see Annabelle come out of the bar. She saw him, eyes narrowing as she stormed toward them.

ANNABELLE WAS IN the middle of her worst nightmare. At first, all she'd seen was her car dangling from the back of the wrecker. After months of avoiding the repo man, he'd caught up with her. She ran across the parking lot, telling herself she had to talk him out of taking her car. She needed it desperately if she hoped to get her grandmother's house sold.

What she hadn't seen at first was Dawson standing in the shadows. When he turned, her heart had dropped like a sack of potatoes. Instantly, she went on the defensive, since that was all she had. That and her badly damaged pride.

"What's going on?" she demanded, hands on her not-so-slim hips.

"I took care of it," Dawson said.

Annabelle looked from him to the wrecker driver who only gave her a satisfied grin and a shrug. She realized what had happened and felt her face burn with shame followed quickly by anger.

"How dare you?" she snapped, turning on Dawson. "How dare you take it upon yourself to pay my bills?"

Dawson pulled off his Stetson and raked a hand through his hair. "I couldn't let him take your car."

"It was none of your business."

"You're right." He put his hat back on and held up both hands in surrender. "I thought I was helping, but clearly..." He cursed under his breath before she swung back around on the repo man.

"This is just a misunderstanding between me and my bank. I will take care of it."

"Sure it is." The wrecker operator nodded with a grin that made her want to retch. "Out of my hands now. Take it up with…" he glanced toward Dawson "…your…friend."

She swung back around to find Dawson studying his boots. Tears burned her eyes but she willed herself not to cry. Just when she'd thought things couldn't get any worse. She didn't have to look into Dawson's brown-eyed gaze to see the truth. He knew.

On top of that, he'd just saved her again. She thought she would die of embarrassment. If only the parking lot pavement would open up and swallow her.

"This must give you a lot of satisfaction," she said, biting off each word.

He glanced up, looking confused.

"I was so full of myself, leaving here to go make something of my life."

"You did what you set out to do."

She shook her head fighting tears. "Only to fail and come back here broke and—" The words caught in her throat as it constricted.

As the wrecker drove off, Dawson closed the distance between them, taking her shoulders in his hands. "You didn't fail."

She let out a strangled laugh and had to look away. "I got fired. Worse, blackballed. I'll never be able to get another modeling job."

"So?"

"So?" she demanded returning her gaze to him. "It's the only thing I know how to do, the only thing I ever planned to do."

"Plans change. I know you. You can do anything you set our mind to."

"Right."

"Don't sell yourself short. You just need a new plan."

She wiped at her tears. "Why are you being so nice to me?"

He released her shoulders. "Why wouldn't I be?"

"Seriously?"

"I was angry for a while, I'll admit it." His voice softened. "I was devastated when you left. But you were right. You needed to go off and follow your dream. And, Annie, you did it."

She heard what sounded like pride in his voice. And he'd called her Annie, his pet name for her.

"So it didn't work out quite like you thought it would. So what?"

So what? She looked away as she tried to swallow the lump in her throat.

"You were right about me, as well. I'm just a cowboy. I'm never going to set the world on fire. I'm happy chasing cows, mending fence, working on my old tractor."

She felt chagrin heat her face as she remembered saying he would be working on some old tractor the rest of his life. "I'm sorry for the awful things I said to you."

"Hell, girl, it forced me to buy a new tractor." He grinned and shrugged. "But I also got the old one running, as well."

She couldn't help but smile at him. "I'm glad you haven't changed. I'm even glad Whitehorse hasn't changed."

"That's only because you'll be selling your grandmother's house and leaving this one-horse town on your next adventure." He smiled when he said it, but the words still stung because she remembered saying them to Mary Sue. It had all been bravado and she felt ashamed.

What if she didn't want to leave? What was there for

her here if she stayed? Those were the words she wanted to say, but they were stuck in her throat.

She opened her mouth, aching for the feel of his arms around her, and closed it again. When she finally spoke, her voice broke. "I will pay you back every dime." With that she turned, and with as much dignity as she could muster, walked to her car and drove away.

Back at the house, she stood for a moment just inside the door. She didn't want to go into the kitchen. She didn't want to see the blood spot on the wall where there might or might not have been an alcove.

But she needed a drink of water. Forcing herself to go into the kitchen, she quickly snapped on the light before glancing toward the wall. A laugh escaped her.

She was exhausted from packing boxes, from worry. From trying to ignore Dawson. From fighting emotions that seemed to overwhelm her at every turn. From living a lie.

But as she stood there, she remembered. There *had* been an alcove there growing up. The reason she hadn't remembered was because her grandmother had kept a hutch there that had filled up the space.

Why hadn't she remembered the hutch? Because it had been covered with knickknacks, plants, newspapers. Her grandmother had always been a collector. A hoarder.

So, when had Frannie gotten rid of the hutch? And why? Why close up that space? It made no sense. She shuddered. Was it possible there was something behind that wall? But what?

"This is silly," she said to the empty room. Anyone who knew grandmother wouldn't suspect her of…of what?

She hugged herself, blaming the crazy thoughts on her exhaustion. Sleep, that's what she needed. Tomorrow everything would look brighter. That made her laugh again because she knew better. Tomorrow she would again be faced with filling boxes and lugging them out to the porch. After that—

Determined not to think about it, she turned off the kitchen light but stood for a moment longer staring at the wall. No dark shadow resembling blood appeared. That was at least something.

ROB STARED OUT at the wide-open spaces in his headlights feeling nervous. It was so isolated out here in the middle of Montana. He hadn't seen another set of headlights for miles on the two-lane highway and that after flying for hours. It was next to impossible to get a decent flight from Florida to Montana—on Thanksgiving Day, no less. He'd been on four different planes, endured hours of layovers and had barely made the connection for the last one. Tired and irritable, he couldn't have felt worse about this so-called job.

Now he wasn't sure he was even on the right road. The rental car had a navigation system, but he hated those things. The rental agent had given him a paper map that now lay on the passenger seat.

According to the map, he just kept going north. If he hit Canada, well, then he'd gone too far. He hoped to find a town, a gas station, someplace he could stop and ask. But he'd driven miles without seeing a soul. Lots of cows, but little else.

Finally, as the sun was coming up, he spotted a gas station ahead and what was reportedly the town of Grass Range though he didn't see much town. He pulled in, bought gas, asked for directions.

"Just keep going up the road. Can't miss Whitehorse," the clerk told him after taking his money.

"Tell me it's bigger than this burg," Rob said.

The clerk, a young woman with red hair and freckles, laughed. "It's bigger."

"There a motel in Whitehorse?"

"Four, I think."

Four? Well, that was better than none, he thought as he climbed back into the rental car. He'd bought some large cookies, two peanut butter and two chocolate chip. He chased them down with a liter of cola as he drove.

He couldn't wait to get to Whitehorse, find out that the dead woman wasn't Bernie's Baby Doll, then head home. He'd missed Thanksgiving, not that he'd ever liked turkey.

As he drove, the country became wilder and more forbidding. He thought about Baby Doll, the woman who'd fooled the family kingpin, the great Bernard "Bernie the Hawk" McDougal.

Was it possible she had been hiding out all these years in this Wild West–looking country? Not the broad the family had described to him. She'd been one cagey woman. Rob couldn't see her way out here in Montana. If he could prove that this Francesca Marie Clementine wasn't Baby Doll, he would be on the first plane out of here.

He relaxed a little, turning on the radio and searching for a station. He found only one. "Shit-kicking music," his friend Murph would have called it. Normally, the two of them did the jobs together. It had surprised Rob when his uncle had wanted him to handle this one alone. Bernie really did think this old chick had been Baby Doll, which also meant he believed that she'd held on to the loot.

Yep, his uncle had to be losing it.

He decided to listen to the country music station. "When in Montana," Rob said as he watched the rental car eat up the miles of rolling ranch land, rugged river bottom and, finally, open prairie.

By the time he reached the outskirts of Whitehorse, he was tired enough that all he wanted to do was find a motel and get some sleep. But he knew his uncle would be calling, wanting an update.

The Grass Range convenience store clerk had been right about one thing. This town was a little bigger. But not much. Which made it almost too easy to find the Clementine place.

Chapter Eight

Annabelle woke to daylight, blinked and covered her head
with the duvet at the memory of the night before. Dawson
knew everything now about her dire straits. Worse, he'd
paid for her car not to be towed. She couldn't have been
more mortified.

Even worse than that, she couldn't spend the day under
the covers hiding out. She had to get up. This house had
to be emptied out before she could sell it. Just the thought
of another day loading junk into boxes made her groan.
How could this now be her life?

That was a question she didn't want to contemplate.
She'd rather fill boxes and lug them out to the porch, she
thought as she threw back the covers and got out of bed.
Feeling sorry for herself wasn't going to get her anywhere.

Last night she'd hated to face coming back to this place.
It was much creepier after dark, especially with a breeze in
the bare limbs of the cottonwoods and the pine boughs. The
house had creaked and groaned more than the first night.

She started toward the kitchen to make coffee. She
wouldn't have a car if it wasn't for Dawson. She wouldn't
even have made it to Whitehorse if he hadn't given her
fuel. Tears welled in her eyes. She quickly wiped them
away with the back of her hand, ashamed of the way she'd
been acting. She'd yelled at Dawson for keeping her car

from being towed. She'd just been so embarrassed. Maybe pushing people away was her one true talent, she thought as she stepped into the kitchen and got the coffee going.

She tried to think of what needed to be done this morning instead of mentally beating herself up. She needed to make another box run and then get back to work. Pouring herself a cup of coffee, she wandered into the living room and stood looking everything that remained. She felt overwhelmed. Not even the coffee helped.

But if she was anything, it was determined. She lifted her chin, telling herself she could do this. Like she had a choice. Finishing her coffee, she returned her cup to the kitchen then went to get dressed in her "work" clothes.

She reminded herself how hard it had been to succeed in the modeling business. Not discounting luck, she'd worked hard to get where she'd been. *Where she'd been*. It still hurt to think that she'd thrown it all away.

Shaking her head to dislodge those thoughts, she went to work, determined to put Dawson out of her mind. But it was so like Dawson to bail her out. Of course he'd want to know why. It had been a perfect opportunity to say *I told you so*.

But he hadn't. If anything he'd been kind. *Too kind*. She grumbled under her breath. She didn't need his pity. She didn't need anyone's pity.

The thought of her dire circumstances—and worse, that Dawson knew—turned her stomach. This was what she'd hoped to avoid. She'd left this town so smug, so sure of herself, so determined to be someone... Now it made her laugh. She was a joke, and the only man she'd ever loved now knew it.

The knock at the door made her jump. For a moment, she thought it would be Dawson, as if just thinking about him had conjured him up.

But it was a pinch-faced little old gray-haired woman who was now peering in the window. She had her hands cupped around her watery eyes and her nose pressed to the glass.

"Can I help you?" Annabelle demanded, opening the door.

"There was a man looking in your windows last night," the woman said. "I live right next door and I looked out—"

"Mrs. Gilbert?" It had been years since she'd seen her grandmother's nosey neighbor.

"You're the trouble one, right?"

"Trouble one?" she echoed.

"The granddaughter Frannie worried about all the time."

"That would be me," she said—as her grandmother would have insisted, owning it.

"I ran him off. The man who was peeking in your windows. Might want to keep your blinds drawn. Those types often come back," Inez Gilbert said as she turned, cane in hand.

Seeing the cane reminded her of the man who'd stopped by yesterday morning. "Did my grandmother have a boyfriend?"

The elderly woman stopped to peer back at her.

"A distinguished-looking man who carries a cane? Said his name was Lawrence Clarkston."

"I saw him. Yesterday morning at your door," Inez said. "Never seen him before in my life. Nor was it him last night."

"So Frannie didn't—"

"She did not," her neighbor said, as she wobbled down the stairs and took off down the sidewalk. "If she had, I would have known."

"I'm sure you would have," Annabelle said under her breath.

Going back inside, she hugged herself. So, who was the

man pretending to be her grandmother's boyfriend? Maybe more scary, who was the man Inez had seen peering in her windows last night?

Catching her reflection and the hideous outfit she was wearing, Annabelle promised herself she would go uptown and buy herself a pair of jeans and a couple of T-shirts.

In the meantime... She looked at the mess—not just in the house but in her life and burst into tears.

DAWSON DIDN'T THINK he had slept a wink. Not long after the sun rose, he drove over to the main ranch house to find his mother and brother in the kitchen.

"Rough night?" his mother asked and handed him a cup of coffee. "I could make you some breakfast."

He shook his head. "Thanks, but I'm not hungry."

"Well, something's gotten under your hide." She motioned to a chair at the table.

He hesitated, even though he knew the reason he'd driven over here so early in the morning was that he needed to talk to her. She'd been his sounding board since he was a kid. Nothing had changed. He glanced at his younger brother already sitting at the table.

"You want me to leave?" Luke asked, pretending to be insulted. "Hell, we both know what's bothering you."

"Language," their mother said as Luke shoved back his chair and started to get up.

"You can stay," Dawson said with a sigh, and his brother dropped back down, grinning. "But not a word of this leaves this room. Agreed?"

Luke nodded. His mother didn't bother. She knew how to keep a secret better than anyone he knew.

Without preamble, he said, "Annabelle's broke. That's why she's back."

His brother laughed. "Annabelle Clementine? What are you talking about? She was just on the cover of one of those fancy women's magazines."

"You read fancy women's magazines?" his mother asked.

Luke's face reddened. "I saw it at Sally's house." He turned to his brother. "This sounds like you just being jealous again, big brother. She left and made something of herself and you stayed here. You've always resented being forced to stay behind to take care of the ranch. Now you're taking it out on her. Why don't you admit it? You're still hung up on her."

"I was wrong. I should have let you leave," Dawson said.

"Your brother means well." Their mother sent a withering look at Luke. "What do you mean, broke?"

"Flat broke." He told her about crossing paths with Annabelle south of town by the river.

"You didn't tell me that," Luke said.

Ignoring him, Dawson continued, "Last night at the bar, her car was almost repossessed. Apparently she hasn't been making her car payment for months." He didn't mention that Annabelle had been wearing the same outfit he'd first seen her in again yesterday at Thanksgiving dinner.

Willie shook her head. "Oh, the poor dear. Something must have happened. You have no idea what?"

"No, but it seems the only reason she's back is to sell her grandmother's house as quickly as possible to get herself out of trouble financially," he said. "More than likely she got in over her head with her supermodel lifestyle." He hated the bitterness he heard in his tone.

"What are you going to do about it?" his mother asked.

Dawson frowned and held up his hands. "Do about it? I gave her gas, I paid to keep her car from being repossessed—at least temporarily, and she told me to stay out of her business."

"She must be so embarrassed," Willie said. "You're the last person she'd want bailing her out."

"Exactly," he said.

"Well, there's a simple solution," Luke said, looking pleased with himself. "Sounds like it will take a while for her to get the house ready to sell, since it's packed with junk that has to be hauled to the dump. Also, Mary Sue doesn't think it will sell fast, especially this close to Christmas. There's time to tell her how you feel."

Dawson groaned. "If I did still have feelings for her, which I don't, what would be the point? I'm a Montana rancher. She's...whatever it is she is. There's a reason we broke up all those years ago. Not to mention that once she has money again, she'll be gone. She isn't interested in Montana or me. The sooner she gets out of town, the better." He finished his coffee and stood.

"Well, if that's the case," his mother said, "then you need to help her."

He stopped in his tracks. "What?"

"You want her out of town? She wants out of town. The solution is right in front of you. Help her get the house ready to sell. Otherwise, who knows how long she'll be around, running out of money."

Dawson stared at his mother. "If this is you matchmaking—"

"Not at all," Willie assured him. "I can see how Annabelle being in town is upsetting you—not to mention costing you money. Help her get the house sold, and if you're right, she'll be gone."

He eyed her suspiciously for a long moment, hating to admit that she might have a point. "Fine. But little brother, you're going to help. Bring the flatbed truck to Annabelle's this afternoon along with some of your friends. We're going to make a trip to the dump."

"Hey, don't involve me in this," Luke complained. "My solution requires a lot less lifting. Also I'm helping the neighbor this morning with his fence."

"Two this afternoon," Dawson said pointing a finger at his brother. "You're the one who is so interested in Annabelle..." He slammed out of the house, letting the door bang behind him.

"Help your brother," Willie said as she rose to get more coffee.

"There's no help for him. He's in love and too stubborn to admit it, as if you didn't know that when you invited Annabelle to Thanksgiving dinner."

Willie looked after her oldest son who was now driving away. "Did he only stay because he thinks I need him to help run the ranch?"

"No, Mom," Luke said, putting an arm around her shoulder. "I was just giving him a hard time. He's a born Montana cowboy and rancher. He's just mad because he didn't put up more of a fight thirteen years ago."

"I'm not sure it would have helped," she said with a sigh. "You need to cut him some slack. For some people, there is only that one person in life. Annabelle has always been the one for your brother."

Luke shook his head. "Guess he's going to be a bachelor till he dies, then."

"Maybe."

He shot her a look. "Don't pretend that you aren't hoping his helping her will make them both realize they love each other."

"Don't be ridiculous. Have I ever interfered in your lives?"

"You really want me to answer that?" he said to her retreating back, but she merely laughed.

Chapter Nine

"What did Annabelle say when she called you?" TJ asked distractedly as she walked with her cell phone to her ear to peek through the curtains at the street below. She'd been writing all day on her latest thriller. That was enough to spook her, a Montana girl living in New York City.

"That's just it," her sister Chloe said with a sigh. "She didn't say anything, really. She just wanted to know why we didn't stay in the house when we were in Whitehorse for Grandma's funeral."

TJ could hear sounds of the newsroom behind Chloe. Like her, she was still at work at the large newspaper where she worked as an investigative reporter. "What did you tell her?"

"That we didn't want to."

"It takes a lot of nerve to call you and demand to know why we stayed at the hotel," TJ said. "She didn't even attend Grandma's funeral. I hope Grandma comes back and haunts her."

"Annabelle did sound scared. I can't imagine staying in that house. You felt it, too. But I wasn't about to tell Annabelle that was the reason we stayed at the hotel."

TJ shivered and hugged herself with her free arm. "Why didn't you tell her?"

"Tell her what? I'm not sure what I felt—let alone what

we might have heard upstairs. I was feeling emotional with grandmother's funeral and remembering going to live there as a girl…and everything."

"We both heard a noise upstairs," TJ said. "It could have been the wind, a branch rubbing against the side of the house or just the house settling. Even though I write this stuff, staying in the house just felt…wrong."

"We are as bad as Annabelle when it comes to sticking our heads in the sand and pretending nothing is wrong," Chloe said. "What if there is something…dangerous going on up there and now Annabelle is in that house?"

"Look, you know Annabelle. She always overreacts to everything. So has she sold the house?"

"She says it will be soon and then she'll be out of there. But you know what it looked like. I would think it would take months just to clean it out, let alone get it ready to sell."

"Chloe, don't you wonder why Grandmother left the house to her and not us?"

"Not really. Annabelle's right. She always was grandmother's favorite. Anyway, if Frannie had left it to all three of us, we would have killed each other over it. The three of us have never gotten along."

"We did once. After high school our lives just kind of went in all different directions. But we're still sisters and Christmas is coming." Chloe said nothing. "I'm glad Frannie left the house to Annabelle."

Her sister chuckled. "I was, too, once that I saw what a mess it was. I like to think it was Grandma teaching her a lesson." TJ laughed. "Can you imagine Annabelle's face when she saw the place?"

Chloe laughed, too, but TJ could hear the hurt in her voice. "The house isn't worth much, so what does it matter?" she asked, letting the curtain drop back into place. It had mattered enough that they'd gotten in a huge fight with their sister and hadn't really spoken for months.

"I suppose you're right."

"I was thinking about going to Whitehorse for Christmas," Chloe said, as if it had just come to her. "Surprise Annabelle. She should have the house ready to sell by then, but if she didn't, maybe help her?"

"Seriously?" TJ glanced outside again, then moved away from the window.

"Remember Christmas in Montana? I wonder if they still have that Christmas dance at the old gym."

"You're really thinking about going?" TJ asked.

"You have to come, too. It's been so long since we've been together. Christmas is the perfect time to patch things up between the three of us."

"I don't know. I have a book out then. My publisher wants me to do a book tour." But TJ was balking at the idea and now that Chloe mentioned it, she was definitely considering Christmas in Montana. Not for the reasons Chloe would have liked, though. "I'll think about it. I have to go." She took another look out the window as she disconnected.

Just the thought of whatever they'd heard upstairs in their grandmother's house—footsteps, the creaking of floorboards, what sounded like their grandmother's walker... The memory made her shudder and she let the curtain drop back again. Frannie's ghost? she thought with a laugh.

Unfortunately there were worse things than ghosts, she thought, as she checked her apartment door to make sure all the locks were engaged.

ONE LOOK AT Annabelle and Dawson could see she'd been crying. He hated that her tears could still affect him the way they did. How had he not seen how hurt and alone she was?

Annabelle leaned against the doorjamb, eyes narrowing. "If you came to get your money back…"

His earlier moment of weakness vanished. He reached over and flicked at her shoulder, making her flinch. "Just trying to knock that chip off your shoulder. I told you. I'm not worried about the money."

"I'll pay you back when I sell the house."

"Fine." He wished he hadn't come here, but the sooner she got the house ready to sell, the sooner it would be bought, even if he had to buy it himself, and then she'd be out of here and things could get back to normal.

Annabelle sighed. "What are you doing here?"

He wished he knew. It had seemed so simple when his mother had suggested it. Help get Annie out of town. But being around her messed with more than his mind or his money. "I'm going to help you pack up the house and take what you don't want to the dump—unless you want to argue about that, too?"

"I know you think I'm a charity case that you have to—"

"You never were graceful when it came to taking help from anyone," he interrupted with a sigh. "Just say thank-you and let's leave it at that."

She clamped her jaw shut for a moment. "I'm also not graceful when people pity me."

He let out a bark of a laugh. "You think that's what this is? Sorry, sister, but you are the last person I feel sorry for. You need to get your grandmother's house ready to sell. You want to sell this house and clear out of town? Fine with me. I have some things to take to the dump. I thought I'd take some of yours." He gave her a challenging look. "But if you don't want my help—"

"Thank you."

He felt his expression soften. She looked dead on her feet already this morning—and even more beautiful even after having been crying. There was something vulnerable about her that he'd only seen a few times. Too bad the cameras had never been able to capture it. She would have been even more famous.

"You're welcome," he said quietly, his gaze still on her. It was hard not to touch her. To run his thumb over those full lips. To brush that errant lock of blond hair back from her soft cheek.

At a low rumble of a growl, his gaze was dragged away. He looked past her to where Sadie had entered the house and now stood just inside the kitchen, the hair standing up on the back of the puppy's neck. From where he stood, though, he couldn't see what the growling was about.

He stepped past Annabelle, worried that the dog had gotten into something she wasn't supposed to. As he entered the kitchen, he found Sadie hunkered down, a low snarl in her throat. What he couldn't see was whatever had her scared. She appeared to simply be growling at the wall.

"Your dog is freaking me out," Annabelle said as she came up behind him.

ANNABELLE SHIVERED AT the eerie, spine-tingling noise the dog was making. "What is wrong with her?"

"Good question. Any reason she would be growling at your kitchen wall?"

"Do you believe in ghosts?" she asked Dawson in a hushed voice.

"Ghosts?" He turned to look at her. "Seriously?"

Annabelle shook off the crazy thought, wishing she hadn't brought it up. "Of course not, but there's a wall that shouldn't be there." She explained about what Mary Sue had told her.

"The plans must be wrong."

"That's what I thought, too, but now…" She glanced at his dog. "Your dog seems to think there's something behind that wall."

"Sadie?" The dog jumped in surprise and, whining, ran to him to cower behind his boots.

Annabelle raised a brow. "I feel like your dog right now."

Dawson was staring at the wall. "I've never seen her act like that before," he said frowning. "Why would your grandmother wall up an alcove?"

"That seems to be the question of the week." She shrugged. "Makes no sense, huh?" She could feel his gaze on her. When she met his eyes, she saw something that made her soften dangerously inside. "I should get to work." Turning, she headed for the third bedroom that was nearly full of her grandmother's collectibles. She grabbed a couple of empty boxes on the way. Behind her, she heard Dawson talking to his pup. It made her smile since he was asking Sadie what was wrong with her as if he expected an answer.

DAWSON LOADED SADIE into his pickup, cracking the windows enough that he could hear her if she needed to get out. It was a crisp, cool November day, the air scented with dried leaves.

It didn't take him long to load all the boxes Annabelle had stacked at the edge of the porch into the back of his pickup. He stretched, thinking of her doing the same. She came out with more boxes full of what could only be considered junk.

"I'll take a load of boxes to the dump, then pick up more boxes," Dawson called up to the porch.

She put down the box and stretched. "Thanks. I was

just going to make some coffee. You want a cup before you leave?"

He shook his head. "I won't be long." She nodded. He could feel her watching him as he drove away. What had made him think this would be easy?

By two in the afternoon, Annabelle had loaded all the empty boxes he'd picked up up on his way back from the dump. He'd helped with the last few and was glad to see his brother Luke arrive with some friends in the ranch flatbed truck.

It didn't take them long to load everything she had packed up. At the dump, he helped discard the contents of the boxes before Luke cut out with his friends. Dawson knew he could have called it a day, as well. There were plenty of boxes for Annabelle to continue packing—if she felt like it. He didn't know about her, but it had been a long, tiring day.

But instead of going home, he drove back to her house, using the empty boxes as an excuse. Along with thoughts of Annabelle, he couldn't get the hidden alcove off his mind. After he'd parked and unloaded the empty boxes in the spot she'd cleared out in the living room, he went back outside.

Annabelle was busy working in one of the upstairs rooms. She'd only given him a tired wave when she'd seen him. He'd seen her surprise. She'd thought he wouldn't be back.

"Let me know when you have those boxes loaded," he'd called up. "I'll bring them down for you."

He wandered into the kitchen, the wall still bothering him. He tried to imagine why anyone would wall up an alcove. Especially Frannie Clementine. It had to have been the owner before her.

Behind him, he heard Annabelle come into the kitchen and pour herself a cup of coffee. She motioned to him. He declined. He had enough trouble sleeping as it was. The last thing he needed was coffee this late in the day.

"Still confused over the wall?" she asked with a chuckle. "I remembered that my grandmother had a hutch there when I was going up. There was definitely an alcove."

"So the plans are right. Why would my grandmother do that?"

He shook his head, but he suspected whatever was in that small space had enough of a smell that his pup was picking up on it. "Aren't you curious at all about what's in there?"

"No and I have no desire to tear into that wall, if that's what's on your mind. I just want to get this house ready to sell."

"There was only one other time that my dog acted like that, now that I think about it," he said, turning to look at her. "We stumbled onto a calf that had been torn apart by wolves."

"There is no dead calf killed by wolves in my wall."

He raised a brow. "There's something in there. Why else close off the alcove?"

"Why is everyone trying to scare me?" She put down her coffee cup. "It's late. We should probably call it a day."

"If I were you, I'd have to know what's in there."

"You aren't me," she snapped. "As you pointed out years ago, we are nothing alike."

His stomach knotted. It was the first time either of them had brought up that part of the past. "So true. You and I have never wanted the same things. And now you just want to get the house sold and get out of town."

"That's right."

"I won't do anything to slow you up." He stepped past her and started toward the front door.

"It's not that I didn't appreciate your help today," she

said, following him out. "Thanks for taking boxes to the dump for me and for getting me more boxes."

"No problem."

"I just don't have time to remodel the kitchen," she said.

He nodded, wanting to take her in his arms and tell her that everything was going to be all right. But he didn't think that was the case. Something was wrong at this house. Maybe there wasn't anything behind that wall. He hoped not. But he could see in her expression that she was running scared and had been for a while.

But he was the last person she wanted trying to comfort her.

He tipped the brim of his Stetson and headed for his truck, all the time mentally kicking himself for the emotions that had his heart aching.

ROB WALKED PAST the house as the last pickup pulled away. Out of the corner of his eye, he saw the young woman standing in the doorway. She pulled off the bandanna that had been covering her long blond hair. Her hair fell to below her shoulders as she turned back inside the house. He could hear her phone ringing as he continued on past.

At the corner, he turned and walked back toward the house. What he'd been able to find out about Francesca Clementine had left him shaken. Maybe it was a coincidence, but the woman had bought the house right after his uncle's Baby Doll had taken off with his loot from the heist.

Now Rob watched the woman inside the house on the phone. From what he could tell, she was alone. He was thinking of circling around to the back of the house when a neighbor came out onto her porch. She squinted in his direction. Small towns. This one was the worst. Everyone seemed to know each other, which meant he stood out like he was wearing a neon sign.

He gave a short nod at the woman and continued walking. He could feel her watching him all the way to the end of the block before the busybody finally went back. It was the same woman who'd seen him last night around the Clementine house. He couldn't let her scare him off again. That his uncle might be right about this one had him excited. He would get into that house, one way or another. But what to do about the granddaughter?

INEZ GILBERT WAS a confirmed busybody. Anyone who didn't like it could just stuff it. At eighty-nine, she had no patience. Not that she'd had much when she was younger. But now she felt as if she didn't have a minute to waste on ignorant fools. And it seemed to her that the number of those people grew in relation to her advancing years.

She prided herself on being more observant than most people. When she was dead and gone, no one would be able to say that she'd let anyone pull the wool over her eyes. She believed that her advanced years had made her a student of the human condition. One look at a person, and she could size him or her up in a minute. She was hardly ever wrong.

That's why, when she'd seen the man walking down the street, looking hard at the Clementine place, she'd known. Something about the way he was walking, something about the way he was looking, something about the way he was dressed. Not to mention, she'd never seen him before last night and doubted he was from these parts.

Picking up the phone, she called the sheriff's office. The dispatcher tried to put her off, then tried to hand her off to one of the deputies.

"I want to speak to the sheriff," Inez said. "Don't make me come down there."

Finally she was put through to Sheriff McCall Crawford. Now there was a sharp woman. McCall had started out as a deputy, but bypassed several men on her way to sheriff. She was respected in the county and had won each election handily. Inez had made sure that everyone at the senior center voted for her. She'd also canvassed the neighborhood to make sure everyone got out and voted for the woman.

"Hi, Inez," McCall said when she came on the line. "I heard there was a problem in your neighborhood." She sounded friendly and not in the least upset that Inez hadn't wanted to talk to anyone but her.

"I saw a man walking past on the other side of the street. He was obviously a stranger, dressed all wrong, and he was staring at the Clementine place in a way that was suspicious."

"Was it possible he was interested in the house because it's for sale?"

Inez appreciated the diplomatic way the sheriff had put the question and smiled. "That stuffy little Mary Sue Linton put a For Sale sign out in the yard, so, yes, I'm aware. But he wasn't looking at the place like he was thinking what it might go for or if he might want to buy it."

"How was he looking at it?" McCall asked.

"Like he was looking for someone. And tonight wasn't the first time I've seen him sneaking around."

McCALL HAD BEEN dealing with Inez Gilbert for years. Most of the department staff found her to be a pain in the neck. But Inez was smarter than they gave her credit for. The elderly woman noticed things, things that often were worth checking out.

"I'll tell you what, Inez. If you see him again, you call me right away. I'll tell the dispatchers to put you right through."

The woman let out a satisfied harrumph. "He's up to no good. Mark my words. I can tell just by looking at people."

"I know." McCall listened to Inez talk about fools for a while and then got off the line. One of the new deputies was passing by. "Martin," she said, motioning him in. "Do me a favor. When you're on duty could you keep an eye on the Clementine place?"

"On Millionaire's Row?"

She smiled, wondering how that area had gotten the name. Apparently a lot of people didn't know what a million would buy. "Let me know if you see anyone loitering around there."

After he left, she decided to call it a day. Her husband was making dinner tonight since it was his day off as a local game warden. Their daughter, Tracey, would have spent the day playing hard since she was on holiday until Monday.

McCall was looking forward to that time after dinner when Tracey was tucked away in bed for the night and she and her husband could just curl up on the couch together.

But as she was leaving, she couldn't help thinking about the man Inez had seen. The county had been quiet for a long while now. There were the usual disturbances that went with any community. But there had been little crime lately. Most of the calls her department got were barking dogs, kids misbehaving, speeding, car wrecks, underage drinking and minor thievery.

It was one of the joys of living here, she thought as she climbed into her patrol car. Her home was in the country, but she made a point of driving the couple of blocks to go down Millionaire's Row. She'd always liked the large houses with their wide porches, though most of them looked as if they could use a little work.

Still, the trees were huge and beautiful when grown out in the spring and summer. In the fall, the yards would be full of fallen leaves. Only a month ago, she'd seen some of the children playing in them and had thought of her own daughter. There was nothing more fun than piles of leaves. But while the leaves were gone now and the trees were stark against the November sky, the branches were so thick and full that they still provided privacy from the street.

She slowed as she neared the Clementine place. A sports car was parked in the driveway. She'd heard that one of Frannie's granddaughters have returned to town to get the house ready to sell. Maybe that's all the stranger was interested in, she thought. As she drove on by, she saw Inez peering out her front window.

McCall gave a flash of her lights and waved. Inez, always on duty, waved back.

ANNABELLE WATCHED DAWSON drive away, reminding herself why they'd broken up all those years ago. She could tell by the set of his jaw and the ramrod stiffness of his back that he was upset with her. Upset because she didn't want him to take a sledgehammer to her kitchen wall? And why? Out of simple curiosity. Like she had time to remodel the kitchen before she sold the house.

She couldn't help being irritated with him. It hadn't been her idea for him to help her clean out the house.

But the moment she had the thought, all her irritation evaporated. The problem between them wasn't her kitchen wall. It was those old feelings mixed with the chemistry that had always arced between them like a live electrical wire. Being so close together most of the day had been hard on both of them.

She felt close to tears as she wandered back into the kitchen and opened the refrigerator. Of course Dawson had come to her rescue. She glanced toward the wall that shouldn't be there.

"What is it you have to hide, Grandma Frannie?" she asked the empty room.

Unfortunately, the refrigerator was almost as empty as the room. She had a few leftovers from her last grocery store trip, but nothing looked good. She closed the door; her stomach rumbled. Glancing at the clock, she saw that the grocery store was open for another twenty minutes.

But she didn't have the energy to drive the few blocks and shop. Turning out the kitchen light, she wandered down to her bedroom and threw herself onto the bed.

Another day or two and the house would be empty. A day or two of cleaning…maybe painting…

She couldn't think about that now. She was too tired. Unfortunately, her mind was still on Dawson. Pulling out her cell phone, she made the call, thankful when his phone went to voicemail.

"I'm sorry. Thank you for your help today. I really appreciated it." She disconnected.

Changing into a flannel nightgown she found in one of the chests of drawers, she crawled into bed. If her model friends could see her now, she thought, loving the feel of the warm flannel. Her last thought, though, was of Dawson as she closed her eyes and dropped off into an exhausted sleep.

Several hours later, she woke with a start. She listened, trying to understand what had awakened her. That's when she heard it. Someone was trying to break into the house.

ROB SWORE AS he saw a light come on at the house next door. That nosey old woman. She'd run him off last night, coming out on the porch with a shotgun, of all things, and yelling at him like he was a stray.

He moved into the shadows where he couldn't be seen. He'd been in town too long. His uncle called him every day, demanding he get into the house, no matter what he had to do.

"You don't understand," he'd tried to tell Bernie. "There's this old woman who lives next door—"

"You can't handle an old woman?" Bernie had demanded. "Am I going to have to come out there myself?"

He'd gotten off the line in the middle of his uncle's tirade. The old man knew nothing about small-town America. Every time he walked around the neighborhood, people stared at him. All day there were people coming and going from the Clementine place. Tonight, he'd told himself, he would get into the house. The problem was that if he had to kill the granddaughter, he feared her body would be found too quickly. It wouldn't leave him much time to search the place, and from what he'd seen looking in the windows, the house was a mess.

But he couldn't keep waiting. Maybe the granddaughter knew about the loot and was looking for it, as well. He couldn't take the chance that she would find it first.

He pried harder at the window and thought he almost had it when a light came on inside the house, making him swear under his breath.

"Move and I'll blow your manhood to kingdom come," said a weathered old woman's voice behind him at the same time he felt the business end of a shotgun shoved into his back.

He swung around, grabbing the barrel of the shotgun and knocking the old woman off her feet. She opened her mouth, but he was on her before she could scream. Clamping a hand over her mouth, he swept her up from the ground. Taking her and her damned shotgun, he headed through the bare-limbed trees that separated the two properties.

Chapter Ten

Dawson woke, head aching. With a groan, he rolled over onto this side and came face to face with Sadie. The look the pup gave him was one of disappointment. "Was I that bad last night?" he asked the dog.

Sadie whined and looked away.

He groaned again, feeling even worse. And all over a woman. Not just any woman. Annabelle Clementine.

Last night, after he'd left her house, he'd started to head home. But then he'd seen Jason's pickup parked in front of the Mint. He'd told himself that he could use a drink. Maybe two. Now he couldn't remember how he'd gotten home.

At the sound of someone in his kitchen, he felt his heart leap. Surely he hadn't gone back over to Annabelle's. And what? Had her drive him home? No.

Swinging his legs over the side of his bed, he saw that he was fully clothed. Hmm. He wasn't sure exactly if that was good or bad. Might depend on how he'd gotten home. He'd never been a drinker—let alone driven drunk. Someone must have helped him off with his boots, though. That meant someone had driven him home last night.

Padding to the kitchen, he peered around the doorjamb, not sure who he would find making coffee—just thankful someone was.

"Jason?"

His best friend turned to grimace at him. "You look like hell."

"I feel worse. Was I...?"

"Drunk?" His friend nodded.

"Morose?"

Jason laughed. "Do you mean did you go on and on about Annabelle?"

Dawson grimaced and headed back down the hall toward the bathroom. "Don't you get tired of being a fool?" he demanded of his image in the mirror. The answer was as plain as the look on his face.

"Talking to yourself again?" his brother asked from behind him, making him start.

"Knock much?"

"You left your door open. You look like hell."

"Thanks. I heard that already." He turned off the water after splashing some on his face and drying himself with a towel. "What are you doing here so early?"

"It's after ten."

He winced as he reached into the medicine cabinet, shook two aspirins into his hand and, chewing them, swallowed them dry.

His brother was grinning at him. "You butt dialed me last night from the bar."

His head began to ache even worse.

"It sounded like you were in trouble."

"Other than having the worst hangover ever, I'm fine."

Luke cocked an eyebrow at that. "So, what is going on with you? If you're going back over to haul more boxes to the dump, I'm sorry but I can't help you today."

"Sure you are."

"That why you have such a hangover?" his brother teased. "Things didn't go well with Annabelle?"

He shot his brother a warning look and walked out of the bathroom to the kitchen where Jason handed him a cup of coffee and offered one to Luke, who heartily accepted.

"So how *are* things going with the two of you?" his brother asked as he pulled up a stool at the breakfast counter.

Dawson didn't even bother to look at Luke, let alone answer.

"Don't get him started," Jason said joining them. "Did I hear that your mother volunteered the two of you for the Christmas Stroll and Parade this year?"

Both groaned. "I hate to ask," Dawson said after taking a sip of his coffee.

"You're going as Santa," Jason said to him and then turned to Luke. "And you're going to be one of his elves."

"Of course I am," Luke said with a curse.

All Dawson could think was that by the time the Christmas Stroll and Parade rolled around, Annabelle would be long gone.

THE LAST PERSON Annabelle expected to see was Dawson. He arrived in his pickup, which she saw was full of more empty boxes. He began to unload them on her lawn. She watched, wondering what he thought he was doing, but at the same time thankful to see that many boxes. She'd been up since daylight, unable to sleep, and had made a half dozen trips to the porch with full boxes already this morning.

She hadn't expected to see him again—not after snapping at him yesterday about the stupid alcove wall. Even with the apology she'd left on his phone. It made her all the more suspicious as to why he was helping her.

Her head ached from lack of sleep. The house had been particularly noisy last night. At one point, she'd thought she heard someone breaking in. But when she looked out, she hadn't seen anyone. After that, she'd gotten up a couple of times only to find the wind whipping tree branches against the outside. Still, at one point, she'd stood at the dark window and could have sworn she'd seen a shadow scurry through the trees and away from Inez's house. The man Inez Gilbert had seen peeping in windows?

She had stared for a long time, but didn't see the shadow again. Still, it had kept her up. At one point, she'd even checked the doors and windows to make sure they were all locked.

Dawson brought a bunch of the boxes up onto the porch. He hadn't seen her standing in the doorway and started when he looked up and saw her. He looked as if he'd had a bad night, as well. He gave her a nod as he went back to pick up more of the boxes he'd unloaded from his truck. Jason and a couple of cowboys she didn't know drove up in pickups and got out. They headed for her, stopped at the edge of the porch for introductions then asked what they could do.

Today she wasn't about to argue. "I have some large things that I need taken down from upstairs to the charity shop," she told them. "Bed frames, side tables and some blankets."

They went to work while she finished filling boxes from upstairs. She'd hoped that she and Dawson might find a minute alone to talk, but he kept his head down loading the boxes she'd filled, seeming just to want to get the work done so he could leave.

On one rare occasion late in the day, both Jason and the crew had taken loads away and hadn't returned yet. She found Dawson on a water break next to the house.

"You don't have to bring your own water," she said as she watched him gulp the cold water from a bottle. It reminded her of when they were kids and shared a hose many times over the summer months.

"I'm fine," he said between gulps.

"You don't look fine." The words were out before she could call them back.

"I might have had too much to drink last night."

She couldn't help being shocked. "That's not like you. At least, not the Dawson Rogers I knew."

"Probably why it didn't take all that much to get me into this shape," Dawson said and finally smiled for the first time that day.

"I didn't expect you back here," she said.

He chuckled at that. "Didn't plan on coming back when I left." His gaze met hers. "I didn't get your message until this morning."

"I am sorry."

"You shouldn't be. We were both tired and I was butting in where I had no business."

She glanced toward the house. "I *am* curious about what might be behind that wall." She chuckled. "Probably just dust bunnies. We'd both be disappointed if we knew."

"Probably," he said, although he knew that wasn't the case. Sadie didn't react like that over dust bunnies. "Maybe it's best if we don't know what's back there or why your grandmother sealed off the alcove. It will just be a mystery." Until the next homeowner realized the space was there and broke into it to find…to find what?

At the sound of Jason returning, they both went back to work. They worked all day. Jason had picked up hamburgers from Joe's In-n-Out for lunch. But that had been hours ago. It was getting dark by the time Jason and the cowboys he'd brought called it a day after loading the last of the boxes. Annabelle thanked them for their help and watched them drive off, leaving her alone with Dawson.

"Why don't I run by the store and get something for dinner?" he offered. He'd taken a peek in her refrigerator when she was out of the room. He doubted she ate much, being a model, but he also worried that she might still be short on cash.

She started to argue that it wasn't necessary, but he waved off her protests and headed for the store before it closed.

It was late. Very few cars were parked in the lot as he went in, not that he was paying much mind. He was bone weary, and he knew it had little to do with the physical exercise he'd had most of the day or even his hangover.

"So you're back from your hunting trip," said a familiar voice behind him.

Amy. With a mental head slap, he remembered telling her that he'd call her when he got back. For a moment he couldn't think of anything to say. They had dated off and on for the past year. If he had to put a name to their relationship, he guessed it would have been called friendship with benefits.

Not that he thought of it that way. In truth, he didn't give it a lot of thought. That was what was nice about what they'd shared. It was…comfortable. He liked her. She liked him.

"Sorry, I'm afraid it slipped my mind," he said honestly as he turned to face her.

She raised an eyebrow. "Slipped your mind?" Divorced, Amy Baker worked at the local hardware store. He saw that she still had on her vest and, like him, had stopped after a long day of work to pick up a few groceries.

Amy studied him as if looking for something in particular. He could pretty much guess. If she'd heard about

Annabelle Clementine returning to town, she was no doubt wondering, like a lot of other people, what was going on. Not that he and Amy had ever discussed his high school girlfriend. But Dawson knew that someone in town would have told her. It was hard to have a broken heart here without most of the county knowing about it.

"How was your Thanksgiving?" he asked, recalling that she planned to go to her aunt's up by the Canadian border and desperately wanting to change the subject.

Her expression made him feel guilty, but that followed quickly by anger at himself. He and Amy had an understanding. Both of them could date other people. Even if he was doing something he wasn't supposed to, he shouldn't have felt guilty.

He groaned inwardly as she said, "Fine," and turned her back on him to sort through the oranges.

Glancing around, he told himself that he really didn't want to get into anything here in the grocery store produce department. Like the post office, this was where you eventually saw everyone in town. It was also where rumors got started like wildfires.

"I'll call you later," he said to her back. She nodded without turning around.

He paid for the chicken wings, bean salad, rolls and a six-pack of beer he'd picked up for his dinner with Annabelle, telling himself he had nothing to feel guilty about.

But by the time he got back to the Clementine place, he was in a bad mood. Annabelle picked up on it right away.

"Your dog pee on your pickup seat?" she asked as he tossed the food he'd bought onto the kitchen table.

He shook his head. He certainly wasn't going to try to explain it to this woman. He wished he'd just gone home. What had possessed him to suggest getting them something to eat for dinner? He couldn't really leave Annabelle without any food, could he?

"Make yourself at home. I'm going to change," she said and left the room.

Change? He blinked. Change into something more comfortable? Had he given her the wrong impression by suggesting dinner? Now he was really wishing he'd followed his instincts and just left.

ANNABELLE WONDERED WHAT had happened at the grocery store. Clearly something, given Dawson's change of mood. She could tell he wished he hadn't suggested getting dinner. She'd smelled the spicy chicken wings the moment he'd walked in the door and heard her stomach rumble.

As she changed out of her dirty clothing, she wished she'd taken a shower while he was gone and changed then. Instead, she'd kept working. Her mind was set on getting this house ready to sell. It occupied all of her thoughts—except when Dawson was around.

"I'm so glad you got chicken wings," she called from the bedroom as she finished changing. No answer, but she didn't let that bother her. She was betting he got bean salad and rolls and beer. That was what he used to get when he planned one of their picnics out in the wilds. The man was a creature of habit. That used to drive her crazy. Now it felt…wonderful and sweet and made her heart ache.

She thought about him coming back this morning, even though he was clearly hungover. That, too, was like Dawson. He wasn't one to whine. Or to take a day off when there was work to do. That he'd come back at all to help her made her heart beat a little faster. It also made her feel guilty. She'd treated him poorly before she'd left and now he was overlooking that to help her.

To get you out of town as quickly as possible, she reminded herself. He wanted her gone. When an old high school friend called after hearing she was back in town, Annabelle had asked if Dawson had anyone in his life.

"I heard he's been seeing Amy Baker for a while," her friend had told her. "But I get the impression it isn't serious. Why? You aren't falling for him again, are you?"

"No, of course not. I'm just here to sell the house. Dawson and I...well, lightning never strikes in the same place twice, right?"

"Wrong," her friend had said with a laugh. "Is there a storm brewing?"

When Annabelle walked into the kitchen, Dawson looked up in surprise. He blinked, taking in what she was wearing and then seeming to relax. Had he forgotten she was there?

"You changed," he said, looking almost embarrassed.

She frowned. "Is that a problem?" She'd put on the T-shirt and jeans that she'd purchased the other day.

The food he'd brought was spread out on the table. She saw that he'd opened a can of beer and was drinking it as he glanced at the contents of the metal box she'd left on the table. Dawson was going through the photos and yellowed newspaper clippings from inside it.

She sat down across from him.

"Help yourself," he said of the food. He stopped looking at the contents of the metal box to enjoy some of the food he'd brought, the two of them eating in companionable silence.

"So what do you make of these?" he asked after a while, as he slid his beer toward her and motioned to the box.

She took a drink before she said, "I haven't really looked at anything in it. I found it under the floorboards in my bedroom. When I opened it, I didn't recognize anyone. Must be from before Frannie moved in."

Dawson shot her a look before he pushed one of the photos in her direction. "Check this out." He went back to reading the newspaper clipping next to his paper plate.

She glanced at the old black-and-white photo. It appeared to be four people in some kind of nightclub setting. Two women, two men. All were dressed to the nines. Other than that, she couldn't imagine what he'd found of interest.

As she pushed the photo back toward him, she saw that he was frowning. He put the newspaper clipping down and looked at her.

"What?" she asked.

"Did you see it?" he asked and nodded toward the photo he'd given her.

"Apparently not." She was tired and the beer was making her lethargic. She would much rather just sit here with him than look through old photographs of people she didn't know.

"Look hard at her," he said, putting his finger under the face of the prettiest of the two women.

She picked up the photo. The woman's pale hair was long and fell over one shoulder. Her figure was quite voluptuous for a woman who was small in stature.

Then she looked into the woman's light eyes and felt her heart begin to pound. "Frannie?"

Dawson chuckled. "Frannie was quite the looker in her younger days, wouldn't you say?"

"That can't be her. This woman is blonde."

"Blonde like her granddaughter."

"But Frannie always had red hair."

He lifted a brow. "Well, at one time, she was a blonde."

Annabelle stared at the photo. It was her grandmother. She hadn't recognized Frannie because she'd looked so different from the grandmother Annabelle had known. And she didn't just look different, she was dressed differently.

Frannie had never worn makeup in all the years Annabelle had known her. But in the black-and-white photo, she was clearly wearing dark lipstick and mascara and eyeshadow.

It was a shock seeing Frannie so young—and sexy—and blonde. The young woman in the photo was smiling broadly and standing next to a handsome man in a pin-striped suit. Annabelle couldn't help but smile back at her grandmother. Frannie looked so happy. Was this the man Frannie had said was her alleged husband? Annabelle had been shocked to find out that Frannie had never married. So who was the mysterious man who'd fathered her son? Could this man be Annabelle's grandfather?

Annabelle speculated that Frannie's white lie about a husband who never existed might have been one reason they hadn't met her until their parents were killed and their grandmother insisted they come to Whitehorse to live with her.

"Even more interesting is the man with her." Dawson carefully smoothed out the old newspaper clipping. It was yellowed and cracked. "His name according to this is Bernard 'Bernie the Hawk' McDougal. He was an Irish mobster."

"What?" Annabelle quickly skimmed the newspaper clipping before staring at the man's mug shot. "He was arrested for a famous heist?"

"Arrested and released for lack of evidence," Dawson said. "The jewels were never found."

She picked up the photograph of her grandmother again.

"Wanna bet they were lovers?" he said. "Check out the way the man is looking at your grandmother."

"You're reading a lot into a photo." Even as she said it, though, she knew he was right. She couldn't help but think of a photo of her and Dawson that she'd kept all these years from their senior prom. The way Dawson was looking at her in the shot—the way she was looking at him… She knew what love looked like.

Her gaze rose to meet his and she wondered if he remembered the photograph. Or if he'd kept his copy. A lump formed in her throat, but it was nothing like the knot in her chest.

"Your grandmother was a gangster's moll," he said with a laugh. "Who would ever have suspected it?" He was grinning at her as he reached for the beer they'd been sharing—just as they had when they were lovers all those years ago. Their hands brushed. She started to pull away, but he caught her, entwining his warm fingers with her own. His grin disappeared. His eyes darkened and his breath seemed to catch.

Her own breath began to come quicker as she lost herself in the warmth of his gaze. She felt her lips part. His gaze shifted to her mouth. Her heart pounded so loudly she couldn't hear anything else. He was going to kiss her.

He gave a slight tug on her hand as he leaned toward her. She held her breath, remembering Dawson's kisses and yearning for this older, even sexier version of him to kiss her as he had on the dance floor that night at the bar.

He was a breath away. She closed her eyes as she closed the last of the distance. Her lips brushed over his, just a feather touch. She leaned in farther.

Her eyes came open abruptly as he let go of her hand. She blinked. He'd pulled away and was now shoving back his chair and rising.

"I've got to go," he said, his voice hoarse with emotion.

"Dawson." She'd wanted that kiss, needed it, and yet as she got to her feet, she knew kissing him again was the stupidest thing she could do. Hadn't Jason warned her not to lead his friend on? That was definitely not what she'd meant to do. As soon as this house sold, she was out of here.

So why did she feel like crying?

BACK AT THE RANCH, Dawson mentally kicked himself as he built a fire and fed Sadie. The pup quickly fell asleep in front of the crackling blaze while he paced, still angry with himself.

He should have been tired after all the boxes he'd loaded and unloaded today. But he felt antsy. At the sound of a vehicle pulling up out front, he moved to the window to see Amy park and get out. He swore under his breath as he opened the door before she could knock.

"I got tired of waiting by the phone," she said, as she stopped at the foot of the porch steps.

"I'm sorry. I've been...busy."

"I heard." She glanced past him into the house. "Is she here now?"

It wasn't like he had to ask whom she was referring to. "No. She's never been here."

Amy nodded and came up the steps. "I thought we should talk." She didn't give him a chance to tell her that he was tired and wasn't in the mood. Clearly she didn't care.

As he followed her inside, he realized that she felt he owed her an explanation. It surprised him, since what they had wasn't serious. At least, for him.

As she turned and he saw the tears in her eyes, he felt a start. It was his night for surprises. Clearly Amy had seen their so-called relationship a lot differently than he had. He thought of his mother's warning.

"Don't hurt that girl," his mother said when he and Amy had first started up after years of random dating.

"She knows it isn't serious," he'd said, and his mother had rolled her eyes.

"It's been serious for her since the first time you took her to your bed."

"It was her bed," he'd said, making his mother roll her eyes again. "Stop trying to get me married off."

"That's not what I'm doing. You shouldn't marry Amy. You should marry someone you can't live without."

"Is this reverse psychology?" he'd joked, uncomfortable with the conversation because there'd only been one woman who fit that bill. And while he and his mother could talk about anything, this was one topic he'd prefer not to discuss with her.

Now, as he looked at Amy, he knew that Willie had been right, as always. He'd thought he and Amy both knew that this wasn't going anywhere. "Amy, I'm sorry I didn't call you."

"This isn't about you not calling me when you returned from your hunting trip," she said. "Although you did say you would."

He nodded. "You're right. Something came up."

Amy let out a bitter laugh. "Something? Don't you mean *someone*?"

"Look, it isn't what you think."

She scoffed. "You didn't just say that."

He groaned inwardly, thinking the same thing.

"It's her, your high school sweetheart, the one who broke your heart."

Yep, he thought, that was the county grapevine's short version of him and Annabelle apparently.

"Annabelle—"

"I know her name," Amy snapped. "Annabelle Clementine. A supermodel no less. What I didn't know was that if she ever came back you would drop everything to be with her."

"That might be the way it looks, but…"

"I don't want to talk about her," Amy said with a shake of her head. She looked around the room for a moment. He could see that she was barely able to hold back the tears.

"I think I know what you want to hear," he said. Her watery gaze met his. "You know I like you." One tear broke loose and cascaded down her cheek. "I enjoy being with you."

"But you don't love me." She nodded. More tears followed.

"I thought that's how you felt about me, as well."

"You never suspected that I might want more?"

"I didn't have more to give," he said, hating himself. His mother had tried to warn him. He should have seen this coming. But he hadn't thought about the future. He'd been living day to day since Annabelle left. "I never wanted to hurt you."

"So you're back with her."

"Good God, no," he said, surprised that she would think that.

She made a swipe at the tears. "Then what is going on?"

"I'm helping her clean out her grandmother's house so she can get it sold and leave town."

Amy stared at him. "You really believe that."

"It's the truth."

She laughed and shook her head again. "And then what?"

"And then nothing."

"You're going to let her leave again?"

"*Let* Annabelle leave?" It was his turn to laugh. "You don't *let* a woman like Annabelle do anything. She's like a force of nature. She does whatever she wants, when she wants, and the best thing you can do is get out of her way before she mows you down."

Surprise registered on Amy's expression. "You make it sound as if you don't even like her."

He took a deep breath, held it for a moment as he considered what she'd said. As he let it out, he said, "Sometimes I want to strangle her. Other times…"

"You're still in love with her."

He started to deny it, but she cut him off.

"All these years? You never got over her. Were you just waiting for her to come back?"

"No." He shook his head adamantly. "I never thought she would come back. Why would I wait for her? Only a fool would…" He swore under his breath. "Like I said, it isn't what you think."

She lifted a brow, clearly not believing a word of it. "She's the one, the one you will always be in love with. The one that got away, the one you will compare all other women to and find them lacking. Is it possible you didn't realize that before she came back? Seriously?"

He felt as if he'd been blindsided. "Look, you have it all wrong."

She was shaking her head. "Stop lying to yourself and worse, to me. We're friends, right?" He nodded, glad she wasn't crying anymore. "So do something about this. If you love her, then don't let her leave again. Tell her."

He laughed and took a step back. "I did that thirteen years ago."

"If you don't, then you aren't the man I thought you were." With that, she turned and walked out, leaving him standing in his living room wondering why she couldn't understand how wrong she was.

"Annabelle doesn't love me. She never did love me. At least, not enough," he said as the door closed behind Amy. He listened to her pickup drive away before cussing Annabelle for coming back and messing up his life yet another time.

Chapter Eleven

Annabelle spread everything from the metal box out on the kitchen table after Dawson left. Once she'd recognized her grandmother in the one photo, she'd been able to find her in others. Bernie, the mobster, was in his share, as well, along with his "associates."

Her grandmother used to tell these outrageous stories of when she was young. She and her sisters had never believed a word of them.

But, it appeared, there'd been some truth to them—maybe more than Annabelle wanted to acknowledge. As she glanced through the contents of the metal box, she reminded herself where she'd found it. Was it coincidence that her grandmother had hidden it under the floorboard in the bedroom Annabelle had stayed in for years growing up? Did her grandmother assume Annabelle would choose to stay in that room when she came back to sell the house?

If the floorboard had been loose and something hidden under it from the time she was a girl until she left at eighteen, she would have noticed it. She was sure of that. Which meant her grandmother had left it for her—just as she'd left her the house. So there was a message in here.

But, for the life of her, she didn't know what it was. Frannie's name was never in the newspaper cutlines. Under one photo, she was referred to as Baby Doll. What was that about? Maybe the woman just looked like here grandmother.

Then why would Frannie have the photos and newspaper clippings?

As she read the news articles, it left little doubt that her grandmother had been involved in some dangerous business as the moll of mobster Bernie McDougal. These men that her grandmother had partied with were criminals. Could it be possible she hadn't known at the time?

Doubtful, Annabelle thought. Her grandmother had been a sharp woman. Annabelle suspected Frannie had known exactly what she was dealing with. She thought of the grandmother she'd known—a soft-spoken, ladylike and diminutive woman. Now, though, she realized there was a lot more to Frannie than anyone in Whitehorse had suspected.

In the clippings, she'd also discovered something that gave her a chill. The heist that Bernie McDougal and one of his associates had been hauled in for questioning about had never been solved—nor the rare jewels ever recovered. But what sent shivers up her spine was that it had been less than a year later that Frannie had bought this house in Whitehorse.

Annabelle recalled her grandmother saying that she used the money from her deceased husband's insurance policy to buy the house. Frannie had been pregnant and given birth not long after that to Annabelle's father, Walter Clementine, said to have been named after the father he'd never known.

Now Annabelle knew that the husband had been a lie. So who was the father of her baby? Carefully she put everything back into the metal box. She couldn't shake the feeling, as she glanced at the wall hiding the former alcove, that she'd only found one of her grandmother's secrets.

That her grandmother had known these men… It made her shudder. Worse, her grandmother had left this for her. Why? Was she trying to warn her?

At the sound of someone on her porch, she jumped. A moment later the doorbell rang. She stuck the metal box into one of the kitchen cupboards as the doorbell rang again. She felt jumpy, almost afraid to see who was standing on her doorstep.

Peering out through the red-and-white gingham curtains, she saw Mary Sue. The Realtor spotted her about the same time. Annabelle quickly dropped the curtain and opened the door.

"Is everything all right?" Mary Sue asked suspiciously.

"It's fine."

"You just had such a weird expression," the woman persisted.

"You startled me, that's all. So, do you have a half dozen prospective buyers to tell me about? How about one?"

Mary Sue shook her head. "I came by to see how you were faring. I heard Dawson and his friends have been helping you."

"No secrets in this town," Annabelle said under her breath as she stepped out of the way to let the Realtor see how much had been accomplished. "All but one of the bedrooms is empty. One bathroom is done and the other one getting there."

"You still have a lot of things to get rid of," Mary Sue noted as she took in the items piled up in the living room.

"These are all to be either sold or donated. I called the antique shop. Mary said she would come look to see if there is anything she can use. I wanted to wait until I had a chance to go through the kitchen."

"You are making progress, I'll give you that," the Realtor said, then *tsked* at the state of the walls in the emptied bedrooms. "Those are going to have to be painted."

Annabelle sighed. "Did you just come by to torment me?"

Mary Sue seemed surprised. "Is that what you think I'm doing?"

Annabelle didn't answer for a moment. "I'm just tired and out of sorts." Mary Sue would be, too, if she'd been working day and night to empty out this place. She hated to imagine how the Realtor would be if she'd just learned that her grandmother had left her a houseful of junk—and box full of disturbing secrets.

"So, you and Dawson…"

Annabelle gave her an impatient look. "Really? Have you had any interest in the house?"

Mary Sue shook her head. "It's a bad time of the year with Christmas coming."

Annabelle groaned. Before she could escort the Realtor out, she had to listen to Mary Sue's other suggestions regarding paint color, possible new appliances, even the replacing of all the carpet in the house with hardwood.

She let out a sigh of relief when she was able to close the door behind Mary Sue. That's when she noticed the dark car parked across the street and realized it wasn't the first time she'd seen it there.

It was, however, the first time she'd realized there was a figure sitting at the wheel behind the tinted glass.

DAWSON OFTEN WENT for a horseback ride to clear his head. Unfortunately, it hadn't done much good today. He kept thinking about his mother's earlier visit and what she'd said about Annabelle. As if Annabelle wasn't on his mind enough.

But he had made a decision, one he thought even his

mother would support, he thought as he returned from his ride.

"We got Annabelle's house pretty much cleared out, but you're right, she needs more help." The words were barely out of Dawson's mouth before his mother took off her apron, tossed it down and said, "So, what are we doing standing around here? Let's pack up some food. I'll get your brother up to help and make a few calls."

When he hesitated, she asked, "That is what you want, right? Jason told me how hard you all have been working to help her get the house ready to sell so she can leave."

He nodded. "That's the plan, remember?"

Within minutes, his mother was on the phone lining up able-bodied men and a couple more trucks.

"I already helped," Luke said when he was rousted from bed.

"So I heard. But today we're getting everything out of the house to begin cleaning and painting," she said, making her youngest son groan. "Get a few of your friends to meet us at the Clementine place."

Luke groaned. "If I call them this early, they'll kill me."

"Tell them your mama said if they don't get up and meet us there—"

"Got it." He threw back his covers, then quickly pulled them over himself again. "Could I have a little privacy?"

"Like you have anything to hide," Dawson joked from the doorway.

He had no idea what kind of reception they were going to get once they reached Annabelle's grandmother's house, but he didn't have to worry.

The moment they drove up, Annabelle opened the door, looking both leery and surprised. She'd already filled a dozen more boxes and had them sitting at the end of the porch.

His mother was out of the truck in a shot, her arms full of food as she charged toward the door.

"Willie?" Annabelle said and looked to Dawson for clarification. As if he could control his mother once she set her mind to something.

"Point me to the kitchen." But his mother was already headed there by the time Dawson reached the edge of the porch.

"I'm going to need your keys to move your car," he said to Annabelle.

She looked a little dumbstruck as two more pickups arrived, both full of boxes. Luke trudged toward the house, a carton full of cleaning supplies in his arms.

As if sleepwalking, she reached back inside for her keys. When she dropped them into his palm, he gave her a quick nod.

But before he could turn away, he saw surprise and something more in her big blue eyes. Gratitude? Surely nothing more. That night outside the bar after he'd kissed her, she'd told him to stay out of her business. Then, last night, she'd seemed willing when he'd kissed her, before his senses had come back to him.

She couldn't be anymore confused than he was about last night. But, in his defense, she'd been real clear about him leaving her alone and he hadn't been listening. Still wasn't. But that didn't mean she hadn't been sincere in what she wanted—and didn't want—from him.

"Dawson," she began.

"Annabelle?" It was his mother calling. She seemed about to say something more to him, but turned back into the house as Willie asked where they should begin. Luke's friends simultaneously began to bring in the cardboard boxes.

Dawson didn't see much of Annabelle after that. He

kept busy hauling the last loads to the dump. Willie had put Luke's friends to work filling boxes with old newspapers and magazines and dragging them out to the porch. If anyone could organize an army, it was his mother.

They broke for lunch. By then, Willie had managed to get both spare bedrooms and a bathroom cleaned. She put Luke and his friends to work painting.

"Neutrals," Willie said in response to Annabelle's surprise. "I called Mary Sue and asked her what we should paint the rooms. I just happened to have some paint. I hope you don't mind."

But Dawson could tell that she didn't believe his mother had never-opened gallons of neutral colors just sitting around anymore than he did.

"I can't tell you how grateful I am for all of this," Annabelle said, her voice breaking. "I don't know how to thank you."

Willie reached across the table to squeeze her hand. "No need. We're practically family." She shot Dawson a look that said they would have been family if it wasn't for him.

He lowered his head and sighed inwardly. His mother didn't think he'd done enough to try to stop Annabelle from leaving thirteen years ago. Maybe she was right about that. But ultimately, nothing on this earth could have kept Annie in Whitehorse—certainly not him.

ANNABELLE COULDN'T MISS the look that passed between mother and son. Dawson appeared uncomfortable, taking a sandwich from the plate his mother passed around and going out to the tiny back porch rather than eating it in the crowded kitchen.

"I'm sure this is your doing," Annabelle said when she joined him on the porch with a sandwich of her own. She sat down beside him to let her legs dangle over the side, much as she had when they were kids.

"My mother?" He shook his head. "You know how she is. She likes to help."

"And she just happened to have a lot of neutral-colored paint she wanted to get rid of."

He grinned over at her. "I told her how anxious you were to get the house sold…" He shrugged.

She looked off into the distance to the line of trees that marked the edge of the Milk River. The backyard was still lush in places, even after a hot summer and long fall. But she could tell the temperature was dropping. Soon the cold and snow would set in. She had to be out of here by then.

"How are you holding up?" he asked.

She smiled, knowing what she must look like in her grandmother's hand-me-down clothes, her hair under a bandanna, smelling of dust and old musty things. "I can see the floor now in all but a couple of the rooms. I'm feeling…better."

He nodded. "What about your grandmother, the photos, the newspaper clippings?"

Annabelle shook her head. "I still can't believe it. Frannie used to tell us stories about these outrageous parties she went to when she was, like, seventeen and all the crazy things men would buy her, furs and diamonds…" She laughed. "We never believed a word of it. I mean, look how she lived here in Whitehorse. I can assure you, there are no furs or diamonds that I've run across in this house."

"I would agree if I hadn't seen the photos."

She drew out the hem of the dirty sweatshirt she had on. "Most everything I've found in her closet looks like this, only with gaudier designs. Frannie didn't even own a car and she used what was left in her bank account to pay the utilities and taxes so I'd have time to sell this place." Her voice broke. "This house was all she had when she died."

She could feel the heat of his gaze as he looked over at her. "She had more than this house. Everyone in town loved her. She was always doing for others. She was rich in friends. To her, that was more important than furs and diamonds," he said as he finished his sandwich and got to his feet.

"You mean her values were better than mine."

He stopped and looked at her. "I wasn't comparing the two of you." He brushed again at the invisible chip on her shoulder.

"Last night…"

"I shouldn't have kissed you," he said quickly and looked away. "You've made it clear how you feel about me, this town, Montana in general."

Had she? "I'm not even sure how I feel about a lot of things," she said, looking up at him.

Willie called from the doorway. "I thought I would start cleaning the kitchen cabinets unless there is something else you'd rather I do."

"No, that's great," she said, pushing to her feet as Dawson hopped off the porch to walk around front. "I'll come help you."

DAWSON OFTEN FOUND himself in awe of his mother. Just watching her in action was a sight to see. The afternoon passed in a blur of activity. The house smelled like cleaning products and paint, which was much better than dust and decay.

"We paint the kitchen tomorrow and finish the rest of the rooms," Willie was saying. "I expect all of you back here after work tomorrow to help."

Luke's friends nodded. His mother commanded respect. He knew no cowboy stupid enough to go against Willie.

Annabelle started to object but his mother cut her off saying, "I'll bring my chocolate cake." As if anyone needed more incentive.

That got grins out of Luke's friends. Willie's chocolate cake was famous.

Dawson hadn't said two words to Annabelle since their talk on the back porch. Mary from the local antique shop had come up and taken what she wanted. After everything had been removed from the house except for a chair in the living room, the bed and dresser in Annabelle's old room, and the kitchen table and chairs, they called it a day.

Everyone began to leave. His mother packed up a few things to take home. When Dawson offered to carry them out to his pickup—since the two of them had ridden in together—his mother waved off his help. "I'm riding with Luke. See if there is anything else you can help Annabelle with."

As if he was fooled by that. Annabelle wasn't, either.

"Thank you, but you've done more than enough," she said as Willie left.

She and Dawson eyed each other in the silence that filled the house following his mother's exit.

"Look, I know you said—"

"Thank you." She met his gaze. "It would have taken me weeks to accomplish all of this..." Her voice broke.

He shrugged. "You needed help. That's what people do here for neighbors." Then he tipped his hat and left, headed straight for the bar. "See you tomorrow," he said over his shoulder.

Chapter Twelve

"What are you doing?"

At that moment, Annabelle was wondering why Mary Sue was calling her, let alone asking her such an inane question. There was music playing in the background and the sound of drunken voices.

"A few people from high school thought you might want to come down to the bar for a drink." She sounded as if those few people were holding a gun on her, forcing her to make this call. A few people from high school? "We're down at the Mint. If you're interested..." Mary Sue also sounded like she'd already had a drink or two. "You have something better to do?"

Now, that really was the question, wasn't it? "I just need to shower and change."

"Great. See you soon." Mary Sue disconnected.

Annabelle considered calling her back and declining. What had she been thinking, saying she would go? But really, did she have something better to do? Fall into bed exhausted. That also had its appeal, but she headed for the shower. When was the last time she'd been out with a bunch of women? She thought of her clubbing days and groaned inwardly. Those days were gone and she wasn't even sure she missed them.

Showered and changed, she pulled her hair up and drove

down to the Mint. A glass of wine sounded perfect. Maybe two. Then back home to bed.

The moment she walked in, she spotted Mary Sue with a handful of young women she wasn't sure she recognized. But as she approached the table and each of the women greeted her, she began to remember them. Mary Sue had traveled in a different circle than Annabelle had in high school. But the school had been small enough that she'd still known everyone.

Mary Sue got her a glass of wine and some of the others pulled up a chair for her. There was the usual chatter around the table—men, mothers and work. Fortunately none of it was about her or why she was back in town. She figured Mary Sue had warned them not to try to interrogate her. She was just starting to relax when she saw Dawson nursing a beer alone at the end of the bar.

DAWSON LOOKED UP from his beer and saw her in the mirror over the bar. He swore under his breath. What was Annabelle doing here? Had she followed him?

He turned on his bar stool, surprised to see that she'd showered and changed, unlike him. She was sitting with a bunch of women, women she'd never associated with in high school. But they all seemed to be getting along as if old friends. Go figure.

He turned back to his beer, determined that she wasn't going to ruin it for him.

At the sound of a commotion and sudden raised voices, he turned, shocked to see that Annabelle was at the center of it. A bar patron who'd clearly had too much to drink was trying to pull Annabelle to her feet, demanding a dance.

"You think you're too good for us since you became some hoity-toity cover girl?" the man demanded in a loud, drunken voice. "You too good to dance with someone like me?"

Annabelle was trying quietly to tell the man that she was just there visiting with friends and didn't want to dance. "I appreciate you asking, but I'm really tired."

"Tired?" The man scoffed and jerked her to her feet and into his arms.

Dawson swore, put down his beer, slid off his bar stool and strode up behind the man. He recognized him as a cowhand from up north by the name of Clyde Brown. He laid a hand on the man's shoulder. "Let's leave the lady alone," he said.

"Lady?" Clyde scoffed as he looped his arm around Annabelle's waist and started to haul her toward the dance floor.

"Let her go," Dawson said quietly, afraid he could see how this was going to play out. Definitely wasn't what he'd had in mind when he'd come here for one beer and a little peace, if not quiet.

"Stay out of this if you know what's good for you, Rogers," Clyde snarled drunkenly.

And just as he'd figured, the cowhand shoved Annabelle. She crashed into the table edge, drinks going everywhere, as Clyde spun around, leading with his fist.

Dawson saw it coming long before the cowhand took the swing. He blocked it and grabbed the cowhand by the back of the collar. "I don't want to fight you. So let's just—"

"She ain't worth fightin' over?"

Dawson looked past the man at Annabelle. Before he could answer, Clyde broke free and took another swing.

From behind Dawson, he heard the cowhand's friends get up from where they'd been at the bar. He swore under his breath as he coldcocked Clyde and swung around to take on the rest.

Chapter Thirteen

Her face flaming from humiliation, Annabelle drove back toward her grandmother's house. She would never think of it as hers. It was her grandmother's, and she was suddenly angry that Frannie had left it to her. True, she needed the money from it to save herself, but right now she could overlook that.

In fact, the more she thought about it, the more she was convinced that Frannie had collected all that junk, filling the house full, just to keep her granddaughter in town for as long as possible. Not that that theory made any sense.

Within a block, she realized that the last place she wanted to be right now was in that house. She turned at the next street and headed east out of town. She had no idea where she was going. A part of her realized she was wasting precious gas, but at that moment, she didn't care.

The night was dark. There was no one on the highway. She drove mindlessly, wishing she never had to stop. The fact that she had nowhere to go after she sold the house terrified her. She had no plan, wouldn't have much money and had no idea what to do next.

At a sign for Nelson Reservoir, she turned off and drove down to the lake. The water shimmered even in the blackness of the dark night. She got out and walked to the edge of the shore, thinking about throwing herself into the icy-cold water. The thought actually made her laugh. As bad as things were, she still wanted to live.

She thought of Dawson, probably still back at the bar fighting those men—and all because of her. She kept seeing the expression on his face when the man he called Clyde had asked if she was worth fighting over.

Annabelle shook away that image, still embarrassed. Dawson had fought the man for her. He'd come to her rescue. Again. She shook her head and breathed in the night air. Mary Sue had gotten her out of there as the bar had erupted into a half-dozen fistfights. She'd passed a patrol SUV, lights and sirens blaring, headed for the bar as she'd left.

If only someone would make an offer on the house. Now it was more than a desperate need for the money. She had to get out of this town. She had to get away from Dawson before she ruined his life as well as her own. Right now he could be sitting in a jail cell because of her. If so, she didn't even have the money to get him out. She owed him money for keeping her car from being repossessed, as it was.

She groaned, suddenly chilled by the November air, and headed back to her car. Just the thought of Dawson choked her up. Why did he have to be so nice to her? She'd hurt him. Why couldn't he act like a jackass and make her glad that she'd left him as well as Whitehorse?

On the drive back, she reminded herself that the house was coming along nicely—thanks to Dawson and his family. Tomorrow most of the rooms would be finished, then there was no reason Mary Sue couldn't start showing the house. By this time next week…

As she pulled into the drive, her headlights flashed across the front of the house. Her breath caught in her throat. She slammed on the brakes, her eyes widening in alarm at the sight of someone inside the house. She cut the lights and sat in the dark staring, telling herself that as upset as she was, she had to have imagined—

The figure moved past the window.

Annabelle threw the sports car into Reverse and stepped on the gas. The car roared backward and into the street. At the sound of screeching brakes, headlights filled the inside of her car. She had only an instant to realize how close she'd come to being hit before her car door was jerked open.

"WHAT THE HELL?" Dawson demanded as he reached in and pulled her keys. "Are you drunk?"

Annabelle stumbled out from behind the wheel and into his arms. He could feel her trembling. "There's someone in the house."

"You can't just back up like that without looking," he snapped before her words registered.

She turned her face up to him. It looked ghastly white. Even her bow-shaped mouth was trembling. "In the house. I saw someone."

Her actions began to make sense as he looked from her to the house. "Stay here."

She nodded, those blue eyes wider than he'd ever seen them.

He considered moving the cars out of the middle of the street, but figured if she really had seen someone in the house... He still had her keys in his hand. "A house key on here?"

She pointed to a large square one.

"Get back in your car out of the cold and stay there."

"Maybe you should call the police."

"I just had a long talk with the sheriff, so no thanks."

"Then be careful."

Was she actually worried about him? He'd fought four cowboys because of her and held his own pretty well.

While her concern was touching, he knew it was just something a person said when they were sending someone into a house after an intruder.

As quietly as he could, he crossed the porch to the front door. He listened for a moment before slipping the key into the lock. Slowly he turned the knob.

The door swung open. A now familiar fresh-paint smell rushed out at him. He listened, heard nothing while he waited for his eyes to adjust to the semidarkness before he stepped in and turned on a light.

He figured if there really had been someone in the house, they were long gone by now. They would have heard the commotion out in the street. They would have seen Annabelle's headlights when she pulled in.

But he wasn't taking any chances as he moved quietly through the house, checking one room after another. There was no sign of anyone. He checked the back door, still locked—just as the front door had been. He checked windows, all locked.

He walked through the living room into the kitchen and turned on the overhead light. Again, no sign that anyone had been here.

He went to the wall concealing the alcove, recalling Sadie's reaction. He'd just squatted down to inspect the white beadboard wainscoting when he heard a sound behind him.

Shooting to his feet, he spun around only to find Annabelle standing in the doorway. She still looked terrified. Her gaze met his. He shook his head, telling himself he shouldn't be surprised that she hadn't done what he told her to—stay in the car.

"Is he gone?" she asked and saw Dawson's expression.

"I couldn't find any sign of anyone being here. Everything is locked up tight. Nothing looks disturbed, not that there is much to disturb at this point."

"But I saw…" She swallowed and shook her head. "Someone." She met his gaze, hoping he would tell her it was possible. She could see that his knuckles were skinned and there was a cut on his cheek near his right eye, the skin around it bruised.

"The place was locked up tighter than a drum. If someone broke in… I didn't see it."

She hugged herself. "So, you're saying I imagined it."

He wasn't saying anything. He looked down at his boots then finally lifted his gaze to her. He saw her bristle. "It isn't that I don't believe you thought you saw something…

"Why are you here?" she demanded.

He felt himself balk at her sudden anger. Right now, he had no idea. "I thought that after what happened at the bar… I only wanted to check to make sure you were all right. I'll move your car."

She said something he didn't catch as he started past her and caught a hint of her perfume. It had the same effect on him that it had thirteen years ago. He increased his stride as he headed for the front door. Remembering how she felt in his arms only minutes ago in the middle of the street, he feared that if he even hesitated, it would only make him do or say something foolish.

"I'll bring you back your keys," he said as he walked out the open front door, thankful his senses were starting to clear in the fresh air of the porch. But as he turned, he saw that the keys he'd left in the door were gone and Annabelle had pulled her car into the drive, but his pickup still sat in the middle of the street. Something about that seemed to mock his behavior tonight.

Hearing her behind him, he said over his shoulder, "Lock up behind me." He almost added that if she had any more trouble tonight to call him. "Call the sheriff if you see anyone around the house again."

He was almost to his truck when he heard the front door of the house slam as if caught by the wind. He looked back to see her pass by the front window. All he caught was a glimpse of her, since she'd turned out all but one of the hall lights. But he could tell that she was crying.

The sight stirred his earlier protectiveness. "Damn it, Annie," he said under his breath. "Why do you have to keep doing this?"

The night had no answer. He saw a light come on in her old bedroom and felt an ache that threatened to double him over.

He had to get her out of Whitehorse. Get her house sold. Get her on the road. No matter what it took. Otherwise... She was going to get into his heart again.

And yet, even as he thought it, he feared it was too late.

ANNABELLE KNEW WHAT she'd seen. A man moving through the house. No ghost of her grandmother, even though, for a moment, there had seemed to be a white light around the figure. No doubt a reflection from her headlights. She didn't believe in ghosts.

She moved through the house searching every closet and cubbyhole, checking the windows and doors herself, turning on all the lights. Dawson was right. The house was empty. All the windows and doors had been locked.

He hadn't believed her. Worse, when she'd come into the house, she'd found him inspecting that stupid wall in the kitchen. Did he think the intruder had escaped through it, somehow?

Exasperated, tired, upset and generally irritable, she stood in the living room trying to decide if she was going to leave all the lights in the house on tonight. It seemed silly, but she was tempted. Angry with herself for being such a chicken, especially given that apparently she'd only imaged the intruder, she went through the house turning off lights until she reached her bedroom.

She was still annoyed with Dawson and realized she had no good reason to be. He'd worked here at the house all day, he'd saved her at the bar, he'd driven over to check on her, he'd braved coming into the house to look for the intruder...

The man just couldn't stop saving her. He must be getting sick of it. Hadn't he pretty much told her that the only reason he was helping her with the house was to get rid of her more quickly?

Well, it wouldn't be quick enough for either of them, she told herself as she started into her bedroom on the first floor and froze.

The loose floorboard where she'd discovered the metal box with Frannie's photos and newspaper clippings was sticking up just enough that only she would notice it. Her heart began to pound as she looked around the room. The board wasn't the only thing out of place.

Her pulse a steady panicked throb in her throat, she saw that someone had moved her bed.

Chapter Fourteen

Annabelle stood nailed to the spot, her mind racing as fast as her heart. *Someone had been in the house.* Dawson wouldn't have pried up the floorboard, but he might have moved her bed when he was searching before she came in.

The thought sent a chill through her, because when she'd searched the house minutes ago, she hadn't looked under the bed. She glanced toward the closet. All that was in it were her grandmother's ugly clothes. No trespasser.

Edging toward the bed, she stopped next to the disturbed floorboard. With her toe, she pushed it back down, knowing whoever had been in here hadn't escaped that way. Now that she was closer, she could see where the legs of her bed had scraped across the floor all the way to the wall. How strange. The bed had definitely been moved.

Slowly, she bent down to peer underneath.

At first, all she saw were dust bunnies, relieved not to find a man hunkered under there. But then she saw something that sent her already thundering heart into overdrive. A scrap of fabric was caught in the corner of one of the floorboards. *Another secret hiding place, Grandma Frannie?*

Rising, she went to the side of the bed. It was heavy, the headboard and footboard made of solid wood. But she got it to move an inch at a time until the bed finally stopped at the wall.

The scrap of fabric appeared to be a gray and white stripe. She touched the cloth. Not an ounce of dust on it. Nor were there any dust bunnies on a large portion of the floor.

As she moved closer, she saw a spot on the floor that had been carved out like…like a handhold. Blinking, she realized what she was seeing. A trapdoor.

She started to try to lift it, but quickly thought better of that. What if the man she'd seen was down there? She pulled out her phone. Her first thought was to call the sheriff. Her second was to call Dawson.

Annabelle was so tired of needing to be saved that she pocketed her phone and went into the kitchen to her grandmother's utility drawer. Willie had managed to get all the top cabinets and some of the lower ones cleared out and cleaned earlier today, but they'd decided to leave this drawer for now because it held all kinds of keys, screws, bolts, nuts and tools, all things that they might need before they were finished.

She brought out the hammer and hefted it, gauging its weight, then grabbed a small flashlight that she quickly found worked. Hurrying back into the bedroom, she found the trapdoor was just as she'd left it. If the intruder was down there, he hadn't tried to get away, because the scrap of fabric was still caught in the corner.

Leaning down, she grabbed the handhold and lifted. The door was heavy but she managed without having to put down the hammer. It groaned upward. She saw that a table leg had been attached so the door could be propped open.

Cautiously she shone the flashlight beam into the gaping hole, surprised to find several wooden steps that dropped down into blackness. What was down there? The piece of cloth that had been caught in the door fluttered down into that darkness. She aimed the flashlight beam into the space, only to see what appeared to be a passageway.

Annabelle listened, chilled to her soul at the sight. *Oh, Grandma, what were you involved in?* She thought of Dawson earlier on the back porch painting Frannie as a saint. Did saints have hidden trapdoors under beds? Or secret passageways dug under their houses?

There was no way she was going down there. Not tonight. Maybe not ever. Exhaustion pulled at her. Slowly she closed the trapdoor. In the kitchen, she dug some nails out of the utility drawer. Back in the bedroom, she pounded four nails through the door and into the floorboards next to it. A crude job, at best, but effective. She put the hammer aside and pushed her bed back into place.

If someone was down there, he wasn't getting out. Not tonight. She told herself she would deal with it tomorrow.

Chapter Fifteen

Annabelle had been hoping to get Dawson alone to tell him about the trapdoor. It was proof that she hadn't been mistaken last night or overreacted or been trying to get his attention. Or whatever it was that he'd thought.

He arrived again with his mother and brother and a small crew armed with rollers and paintbrushes. Everyone fell into line with Willie cracking the whip. Drop cloths were put down, paint cans were popped open, rollers and brushes were handed out and in no time the once-dingy walls took on new life.

Annabelle and Willie emptied the rest of the cabinets in the kitchen and cleaned them in preparation for the painters. Dawson had hauled away the last of the junk. All that was left behind was what Annabelle would need to live here until the house sold.

Willie had asked if Annabelle wanted her to empty the closet in her bedroom of her grandmother's things, but she'd declined, saying she would do it later. The truth was, the clothes were the last of her grandmother's belongings. She'd kept the cookie jar where Frannie had put her "loose change" as well as a few other personal things including several boxes of Christmas tree ornaments, but the truth was, her grandmother hadn't had much worth hanging on to.

"Tell me," Willie said as they cleaned the last cupboards. "What was it like, modeling?" She sounded genuinely interested.

Annabelle rinsed out the rag she'd been using before she answered. "It was hard work. Hardly anyone believes that. They think you just stand there, turn one way then another, smile and go about your day. It was hours of shooting, often either in the cold or the heat. And that wasn't even the worst part."

She stopped, realizing that she'd said more than she'd originally planned. But Willie was looking at her expectantly, as if waiting for the rest.

"There is the not eating, but you get used to that. The working out every day of the week to keep in shape. The always being made up in expectation of someone snapping your photo on their cell phone and selling it to the tabloids, with an accompanying story about how sick you look, how fat, how tired, how ill-dressed. So you're always 'on' except when you're alone in your apartment."

"I'm guessing that still wasn't the worst part," Willie said.

Annabelle let out a bitter laugh. "No. There are the men who have power over your career and the desperate young faces who want your job. At first, it was wonderful, unbelievable. The parties, the money, the famous people you get to meet, seeing your photo on the cover of a magazine." She shook her head. "But none of it is real. Your photos are all doctored. That's not really you on the cover or in the ads. Because even if you look good, you don't look good enough without Photoshop."

She took a breath, shocked that she'd let all of that out—especially to Dawson's mother.

"So, you're going back after you sell the house?" Willie asked.

Tears stung her eyes. "I don't have a choice. I'll never work again at the level I did before, but it's all I know."

Willie scoffed at that. "We all have choices. Some are harder than others. What I'm hearing is that you feel trapped. Sounds like you're the only one who can change that. Just make sure you don't latch on to the first life raft that comes along. It wouldn't be fair to anyone to find yourself trapped in some other way, now would it?"

Just then, Luke came in to announce that the other rooms were done.

But Annabelle had gotten the message loud and clear. *Willie's son wasn't a consolation prize for the mistake she'd made with her life.*

After a quick lunch, Annabelle and Willie painted trim in the bathrooms, neither talking. Willie'd had her say. Annabelle didn't blame her for the warning.

Several of the crew had to leave, which left Dawson and Luke to paint the kitchen.

"I can't believe how different this house looks," Willie said after they'd cleaned their brushes and wandered through the finished rooms. She stopped at Annabelle's bedroom. "You sure we can't paint this room today? We can move the bed and—"

"I'd like to do this one myself," Annabelle said.

"Sure, sweetie, if that's what you want."

"I appreciate everything you've done," Annabelle said quickly.

Willie patted her arm. "Honey, we were glad to help. Now you can get it on the market."

She nodded, afraid she would cry. There was so much she wanted to say. She'd hurt this woman's son, and yet here was Willie helping her. Or maybe she wanted Annabelle out of town so she didn't hurt her son again.

WHEN THEY WERE finishing up for the day, all Dawson wanted to do was make a quick getaway. But his mother seemed to be dragging her feet. The house was coming along nicely. The only room that hadn't gotten painted was Annabelle's bedroom. According to his mother, she wanted to paint that one herself.

More than likely she was just ready for them all to clear out. He knew *he* was ready. Every moment he was around her, he was intensely aware of her. It wore him out. It was time to let them both get on with their lives.

He'd just picked up the cooler his mother had packed and started for the door, when Annabelle said, "Dawson, could I speak to you for a moment?"

He knew he must have looked like a deer caught in headlights.

"Privately?" She motioned him back into the house.

"I'll catch a ride with Luke again," his mother said quickly and grabbed up her belongings. "I need to talk to him anyway." She was out the door before Dawson could argue.

Now, with just the two of them alone in the house, he shot Annabelle a weary look as he put down the cooler. "If this is about last night..."

"There's something I need to show you," she said without preamble and headed for her bedroom.

He watched her go for a moment before following. At the bedroom door, he stopped. She was standing by the bed. For a moment, he thought she'd brought him in her to...to do what? Seduce him?

She shoved the bed with all her strength, sending it skidding across the floor until it hit the wall.

He blinked in shock, his mind racing. What the—

She pointed at the floor. His mind was still on Annabelle standing next to a bed in her bedroom and him thinking... His gaze dropped to the floor. He stared.

"Are those nails?" he asked. They were sixteen-penny nails, large enough that even with half of them embedded in the wood, the other half was sticking out a good three inches. All he could think was that she'd lost her mind—until he saw the handhold carved into the floor and realized he was looking at a trapdoor.

"What the hell?" he said as he moved closer.

She nodded at his surprise.

"Did you know that was under your bed?"

"Not until last night when I came back into my room and found my bed had been moved."

So they were back to her believing that someone was in her house last night?

"Remember the metal box I told you I found under the floorboards? That same floorboard had been pried up and hadn't been pushed back down all the way. I knew someone had been in here. When I knelt down, I saw that the dust bunnies under the bed had been disturbed. Also there were marks on the floor where the bed had been moved."

He had to give her credit, that was pretty observant of her. When he'd searched her house for an intruder, he hadn't noticed any of that. "It must just be an opening to the crawl space under the house. Did you—"

"I took a look, but no, I didn't go down there. But *someone* did. I found a piece of cloth caught on the trapdoor. It hadn't been there long since there was no dust on it."

He stared at the trapdoor with the nails sticking out of it for a moment. "I'm assuming you have a hammer."

She reached over to the bureau, retrieved the hammer and handed it to him. "That's not all. Remember the metal box with the photos and newspaper clippings? I had put it in an empty drawer in the kitchen. Well, it's gone."

He looked up at her. "But it didn't appear that anyone had broken into the house. Unless…" He glanced down at the trapdoor. "Sorry, I didn't believe you last night."

She nodded, seeming to let it go.

It took a few minutes to remove the nails. She'd hammered them down pretty good. He handed them to Annabelle, and after the last one, she gave him a flashlight. It was small and not all that powerful, but he figured he wouldn't be going far. He'd seen trapdoors in other homes that were merely a way to get down to the crawl space if needed.

That's why he was surprised when he shone the flashlight beam down into the hole and saw the footprints on what appeared to be steps. He glanced at Annabelle. She flashed him an impatient look that said maybe it was high time he started trusting her. Now that was definitely something he wasn't going to ponder right now.

"I'll go down and see—"

"I'm going with you." She had her arms crossed, and her jaw set, and determination burned in those blue eyes.

"I can tell you right now there are going to be spiders, cobwebs, maybe even mice and only God knows what else down there."

ANNABELLE DID HER best to hide her shudder. "I'm going."

He shook his head. "Suit yourself, but don't say I didn't warn you."

She still had the bandanna covering her hair and wore the baggy jeans and ugly sweatshirt. Perfect for a tour of the hidden space under the house.

Dawson took a tentative step onto the top stair, then dropped down the next three. The steps were wide apart.

When he reached the earthen floor, he turned to offer her a hand. She hesitated only a moment before taking it. Even with his help, she had too much momentum and ended up in his arms.

He chuckled. "If that's all you wanted, we could have stayed up in your bedroom."

"Funny," she said, pushing herself off his rock-solid chest.

He turned to shine the flashlight beam under the house. "Huh?"

She too was surprised to see that they were standing in what appeared to be a narrow trench. "Isn't this awfully deep for a crawl space since we don't have to crawl?" she asked.

He shot her a look. As he shone the light toward the rear of the house—and the darkness, he said, "If you are still determined to come along, stay right behind me."

Once away from the trapdoor, the damp, earthy air became close. The flashlight beam punched a small hole into the absolute blackness ahead. She grabbed hold of his tooled leather belt. When she tried to see around his broad shoulders, a spiderweb hit her in the face. She shuddered and wiped crazily at it with her free hand.

"You all right back there?" he asked, amusement in his tone.

"Fine."

He stopped. The flashlight beam flickered upward and she saw that they had reached the back of the house. "Watch your head," he said as he ducked under the edge of the foundation.

This time when she glanced past him she saw that this underground space didn't end under the house. It made a sharp right-hand turn and then appeared to keep going. They would have to either crouch down or crawl.

"What is this?" she whispered, although she doubted anyone could hear them this far underground. That thought sent a chill through her.

"It appears to be a tunnel."

"A tunnel? A tunnel to where?"

"Good question," he said. "I'm not sure you should go any farther. We have no idea how long it's been here. If it were to cave in—" She started to argue, but he stopped her. "One of us needs to be able to call for help if the other doesn't come back. You want to see where it goes? Or..." He turned her around. "Or do you want to make your way back to the bedroom? Just keep walking until you reach the light." As much as she hated to admit it, he made a good point. "Give me five minutes once you reach the bedroom. If I'm not back, call for help because part of your backyard would have caved in on me."

"Maybe you shouldn't—"

"Sure you can find your way back?"

She swallowed the lump in her throat and nodded. He gave her a little push and she started walking. It was pitch black all around her. She put out her hands. Spiderwebs brushed her fingers. She stumbled and had to grab hold of the dirt bank next to her. She thought she heard a scampering sound and wanted to run.

But she kept her gaze on the faint light ahead and walked as swiftly as possible. When she reached the steps up into her bedroom, she turned to look back. All she could see was darkness. Not even a faint flashlight beam.

She pulled herself up the steps into her bedroom, grabbed her cell phone and set the timer for five minutes. That's when she saw the spider on her sweatshirt sleeve.

Annabelle had been a runway model, but she'd never undressed that fast in her life. Opening the window, she tossed the clothes and bandanna, spider and all, out the window. She could still feel spiderwebs in her hair. Phone in hand, she streaked across the hall to the bathroom. Turning on the shower, she jumped in, letting the warm water wash away the dirt and dust and spiderwebs as quickly as possible. The alarm would be going off in a few minutes. If Dawson hadn't come back...

DAWSON FOLLOWED THE TUNNEL, aware of the fresh prints in the soil ahead of him. Annabelle was right. Someone had recently been in this tunnel, which would explain how someone had gotten into the house without breaking in.

As he shone the flashlight into the blackness ahead, his mind raced. How long had this tunnel been here? Had the first owners of the house dug it? For what?

He'd read stories about secret passageways. In Mexico, wealthy Spanish silver families years ago had tunnels dug under their houses to get their families and silver out in case of an attack by outlaws. But what would a family in Whitehorse have to fear? What would a sweet old lady like Frannie Clementine have to fear? Or to hide?

He thought of the newspaper clippings and the walled-up alcove. *Oh, Frannie, what secrets did you have?* Maybe more to the point, why leave the house just to Annabelle? *Was there something here that you wanted only her to find?*

His flashlight beam shone on what appeared to be more stairs ahead. Reaching the end of the tunnel, he climbed up a step to push on another trapdoor. It creaked open, but only a fraction of an inch. That was enough though to see where the tunnel ended—in the old garage behind the house. Someone had pushed several heavy bags of sand onto the door. To hide it?

WHEN THE ALARM on her phone went off, Annabelle was just stepping from the shower and ready to call the sheriff for help if Dawson hadn't— She let out a shriek as the bathroom door swung open and jumped back into the shower to cover herself with the plastic curtain.

"You do realize that shower curtain is see-through, don't you?" Dawson drawled as he stepped into the steamy room and turned off her phone's alarm.

"You scared me half to death," she snapped. "I was ready to call the sheriff so we could start digging for you. You could have knocked."

"I did. When I saw your clothes flung all over the yard, I got worried."

"There was a spider…"

He nodded, still looking at her. She had to give him credit, though, his gaze was on her eyes. But she could tell that he was enjoying himself. He'd caught her at a distinct disadvantage.

"Well?" she demanded.

"The tunnel kept going all the way to the old garage. There was another trapdoor. Someone had pulled several bags of sand over on it recently, I would suspect so no one else found it."

"I wasn't asking about that. I meant that you should leave the bathroom and let me get dressed."

He glanced around. "It seems you didn't remember to bring anything to wear. It's a good thing the tunnel didn't cave in on me."

"I was ready to call for help." She cocked her head at him. "A gentleman would leave."

He chuckled at that, his gaze locking with hers. "You and I are way past that, Annie."

Her heart did a dip-tee-doo at the sound of the pet name. He'd only called her that when they were alone and always when they were intimate. The heat of the shower had warmed her cheeks, but nothing like the sound of that cherished name on his lips.

Without breaking eye contact, he handed her a towel.

Her pulse throbbed under her skin as desire rippled through her. In his eyes, she could see that he remembered what they'd shared right down to the last kiss, the last caress, the last time they'd made love.

She let go of the shower curtain to pull the towel around her. When she did, his eyes definitely weren't on hers.

Chapter Sixteen

Rob walked along the edge of the Milk River. He could only assume it had gotten its name because it resembled chocolate milk. The river was more like a wide ditch. It backed up onto Frannie Clementine's property.

After the old lady had been a problem, he'd known he couldn't keep walking around the neighborhood. Unfortunately, there were a lot of old ladies like her. Driving past was almost as bad. He swore most of the neighbors spent their time at the window looking for trouble.

He'd gone through the metal box of photos and newspaper clippings last night. If he'd had any doubt that Francesca Clementine was his uncle's Baby Doll, he no longer did. He had to get back into that house, but it had been a beehive of activity. He'd watched box loads of belongings being hauled out.

After following one of the trucks, he'd realized with a sinking feeling that all of it was going to the dump. All but some old furniture that he'd seen dropped off at a local charity shop. What if the granddaughter didn't realize what she was throwing away?

He told himself that wasn't possible. She wouldn't throw away priceless gems. He had to believe what he was looking for was still in the house.

Anxious, he wanted to end this. The motel in town

was adequate but nothing like his home in New York. The weather was colder and he couldn't get any of the food he'd grown accustomed to in the city. It made him jumpy and irritable. Everywhere he went he saw cowboys and pickups. Last night he swore he heard mooing cows. He'd looked out his window to see a semi parked across the street. Sure enough, the back was loaded with cattle.

"I have to get out of here," he said to the wintry-looking landscape. The temperature had dropped and a fog had rolled in. Now everything was covered with frost. He kept slipping on the icy grass along the edge of the river. So help him, if he fell in, he was going to kill someone today.

Last night he'd seen the trapdoor in the old barely standing garage and thought he'd hit the jackpot. But once he'd dropped down in it, he realized it was a tunnel. Following it, he'd ended up in one of the bedrooms. It had taken all of his strength to move the bed aside enough that he could get the trapdoor all the way open.

Once inside, the house had proved to be uninteresting. He'd found the metal box with the photos and newspaper clippings, confirming what he already knew. Francesca had been Baby Doll. But that's all he found.

So what was the point of the tunnel? He hadn't had enough time to search the house well. He didn't think the loot was hidden in the tunnel. It seemed more like an escape route. The old lady must have had it installed in case someone discovered who she was, what she'd done and just how much stolen loot she had gotten away with.

Now he stopped at the back of the house. He could see only a portion of it through the dense, bare-limbed trees and the rock wall next to the river. On the other side was the old garage. He studied the property for a few long minutes trying to decide what to do next. From what he'd seen

in the house, the crew who'd been helping the granddaughter should be about done.

The granddaughter would finally be alone. He was
counting on it. The first step would be seeing what she
knew. Then disposing of her. He could hide her body in
the tunnel while he tore the house apart.

He'd been so sure that the woman in the obit wasn't
his uncle's Baby Doll. Then he'd been certain that, if she
was, she'd blown the loot long ago. Then he'd discovered
the tunnel and that had changed everything. The way he
saw it, Frannie Clementine had the tunnel dug as an escape route in case she was found out. She would have
been afraid of what Bernie would do if he found her. The
woman wasn't stupid.

But if she was that afraid, then Rob's instincts told him
she probably lived on the cash and gold but wouldn't have
dared fence the jewels. She would have known that Bernie and his associates were all waiting for even one of the
pieces to surface. Which meant the gems were still in that
house. All he had to do was find them.

"You know what this means," Dawson said, rising up on
one elbow.

She looked into his eyes, her heart pounding. When
she'd awakened, all she could think was that this was what
everyone had tried to warn her about. But being with Dawson had felt so right. She still loved him. Had never stopped
loving him.

That didn't mean she knew what she wanted to do with
the rest of her life. She thought about Willie's warning.

"You know what we have to do now," he said.

A dozen thoughts raced through her mind. Her mouth
went dry. Did he think because they'd made love and fallen
asleep in each other's arms that it meant she was back?

That they would take up where they'd left off? All her conflicted feelings for him aside, her life was a mess. She couldn't commit to a paint color if she had to, let alone what she wanted to do with the rest of her life right now.

"We have to bust open that wall in the kitchen."

She stared at him in disbelief. "What?" That was the last thing she'd expected him to say. He must have seen her relief because his brown eyes dimmed a little. His look said, *It's okay, Annie. I know you don't want me.*

Annabelle wanted to cry out that it wasn't true. She'd never wanted anyone the way she did him. But everything was so complicated right now. She would never know if he'd just been an easy way out. Worse, he'd never know if that hadn't been the case.

DAWSON HAD SEEN the panic on her face when they'd awakened in each other's arms. The passion was still there between them, the chemistry, even the love. Last night had proved it. But it wasn't enough to keep her in Montana, maybe especially with a Montana cowboy like him. She'd been out in the world. She'd lived a glamorous life. Being a ranchwoman was a far cry from the way she'd been living in California.

"Annie, the tunnel, the metal box, all of it," he said, hoping she didn't see his disappointment. Had he really expected last night to change anything? "Who knows what other secrets your grandmother had, but given what we do know…we have to open that wall."

A laugh escaped her. He saw her relief and felt his heart drop even more. Obviously last night hadn't meant the same things to her that it had to him. Still, he wouldn't have changed anything. They'd wanted each other, needed each other. Even as he'd taken her in his arms, he'd known it was temporary and he hadn't cared one damn bit.

This morning…well, only a fool would have thought that making love with her would change everything.

"WE HAVE TO look at all the evidence," Dawson said as he climbed out of bed and began pulling on his clothes. So they weren't going to talk about last night. Apparently they were back to business as usual, which meant getting this house sold and her gone.

"No woman has an escape tunnel unless she has something to hide," he was saying.

She felt bereft as she watched him dress and leave her bed. As much as she wanted to call him back, to try to explain… "Maybe the original owner—"

"The original owner didn't have it dug. This was the bedroom you grew up in, right? Was that escape hatch under the bed?"

She shook her head. Nor had the board been pulled up to hide a metal box. But there had been an alcove in the kitchen that was now gone. She didn't want to believe that any of this was true because of what it said about her grandmother. What it said about Annabelle herself. There was a reason her grandmother had left only her the house, she was starting to realize.

"We're talking about Frannie," she said as she got up and quickly dressed. She saw that Dawson had retrieved her clothing from the yard, sans spider. She dropped it into the hamper and put on her own jeans and one of her new T-shirts. "You remember Frannie? Local do-gooder, tiny, sweet, always helping others."

"I remember her. But you're forgetting. Sweet Frannie had a past. She was a mobster's moll."

She turned her back to him as she dressed. "We don't know that," she argued over her shoulder. "Just because she had her photo taken with that mobster a few times…"

She knew she was clutching at straws, but this was Frannie. The grandmother she wanted to believe had left her the house because they were so much alike.

Slowly she turned to look at Dawson. He was so handsome that sometimes it took her breath away. Big, strong, broad shouldered, slim hipped and all cowboy. But also tender and sweet and as trustworthy as the day was long. "You're determined to tear into that wall, aren't you?"

"Just as determined as you are not to touch it. I know you're scared…"

He had no idea. She swallowed. She'd come this far. "Okay."

"We have to open that wall," Dawson said. "We have to know what's back there. Maybe nothing."

"You don't believe that."

"No, I don't. All these secrets… You have to admit, walling up the alcove like that…"

She nodded.

"I promise to fix it better than new so you can sell the house. I'll do it quickly so it doesn't hold up the sale. If there is nothing behind it, you'll be gaining an alcove. It will add to the value of the house."

Annabelle mugged a face at him. "And if there is something behind that wall that shouldn't be?"

He shrugged. "Better to find out now than later."

She headed into the kitchen, suddenly scared. She hoped her grandmother had merely lost her marbles, decided she didn't like the alcove and had someone come in and wall it up. Or maybe she did the work herself. Her grandmother was a master at a lot of things around the house, as Annabelle recalled.

Now that she'd remembered the hutch that had been in the alcove…that meant that her grandmother had to have closed up the space sometime in the thirteen years that Annabelle had been gone.

"I have a sledgehammer in my toolbox in the back of the truck," Dawson said from behind her. "And a better flashlight."

Annabelle nodded and listened as he hurried out to his pickup. Her gaze was on the wall. In the morning light, it appeared innocent enough. It was what might be behind there that had her terrified. *Oh, Grandma, how many secrets do you have?* Maybe more important, what was Frannie expecting her to do about them?

Dawson returned quickly. He hesitated, looking over at her. She nodded and he hefted the sledgehammer.

"You want to do the honors?" he asked.

She shook her head. She didn't want to know what was behind there. She'd already learned enough disturbing things about Frannie and feared they were about to learn even more.

Dawson stepped back and swung the sledgehammer, making a huge hole in the Sheetrock. He swung again, making an even bigger hole. The third time, the Sheetrock crumbled enough that they could see into the hole.

He put down the sledgehammer and picked up the large flashlight he'd brought from his pickup. This one had a broad, strong light. Glancing at her, he said, "Ready?"

She nodded. There was no going back now. She stepped to the hole as Dawson shone the light into the darkness beyond it. The first thing that hit her was the smell.

He let out a curse. Annabelle couldn't speak. *Oh, Frannie, what have you done?*

Chapter Seventeen

Sheriff McCall Crawford stepped into the kitchen. She'd never been in Frannie Clementine's house. Few people had. While always up for helping others, she'd kept to herself the rest of the time. McCall had known the woman was a hoarder and her house was full to the brim. No wonder she didn't have friends over—not even her neighbor Inez Gilbert.

"In here," Dawson Rogers said now, as he motioned toward the large hole in the wall at the end of the room. McCall wondered if he and Annabelle Clementine were back together since her return. News of the supermodel's return had the entire county talking—and speculating.

He handed her a flashlight. McCall took it as she looked at Annabelle standing with her back to the kitchen counter, arms crossed around her, a scared, stony, shocked and worried look in her eyes.

Turning on the flashlight, McCall stepped to the hole and shone the light in. What she saw shouldn't have surprised her. When Dawson had called and said they'd found something at Frannie Clementine's house that they thought she should see, she hadn't been sure what to expect. Being in law enforcement she was seldom surprised.

At first, all she could see was the rotted, once-clear plastic the body had been wrapped in. Sometime over the years, the decaying body stuffed in the hole had burst the rotting plastic. It appeared that the gelatinous remains of the body had run out, soaking into the floorboards. The rest of the body had rotted along with the plastic and was now little more than a gluttenous blob and bones.

With a sigh, McCall straightened and looked at the granddaughter. "You have any idea who this might have been?" she asked.

Annabelle shook her head. Her blue eyes were wide with shock and fear and no doubt revulsion.

McCall looked to Dawson. "How about you?"

"Not a clue."

"Any reason you decided to look in this wall?" the sheriff asked and listened as he explained about his puppy's reaction. "So this used to be an alcove that you believe your grandmother walled up?"

"For obvious reasons," Dawson said before Annabelle could answer. As he did, he reached over and took the young woman's hand, making McCall wonder again what their relationship now was. Idle curiosity, since everyone in the county knew that she'd broken his heart when she left town all those years ago.

This latest discovery would only add to the intrigue, McCall thought as she looked past them to the window. A small crowd had gathered. Taking a quick inventory, she realized someone was missing.

"Has anyone see Inez lately?" she asked.

ANNABELLE LOOKED AS if she was in shock. "You can't stay here tonight," Dawson said, feeling guilty. He'd been determined to open up this wall even though he'd known she hadn't wanted to. Had he expected to find a body? Or was he thinking he might find the missing jewels from the

Marco Polo exhibit heist they'd read about in the newspaper clippings Frannie had saved in the now missing metal box?

"I have a guest room," he added, seeing how anxious Annie already was.

"He's right," McCall said. "You can't stay here. In fact, I need you both to clear out while we take care of this." She turned to the deputy who came through the door. "Run over to the neighbor to the south and see if Inez is all right."

The deputy seemed surprised that Inez wasn't already over there finding out what was going on. Clearly so was the sheriff.

She looked to the two of them. Annabelle seemed rooted to the floor. "If you need to get a few personal things," the sheriff said, "do that. I'll let you know when you can get back into the house."

Dawson already had Annie's hand in his. Hers was freezing cold. He gave her a little shake. "The sheriff needs us out of here."

"Who is that?" she asked, motioning toward the former alcove.

"We won't know for a while," McCall said and looked to Dawson. "You'll see that she's okay?"

Those words finally seemed to bring Annabelle out of her stupor. She nodded, saying, "I'm fine," even though it was clear she wasn't. She numbly followed him out to his pickup. The street was full of people. Some called to him, asking what was going on. He merely shook his head and hurriedly loaded Annabelle into the passenger seat, then ran around to slide behind the wheel.

Annie was staring at all the gawking people. "Everyone is going to know what Frannie did."

He wanted to argue that they didn't know it had been Frannie's doing, but he doubted she would believe that any more than he did. Once they'd seen the photos of her with the mobster, they'd stopped being sure what Frannie might have done.

He drove toward his ranch. Annabelle stared out the side window, appearing to fight tears. "I'm sorry," he said.

"It's not your fault."

"I never should have opened that wall."

She finally looked over at him, her blue eyes swimming. "She had to have killed him and then closed off the alcove to hide his body." She shook her head as if trying to chase away the memory of what she'd seen. "This is why she left me the house and not my sisters."

He wasn't sure how that computed.

"I just don't know what I'm supposed to do with this," she said. "She wanted me to know about her past. She left it all for me, including what we found behind the wall."

"I doubt your grandmother meant for you to find the body," he argued.

She gave him a patient look. "Why do I feel as if all of this is a warning?"

NEWS OF THE discovery traveled like quicksilver through the town. Rob heard people talking about it everywhere he went. He wasn't sure what rumors to believe. But the bottom line was that a body had been found in the house—and no jewels, as far as he knew.

Back in his motel room, he called his uncle and told him.

"They have any idea who the man is?" Bernie asked.

What shocked Rob was that his uncle didn't sound all that surprised. "Not yet. Why? Do you think you know him?"

Silence, then finally Bernie said, "I might."

Rob swore. "Someone you had looking for her?"

"I had a lot of people looking for her. Mickey Frazer, remember him?"

"Wait. He disappeared like fifteen years ago?"

"Maybe less than that."

"I thought the speculation was that he got hit by the Italians."

His uncle chuckled. "I might have started that rumor since he was always fighting with a few of them."

Rob couldn't believe this. "So how did he end up dead in some wall in Whitehorse, Montana?"

"If I had to guess? He found Baby Doll and she did him in, stuffed him into a wall and covered up the whole thing before he could contact me with her location. If that was his plan. So, what about the jewels?"

"The place is now crawling with cops," Rob complained. He wasn't about to tell his uncle that part of the reason was the death of the neighbor, a woman named Inez Gilbert. She'd been found at the bottom of her basement stairs with a broken neck. "If any of the loot is left—"

"It's there and I want it, understand?"

Oh, Rob understood perfectly. "How do you expect me to find it—if it is there? They are still digging Mickey's remains out of that wall. If the gems were in there with him... Well, they're gone, okay?"

"She wouldn't have put them in the wall with a guy like Mickey Frazer. No, she would have hidden them somewhere else. Remember, the woman was smart, cagey. So find the jewels."

"I don't get it," Rob said. "Why take the jewels if she wasn't to sell them or fence them?"

"Truthfully, I think she thought she was saving me from a prison sentence. As it turned out, she probably was. The Feds turned the city upside down looking for those gems. They would have found them if Baby Doll hadn't absconded with them. Maybe she thought she was doing me a favor."

"Yeah, I bet that was it."

"Just find them."

Rob stared at his phone, realizing that his uncle had hung up on him. He cursed a blue streak as he disconnected. A thought struck him. Once the cops were through over at the house, he could get into it. The granddaughter wouldn't stay there now. He knew how to get in—and out—without notice. All he had to do was wait until the cops cleared out.

"We get an ID on the body?" County Attorney Rand Bateman asked from McCall's doorway.

"Frannie made it easy. The man's leather wallet was in the hole with him." She picked up the plastic bag with the New York driver's license in it and held it up. "Michael James Frazer. From what I've been able to find out, he was involved in the Irish mob in New York City."

"Cause of death?"

"The coroner found blade marks on his ribs."

Rand shook his head. "Unbelievable."

"That's not the half of it." She motioned to her open computer. "Ever heard of the Marco Polo Heist?" He shook his head. "Me, either. Way before my time. But fifty-six years ago, it was big news. Several men died during the robbery. Only one was believed to have gotten away, Bernard 'Bernie the Hawk' McDougal, an Irish mob kingpin. The men killed all worked for him. There was never enough proof to arrest Bernie, but he was questioned about the heist, according to what I've found out so far."

"What could any of that have to do with Frannie Clementine?"

McCall leaned back in her chair. "Michael 'Mickey' Frazer would be seventy years old now if he had lived. But that's not the interesting part. Guess who he worked for?"

She nodded. "Bernard McDougal. Although Bernie was suspected in the Marco Polo Heist, he was never convicted and the gems were never recovered. Now one of his men ends up dead walled up in Frannie's house. The coroner says he's been there for from ten to fifteen years."

Rand swore under his breath. "So the body wasn't in the house when Frannie bought it."

McCall shook her head. "In the wall we found newspapers she must have used to wipe up the blood. The dates on the papers bear out the fact that she was the owner of the house when the body went into the wall about twenty years ago. Frannie had to have known—even if she didn't personally put the body in the space and wall it up."

Rand had been standing, but now he pulled up a chair and sat down. "I knew Frannie Clementine most of my life. She went to our church. Hell, we had her over to dinner." He met her gaze. "I don't believe it. What did the granddaughter say?"

"She seemed to be in shock. I'm sure what we found took her by surprise, but I am curious what made them open the wall."

"Them?"

"Dawson Rogers was with her. He told me his puppy sensed something about the wall that scared her. There was a definite smell. Also, when Annabelle was getting the house ready to sell, she realized that an alcove had been walled over. I think they were just curious."

"How could Frannie have kept something like this a secret for...?"

"I don't think there would have been a smell since the body was wrapped in multiple plastic sheeting, trussed up like a turkey, but the plastic had rotted and the some of the contents had leaked out."

Rand cringed. "And the Gilbert woman?" he asked, as if anxious to change the subject.

"Apparent accident."

The county attorney eyed her questioningly.

McCall shook her head. She didn't want to admit that she had a feeling it hadn't been a sad mishap. Inez had been wearing a coat and boots, as if she'd been outside. Also, deputies hadn't been able to locate the old woman's shotgun. McCall knew for a fact that she kept it by the front door. Inez had bragged about it, saying she liked to have it handy. Now it was missing.

DAWSON WOKE WORRIED about Annie. He got up to find the guest room empty. He found her sitting at the computer in his office. She looked up, startled to see him in the doorway.

"I didn't think you'd mind," she said.

He shook his head. "What are you looking at in the middle of the night?"

"The sheriff, when she called earlier, asked me if I'd ever heard of a man named Michael 'Mickey' Frazer."

Dawson stepped into the room and sat down on the edge of his desk. "Is that who was in the wall?"

She nodded. "McCall had found out the Marco Polo Heist and that Mickey worked for Bernie McDougal. What she doesn't know is the connection between Frannie and Bernie. Without the photos..." She broke down. "Isn't it bad enough that everyone will know Frannie was a murderer? Do they have to know that she was a mobster's moll?"

"Annie." He wanted desperately to comfort her but he was trying to keep his distance. Making love the other night had been a mistake—at least, he could tell she thought so. He knew better than to let it happen again—for his own heart's sake if not hers.

"Worse, I don't understand is how deep my grandmother is involved in all this," she said between sobs. "She had to be the one who killed that man and put him in the alcove and then walled it up. Along with jewels taken in the Marco Polo Heist there was a whole lot of cash. Apparently the museum hadn't taken the deposit to the bank. Because the Marco Polo exhibit had been so popular, there were thousands of dollars in a safe that was blown open. And I thought my grandmother lived all those years on my grandfather's insurance policy."

"Annie, you can't let this—"

"She must have been in on the heist. She was definitely in New York City at the time. Robbery is nothing compared to murder and hiding a body in your house behind a wall."

Dawson reached over and shut off the computer. "Come on, it's almost daylight. Let's get out of here." She let him pull her to her feet. "Get changed. I'll saddle up the horses."

THE SUN ROSE fiery red over the prairie. Annabelle breathed in the sweet scents of the late-fall day. She could see her breath in the cold morning air, but it felt good to be on a horse again. Good to get away from her troubles for a while.

She looked over at Dawson. Now, there was someone who felt at home in the saddle, she thought. Past him the Little Rockies loomed up into a brilliant blue sky. The breeze carried the scent of the pines as well as the creek next to them. Only a few golden leaves still remained on the cottonwoods. Fall here had always been a beautiful time. She realized how much she'd missed the seasons, missed a lot about Montana.

Her gaze went to Dawson again. Her heart ached. She was surprised by how much she'd missed him. Her life in California had been filled with busy, long, stress-filled days trying to make something of herself. She'd forgotten what it was like to just relax and enjoy the day.

"Better?" Dawson said.

She nodded and looked away, realizing she'd been staring at him. He'd aged wonderfully. If anything, he was more handsome. There was a confidence to him that had also grown. Dawson Rogers knew who he was, what he wanted, what tomorrow would bring and he was good with that.

Tears burned her eyes; she turned to swipe at them.

"It's going to be all right," he said softly as he rode beside her. "Once the sheriff is finished at the house, I'll go in and make that kitchen like new. You'll get the house sold and—"

"Dawson," she said, her voice breaking as she turned toward him. "I don't care about the house, about any of that."

He swung off his horse. The next thing she knew his big hands were on her waist and he was lifting her down and into his arms. She let the tears come again, crying her heart out, soaking his jean jacket with her tears.

One hand smoothed her hair, while the other held her tightly to him. He said soothing words, whispered into her hair as he let her cry.

When she finally was able to stop, he handed her his bandanna. She wiped her eyes and blew her nose. He took the bandanna back, stuffing it into his pocket. She couldn't help but smile at him. He'd always been there for her. Always.

"I love you." The words came out on their own accord. She couldn't have stopped them even if she had wanted to. "I love you so much."

He nodded. "I love you, too." His voice sounded rough with emotion.

"The other day after we made love—"

"You don't have to explain," he said. "I know."

"You do?"

"We both got lost in the moment. I'm not sorry, but I know that it didn't change anything."

Hadn't it?

"Come on. Let's head back. I suspect the sheriff will be calling."

She looked into his face. There was so much she wanted to say to him. "I need to tell you—"

"You don't have to say it," he said, handing her the reins to her horse. "I know you appreciate my help. That's what old friends are for."

She took the reins, feeling her heart breaking all over again. She realized he wouldn't trust anything she said at this point. She'd just had her second emotional breakdown. Given what had been found in her grandmother's kitchen wall, of course, she would be emotional.

But it was Dawson, being back here with him, that was killing her. She hadn't known what she wanted, but looking at him right now, he was all she wanted.

"Is there someone else?" she asked as he gave her a boost up into her saddle.

He seemed to hesitate for a moment. "I've been seeing Amy Baker," he said, swinging up into his saddle. He reined his horse around. The sun had come up making the day shine. "That sun sure feels good, doesn't it? I'll make us some breakfast when we get back. You still love French toast?"

DAWSON HAD NEVER thought of himself as a coward, but he'd had to cut Annie off from whatever she was going to tell him. He couldn't bear the thought of her telling him that their lovemaking hadn't meant anything. That she was still heading back to her life in California once the house was sold.

Those were all things he already knew on an intellectual level, but he'd let his heart hope for a different outcome. Sometimes the way she looked at him, he would swear… But he knew that she'd been through so much, she probably didn't even know what she needed. He didn't want her making the wrong decision. But he didn't want her staying with him for the wrong reasons, either. He honestly didn't know what was right for her and he doubted she did either right now.

Back at the ranch, he'd sent her inside while he unsaddled their horses. Holding her earlier had made him want to throw down one of the horse blankets and make love to her out there in the wild. He wanted her so badly…

He pushed that thought as far back into his heart as he could. Once her house was sold… It was the mantra that kept playing in his head. But when he thought about her leaving, it almost knocked him to his knees.

"There you are."

He turned at the sound of his mother's voice.

"Are you all right?" she asked, closing the distance between them to look into his face as if she could read him like a child's book. "Oh, Dawson."

He shook his head, swallowing the lump in his throat. "I'll be fine."

She shook her head. "I heard what happened at the house. Annabelle's staying with you?" Her gaze searched his face.

"It isn't what you think. She's staying in the guest room." He'd never seen his mother cry, but right now she looked close to tears. He put his arm around her. "Once the sheriff lets her back into the house, I'll go over and get the kitchen fixed and then the house should be able to go on the market."

Her mother was shaking her head. "Who's going to buy it knowing…"

He'd thought of that and was sure Annabelle had, too. "I might have to buy it."

Willie nodded. "Okay, son. You could use it as a rental, I suppose. You're that anxious to get her on her way?"

"I have no choice."

"I suppose not." She sounded as sad about that as he did.

ANNABELLE HAD SEEN Willie drive up and head out to where Dawson was unsaddling the horses. She watched them for a moment before stepping into the bathroom to check herself in the mirror. Her cheeks were still pink from the November air. Her eyes weren't as bad as she thought they would be considering all the crying she'd done earlier. She couldn't help being embarrassed. Dawson, as usual, had been kind and understanding. It was his tenderness that kept breaking her heart.

Her cell phone rang. She stared down at the number. Clarisa? It was one of the models she used to work with. Her phone rang again. She thought about not answering it. She'd spoken to hardly anyone she'd worked with since everything went south. Clarisa was one of the new, younger models, but a sweet girl who was just starting in the business.

The phone rang again. Curiosity made her take the call. "Hello?"

"Annabelle, I'm so glad I got you. I was worried you wouldn't pick up. So, have you heard?"

Apparently not. "Heard what?"

"About Chambers. More models have come forward after hearing what happened to you. At first, everyone was

scared to speak up, but then they did, one after another."
Clarisa was laughing. "Chambers was arrested yesterday
on assault charges. Everyone is talking about it. It happened because of you."

She couldn't believe what she was hearing. When she'd
reported Gordon Chambers, she hadn't been believed.
Gordon owned the top modeling agency in Southern California. If you crossed Gordon, your career was over. Annabelle had dodged his advances until he'd offered her a
modeling job she would have given her eyeteeth for—but
not at the cost of sleeping with him.

She'd told him what he could do with his job and then
gone to the authorities, for all the good it had done. Chambers had instantly blackballed her. Word went out. She'd
known he could hurt her. She hadn't realized how badly.
He was telling everyone that she was impossible to work
with and denying her charges. That's all it took and she
couldn't get another job.

"I have even more good news," Clarisa was saying. "I
ran into Thomas Darrington the other day. He asked if I'd
seen you. Apparently he'd heard about Gordon blackball-
ing you. Anyway, I brought him up to speed. He said he
wants you for a big spread he's going to be doing after the
first of the year. Girl, I really think you can have just about
any job you want now. A lot of people had the same problem with Gordon and you brought him down."

Only she hadn't brought him down. She'd only started
the ball rolling. She took a breath and let it out. Her heart
was pounding. She could go back. She had a job. She'd always liked working with Thomas Darrington, an up-and-
comer in the business and someone she'd worked with
before. Thomas had made her an offer she couldn't refuse.
She could have her old life back. According to Clarisa, it
was waiting for her.

"You need to take down Thomas's number and give him a call," her friend was saying. "He's really anxious to talk to you."

She found a notepad on Dawson's desk and wrote down the number. "Thank you for letting me know."

"I was afraid you hadn't heard," Clarisa said. "You were always so nice to me when some of those other models..." She laughed. "I hope you come back. Give me a call anytime. Also, I know a model who's looking for a roommate, if you're interested."

Annabelle disconnected and looked down at the number she'd written on the notepad. Next to it, she'd written *Thomas. Modeling job.* She still couldn't believe it. Just when she was at her lowest.

At the sound of Dawson's voice, she stuffed the note into her jeans pocket. As happy as she'd been just moments ago, she felt that awful pull on her heart. Could she really go back and leave here? Leave Dawson?

"Annabelle?"

Just the sound of his voice made her close her eyes for a moment, as if memorizing it. She loved him. He was all Montana cowboy. He'd never leave here. If she left him again, there would be no coming back.

Chapter Eighteen

Dawson noticed the change in Annabelle when he and his mother entered the house. They'd all congregated in the kitchen, with Willie talking about how it wouldn't take long to get the house back in order and on the market.

Annabelle was quiet, nodding, but saying little. When their eyes met, he saw pain in them. There seemed to be a sadness to her, a resignation. He told himself he was glad he'd stopped her when they were out on horseback. More than ever, he felt that she'd been about to tell him what he already knew. That she was leaving as soon as the house sold.

He whipped up French toast, talking his mother into staying and joining them. He didn't want to be alone with Annabelle. He told himself that if he kept busy...

They'd turned the conversation to the weather and the upcoming holidays when Annabelle's cell phone rang. She pulled it out and glanced at the screen as if she'd been expecting a call. At her frown, he surmised that it wasn't the one she'd been waiting for.

Excusing herself, she stepped away from the table. He and his mother both pretended not to listen, but it was clearly the sheriff calling to say they were finished at the house and she could move back in.

"You'll get the work done for her?" Willie asked.

He nodded as Annabelle returned to the table.

"Honey, you dropped something." His mother knelt to pick up what appeared to be a sheet from his office note-pad. She glanced at the writing on it before handing it to Annabelle. Dawson couldn't miss what was written there. If he'd had any doubts, any hopes, they were dashed.

He watched Annabelle stuff the note into her pocket quickly. Her gaze locked with his for a moment and she seemed about to say something when Willie spoke.

"Dawson and I were just discussing your kitchen," his mother said. "Are we going to close off the alcove again or open it up?"

"You have both already done so much," Annabelle said.

"We finish what we start, isn't that right, Dawson?"

He was still looking into Annie's blue eyes, feeling his heart breaking all over again. He mentally cursed himself for letting it happen. Of course he'd fallen for her again. Hell, he'd never stopped loving her.

"I'll get right on it. The sooner the better," he said and got up to clear away the dishes.

"Let me help you with those," Annabelle said, but he quickly cut her off.

"I've got them."

"Yes," his mother said, as if seeing that he needed to be alone. "Annabelle, why don't you and I go back to the house and see what we need to pick up?"

Annabelle started to say something, but he heard his mother whisper, "Let's leave Dawson alone for a while, okay?"

ANNABELLE STARED AT Dawson's back. He'd seen the note. So had his mother. She wanted to tell him that she was torn, that she didn't know what she wanted, that she couldn't bear leaving him again. But she couldn't do that to him again. She'd put him through enough, so she left with Willie.

For much of the way into Whitehorse, neither of them spoke.

"Want to talk about it?" Willie finally asked.

"You saw that I've been offered a modeling job back in California. I'll admit that at first I was excited. I thought for sure I'd never get to work again."

"So it's good news."

She looked over at the older woman. "I can go back to that life. In fact, they want me back." She told Willie why she'd left and what had apparently happened.

"I'm so sorry," Willie said. "That must have been awful."

"Yes, it was. But the others came forward. They backed me up."

"So there is no reason you can't go back to the life you had."

"You know there is a reason," Annabelle said. "Just the thought of leaving Dawson again..." She had to look away as tears welled in her eyes. Determined not to break down again, she said. "I don't think I can leave him."

Willie looked over at her as they pulled up in front of the house behind Annabelle's car. "You love him."

"With all my heart. I always have. But I wanted to see what I could do outside of Whitehorse."

"What do you want now?" Willie asked, but before she could answer there was a tap on the window.

They both turned to see Mary Sue standing there as if waiting for them. Willie hesitated a moment, as if not wanting to quit their conversation, before she turned to put down her window.

Annabelle felt a moment of relief. What did she want to do?

"I thought you might need me," Mary Sue was saying. "The sheriff called me to say that the house was open. I suppose we'd better see how bad it is and decide what to do."

Willie agreed and put up her window. As Annabelle started to get out, the older woman touched her sleeve. "You know how I feel about you and about my son. Make the right decision for yourself. If you stay for the wrong reasons, you'll resent him and the life he has to offer you." She dropped her hand, smiling sadly. "I just want you both to be happy."

DAWSON HAD NO idea how much work undoing Frannie's remodeling in the kitchen would take. All he knew was that he had to do it quickly and then hope the house sold. If not, he would buy it. He'd already made up his mind. He would just have to do it through a subsidiary of the ranch corporation so Annabelle didn't know it was him buying it.

He wasn't far behind his mother. In fact, he drove up right as Annabelle was opening the house. Mary Sue was here, no doubt to see how bad it was going to be. That, or morbid curiosity. He imagined that would be the case for a lot of people once the house was on the market. Another reason he had to act quickly and probably buy the place. He didn't want Annie to have to go through that.

She opened the door and he saw her grimace. There was a definite smell. They all trailed inside. He pushed his way through, wanting to see how bad the kitchen was, to spare Annabelle if it was as bad as he suspected.

But she wasn't having any of that. She was right behind him. The alcove was wide open. The sheriff's department had made the opening larger to get the body out. It appeared that McCall had had someone clean up the floor.

But the frame of the stained wall was still there. That was the first thing that would have to go.

He turned to find Annabelle staring at the hole. "Want it walled back up or opened?" he asked.

"Open. But I can't ask you to—"

"You aren't asking. I'm going to get my tools, tear the rest of this out, take up the floorboards. The flooring in the kitchen will have to be replaced but there isn't that much. It won't take long. I was thinking a nice hardwood floor." Before she could object because of the price, he added, "It will help sell the house, trust me."

She closed her mouth and nodded. "I do trust you. I already owe you so much."

"I'm sure money won't be a problem once you're back at work."

ANNABELLE DIDN'T GET a chance to reply as Mary Sue and Willie came into the kitchen. Mary Sue was complimenting everything that had been done. Willie offered to show her the rest of the house. The two of them left as Dawson headed for his pickup and tools.

She stood in the kitchen feeling almost dizzy. So much had happened. The poor old woman next door had died after falling down her stairs. Not to mention Annabelle's grandmother had walled up a man in her kitchen.

"Is there anything I can—"

Dawson cut her off as he returned with his tools. "I've got it. I called for the subfloor sheeting and the lumber to be delivered. This won't take long."

She nodded and stepped out of his way as he strapped on his tool belt. He couldn't have looked more sexy, she thought and quickly moved out of his way.

From upstairs came voices. Willie and Mary Sue were visiting, discussing people they both knew. It seemed most people in Whitehorse were related to each other in some way.

Annabelle walked down to her bedroom. It was the last room of the house to be painted and cleaned out. She closed the door and called Chloe. "Hi," she said when her sister answered.

"What's wrong?"

She let out a nervous laugh. "You can tell by that one word?"

"I know you, remember?"

Yes, unfortunately, her sisters did know her. That's why they didn't like her. "Something's happened." She explained about the walled-up alcove and what had been found inside.

"You can't be serious. A man's body?"

"I'm afraid so. Would you let TJ know? From what the sheriff has told me, it's been in there for years. I remembered there used to be an alcove there. Do you remember it?"

"I suppose. It's just been so long. I'm not sure I would have remembered. You're saying this happened when?"

"After we all left home. That's what the coroner thinks so somewhere in the past thirteen years."

"How did he get into the wall?" Chloe asked.

Annabelle stifled a laugh. The question was so like her sister. *Oh, he just crawled into the alcove and curled up to die while Grandma built a wall around him.* "He was murdered, wrapped in plastic and walled up in the kitchen."

"They can't think Grandmother did that!" her sister cried.

"I'm afraid that's exactly what they think." Annabelle thought of the photos and the newspaper clippings. It was all going to come out. She figured warning her sisters was the kindest thing she could do.

She told Chloe about what she'd found under the floor-board and under her bed, along with what she found in the metal box.

"That is the most ridiculous thing I have ever heard," Chloe snapped when she was finished. "Our grandmother was not a mobster's girlfriend."

"The dead man worked for the mobster. The sheriff thinks the man followed Grandma from New York and that the reason she killed him probably has to do with the Marco Polo Heist, a famous robbery back in New York. They've never found the jewels or the money that was taken."

Chloe had fallen silent.

"I'm sorry to hit you with all of this, but it is going to come out," Annabelle said.

"What is that noise?"

"Dawson is in the kitchen removing the rest of the wall and putting down new flooring."

"That house is never going to sell."

Annabelle thought her sister was probably right about that. Murder houses weren't that popular. "I will probably be returning to California and keeping the house on the market. I've been offered a really good modeling job." Annabelle glanced in the direction of the kitchen. "Unless I decide to stay."

"You're thinking about staying? You have to stay at least until Christmas. TJ and I have already bought our tickets. We were going to surprise you. Surprise! We're coming up there to help you sell the house and have Christmas together. We were planning to be there a few days before Christmas Eve."

"Really?"

"Would that be all right or do you need to get to your job before then?"

"No, it would be wonderful." Annabelle was having

trouble believing they really were coming back to help her so the three of them could have Christmas together, especially after she'd just told them the news.

"Now, more than ever, I feel like we should be together for the holidays," Chloe said.

Annabelle was fighting tears when she heard the knock at her bedroom door. "I couldn't be happier," she said, her voice breaking. "I have to go, but I will talk to you soon."

"Am I interrupting?" Willie asked when Annabelle opened the door, still fighting tears.

She shook her head. "That was my sister Chloe. She and TJ are coming up to spend Christmas with me."

"That's wonderful." Willie hugged Annabelle. "I'm happy for you." As she pulled back, she said, "Dawson thought things would go faster if you came out to the house and stayed at the ranch until he's finished."

She could see what the two of them were trying to do. "Thank you, but I'm staying here."

"Are you sure?" Willie asked, glancing over her shoulder toward the kitchen.

"I'm sure." Annabelle smiled. "My grandmother left me this house because she knew I was the one who could deal with all this."

"Yes, you're plenty strong," Dawson's mother agreed.

He called from the kitchen, wanting Annabelle to see if she liked the hardwood floor he'd ordered.

"I'm going to take off, then," Willie said. "If you change your mind…"

"I know where you live," Annabelle said with a smile. "Thank you again for everything."

"You bet," Willie said and called goodbye to her son as she left.

Dawson looked surprised. "I thought she was going to ask you to stay at the ranch."

"She did. I'm staying here."

He didn't look happy to hear that. "It's going to be noisy and dusty."

"I'll make do. My sisters are coming up for Christmas." She laughed at his surprise.

"So you're staying that long? What about the job offer?"

"It wouldn't start until after the holidays. But I'm not sure I'm going to take it, anyway. I still have to get the house sold."

"Maybe you'll get lucky and the house will sell and there won't be anything keeping you here after the holidays," he said and turned away to show her the flooring.

"It's beautiful. Thank you. I'm getting better at accepting help, don't you think?"

He glanced over at her. "You are."

"Who says people can't change?" With that, she turned and left him to it.

Rob couldn't believe how quickly the house had filled up again after the sheriff's department finished its investigation. He'd kept his ear to the ground, but it seemed there hadn't been anything else of interest found.

"I think the old girl got rid of the loot," he grumbled to himself. "Maybe she didn't even try to fence it. Could have sold it to a private collector. It wasn't like she hadn't met the kind of people who would have been interested. And now my uncle thinks she did him a favor? The foolish old coot definitely has dementia."

Still, he knew what his uncle would have said. Someone would have talked if they'd bought the gems. That was the problem with even the filthy rich, they liked to brag. If one of them had bought the jewels from Francesca Clementine, word would have gotten back to Bernie. And the old gal would have died a long time ago.

So she'd kept it for whatever reason. Hidden them like she had poor Mickey's body. He cringed at the thought of being walled up in a house like that. Sure, the goon was dead, but still.

Frannie, as everyone referred to her, had stiffed Bernie, gotten out of town and come out West telling everyone she was a widow. The woman probably couldn't have told the truth if her life depended on it. She couldn't have found a husband, gotten knocked up and become a widow that quickly, unless...

He frowned. Not long after arriving, she'd bought the house and given birth to a son, according to the local gossips he'd overheard at the café downstairs in the hotel. As far as anyone knew, she'd never had a full-time job other than raising her grandkids when they'd come to live with her when they were young. His frown deepened.

He stopped pacing to count on his fingers, then swore.

His uncle had wondered for over fifty years why she'd left like she had. He counted again to make sure before he picked up the phone. "You aren't going to like this," he said and then told Bernie. Let him do the math.

"I'M CALLING IT a day," Dawson said as he put away his tools. He'd looked up to find Annabelle standing in the doorway.

"I can't believe how much you got done," she said. "It looks great. I like that that stupid wall isn't still there."

"You sure you aren't going to have nightmares tonight?" he asked seriously as he closed his toolbox and straightened.

"No," she said, realizing it was true. "It's funny, but this house seemed more creepy with that wall. Now that's it's gone and what was behind it, I'm fine." She shook her head. "At least I know now why my grandmother left the house to me." She had to smile. "She said I was a lot like her."

"I hope not," Dawson said with a laugh.

"I guess we'll never know for sure what happened here. If McCall is right, then it all has to do with that museum exhibit on Marco Polo and the stolen jewels. I'd like to think the man's death was self-defense—and that grandmother did what she had to do to protect us all. If she was running from her mobster boyfriend... We already know that she was pregnant, probably with his child. It's funny. She always seemed so...content, as if she'd made her peace with the past and everything else."

"She did a good job of raising you girls and everyone in this community loved her."

"Well, they *did*. Wait until they learn about the man she kept in her wall."

"This town is pretty forgiving. Your grandmother did so much good in this community. That's what will be remembered."

"I hope so."

He stood for moment just looking at her. She felt the chemistry sparking between them and a whole lot of good past history making the kitchen suddenly seem too warm. "I should get goin'."

Annabelle stepped out of his way and let him walk out. She was staying for Christmas. There would be time to see how he felt about her maybe staying around. She watched him drive away and then closed the door and locked it.

"I wasn't sure you'd be back to the ranch tonight," Willie said as Dawson walked into her kitchen to find her standing over the stove.

"I don't know why not," he said and leaned in to see what she was busy stirring. "Chili?"

She nodded. "The way you and your brother like it."

"I thought we'd be eating leftover turkey for a few weeks," he said as he leaned against the counter to watch. When his mother was fretting over something, she cooked. He didn't have to ask what was bothering her.

"That huge old turkey carcass got picked clean at Thanksgiving," Willie said. "That's what's nice about having a lot of people over. Not a lot of leftovers."

"You don't mind me using some of the ranch funds to buy Annabelle's house?"

"I think it's a good investment."

He wasn't so sure about that. "I figure the sale will go through pretty quickly so she should be able to leave right after the holidays."

"Sounds like you have it all worked out." Willie stopped stirring the chili to turn to face him. With a sigh, she said, "I'm worried about you."

"I'll be fine."

"She doesn't want to go." Willie made it sound as if it was hard for her to tell him that.

"What would make you think that?"

His mother gave him a look. "You live as long as I have and you know things. She just doesn't know how to tell you so neither of you think she's taking the easy way out."

He shook his head. "Don't take this wrong, but this time, you're wrong." He started to turn away but she caught his arm and pulled him back.

"I was thinking as I was making this chili. Maybe it's time for some sort of grand gesture, you know, like they do in movies, to let her know how you feel."

Dawson chuckled at that. "She knows how I feel, Mama." He hadn't called her that since he was a boy.

She let go of his arm. "You want some chili?"

"I'm not hungry, but thanks." With that he left and headed to his own home, knowing that without Annie there it would feel empty—just like he felt.

ANNABELLE WOKE WITH a start. For a moment, she thought the sound had come from under the bed, but Dawson had secured the trapdoor with the nails. No one was coming up through that door.

She lay in bed listening. There was a strange light coming through the curtains. She frowned and quietly climbed out of bed to look. After a longer than normal Indian summer, winter had come while she was sleeping.

The first blizzard of the season had blown in. She could tell that the temperature had dropped drastically from the ice that was forming on the inside of the old windows. The sky, which should have been dark, was a pale gray color as huge snowflakes whirled in the wind, sticking to anything they touched.

She shivered and climbed back into bed, telling herself she must have heard the wind. Gripping the covers under her chin, she lay still, listening to the wind—until she heard a sound that sent her pulse into overdrive. The front door had just blown open!

ROB HAD KNOWN his uncle was going to be furious.

"She was pregnant? Pregnant with my kid?"

"If you do the math—"

"I did the math. I had a son I knew nothing about? Where is he now?"

"Died in a car wreck with his wife when the youngest kid was, like, four or five, I heard. You can't believe the way people talk in these small towns. If you stay here long enough, you hear—"

"So that's my grandkid staying at the house," his uncle said, clearly not listening to him. "My granddaughter. And Baby Doll kept this all from me." He was swearing again.

"So, what do you want me to do?"

"What I told you to do. Find the damned loot. But don't touch a hair on my granddaughter's head. You got that?"

He couldn't believe the old man was getting sentimental in his old age.

"I got it. But what do I do if she catches me in the house?"

"Figure it out. But don't you hurt her. Not one hair."

He'd hung up doing some cussing of his own. Then he'd gotten dressed and started to leave the motel, only to find that a snowstorm had blown in. Just his luck. But he couldn't put this off any longer. He would break into the house and finish his search. If he was right, no way would the granddaughter be staying in the house—not after a body had been hauled out of it.

ANNABELLE SCRAMBLED OUT of bed and rushed into the living room to close the front door. She turned on a light and was about to bolt the door, when she heard a noise behind her. Turning quickly, she saw the snowy footprints melting on the floor a second before she came face-to-face with Lawrence Clarkston, the old man with the cane who'd sworn he was Frannie's beau. He'd lied, according to Inez. Worse, she'd noticed his car parked in front of the neighbor woman's house across the street.

She stared at him, shocked to see him standing in the empty living room. Even more surprised to see the gun in his hand. He motioned for her to step away from the door.

"Where's the jewels?" he demanded. "I know your

grandmother still had them when she died. She might have
spent the money, but she still had the gems."

Annabelle groaned. "I don't know anything about any
jewels."

"My brother followed your mother out here. I never
knew where he ended up. She'd changed her name, her
looks, everything. I'm amazed Mickey was even able to
get a lead on her. Bernie was losing his mind trying to find
her. He's been looking for her for years. My brother finds
her and she kills him!"

She didn't know what to say. "If you knew your brother
found her—"

"He called, told me he'd found her but didn't give me
any specifics. Damned fool. He thought he could keep the
jewels for him, fence them and not have Bernie find out.
I was trying to talk him out of it, telling him how dangerous it would be." He laughed. "Instead, Bernie's Baby
Doll kills him?"

"He must have told you something since you showed up
at my door days before the body was found," Annabelle
said. She didn't know who or what to believe. This old man
had lied to her once already.

"I've kept my ear to the ground for years. When I heard
where Bernie was living now, I made sure I got a room
down the hall. He doesn't know me from Adam, but I know
him. He corrupted my brother. Mickey was a good guy before he met Bernie."

"So Bernie knows about Frannie?"

He nodded. "You know why they called him Bernie
the Hawk? 'Cuz he had an eye for the ladies—until your
grandmother came along. He fell so hard for that woman.
My brother said anyone could have told him she was trouble, but no one had the guts. I laughed my ass off when I
heard that she stole it all and disappeared."

Her mind was racing. She glanced around for a way out. Since they'd pretty much cleaned out the house, there was no handy weapon. The door was a few steps behind her, but she doubted she could turn and reach it before the man shot her.

"Look," he was saying. "Mickey wasn't all that bright. I thought he'd taken off with the jewels. But when I happened to see the newspaper in Bernie's trash at the rest home, I got curious. Bernie was all excited. Everyone at the home was talking about it. I went online, saw the Milk River Courier newspaper and checked out what Bernie had cut from it. The moment I saw your grandmother's face..." He smiled. "Bernie must have felt the same thing. Your grandmother was a looker. Played Bernie like a Stradivarius. Did you know she never told him her real name? He just called her Baby Doll."

The old man took a breath. "When I found out that Bernie had sent his worthless nephew, Robby, out here, I thought it was going to be another wild-goose chase. How wrong I was. So hand over the jewels and I'm out of here."

She started to tell him again that she really didn't know anything, when they both jumped at the sound of glass breaking.

Lawrence swore and said, "Stay right here." The moment he started toward her bedroom, she quickly unlocked the door. She didn't think the old man could move fast enough to catch her and once she was outside in the blizzard—

Annabelle had the door open and was almost outside when she slammed into a dark figure that appeared out of nowhere. She realized he must have thrown something at her bedroom window to distract the old man. This man wasn't old. He was big and strong and he literally lifted her up by her shoulders and thrust her back inside the house.

He'd just slammed the door behind him when Lawrence came running into the room, gun firing.

The younger man pushed her out of the way and drew his own weapon, firing at the approaching target. The old man staggered and went down. "Larry the Loser? What the hell is he doing here?"

She watched in horror as the younger man walked over and picked up the gun the old man had dropped. He pocketed it. Everything had happened so fast that she hadn't even moved. Now, as she started to bolt for the door, he turned to point his gun at her.

"Tell me you aren't going to give me as much trouble as your grandmother did my uncle," the man said.

"Your uncle?" she managed to get out. This must be Robby, the guy old man had mentioned.

"Bernie. He said to say hello. You realize he's your grandfather, right?"

Annabelle felt as if she'd fallen down a rabbit hole. "Yes, my grandfather."

"So, just give me whatever is left that she took from my uncle and I'm out of your hair, so to speak."

She groaned. "I just told that man I don't know anything about any loot."

"You threw a lot of stuff away. You're sure you didn't come across some jewels? Rubies, pearls, diamonds, emeralds?"

"My grandmother didn't have anything like that. She didn't wear jewelry, so she didn't even have costume jewelry."

"Didn't wear jewelry?" He scoffed at that. "My uncle weighed down that woman with diamond necklaces and earrings. On her birthday, he gave her an emerald ring that set him back a small fortune. You're telling me she got rid of all of his gifts?"

"Apparently. I suspect that's how she lived as long as she did. I never saw any jewelry, ever." She took a step closer to the door.

He waved her back with the gun in his hand and a shake of his head. "We're still talking here."

MAKE A GRAND GESTURE. Dawson couldn't get the phrase out of his head. What exactly did his mother expect him to do? Show up like he had the last time, with an engagement ring and a bouquet of roses—both things he couldn't afford. That had been his grand gesture and look where it had gotten him.

No, he was fresh out of grand gestures. But as he drove through the blizzard toward home, he couldn't get Annabelle off his mind. He hadn't liked leaving her in that house alone.

He wasn't concerned with ghosts. He didn't think she would be, either. She was a strong woman and she was handling all of this remarkably well.

Still, when he reached the turn-off to his house, he kept going in the direction of town. He told himself it wouldn't hurt to drive by her place. It was late, since, after talking to his mother, he'd gone out to the barn and worked on his old tractor for a while. It had seemed a symbolic thing to do. Also the damned thing wasn't running again.

The snowstorm roared around him making it difficult to see where the road started and ended. He felt the need to drive faster, to get there quicker, and told himself he was letting his imagination run away with him. Maybe he was more spooked by what they'd found at the house than Annie was. Annie. He did much better when he thought of her as Annabelle.

Through the falling, whirling snow, he caught a glimpse

of the lights of Whitehorse. He told himself she'd be in bed, sound asleep, not having given a thought to him.

But still, he sped up a little on the outskirts of town. It wasn't far now.

ROB STUDIED HER. He thought she was telling the truth. He'd been hanging around long enough to know that this woman had been some kind of supermodel until she fell on hard times and came back here to sell her grandmother's house. He'd even heard that her fancy sports car out in the yard was almost repossessed for lack of payment. Someone at the local bar had seen Dawson Rogers write the repo man a check. The car had already been hooked up to the wrecker. A few more minutes and it would have been gone.

"Look, I need to call my uncle with this news. He won't be happy. Normally he would tell me to torture you until you told me the truth. But the fact that you are his flesh and blood and Baby Doll's granddaughter, I think he'll cut you some slack. You have to be honest with me, though, okay?"

Her mind had been racing. "You found the tunnel," she said as she was putting things together. "I would imagine you already looked down there and in the garage. I don't know of any more hiding places. I never knew any of this about my grandmother. It all came as a shock, including the dead man in the wall."

Rob was considering that when he heard a sound behind him. He spun, just not quickly enough. For a moment, he couldn't figure out what had hit him. But glancing over his shoulder, he saw the sword blade sticking out of his back. When he looked at the old man he'd thought he killed, he saw that he was holding the shell of his cane.

Rob lifted the gun to fire, but as he turned, it felt as if someone had cut his strings. Before he could get a shot off, he slumped to the floor at the old man's feet. "Bernie isn't going to like this, Larry," he choked out before everything went black.

ANNABELLE WATCHED ALL of this play out before her eyes as if in a bad dream. It wasn't until the younger man slumped to the floor that she found her feet.

She made a run for the door, but the old man was faster than he looked even wounded. He grabbed a handful of hair and jerked her back. His rancid breath washed over her face as he pulled her close and whispered, "He might have believed you, but I'm betting you're going to tell me where the loot is before this night is over because I could care less if you're Bernie's granddaughter."

She could hear the storm raging outside. The old man jerked her hair harder, making her cry out in pain. She could see that he was bleeding, but clearly the gunshot wasn't going to kill him. Apparently he'd been listening to her conversation with Rob.

"Let's go in this room down here," Larry said. "Your bedroom. I saw through the window that it's about the only room with stuff still in it. Is that where the loot is?"

"I told you just like I told the other man. There is no jewelry."

"Right," the old man said, giving her a hard shove. "Maybe I can help jog your memory."

She stumbled into her room, banging against the closet door where her grandmother's clothing still hung. Her mind raced to think if there was something in here that she could use for a weapon. She spotted her hammer on the dresser.

Larry went to the closet. Keeping one eye on her, he began to tear Frannie's clothes from their hangers. One gawdy sweatshirt after another hit the floor.

Annabelle inched a little closer to the dresser and the

hammer sitting on top. Larry saw her out of the corner of his eye and lunged at her, throwing her across the bed. He smacked her across the face, holding her down as he reached to grab the cord on the blinds. She tried to kick him in the groin only to have him slap her harder.

The cord snapped off and he roughly rolled her onto her face on the bed and began to tie her hands together behind her back.

"You're hurting me," she cried out.

"I've only just begun. You try anything and I'll kill you because, according to you, you know nothing, right? I can hog-tie you and I will if you move again."

She rolled to her side and watched him as he went back to the closet. He pulled down boxes of old shoes, throwing them onto the growing pile until the closet was empty.

He was breathing hard when he came back over to where she lay. "Okay, girlie, now we're going to get down to business." He pulled a knife from a scabbard under his pants leg. She tried to recoil, but he grabbed her hair again as he laid the edge of the blade against her cheek. "You were your grandmother's favorite, according to the woman across the street who I visited for a while recently. These little old ladies are so helpful. If Frannie confided in anyone, it would have been you. Tell me where it is!"

DAWSON SAW THE lights on Annie's bedroom and the living room the moment he pulled up. He couldn't explain what had him so afraid. Just a bad feeling. He rushed up to the house and pounded on the door. She would think he was crazy. Think he was butting into her life. Again. But he didn't care. He had to see her. Had to see if she was all right.

The light in the bedroom went out.

"Oh, no, you don't," he said as he pounded harder.

"Annie, you might as well open up, because I'm not going anywhere until you do!" he yelled.

The light came back on in the bedroom. A few minutes later, the door opened a crack.

Annabelle's pale face peered out. "What do you want?" she demanded, her voice cracking.

He noticed there was a red mark on the side of her face. Had she been asleep?

"You need to leave." Her blue eyes seemed to plead with him. "Please."

"I just had to be sure you were all right. I know it sounds crazy but… Could I come in for a moment?"

She shook her head. "No. Now, please go." She began to close the door.

As she was closing the door, his bad feeling was even stronger, now that he'd seen her. Before she could get the door all the way shut and locked, he slammed his hand into it, forcing her back so he could enter.

Bursting into the empty living room, he shoved to the side. As he turned, he found some old man holding a gun to Annie's temple.

"Close the door," the old man ordered. "Lock it. Play hero and she dies."

Off to the side, he could see a body with a sword sticking out of it. His throat constricted. He'd been right about Annie being in trouble. But now he might have made it worse.

ANNABELLE LET OUT a cry as the man jabbed the gun against her temple and twisted her arm behind her as he dragged her to him. He was much stronger and quicker than he looked.

"Close the door," Larry ordered. "Now!"

Dawson did as the man asked. "What's going on?" He sounded so calm.

"He thinks my grandmother had the jewels from the heist and that I know where they are," she said, her voice breaking. If only Dawson had just left like she'd asked him. She couldn't bear the thought that he was going to die because of her.

"That's ridiculous," Dawson snapped. "She didn't even know about the heist or her grandmother's relationship with Bernie McDougal."

"Or about my brother being murdered and walled up in her grandmother's house?" the old man said.

"I was the one who wanted to know what was behind that wall. Let her go. She doesn't know anything."

"Maybe. Maybe not. But unless you want to see her die, you'll do exactly what I say." Larry motioned with the gun for Dawson to go down the hall toward her bedroom.

She didn't believe for a moment that he would let them go when he didn't find anything. Or even if he did.

Dawson was ahead of them as they started toward the bedroom. She feared what would happen once they reached there. Larry still had her arm pulled behind her, but the gun was no longer to her head. She knew it was risky, but she saw no other way. "Dawson!" she called and spun around, even though it hurt her arm.

She kicked Larry as hard as she could in his private parts. As she did, she grabbed the gun. The old man doubled over, but his grip on the gun was still too strong for her to wrestle it from him. She feared he would get off a shot at Dawson before she could. From behind her, she heard the sound of Dawson's boots on the old hardwood floor as he rushed toward them. As he did, he pulled the sword from Robby's body.

He drove the blade into the man's side, forcing him back.

Larry's grip on the gun gave. She jerked it from his hand as he stumbled back and dropped to the floor.

Dawson took the gun from her and held it on the man. It had all happened so fast. She felt dizzy, fear still coursing through her even with a sense of relief. Was it really over? Or would there be others who would come looking for the loot?

Trembling, she listened to Dawson make the call to the sheriff. Then he pulled her into his arms as they stood over the old man until they heard the sound of sirens. Moments later, deputies were streaming through the front door.

Chapter Nineteen

Annabelle didn't know how long she'd been asleep when she felt something warm and wet touch her cheek. Her eyes flew open. She jerked back, a laugh escaping her lips as Dawson's puppy gave her another kiss.

"Sadie, no," he cried as he rushed into the room. "She has been wanting to come see you for hours. I thought I'd closed the door all the way after I checked on you earlier. How are you?"

"Good, thanks to you."

"Well, when you're ready, I made you something special for breakfast." With that, he called the puppy, who scampered out and the door closed.

Annabelle looked around for her clothes and groaned when she realized that last night she'd thrown on one of her grandmother's sweatshirts and her jeans. She pulled on the sweatshirt, thinking about her grandmother. Was she really like Frannie? Her grandmother had been a survivor. Annabelle guessed she could say that about herself too.

"Something smells good," she said as she walked into Dawson's kitchen.

"I thought you might be hungry. You slept a long time. It's almost noon."

She couldn't believe it. Then again, last night she remembered his arm around her all the way out to his house.

He'd helped her inside and into the bed. She remembered trying to thank him, but he'd already closed the door. The next thing she knew, she was waking to Sadie's kisses.

"You saved my life last night," she said, her voice breaking. "If you hadn't come back to look in on me…"

"For once my instincts were right," he said and turned back to dishing up the Mexican quiche he'd made.

The smell of it brought back other memories of the two of them. Dawson had always been a great cook. There wasn't anything the man couldn't do.

"Your instincts weren't wrong thirteen years ago," she said as he put a slice in front of her along with a bowl of fresh fruit. "I wanted so badly to marry you. The ring, the roses…" Her voice broke again. "But I couldn't."

He nodded, his brown eyes serious. "I know. There were things you had to do. I was incredibly selfish asking you to give up your dream."

"I'm not going back to modeling. I know you said you're seeing Amy now, but—"

"Annie, you can't make a decision like that so soon after everything that's happened."

"I'm not going to change my mind. Also, I'm going to give Amy Baker a run for her money. I want you back, Dawson."

He shook his head. "Annie."

"My life was so up in the air the night we made love. But I'm perfectly clear on what I want now. I love you. I'll wait for you. I'll talk to Mary Sue about keeping the house and I think I can get a job down at the grocery store. If not there, then—"

He reached across the breakfast bar and took her face in his big hands. Bending, he kissed her. She forgot all about the quiche. All about everything except being in this man's arms again. She kissed him back as he swept her up and carried her to his bedroom.

They made love slowly until neither of them could stand it any longer. And then they let the chemistry burn between them in a fire that Annabelle knew would last the rest of their lives.

Later, lying naked in his arms, she looked up at him. He was her Montanan and she was finally home.

"WHEN I SAID maybe you needed a grand gesture," Willie cried when they came in the kitchen door, "I didn't mean almost getting yourself killed." She rushed to her son, cupping his face in her hands and just looking at him, as if too thankful to speak.

"But I got the girl," he said and smiled.

"Oh, you boys are going to be the death of me," Willie said and stepped to Annabelle and hugged her tightly. "You're staying."

She nodded. "I'm not going anywhere." Dawson put his arm around her.

Willie smiled at them. "I'm so glad the two of you are all right."

"The nightmare is over," Dawson said.

"I wish that were true. It won't be over until the jewels from the heist turn up," Annabelle said. "We can't even be sure that my grandmother had them. Obviously, my grandfather still believes she does and so do his…associates. He believes she stole them when she took off without a word and disappeared. He's been looking for her and the loot for more than fifty years. I doubt he will stop now."

Willie shook her head, as if in wonder, and Annabelle realized she was staring at her ugly sweatshirt. "It was my grandmother's. She has a closet full of them."

"I bet she does," the older woman said. "I've never seen

anything like it. I noticed you were wearing a clown one the other day. What is this one?"

"A unicorn," Annie said with a groan.

"May I?" Willie asked as she began to pry at one of the green stones that made up the ground the unicorn was standing on. "It's been a while since I've seen an emerald, but I'd swear this is one."

"What?" Dawson and Annie said in unison.

Willie handed the stone to her son. "I think we've found what happened to the missing jewels. Your grandmother knew there would be others coming to find them, so she hid them in broad daylight."

Dawson looked at Annie. "I think she's right. You say there are a dozen of these in her closet?"

Annabelle nodded in disbelief. "We need to call the sheriff."

"ARE YOU SURE you want to keep the house?" Dawson asked as he finished setting up the last of the furniture in the spare bedroom. Fortunately, they'd been able to retrieve a lot of it from the charity shop, assuring them it would only be temporary.

"My sisters are coming home for Christmas. I think we need to stay here. At least for the holidays. This is where we were raised."

"I was planning to buy the house, anyway," he confessed as he stepped to her to take her in his arms and kiss her.

"Aren't you tired of rescuing me yet?"

"No chance."

They both turned at a knock on the door. A deliveryman stood on the porch. When Annabelle opened the door, he asked her to sign for the large envelope he held in his hand. She signed, curious.

After he left, she stepped back inside and showed Dawson. "It's from Bernie in New York. Do I dare open it?" She looked at him and then laughed, thinking of the wall over the alcove. Her future husband was even more curious than she was.

She tore into it to find a letter-sized envelope inside with a note attached to it.

I'm one of Bernie McDougal's nurses. He asked me to make sure you got this. It was his dying wish.

She looked up at Dawson and slowly opened the letter.

My dear granddaughter,
I'm sorry I'll never get to meet you.

But I wanted you to know how much I loved your grandmother. Whatever she might have done, it was to protect the child she was carrying and later her three granddaughters.

My nephew told me that everyone said you were the one most like your grandmother. In that case, I know you must be beautiful and have her spunk. So I also know that you will do just fine.

I wish you well. You will be safe now,
Bernie, your grandfather

Annabelle had tears in her eyes as she refolded the letter. She looked at Dawson. "Aren't you worried that I might have inherited some of my grandparent's genes?"

He laughed and pulled her to him. "I can handle it."

She smiled up into his handsome face. "I know you can, cowboy."

Annabelle cuddled against Dawson. She'd come home and there was no other place on earth that she wanted to be.

Her sisters would be here soon. It was going to be a wonderful Christmas, she thought, as she looked around the house Dawson and his mother had helped her get ready for her family.

Outside the snow continued to fall. Nothing like a white Christmas, she thought.

She only had one wish. That her grandmother were here to share it with them. Then again, she thought with a smile, knowing Frannie the way she did now, she figured she was here in spirit.

* * * * *

FINGER ON
THE TRIGGER

DELORES FOSSEN

Chapter One

Something wasn't right.

Rachel McCall was sure of it. Her heartbeat kicked up a notch, and she glanced around Main Street to see what had put the sudden knot in her stomach.

Nothing.

Well, nothing that she could see, anyway. But that didn't help with the knot.

She walked even faster, trying to tamp down her fears. It had been only a month since someone had tried to kill her father and had kidnapped her mother. That wasn't nearly enough time for her to force the images out of her head. The sound of the shot. All that blood. The fear that she might lose both her parents.

There were images and memories of the other things that'd happened over the course of those two days, too.

Remembering that wouldn't help her now, though. She had to get to her car, and then she could drive back to the inn on the edge of town and figure out why this "not right" feeling wouldn't budge.

She continued to walk from the small pharmacy up the street to where she'd parked her car. There had still been plenty of daylight when she'd gone into the pharmacy twenty minutes earlier to wait for her meds to be ready, but now that the storm was breathing down on her, it was dark, and the sidewalks were empty. There were so many alleys and shadows. Enough to cause her nerves to tingle just beneath her skin.

Rachel silently cursed herself for not parking directly in front of the pharmacy, but instead she'd chosen a spot closer to the small grocery store where she'd first picked up some supplies before going for the meds. That grocer was closed now—as was seemingly everything else in the small town of Silver Creek.

She'd chosen this town because in many ways it'd reminded her of home. Of McCall Canyon. But bad things had happened there, and they could also happen here.

The moment her car was in sight, she pressed the button on her key fob. The red brake lights flashed, indicating the door was unlocked, just as a vein of lightning lit up the night sky. A few seconds later, the thunder came, a thick rumbling groan. And it was maybe because of the thunder that she didn't hear the footsteps.

Not until it was too late.

Someone stepped out from one of those dark alleys. She saw only a blur of motion from the corner of her eye before that someone wearing a white cowboy hat pulled her between the two buildings.

The scream bubbled up in her throat, but she didn't manage to make a sound before he slid his hand over her mouth.

It was a man.

Rachel had no trouble figuring that out the moment

her back landed against his chest. But she didn't stay there. The surge of adrenaline came. And the fear. She rammed her elbow into the man's stomach, breaking free, and turned to run. She didn't make it far, however, because he cursed and hauled her back to him.

"Shhh. Someone was watching you," he said.

She continued to struggle to get away, until the sound of his voice finally registered in her head. It was one she definitely recognized.

Griff.

Or rather, Texas Ranger Griffin Morris.

How the heck had he found her? And better yet, how fast could she get rid of him?

Rachel pushed his hand away from her mouth and whirled around to face him. She hoped the darkness didn't hide her anger. Even if it did, Griff didn't seem to notice, because his attention was focused across the street.

"Shhh," he repeated, when she started to say something.

Rachel nearly disobeyed him on principle just because she didn't want Griff telling her what to do. But she wasn't stupid. His own expression told her loads. Something was wrong. The knot in her stomach hadn't been a false alarm.

She followed Griff's gaze and tried to pick through the darkness to see if she could figure out what had caused him to grab her like that. There was a row of buildings, mom-and-pop type stores, all one and two stories high. Like the side of the street that Griff and she were on, that one had alleys, too. If someone was hiding there, she couldn't see him.

"Who's watching me?" she whispered. That was just the first of many questions she had for Griff.

He didn't jump to answer, but merely lifted his shoulder. Since he still had his left arm hooked around her waist, she felt his muscles tense. Felt the handgun that he'd drawn, too. Apparently Rachel wasn't the only one who'd thought something was wrong.

"Is this about my father?" she pressed.

That only earned her another shoulder lift. For a couple seconds, anyway. "Your dad's alive, by the way. Just in case you want to know."

She hadn't needed Griff to tell her that. Rachel had kept up with the news about his shooting. Her father had survived the surgery and had been released from the hospital. She hadn't wanted him dead. But Rachel no longer wanted him in her life.

That applied to Griff, too.

"I got here about five minutes ago," Griff went on. He tipped his head toward the end of the street. "I parked up there and came to your car to wait for you. That's when I saw the guy across the street. He's about six feet tall, medium build and dressed all in black. I didn't get a look at his face because he stepped back when he saw me."

Even though Griff and she were at odds—big odds— she believed everything he'd just said. Griff wasn't the sort to make up something like that just to get her in his arms again. Though it had worked. Here she was, right against him. Rachel was about to do something about that, but Griff spoke before she could put a couple inches of space between them.

"Keep watch of the alley behind us," he said. "I don't want him backtracking and sneaking up on us."

That tightened the knot even more, and Rachel wished she'd brought her gun with her. Too bad she'd left it at the inn.

"There might be nothing to this," she whispered. However, she did turn so she could keep an eye on the back alley. "Unless…" She almost hated to finish that. "Has there been another attack? Did someone try to kill my father again?"

Griff didn't answer right away, but he did spare her a glance. He looked down at her just as she looked up at him. Their gazes connected. It was too dark to see the color of his eyes, but she knew they were gunmetal gray.

Rachel also knew the heat was still there.

Good grief. After everything that had happened, it should be gone. Should be as cold as ice. But here it was, just as it always had been. Well, it could take a hike. Her body might still be attracted to Griff, but she'd learned her lesson, and she wouldn't give him another chance to crush her.

"There have been new threats," he finally said. A muscle flickered in his jaw. "Both emails and phone calls. Have you gotten any?"

She shook her head. "No, but then I closed my email account and have been using a burner cell."

Of course Griff knew that, because he was the reason she'd gone to such lengths. Rachel had been trying to get away from him.

"How'd you find me?" she snapped. "*Why* did you find me? Because I made it clear that I didn't want to see you."

There was too much emotion in her voice. Not good. Because it meant she was no longer whispering. Rachel tried to rein in her feelings so she could keep watch and put an end to this visit.

"Your meds," Griff said.

Because she was still doing some emotion-reining, she didn't immediately make the connection. Then Rachel remembered she'd needed the pharmacist to call her former doctor in McCall Canyon to verify the prescription for her epilepsy medicine. Without them, she would have had a seizure, something that hadn't happened in two years.

Rachel cursed herself for that lapse. She should have figured out a way to get the meds without anyone having to contact Dr. Baldwin. Of course, Dr. Baldwin shouldn't have ratted her out to Griff, either, and as soon as she could, she'd have a chat with the man about that.

"I'd been so careful," she mumbled. She hadn't meant to say that aloud, and it got Griff's attention because he glanced at her again.

"No. You haven't been. You shouldn't have parked here. If I could find you, then so could the person who made those new threats."

She couldn't argue with that, but what Rachel could dispute was that the person who'd made those new threats might not even be after her. Yes, a month ago someone had put a bullet in her father's chest while he'd been in the parking lot of the sheriff's office where both her brothers worked. But that person, Whitney Goble, who'd been responsible for the shooting, had tried to kill Rachel's father so Whitney could set up someone else that she wanted to punish. Now, Whitney was dead.

Not that it helped lessen the memories just because Whitney was no longer alive.

No. Because of everything else that'd happened in the twenty-four hours following the shooting. That's when they'd learned that her father also had secrets.

Well, one secret, anyway.

That, too, twisted away at her. Just as much as reading the threat he'd gotten and seeing him gunned down in the parking lot. But the truth was her father had been living two lives and had a mistress and a son living several counties over. Her brothers, Egan and Court, hadn't known. Neither had her mother, Helen.

But Griff had.

Of course, Griff hadn't breathed a word about it. Not after the shooting. Not even when later that night she'd gone to his bed to help ease the worry she was feeling for her father. That's why the cut had felt so deep. Griff had known, and he hadn't told her.

All of those emotions came flooding back. "I don't want you here," she said.

If her words stung, he showed no signs of it. "Yeah, I got that, but I made a promise to your mother that I'd keep you safe."

It didn't surprise her that her mother had made that request. Or that Griff had carried it out. But there was possibly another side to this. "Are you using this as a way to mend fences with me? Because if so, it won't work."

He didn't even acknowledge that, but Griff did push her behind him. He brought up his gun as if getting ready to fire. That put her heart right in her throat, and Rachel came up on her toes so she could see over Griff's shoulder. She shook her head and was about to tell him she didn't see anything.

But she did.

Rachel saw someone move in the alley to the right of the small hardware store. Since it was only 8:00 p.m., she reminded herself that it could be someone putting out the trash. However, that knot in her stomach returned. It was a feeling that her brothers had always told her never to ignore.

Was this the person who'd made those new threats against her family?

Maybe. Whoever it was definitely seemed to be lurking. And looking in their direction. Rachel doubted the person could see them because Griff and she were deep enough in the shadows on this side of the street. Or at least they would be unless there was more lightning. Which was a strong possibility. She could hear more thunder rumbling in the distance.

"Why would someone want to hurt me?" she whispered.

"To get back at your father. At Warren," Griff answered without hesitation. "Everyone in the McCall family could be at risk. Don't worry," he quickly added. "We have a guard on your mother's room at the hospital."

Good. Because her mother was mentally fragile right now. Suffering from a breakdown. Helen didn't need to be fighting off idiots obsessed with getting back at Warren.

Rachel felt the first drops of rain hit her face. They

no doubt hit Griff, too, but they didn't cause him to lose focus. He kept watching the man across the street. But the guy wasn't moving. She did see something, however. The flash of light, maybe from a match or lighter. A moment later, a small red circle of fire winked in and out.

That caused her to breathe a little easier. "He's just smoking."

But Griff didn't budge. "He's carrying a gun."

Rachel certainly hadn't seen anything to indicate that, but she took a closer look. She had to wait several snail-crawling moments, but she finally saw the glint of metal. Maybe a gun in his right hand.

More raindrops came. So did the vein of lightning that lit up the sky, and Griff automatically moved her deeper into the alley. He also took out his phone.

"I'm calling the locals for backup," he said, without taking his attention off the man. "Yeah, it's me again," he added, speaking to whoever answered.

That probably meant Griff had already been in touch with local law enforcement. In fact, he'd probably called them as soon as he'd figured out she was in Silver Creek.

"Do a quiet approach," Griff instructed. "If you can, try to get someone behind this guy so we can take him into custody." He ended the call and put his phone away.

She doubted it would take long for someone to arrive, but it would feel like an eternity. And might be completely unnecessary.

"If he means to do me harm, why hasn't he fired at me?" Rachel asked.

Again, Griff took his time answering, but judging from the sound of agreement he made, it was probably something he'd already considered. "Maybe he's waiting for a clean shot."

That gave her another jolt of memories. Of her father's shooting. They hadn't seen the gunman that day because she had fired from a heavily treed area behind the police station. But it had indeed been a "clean shot" that went straight into her father's chest. It was a miracle he'd survived.

"We can cut through the back of the alley and then get to my truck that's parked up the street," Griff whispered. "That way you're not out in the open."

"My car is right there," she pointed out. "Only about ten feet away. And the doors are already unlocked."

"If this man wants you dead, he could shoot you before you get inside."

That caused her breath to stop for a moment. Griff normally sugarcoated things for her, but apparently those days were over. Maybe he truly understood that their friendship—and anything else they felt for each other—was over, too.

"There's a deputy," Griff said.

Rachel immediately looked out and spotted a man on foot coming up Main Street. He had his gun drawn and was ducking in and out of doorways of the various shops. He was still three buildings away when the guy who'd been watching them turned and started running out the back of the alley. He quickly disappeared from sight.

"He's getting away," she blurted out.

"The sheriff might have had time to get someone back there." Griff didn't sound very hopeful about that, though. "Come on."

He took hold of her arm to start them moving, and she saw his truck. It was indeed at the back of the alley. But they had barely made it a step before a deafening noise blastcd through the air. Not lightning or thunder from the storm. The impact slammed Griff and her into the side of the building.

And that's when Rachel saw that her car had exploded into a giant ball of fire.

Chapter Two

Griff didn't bother to curse himself for not being able to prevent this from happening. No time for cursing and regrets.

He had to get Rachel out of there. And it didn't matter if she no longer trusted him—that explosion should be plenty enough proof to her that someone wanted her dead.

"This way." Griff hooked his arm around her waist to get her moving.

He didn't take her out onto the sidewalk, though. It was too risky for them to go there, because the person who'd just blown up her car could be waiting for them to do just that. Nor did he want to stay put in case there was a second explosion.

The rain started to pelt them, and the lightning suddenly seemed way too close. It definitely wasn't a good time to be outside, especially since there were metal gas pipes leading into the buildings.

"Was that really a bomb?" Rachel asked. Her voice was as shaky as the rest of her, and she seemed to be talking more to herself than to him.

Griff wasn't sure exactly what it had been. Definitely

some kind of explosive device, and that meant some-one—probably the guy from the alley—had put it on Rachel's car. He could have done that after she'd parked and gone to the pharmacy, but if so, it was a huge risk. Because someone could have spotted him.

Of course, the idiot could have planted it hours ago and waited until now to detonate it. Even if it didn't kill Rachel and him, it created enough of a diversion for the goon to get away.

Griff kept them moving. Not too fast, though. He needed to try to listen, to make sure someone wasn't coming up behind them.

Or in front of them.

Because it was entirely possible the bomber had a part-ner somewhere in the maze of alleys. One who could be waiting to ambush them.

"Stay close to me," Griff warned her. "We'll go to my truck."

Rachel immediately started shaking her head. "What if he planted a bomb on it, too?"

"It wasn't out of my sight long enough while I've been here."

Which wasn't long at all. As soon as he'd gotten word that Rachel was in Silver Creek, Griff had come to find her.

Normally, it would have been a forty-five-minute drive from McCall Canyon, but he'd shaved off the minutes to make it in just half an hour. And he was damn lucky he had, too. Because if he hadn't gotten to Rachel in time, she would have tried to get into her car and would have been blown to smithereens.

A thought that felt like a knife to his heart.

Rachel and he weren't a couple. Never had been, really. But Griff wouldn't have forgiven himself if he hadn't been able to save her. And her father wouldn't have forgiven him, either.

"Keep watch behind us," Griff told Rachel, repeating the order he'd given her earlier, and he passed her his phone. "Text the sheriff, Grayson Ryland. That's the last number I called. And tell him where we're going."

He could feel her doing that, hopefully managing to do so while he kept her moving. However, Griff stopped as soon as he made it to the end of the alley. He peered around the corner of the building, but it was too dark to see much of anything. Hearing was a problem, too, thanks to the rain and thunder. He did hear a dinging sound, and figured that meant Rachel had gotten an answer to the text.

"The sheriff says he and his deputy are in pursuit of the guy who was in the alley," she relayed.

Good. Griff didn't want him getting away. If they caught him, they might finally have answers as to who was trying to kill the McCalls.

And why.

Griff and Rachel's brothers had been investigating that for nearly a month now and had come up empty. Even if Sheriff Ryland and his deputies didn't manage to nab this bomber, maybe they'd be able to get some DNA off the cigarette that the guy had almost certainly ditched somewhere in the alley. Of course, the storm wasn't going to help with that, which meant time was critical right now.

Thanks to another bolt of lightning, Griff was able to

get a glimpse of the darker spaces in the alley. He didn't see anyone lurking there, so he stepped out to get a better look.

Not good.

Because all he managed to see was a gun. And that glimpse happened at the exact same moment that a bullet slammed into the brick wall right next to where Griff was standing.

Rachel gave a sharp gasp and grabbed hold of his shoulder, pulling him back just as another shot came at Griff. An inch closer and he would have been a dead man.

Griff cursed and pushed Rachel even deeper into the alley, putting his own body in front of hers. It was far from ideal, mainly because the smoke from the explosion was spilling into the alley and making its way toward them.

Hell.

First an explosion, then lightning. Now a gunshot. This was not the quick in-and-out that Griff had planned for Rachel.

"Did you see the shooter?" she asked. She was shaking even harder now.

"No. But he's to our left." In the opposite direction from Griff's truck. Still, the guy was in the catbird seat right now because he could be hiding behind heaven knew what, just waiting for them to step out so he could shoot them.

Maybe this was the same guy who'd been in the alley across the street. If he knew the layout of the buildings, he could have possibly made his way here. But it was just as likely there were at least two of them.

That didn't help settle Griff's raw nerves.

His phone buzzed, and since Rachel was still holding it, he motioned for her to answer. She did, and even though she didn't put it on speaker, she held the phone close enough for him to hear.

"Did you fire that shot?" Sheriff Ryland asked.

"No. The shooter's somewhere in the alley. I'm taking Rachel back to Main Street."

Shock flashed through her eyes, and Griff could tell from her tensed muscles that she didn't think that was a good idea. He didn't believe it was an especially good one, either, but staying put was too dangerous. If there were indeed two attackers, then they could try to trap Rachel and him in the alley.

"Hold tight for a few more minutes if you can," Sheriff Ryland said. "I'll try to make sure the street is clear."

It was a generous offer, one that Griff accepted, but he knew it was going to be tough for the sheriff to manage. The smoke would be cutting his visibility, too, and they weren't out of the woods yet. There was still the possibility of a second explosion.

Griff moved Rachel to the center of the alley. "Stand with your back to mine and face Main Street," he instructed. That way, he would be in a position to shoot the attacker who'd fired those shots at him.

He took out his reserve weapon from a slide holster in his jeans and handed it to her. Griff prayed she wouldn't need it, but at least if she did, Rachel could shoot. He knew that because he'd been the one to teach her.

That reminder brought back some unwanted thoughts. Rachel's and his lives had been intertwined since he was twelve years old. That's when Griff had moved to Mc-Call Canyon and started doing odd jobs for her father at the McCall Ranch. That meant they had twenty-four years of memories. Some had been bad, really bad, but this would be at the top of the heap.

She took his gun, automatically positioning it the way he'd taught her. Griff hated that he had to put her in this position. Hated that she was in this kind of danger. Later, when they made it out of this, he would need to do something to fix it, to make sure it never happened again.

Of course, Rachel might not let him fix anything. She might try to go on the run again.

"Who's doing this?" she whispered.

"I don't know." Griff wished he did. "But if you've got any ideas, I'm all ears." He expected her to say no.

She didn't.

"Marlon Stowe," she said.

The name meant nothing to Griff, but judging from the way she shuddered, it meant plenty to Rachel.

"Who the hell is he?" Griff demanded.

He wanted to hear every word she said, but he also didn't want anything they were saying to cause him to lose focus. He had to keep watch, and listen, for that shooter.

Rachel shook her head. "It's just some guy who works at the inn where I'm staying. The first week I was there, I saw him and his girlfriend get into a serious argument. I intervened when I thought he was about to hit her, and after the girlfriend and I talked, she broke things off with Marlon and moved out of town. Marlon blames me for that."

Griff was slammed with emotions. Anger that some clown wouldn't leave Rachel alone.

"It's probably not him, though." Rachel gave her head another shake. "I don't think he was mad enough, or crazy enough, to want to kill me."

Griff would soon find out if that was true. Once he had Rachel safe, he would make it a top priority to find out everything he could about this guy. Rachel had been through entirely too much to have to deal with a hothead.

"It's more likely that this is connected to my father and those new threats," Rachel added a moment later.

Griff didn't voice his agreement. Didn't ask her to elaborate, either. That's because he knew what she meant. This could go back to her father's mistress. Or maybe to someone else Warren had ticked off when he'd carried on a three-decades-long affair.

The rain started coming down harder, and Griff felt Rachel shiver. He didn't think it was solely from fear this time. It was May, which meant the temps were already high, but the rain was cold, and their clothes were past the damp stage. The water was starting to stream down their bodies.

His phone dinged again with another text message. "The sheriff says he doesn't see a shooter anywhere near your truck. His deputy is still pursuing the bomber on foot."

Good. Maybe that meant the bomber wouldn't double back. But even if he was trying to do that, it was too dangerous for them to wait around and find out. If the guy had managed to plant one explosive, he could have others on him.

"Let's go," Griff told her.

She nodded, shoved his phone in her pocket and got moving. While they made their way back to the front of the alley, Griff tried to keep watch all around them, and Rachel was doing the same. He prayed it would be enough.

"Stay down," he muttered, when they reached Main Street.

There wasn't much left of her car, but still plenty of flames and smoke. Both could conceal a shooter, but could hopefully give Rachel and him some cover, too.

As he'd done at the back end of the alley, Griff leaned out from the building and looked around. There were plenty of places a shooter could hide. Too many. And Griff didn't see either the sheriff or a deputy. Still, he couldn't wait any longer.

"Keep low and watch where you're stepping," Griff warned her.

In addition to the limited visibility from the smoke, there were bits of car parts, metal and glass all over the sidewalk. He didn't want Rachel getting tripped up once they started to move.

Griff took out his truck keys, said a quick prayer and stayed in front of Rachel when they stepped out from cover. He didn't have to tell her to move fast because she did it automatically. She also started to cough.

The smoke quickly began to burn his eyes, so Griff picked up the pace as much as he could. He also continued to keep watch. Especially behind them. He didn't want that shooter coming out of the alley and gunning them down.

It seemed to take way too long to get to his truck, and the moment he reached it, he unlocked the driver's-side door and threw it open. He was about to push Rachel inside when he heard a sound. Not on the street.

But from above.

Griff glanced up just in time to spot the man on the roof of the one-story building. Even though he didn't have a good view of the guy's face, he had no trouble seeing his gun. A gun the man fired.

The bullet ripped through the rear window on his truck and exited the windshield. The only reason it missed Rachel was because she moved a split second before the guy pulled the trigger. She dived across the seat, and in the same motion caught Griff's arm to pull him in, as well.

He shook off her grip, turned and took aim, firing two shots at the man on the roof.

That sent the guy ducking for cover, and Griff took advantage of that. While he would have liked to go after this moron and arrest him, he couldn't put Rachel at risk like that. He had to get her out of here. And not just off Main Street and out of the line of sight of this shooter. He needed to get her away from Silver Creek and whatever the heck was going on here. He had to take her to McCall Canyon so they could regroup and catch these SOBs.

Griff jumped behind the wheel, got the engine started and hit the accelerator.

"Get down!" he warned Rachel.

She did.

Just as bullets slammed into the back window.

Chapter Three

Griff and she had managed to get away from a killer.

She kept reminding herself of that. Kept reminding herself, too, that they were alive. But it might be a long time before that all sank in. Especially since the would-be killer had managed to escape. He was still out there. Maybe regrouping. Perhaps planning another attack. And maybe next time, Griff and she wouldn't be so lucky.

With that terrifying possibility going through her mind, Rachel looked out at the McCall Canyon sheriff's office when Griff pulled to a stop in front of it. She took a deep breath, trying to steel herself.

It didn't work.

Of course, there wasn't much that would help steady her right now. She was going to have to face her family, and there probably wasn't enough steel in her backbone to get her through that. Because she was already close to the breaking point.

If Griff hadn't pulled her into that alley when he did, she would have died in the car explosion. Ditto for him getting her to his truck so they could get away. While she was very glad to be alive, she couldn't forget that in those blink-of-an-eye moments, the outcome could have been a whole lot different. Griff and she could both be dead.

"Thank you," she told him.

He'd already reached to open the door of his truck, but he stopped and looked at her as if she'd lost her mind. That's when she realized he'd misinterpreted what she'd said.

"I'm not thanking you for bringing me here," Rachel corrected. "But for saving my life."

Griff just sat there, perhaps waiting for something else. Maybe for her to blast him for finding her when she'd made it so clear that she hadn't wanted to be found. She hadn't wanted him in her life, either. However, that was an argument that could wait. For now, she had two other items on the agenda.

Her brothers.

Both Court and Egan were right there in the squad room when Griff and she went in. Anyone who saw her brothers together like this had no doubt they were related. They had the same dark brown hair and intense gray eyes. Rachel had obviously gotten their mother's genes, since her hair was blond and her eyes blue. Still, there was enough family resemblance for people to tell she was a McCall, too.

Thankfully, there were no other lawmen around, not even a dispatcher. And she was especially thankful that her father wasn't here. Since this probably wasn't going to be a pleasant conversation, Rachel preferred that as few people as possible were present.

Griff's phone dinged with a text message—something that had been happening during most of the drive from

Silver Creek. He'd had Rachel read those to him so he could focus on the drive, but he didn't make that offer now. He stepped to the side, probably not only to read the text but to give her some time with Egan and Court.

As Griff had done in the truck, her brothers just stared at her for a moment. They looked her over from head to toe, their gazes lingering on the jacket she was wearing.

It was Griff's.

He'd given it to her in the truck when she'd started shaking. Not just because she was wet from the rain, but because the adrenaline had still been slamming into her. She'd gladly accepted the jacket. And had tried not to notice that it carried Griff's scent.

Rachel failed at that, too. She noticed.

Court was the first to budge. He cursed—the profanity definitely meant for her—and then he pulled her into his arms. "Leaving town like that was a really stupid thing to do," he whispered to her, while he brushed a kiss on her cheek.

"I didn't have a choice," she whispered back.

Court pulled away, studied her eyes, then he nodded. Perhaps that meant he understood that what their father had done had shaken her so badly that she'd needed to put some distance between them. What Court probably didn't know was that the deepest cut had come from Griff.

Again, though, that was an argument with Griff she'd need to postpone, because she had to face Egan. Unlike Court, he didn't come to her. Her other brother stood there, giving her one of his infamous glares that no doubt worked on criminals. Not kid sisters, though. Rachel went to him and hugged him. It was like hugging a statue,

because his muscles were rock hard. But then she felt
him relax.

"I was worried about you," he said against her ear.
"Don't you *ever* make me worry about you like that
again."

No need for her to tell him that she'd been concerned,
too. Not just with leaving McCall Canyon, but with everything that had gone on tonight. Concerned and scared.
All their lives had changed on a dime when their father
had been shot, and the changes apparently weren't over
yet. Griff had said there were new threats, and with the
attack, it could mean the person who'd made those threats
wasn't finished with her family.

Or not.

This might not be connected at all, which made it
all the more frustrating. Someone wanted her dead, and
she not only didn't know who, Rachel didn't know why.

"Griff said you weren't hurt," Egan added. "Is it true?"

"I'm okay," she settled for saying.

He let the hug linger a few more seconds before he
moved back and looked at Griff. "Tell me how we catch
the SOB who tried to kill Rachel."

On the drive over, Griff had filled Egan in on the ba-
sics while on speakerphone. Well, he'd done that after
they'd been sure the shooter wasn't following them. He
had also had several conversations with Sheriff Ryland.

What Griff hadn't done was talked to Rachel.

Like Egan, he was clearly still fuming that she'd left
town and then had gotten herself into a dangerous situation. She hadn't purposely run toward the danger. She'd
been running to get away from Griff and her father. Now,

here she was—right back with them. Or at least she soon would be with both of them because she was certain that either Egan or Court had already called their father.

Griff quit reading the text on his phone and shifted his attention to Egan. "Sheriff Ryland is getting us footage from a security camera outside a bank that was just up the street from where Rachel had her car parked. We might be able to see who planted the explosive device."

Rachel wasn't holding out hope. If the guy was bold enough to do something like that on Main Street, then he was probably aware of the position of the camera. Still, they might get lucky. If not, maybe someone had even seen the person and could give them a description.

Egan hooked his arm around her and got her moving to his office, which was at the back of the squad room. Once he had her there, he practically sat her in the chair next to his desk, then got her a bottle of water from his fridge.

She'd been in this office many times—when it'd been her father's, and then for the past four years since it was Egan's. It hadn't changed in, well, forever. Same desk. Same filing cabinet. Same fridge.

The picture was there on the wall, of course. A photo of Egan, Court, her and their late brother, Warren Jr.— or W.J. as folks had called him. W.J. had been dead for nearly a decade now. Shot and killed in the line of duty when he'd been a deputy sheriff on call at a domestic dispute that had turned deadly.

The pain and grief from losing him felt as fresh as if she'd just lost him hours ago instead of all those years. That was the picture she had in her head. Her brother dead. His life cut much too short because he'd been wearing a badge and trying to do the right thing.

And that was the reason Rachel had sworn she would never fall for a cop.

That included a Texas Ranger like Griff.

"Tell me about this dirtbag who's riled at you," Egan insisted.

That was his big-brother tone, and it caused her to sigh. Egan had always been protective of her, which was why he often shot Griff scowling looks. Like now. Neither their father nor Egan had ever thought Griff was the right man for her. And he wasn't. He'd proved that last month.

"His name is Marlon Stowe," Rachel answered, after she had a long sip of the water. "His folks own the inn where I was staying, and he works part-time in the office there. He believes I'm responsible for his girlfriend leaving him. I suppose I am," she added.

"I've already requested a background check on him," Griff explained. "I'm waiting on a call about him now." He took out his phone and showed her the photo on the screen. "That's the guy, right?"

She nodded. It was Marlon's DMV photo that Griff had apparently gotten in that text. "His hair's a little lighter in this picture than it was the last time I saw him." Marlon definitely didn't look like a cowboy. He had the clean and polished appearance of a businessman. One with a tense edge to him.

"Checking out Marlon is a good start," Rachel continued. "He gives me the creeps, but he hasn't been around the inn for the last week or so. Plus, he's never been... actually physically aggressive. He just made it very clear that he was furious with me because I convinced his girl-friend to leave him." She paused. "You're sure our half brother or our father's mistress isn't behind this?"

Griff quickly shook his head. "Your half brother is a cop. And no, there's no indication whatsoever that he's dirty. His name is Raleigh Lawton, by the way. He's a county sheriff."

She knew that. Rachel hadn't been able to resist look-ing him up online. "We're certain Raleigh is really War-ren's son?"

"Warren says he is," Griff confirmed. "Raleigh re-fused to have a DNA test. He wants nothing to do with Warren, your brothers or you."

Rachel didn't fault him for that, since she felt the same way about Warren. "How about his mother then?"

Her name was Alma Lawton. Rachel knew plenty about her, too, but it wasn't *plenty enough* to understand why her father had carried on an affair with the woman and had a child with her.

"I've already called Alma," Court said. "She'll be in first thing in the morning for questioning."

Rachel was betting the woman wouldn't care much for that, and it almost certainly wasn't the first time her brothers or Griff had brought the woman in. No. Because Alma was once a person of interest in her father's shoot-ing and could have been connected to the actual shooter, Whitney. After all, Alma had been his mistress for years, and it was possible she'd just gotten tired of waiting for Warren to leave his family for her.

But that wasn't motive for Alma to go after one of Warren's kids.

Was it?

Maybe if the woman wanted to punish Warren, she might believe that was the way to do it. But there were a lot of "ifs" in that theory. It was possible that Alma was the one who'd ended the longtime affair, and if so, that would mean she didn't have a motive for what was going on.

"We haven't told Mom about the attack," Court went on. "We thought that was best, considering."

Yes, considering that their mother was in a mental hospital. That was something else she could thank her father for doing. Hearing the news of her husband's affair and his other life had sent Helen over the edge.

"I won't say anything when I talk to her," Rachel assured them. Which would be soon. Rachel had been calling her every day for the past month, and she wouldn't miss the call tomorrow, either.

"You haven't asked about Dad," Egan said. He didn't wait for her to respond. "He got out of the hospital about two weeks ago, and he's upset that you ran off before he had a chance to explain."

Rachel could practically feel her blood pressure soaring. "Well, you can tell him I'm upset that he couldn't be faithful to his wife."

She didn't bother to take the venom out of her voice but hated that she'd aimed it at Egan. Court was more of the forgiving sort and had probably worked out a way to make amends with Warren, but Egan was likely just as bitter about this as she was. The difference was that he hadn't left.

Egan grunted in agreement and tipped his head to

Griff, sending another scowl his way. "Griff told us what happened between you two the night Dad was shot. That you landed in bed for comfort sex."

Rachel snapped toward Griff so fast that her neck popped. She was certain *she* was scowling at him now.

"I thought they needed to hear what'd happened," Griff said, his mouth tight. "I wanted them to know that you might have left because of me and not Warren."

"I left because of both of you," she snapped. And intended to say a whole lot more to Griff—in private.

Mercy. He had no right to tell her family about that.

"I'm guessing it's over between Griff and you?" Egan asked.

"Yes." Rachel snapped that response, too.

And she scowled at Egan when he gave her that big-brother look again. Egan didn't have to come out and say it, but she felt a mental lecture coming on. One where he would say something about hoping she'd remembered to practice safe sex. She had.

Or rather, Griff had.

They'd used a condom, but with the way her life had been going, she'd taken a pregnancy test two weeks later just in case. It'd been negative. So at least her mistake of sleeping with Griff hadn't resulted in a pregnancy.

The mental lecture was still going on between Egan and her when the front door opened. Griff, Court and Egan all reacted by drawing their guns. But they all soon holstered them again, Court and Griff making grumbling sounds. Rachel knew the reason for the grumbles.

Their visitor was the district attorney, Brad Gandy.

It was an understatement that Brad and Griff didn't get

along. She was the main reason for that. Brad had always had a thing for her. And Court had been on Griff's side. In fact, Court was the only McCall who'd ever wanted to see Griff and her together. Of course, that probably didn't apply now that Court knew Griff had slept with her while keeping Warren's dirty little secret.

Brad made a beeline to Egan's office, volleying glances at all of them when he stepped inside. His eyes narrowed a bit when his attention landed on Griff. Griff's only reaction was to scowl even harder than he already was.

The two men were definitely a huge contrast. Brad, in his pricey gray suit, looked as if he'd just stepped out of the courtroom. Griff was pure cowboy in his jeans and Stetson.

"Rachel," Brad said on a rise of breath when he'd finished with his glances. "I heard about someone trying to kill you. God, I'm so sorry." He went straight to her and pulled her into his arms.

She tried not to go stiff. After all, Brad and she had once dated in college, and he'd hugged and kissed her back then. However, it didn't feel right for that little display of affection to happen in front of her brothers. Or Griff.

Especially Griff.

Rachel silently cursed him. And the blasted attraction. She wished she could make herself immune to him.

Brad eased back, making eye contact with her. Except it wasn't just mere contact. He was looking at her as if examining her, to make sure she was all right. She wasn't, but Rachel tried to appear a lot stronger than she felt as she stepped out of his grip.

"How'd you know about the attack?" she asked, and she prayed it wasn't on the news. Rachel didn't want her mother to find out that way—or any other way, for that matter.

Brad flinched a little. Maybe because her tone had been so brusque. Or maybe because she hadn't greeted him with the same enthusiastic hug he'd given her. "I'm friends with the DA in Silver Creek."

She glanced at Griff, and before she could voice her concern about that, he took out his phone once more. "I'll make sure no one at the hospital mentions it to your mother." He stepped outside the office to make the call.

Rachel made a mental note to thank him for that, too. Another mental note to make arrangements to put some distance between Griff and her. She needed to think, and right now, her head wasn't cooperating. She was dizzy and exhausted, and being around Griff had a way of making her not think straight. The blasted attraction kept getting in the way.

"Are you really okay?" Court asked her.

That's when Rachel realized she was massaging her right temple. "I'm not about to have a seizure. And I've been taking my meds."

Of course, that didn't mean a seizure wouldn't happen, but if it did, there was nothing she could do to stop it now.

"Please tell me you know who tried to murder Rachel," Brad said to Egan.

Egan lifted his shoulder. "Sorry, my ESP isn't working so great tonight. But I've got a lead, and I'll question Alma Lawton."

"Alma!" Brad spat out the name like he would profanity. Maybe some of his tone was due to Egan's smart-mouthed remark. "Yes, definitely talk to her. She hates every one of you. What kind of lead do you have?" he pressed.

Egan hesitated, as if debating if he would tell him. Brad and he were on the same side of the law, but Rachel figured sometimes it didn't feel that way. They'd butted heads on several cases over the years. However, Rachel thought the underlying current was because Egan didn't want her to be with Brad any more than he wanted her to be with Griff.

At the moment, she felt the same way—despite the simmering heat between Griff and her. There was heat, too, when it came to Brad, but it was all one-sided.

"Marlon Stowe," Egan finally answered. "He's a guy who might blame Rachel for his girlfriend leaving him. Did the Silver Creek district attorney happen to mention him to you?"

Judging from the way Brad's mouth tightened, that would be a no. "When are you bringing him in for questioning?"

Egan shrugged. "When I've got probable cause, and right now—"

"You've got it," Griff interrupted, stepping back into the room. He looked at Egan and then tipped his head to the laptop on the desk. "First things first. Sheriff Ryland just emailed you the surveillance footage from the bank camera."

That sent both Court and Egan to the computer. Rachel would have joined them, but it was obvious Griff had something else to say.

"Marlon's ex-girlfriend from a year ago took out a restraining order against him because he was stalking her," Griff continued. "Sheriff Ryland said Marlon also hit her, but she wouldn't press charges against him. There are rumors that he hit his last girlfriend, Taryn Harrison, too. That's the woman you saw with Marlon while you were staying at the inn."

Yes, and Marlon blamed her for the breakup. Rachel felt the chill slide through her. Here, she'd left McCall Canyon to escape, and instead she'd crossed paths with a bully. One who might be unhinged if he was indeed into stalking.

Brad turned toward her. "See? This is why you should have never left," he snapped. "Did that man touch you?"

"No. He just said I should mind my own business." She stopped, thought of something else. "But the next time we crossed paths, he seemed to know who I was. I mean, I was using an alias. I'd told everyone there at the inn that my name was Margaret O'Malley."

"Mom's middle and maiden names," Court supplied, looking up from the laptop. Egan kept his attention planted firmly on the screen.

She nodded. "I lied and told them I didn't have any ID because my wallet had been stolen. I used cash to pay for the room."

"Cash that you withdrew from your bank account right before you left town," Brad said.

So obviously he'd checked on that. That wasn't a surprise, not really. They'd probably all been looking for her. It was ironic that Griff had been the one to find her.

"What made you think Marlon knew who you were?" Griff asked.

She almost dismissed it, but that would mean dismissing the knot in her stomach. After what'd happened, it was best if she listened to it.

"When I was paying for my room last week, Marlon was in the office, and he wrote the receipt," she explained. "He started writing my name with an *R*, then he quickly scratched it out and wrote 'Margaret' instead. I think he'd been about to put down 'Rachel.'"

Brad made a sound to indicate he was giving that some thought. "Maybe he saw you on the news. After Warren's shooting," he clarified.

It was possible, but Griff didn't look as if he was buying it, either. Good. She wanted him and her brothers to dig into Marlon's activities and see if there was something to find.

"Hell," Egan said. "There's someone on the footage."

Brad hurried behind the desk to have a look, but Griff stayed right next to her. Egan turned the screen so they could see, and it didn't take long for her to realize they were looking at the man who'd been in the alley.

A man she instantly recognized.

Oh, God.

Chapter Four

What the hell was Warren doing on the Silver Creek surveillance video?

That was the question Griff was very anxious to ask the man. Apparently, he wasn't the only one who had an urgent need to know, because Rachel whipped out her phone and pressed in her father's number. Since Griff had been about to do the same thing, he just waited for Warren to answer.

But he didn't.

After a few rings, the call went to voice mail. "Call me now," was all that Rachel snapped into the phone when she left her father a message.

Since Warren was worried about Rachel and had spent the past month trying to find her, he would no doubt do just that. Well, he would unless he'd done something stupid.

"It appears you've got a new person of interest," Brad said, his mouth tight and his eyes narrowed as he stared at the screen.

Griff didn't like that Brad had jumped to the worst-case scenario. Of course, he'd never been a fan of Warren, because they, too, had clashed when Warren had been sheriff.

"It doesn't make sense," Griff said to Rachel. "Warren wouldn't hurt you. He wouldn't hurt any of his kids."

"Not unless he was finished with me," Rachel quickly pointed out. But even she had to wave that off. "No. He wouldn't hurt me. Not intentionally, anyway." She pointed to the screen. "So why is he there?"

Griff had a theory, and this was going to be a good news/bad news kind of deal. "Maybe Warren found out where you were and went to check on you." That was the good news. "And maybe while Warren was watching you, he could have gotten caught up in the attack."

After everything she'd been through tonight, Griff hated to point that out to her, but Rachel was smart and would have soon come to the same conclusion. Plus, that was still better than thinking Warren could have had any part in that explosion or the shots being fired.

"I'll call the Silver Creek sheriff," Egan volunteered, taking out his phone, as well.

"And it might be jumping the gun, but I'll see if I can have Dad's cell phone traced," Court added. He stepped away as if to start doing just that, but then volleyed glances at Brad, Griff and his sister before his attention settled on Griff. "Why don't you go ahead and get Rachel out of here so she can get some rest?"

Since Rachel was no doubt on the verge of an adrenaline crash, that was a good idea, but judging from the way her forehead bunched up, it was going to be hard for Griff to sell her on doing that. He definitely didn't want to use her epilepsy to get her to leave. Over the years, he'd learned that she didn't want any special considerations because of it. Still, the stress might trigger a seizure. He'd been with her once when that'd happened. They'd been teenagers then, but he'd never forgotten it.

"I can take Rachel to my place," Brad suggested. "I've got a great security system, and it's not somewhere that the gunman would expect her to go."

Griff wanted to nix that suggestion right off, but had to admit that was because he didn't like Brad. He didn't want Rachel under Brad's roof at any time, but especially not when she was so vulnerable.

Of course, that might be his own guilty conscience at work. Rachel had certainly been vulnerable after learning of her father's affair, and that hadn't stopped Griff from sleeping with her.

Apparently, Rachel had her own concerns about Brad, however, because she shook her head. "Thanks, but your place is over a half hour's drive from here. I don't want to be that far from the sheriff's office in case they catch the shooter. I want to be here if they get a chance to question him."

Griff figured there was no way to stop her from observing the interview. No way to stop him, either, since this idiot had nearly killed Rachel and him. But first they had to catch the guy, and he was most likely long gone by now.

"If you don't want to ride all the way out to the ranch," Griff suggested to her, "my house is closer."

She looked at him, and he saw the concern she had about that. Rightfully so. The last time she'd been at his house, they'd landed in bed. No way would that happen again. Not now, maybe not ever.

"The Silver Creek cops haven't seen Dad," Egan relayed when he got off the phone. "But they'll look for him while they continue their search for the shooter."

Maybe they'd get lucky and find both. Griff just didn't want the cops to find Warren and the gunman together. Because if that happened, it meant Warren was either a hostage or had been involved in some way. That involvement might not necessarily be of his own doing, though.

"There's nothing else you can do here," Court chimed in, glancing at Rachel. "Griff could drive you to the ranch or his place, and I could follow to make sure you get there all right."

In other words, Court would go to make sure they weren't attacked along the way. It was a possibility, but since the other attack had happened on Main Street in Silver Creek, the ranch was probably safer than keeping her here. The ranch had a security gate, so someone couldn't just come driving through. Of course, there were fences that could be scaled, which meant Griff would need to alert the hands to keep an eye out for anyone suspicious.

Rachel huffed and then finally nodded. "The ranch. It'll give me a chance to catch up on some paperwork that I'm sure has been piling up since I've been gone."

It had been, because Griff had heard Warren, Court and Egan complaining about it. Normally, Warren and his sons handled the livestock supply, but Rachel managed the ranch's finances and day-to-day operation. The McCall Ranch was big so it was a full-time job. With Warren recovering from the shooting and Rachel's mom in the hospital, the business side of things had been neglected during Rachel's absence, and it was costing the McCalls business.

"Does this mean you're moving back?" Court asked.

"No." Rachel didn't hesitate, either. "But I'll try to organize the paperwork so that whoever Dad hires to take my place will have an easier transition." She paused. "I don't want the ranch to lose business, for Egan's and your sakes. It's your home."

Court went to her, brushed a kiss on her forehead. "It's your home, too. And you don't have to stay under Dad's roof. You can do what I did and build a place of your own on the ranch grounds."

She gave no indication whatsoever that she would consider that, but she did give her brother's arm a gentle squeeze. Maybe Court would be able to help mend the fences between Warren and Rachel. Of course, there was a lot of mending to be done, and now that had to include a good explanation of why Warren had been in Silver Creek tonight.

"Rachel, I can drive you out to the ranch," Brad volunteered. "That way, Griff could stay here and work the investigation. I'm sure he has plenty to do."

Griff did have plenty, but he could do it at the ranch. He also didn't like the way Brad was pushing this.

"We don't need Griff here," Court argued. Griff really needed to buy Court a drink for that. "And I'd rather Rachel be with a lawman. No offense, but if the shooter comes back, a Texas Ranger would be better able to protect her than a DA."

Brad's mouth went tight again, and he looked at Rachel, no doubt hoping that she would choose him over Griff for protective custody.

Rachel glanced at both of them and took a deep breath before she answered. "I'll go with Griff. But I'll be at the ranch just for tonight. I'll make other arrangements tomorrow."

It didn't sound as if she wanted Griff in on those arrangements, but there was no way Egan and Court would just let their kid sister go someplace that wasn't safe. Well, as safe as they could make it, anyway.

"We can use the cruisers out front," Court suggested, and he turned to Griff. "I can have someone bring your truck to you."

Griff thanked him, and after Rachel said a quick goodbye to Egan, she followed Court and Griff to the front. Court went out first, glancing around to make sure no one was out there. Once Court had given him the all clear, Griff got Rachel moving as fast as he could. Brad was right behind them, and for a moment Griff thought the man might try to get into the cruiser with them, but he stopped at the passenger door. He kept his attention nailed to Rachel as if he hoped she would change her mind.

She didn't.

Rachel looked everywhere but at Brad as Griff drove away. He spared the DA just a glance, to make sure he stayed put, but Griff was more interested in making sure Court was right behind them and that no one else pulled out to follow them. He didn't see another vehicle other than Court's cruiser and hoped it stayed that way.

"Sorry about this," Griff said. "I know you don't want to be with me—"

"I don't." Then she paused. "But I don't want to die. Nor do I want to tie up Egan and Court to babysit me."

She probably had meant that to be a dig, and Griff didn't mind if it was. He didn't want to tie up her brothers, either. He needed them to focus on catching whoever was behind the attack. Griff would help with that, too, but the sheriff's office wasn't his jurisdiction, and he could work the case from his laptop.

"This doesn't mean things are good between us." Rachel tacked that onto her comment.

He nodded. "It won't make sense to you, but I don't want things to be *good* between us. I screwed up, and I don't expect you to ever forgive me for it."

Her expression let him know that she wasn't buying that he was being genuine about that. Well, she should. Because it was true. If it'd been just keeping Warren's secret, then in time she might have relented. But Griff had slept with her, and he didn't see a way past that.

Since their *relationship* was a touchy subject, Griff moved on to something else. Something that could end up being touchy, too, but he was getting a bad feeling in his gut about the DA.

"Is it my imagination or is Brad…clinging more than usual when it comes to you?" Griff asked.

She shot him a look as if that was something she might not want to discuss with him before she sighed. "He's clingy," she confirmed. "Before things fell apart at home, Brad had been pressuring me to go out with him again. And you should know that my father was encouraging it."

That didn't surprise Griff, but it still stung. It was also a reminder that as much as he loved Warren, Warren had never felt Griff was worthy of Rachel. And he wasn't.

But it bothered Griff that Warren thought Brad was the right man for his daughter. Brad wasn't anywhere near good enough for her, but then Griff admitted that he was biased about that.

"I think Dad was starting to believe I'd become an old maid," she added in a grumble.

Nowhere close to that. Rachel was only thirty-one. Since Griff was five years older, that'd been another reason Warren had wanted him to keep his distance from Rachel. It had been a big deal when she was just sixteen, but no longer seemed an obstacle. However, there were other obstacles now, including the fact that Rachel might never trust him again.

Griff continued to look around. So did Rachel, and because she was so quiet he heard the rhythm of her breathing change. For one heart-stopping moment, he thought it was because she'd seen someone lying in wait for them, but he soon figured out it was because the ranch had come into view.

He hated that this place was no longer a sanctuary for her. No longer a home. And he wondered if it ever would be again. Her mother would be getting out of the mental hospital soon, and it was entirely possible that Helen would file for a divorce. No one would fault her if she did. But that meant one of Rachel's parents would almost certainly move.

Griff turned onto the ranch road and immediately spotted several hands near the gate. They opened it for him, and he drove through. As planned, Court turned around and headed back toward town. Griff kept watch in the rearview mirror to make sure the hands closed the gate behind them. They did.

Rachel eyed the main house and then Court's place, which was just up the road. "Is Rayna living there now?" she asked.

Rayna Travers was Court's girlfriend and likely soon to be his fiancée. "No. Not yet. She's still living at her place." A small horse ranch not far from there.

Rachel's eyes widened. "She's not alone, is she? Because the shooter could go there."

He quickly shook his head. "She's at a horse show in Dallas. I'm sure Court has someone watching out for her."

In fact, there was no doubt in Griff's mind about that. Court was clearly in love with Rayna and would take plenty of precautions to make sure she was safe. Ditto for taking those precautions for his sister. Both Court and Egan would work this case to make sure the danger ended fast. Griff just hoped it was fast enough that there wouldn't be another attack.

"So far, Rayna hasn't been included in the new threats we've been getting," Griff added.

"*We?* You've been getting them, too?"

He nodded. "Court, Egan and your dad, as well. And your mom. Obviously, we haven't let her know about that, and yes, we've alerted the hospital. Egan hired a private guard to watch her."

The guard wasn't only because of the new threats, though. It was because a month earlier someone had kidnapped the woman, and Egan and Court wanted to make sure that didn't happen again.

A heavy sigh left Rachel's mouth. "How bad are the threats?"

Bad. In fact, they still twisted away at him. And while he would have liked to have sheltered Rachel from knowing the exact words, he wouldn't keep this from her. He'd learned his lesson about doing that. Besides, if he sugar-coated it, she might not take it as seriously as she should.

"The person who sent them wants Warren to suffer," Griff answered. "He or she says Warren will watch his children die one by one until he has nothing left but misery in his life."

Rachel shuddered and turned away from him. "Please tell me you have a suspect."

"Too many of them," he admitted. "Along with Alma Lawton, who could be connected to Whitney, there are plenty of criminals who'd like to get back at Warren for arresting them. We're making our way through the case files now."

But the investigation was moving at a snail's pace since they were basically having to use the looking-for-a-needle-in-a-haystack approach. Because it might not be an actual convicted criminal who was doing this, but rather someone connected to a person who Warren had managed to convict. Warren had made more enemies than friends during his long reign as the sheriff of Mc-Call Canyon. He'd made an ample share of enemies in his business dealings, too. So, yeah, definitely slow going.

Rachel looked up at the house when Griff pulled to a stop in front of it. The porch lights were on, and Griff spotted one of the hands in a truck parked in the side driveway.

"You know the drill," Griff reminded her. "Move fast."

She did. Rachel got out of the cruiser and hurried up the porch steps, but the door opened before they reached it. Griff automatically went for his gun, but it was only

Ruby, the McCalls' longtime cook and housekeeper. The woman was more family than employee, and immediately pulled Rachel into a hug.

"I'm so glad you're home," Ruby whispered to her.

Griff hated to cut the reunion short, but he didn't want Rachel out in the open any longer than necessary. That's why he took both women by the arm and maneuvered them inside.

"Are you all right?" Ruby asked, pushing Rachel's hair from her face. "Egan called and said there'd been some more trouble. I figured we'd already had enough of that."

"We have," Rachel assured her. "And I'm fine."

No, she wasn't. She looked ready to collapse, and Ruby must have noticed.

"Should I do anything special to be certain that she stays safe?" Ruby asked Griff.

"Make sure all the windows and doors are locked and set the security system. I'll call the head ranch hand and see where he has guards posted." Griff took out his phone to do that, but Rachel's cell rang.

She sucked in her breath when she saw the screen, so Griff knew this was important. He went to her and saw the name.

Warren.

Rachel's hand was trembling when she pressed the button to put it on speaker. "Where are you?" she snapped.

"Rachel?" It was Warren all right, but he sounded groggy or something. "Is that you?"

"Of course it's me. You called my phone, remember?"

"What?" Warren mumbled something else that Griff didn't catch. "Are you all right?"

"No, I'm not," she answered, her tone edged with anger. "Are you in Silver Creek? And did you attack Griff and me tonight?"

Griff expected Warren to jump to deny that last question. He didn't. Instead, Warren groaned. "Someone tried to hurt you," he said, but he slurred his words, making Griff wonder if the man was drunk.

"No, someone tried to *kill* me. Was it you?" Rachel demanded, her voice much louder than before.

"God, Rachel." Warren groaned again. "I'm so sorry. But I just don't know."

Chapter Five

Rachel paced across the living room of the ranch house, each time checking out the huge bay window as she walked past it. There was no sign of Egan or her father yet, but according to Egan's last text, they should be here any minute.

Maybe then she could get answers.

Answers that she certainly hadn't gotten the night before, when her father had called her. He'd sounded disoriented, maybe even drunk, but she'd never witnessed him having more than a beer or two. Certainly not enough alcohol to make him forget where he was. Or if he'd had something to do with the attacks.

She heard Griff's footsteps, but even before she could see him, he grumbled out a warning. Probably because he heard her footsteps, too. "The pacing won't help. They'll get here just as fast if you're sitting."

Yes, but there was no way she could sit with all this restless energy inside her.

Griff came from the direction of the kitchen, carrying two mugs. She could tell from the smell that one was the strong coffee he favored. The other was her usual tea, which he handed to her.

"Ruby fixed it," Griff added, "so it should be good."

Rachel had a sip, nodded. It was exactly the way she liked it, and she made a mental note to thank Ruby the next time the woman came in to check on her. Which would no doubt be very soon. Ruby had been making those checks ever since Griff and she had arrived at the ranch the night before, and the frequency had increased in the past hour, since Egan's text.

"I talked to Court a couple of minutes ago," Griff said. "Your father is more lucid this morning."

"But?" Rachel definitely heard the uncertainty in his voice.

"But he has some memory gaps about last night. In other words, don't expect him to be able to tell us a lot more than we already know."

She shook her head. "He has to tell us more. I need to know why he was in that alley."

Griff made a sound of agreement and sipped his coffee. He didn't sit, but instead joined her at the bay window. At first she thought that was because he was anxious to see Egan and Warren, too, but he gently took hold of her arm and moved her back. Only then did she remember that it probably wasn't safe to stand in plain view like that, because there could be a sniper in the area.

She silently cursed. She hated that she had to be cautioned about that kind of threat in a place where she'd once felt so safe.

"I just assumed if the doctor released Dad from the

hospital, it meant his memory had fully returned," Rachel grumbled.

She didn't really expect Griff to have an answer to that, because he'd already told her the details of his conversations with both her brothers. Her father had had an overnight stay because the doctor had wanted to run tests on him to see why he was so disoriented. The tests had been inconclusive, but all the results weren't in yet. She was hoping when they had those results back, they'd have answers to go along with them.

Rachel got up and went to the window again when she heard the sound of an approaching vehicle, and spotted Egan's cruiser as he pulled to a stop in front of the house. She'd thought she had steeled herself enough to see her father. She hadn't. When he got out of the car, he looked frail and old. It seemed as if he'd aged a decade in the past month.

Griff went to the front door and opened it after he disarmed the security system, then he helped Egan get Warren up the steps. Her father was short of breath by the time he made it inside.

"Rachel." His gaze immediately connected with hers, but he didn't come toward her. Probably because he didn't want to risk her turning away from him.

She nodded a greeting, and because she suddenly felt a little unsteady, sank down onto one of the chairs in the family room. Griff led her father in there, too, and had him sit across from her.

"Nothing yet on the rest of the test results," Egan volunteered. "The doctor wants Dad to take it easy for a day or two."

"I don't want to take it easy," Warren immediately protested. "I want to find the person who tried to kill Griff and Rachel. Because I'm betting that's the same person who did this to me. He must have drugged me. My guess is it was some kind of barbiturate, since I've got memory loss."

Yes, Rachel suspected that, as well, but her father wasn't in any shape to go looking for a would-be killer. But that did lead her to something that had been eating away at her.

"If the shooter got close enough to you, then why just drug you?" she asked her father.

Warren shook his head. "I don't know. If he wanted me dead, he could have killed me then."

He took the words right out of her mouth. Words that chilled her to the bone. Because this monster could be toying with them. Or maybe her father wasn't even the target.

Maybe she was.

And that led her right back to Marlon.

Of course, it could be Alma, too, if she'd wanted to punish Warren by making him witness the death of his daughter. Rachel hoped Egan and Griff didn't give her any hassles about watching the interviews they had scheduled with both of them. Not that she expected either of them to blurt out confessions, but they might say something to give them away.

"What exactly do you remember about what went on last night?" Griff asked Warren.

That caused Rachel to shift her attention back to her father, but after one look at his downcast expression, she doubted he was going to give them much. Still, anything was a start.

He dragged in a long breath before he started. "I went to a bar in San Antonio to meet with Buddy Hoskins. I thought he might know something about who was sending us those threats."

Buddy Hoskins. She knew the name. Buddy was one of her father's criminal informants when he'd still been sheriff. From what Rachel could remember, the man had a drug habit and a long arrest record. Her father had never brought him to the house, but she'd seen him once at the sheriff's office.

"Why would Buddy know anything about the threats?" Griff pressed.

"He didn't say when he texted me to set up the meeting. Buddy just said he'd heard some talk and wanted to pass it along to me. I figured the reason he wanted to tell me in person was so I'd give him some cash."

That didn't surprise her, but considering everything that had gone on, the meeting could have been a setup.

"Buddy texted you," Griff said. "Is that the way he usually gets in touch with you?"

"Sometimes. Usually he calls, though." Warren groaned and scrubbed his hand over his forehead. "You think it was someone else who sent that text, to lure me to that bar?"

"Possibly. Did you actually meet with Buddy?" Griff pressed.

"I don't think so. If I did, I don't recall seeing him. I got to the bar, ordered a beer and the next thing I remember is waking up in the hospital. Everything in between is a blank."

"For now it is," Egan said. "The doctor thought there was a chance you might get those memories back in a day or two."

Rachel sighed before she could stop herself. A day or two might be too late for Griff and her. Heck, for all of them.

Egan checked his watch and then looked at Griff. "Can you hold things down here while I go back to the station? I've got a mountain of paperwork to do before the interviews."

Griff nodded, though he did cast an uneasy glance at Rachel. Maybe because he wasn't certain how she felt about being in the same house with her father. She wasn't certain about how she felt, either, but it wasn't safe for her to leave until she'd made other arrangements. Something she needed to get started on, since it was obvious she wasn't going to get answers from Warren. She also couldn't rely on her brothers to help with those arrangements, since she wanted them working this investigation.

Rachel stood to face her brother. "What time are Marlon's and Alma's interviews?" she asked.

"The first is at noon. The other, two hours later," Egan answered, and then he shifted his attention to their father. "Can you get to your room by yourself or do you need help?"

It was possible that Warren answered, but if so Rachel didn't hear him. That's because she felt a tingling feeling in her stomach, then saw a glowing light. Mercy, she knew what that was: an aura. And it always happened right before a seizure.

Rachel looked at Griff to tell him what was happening, but it was too late. Still, he seemed to know, because he lunged for her, catching her in his arms before she fell to the floor.

"I'M FINE," RACHEL grumbled to the doctor.

Griff didn't believe her, and obviously neither did Egan, since he gave her a big-brother stare-down. Ditto for Dr. Henry Baldwin not believing her, since he continued to examine her. He had already taken a blood sample.

"This checkup is just a precaution," Dr. Baldwin explained. He'd given her several variations of that assurance in between listening to her heart and checking her pupils.

"I've been taking my meds," Rachel went on. That, too, was something she'd been repeating since Griff and Egan had rushed her to the hospital.

Over the years, Egan had no doubt witnessed his sister having many seizures, but it still seemed to shake him up. It had certainly done that to Griff. That was in part because Rachel had said she'd been seizure-free for two years. It was always possible for an epileptic to have a seizure, but Griff definitely didn't like the timing of this one.

"Is this stress related?" he asked Dr. Baldwin.

The doctor only lifted his shoulder. "Maybe, but these things happen with or without stress. If there are any red flags, the test results might show it. *Might*," he emphasized. "In the meantime, I want her to get plenty of rest. The same for Warren. Please tell me he didn't come to the hospital with Rachel and you."

Egan shook his head. "He didn't. I insisted that he stay put."

Warren had thankfully done that, but it hadn't stopped the man from texting both Egan and Griff to get updates on Rachel's condition.

The doctor helped her to a sitting position on the examining table. Griff could tell from her slight grimace that she was exhausted. That was the usual symptom after she had a seizure. Of course, this one was worse, since she'd hardly slept the night before.

Even though she was a little wobbly, she got off the table and tried to look a lot stronger than she likely felt. She gave Griff a warning glance when she thought he might start toward her to help, but he stayed put. He also knew from experience that it wasn't a good idea to treat Rachel with kid gloves after something like this.

"I'll call you if there's anything in your test results," the doctor said, looking at the tablet that contained her medical records. "Oh, and right before you two brought Rachel in, I got back the blood work on Warren."

Rachel, Egan and Griff had already started for the door, but that stopped them.

"I'll call and tell him," the doctor went on, "but since this is a police matter, I can give you the results. Warren was definitely drugged. Someone gave him a huge dose of Rohypnol."

That was the date-rape drug, and it explained the memory loss. However, it didn't prove why someone had given it to him in the first place. Unless...

"This was to set up Warren," Griff concluded. "Someone drugged him and drove him to that location so he'd be blamed for the car bombing." And therefore blamed for Rachel's murder.

That was the only scenario that made sense, since Griff was positive that Warren hadn't tried to kill his daughter, or anyone else for that matter. Still, who would do this, and why? There was only one person with that kind of motive.

Alma.

When Griff looked back at Rachel, he realized she was volleying glances between Egan and him. "We should go to the sheriff's office and wait for Alma," she said. "She'll be coming in soon for her interview."

Yes, she would be, but taking Rachel there definitely wouldn't give her the rest that the doctor had just ordered.

"If I go home," Rachel added, "I'll only be pacing and waiting to hear the outcome of the interview. I can pace and wait at the sheriff's office."

Egan, Griff and the doctor all huffed, but Griff knew that's exactly what she'd do. No way would Rachel be able to relax until they had some answers. Whenever that would be.

Egan's phone buzzed, and when he glanced at the screen, he mumbled something about this being a call he had to take, and stepped out in the hall to answer it.

"You have any other questions?" the doctor asked, glancing from Griff to Rachel. Both shook their heads. "Fine, then just make her sit down as much as possible," the doctor instructed. He patted Griff's arm on the way out. "Good luck with that."

He'd need luck and a whole lot more to get Rachel to cooperate, but Griff waited until the doctor was out of the examining room before he said anything to her. "I want to focus on this case, and I can't do that if I'm worried about you."

She blinked as if surprised by his words. Maybe because she didn't want to hear that he was still worried. Or that he cared for her. Which he did.

"The odds are slim to none that I'll have another seizure today," she said, "and I can rest when I get home after the interviews." She stopped, though, and gave a frustrated sigh. "I was going to make arrangements for another place to stay."

That didn't surprise him. Rachel probably wanted some breathing space away from Warren and him. But considering the fact that he'd just rushed her to the hospital, breathing room probably no longer seemed like a smart idea.

Even though Griff didn't say a word, it was obvious she was playing out his argument in her head, because she huffed. "Fine. I'll stay one more night at the ranch if you don't give me any hassles about watching those interviews."

Griff didn't want to give in to that, but the truth was he couldn't stop her. Sure, he could tell Egan to keep her out of the observation room at the sheriff's office, but she had a right to hear what Marlon and Alma had to say. And that's why Griff finally nodded.

When they went into the hall, Egan was just finishing up his call, and he turned to them. "That was the Silver Creek sheriff. They found a dead body about five miles outside town. Male, about fifty years old, and he was killed with a single gunshot wound to the head. They think he might have been the person who set the bomb because he had some explosive paraphernalia in his truck."

"He's really dead?" Rachel asked. She made a sound of relief when Egan nodded, but there was no such relief on her brother's face.

"The truck was stolen, and the dead guy had no ID," Egan went on. He started walking toward the exit, and Rachel and Griff followed. "There was also no gunshot residue on his hands."

So he probably wasn't the man who'd tried to gun them down, and that meant there had to be two of them. Maybe more. That wasn't exactly a settling thought. Because even though this guy was dead, another would-be killer could still be out there.

With that reminder fresh in his memory, Griff made sure Rachel hurried when they went outside to the cruiser. He also kept watch as Egan drove toward the sheriff's office. Along the way, Griff updated Egan on his father's test results, while he also kept an eye on Rachel. She definitely didn't seem steady, but there was nothing he could do about that.

She looked at him, their gazes connecting, and for a split second he saw just how bad her fatigue was before she shut down. Of course, she couldn't turn off her emotions, because coupled with that fatigue was still plenty of disapproval that he was the one sitting beside her. Or at least he thought it was all disapproval.

Until she glanced at his mouth.

One quick look at her, and he saw something else. The heat. Maybe she was remembering the night they'd spent together or the fact that they'd skirted around this attraction for each other for years. Either way, she wasn't having an easy time dismissing it, because she scowled and mumbled, "Really?"

For some stupid reason, that made him smile. And it seemed to ease her scowl a bit, too. She didn't exactly return the smile, but she no longer looked ready to punch him. Maybe that meant they'd reached some kind of truce.

Egan pulled to a stop in front of the sheriff's office, and Griff spotted his sister, Deputy Thea Morris, in the squad room. He knew from what Egan had said earlier that she was manning the place by herself while the other deputies were out working on the investigation. But his sister wasn't alone.

When Egan, Griff and Rachel went inside, they saw Alma standing there. Griff had already met the woman. Had met her attorney, Simon Lindley, but this was Rachel's first time seeing the pair.

Alma's attention immediately went to Rachel, and the woman's mouth went into a flat, disapproving line. "You're the reason I'm here," she snapped. "Well, I don't like it, and I'm tired of you McCalls and this vendetta you have against me."

Griff was about to return some verbal fire, but Rachel stepped in front of him. "Someone tried to kill us." Her voice was surprisingly strong, considering she'd had a seizure a couple hours earlier. "It's not a vendetta. We just need to know the truth so the attacks can be stopped."

"Well, you're not going to learn the truth by going after my client," Simon protested. He volleyed his attention between Griff and Egan. "This will be the last time you drag her in for questioning. If you try it again, I'll sue you for harassment. My client has done nothing wrong."

"Where was she last night?" Griff asked, the moment Simon had finished his little rant.

"I was at home," Alma said, at the same time that Simon spoke.

"She doesn't have to answer that!"

Egan huffed. "She'll have to answer it if she wants to get out of here anytime soon. But, hey, that's your call if you want to wait around here for a couple of days for the DA and me to decide if we're going to file charges."

That put Alma's mouth in an even flatter line. "What exactly do you suspect that I've done?"

Egan lifted his shoulder. "Maybe blew up a car. Drugged a man. Shot at people. Oh, and put a bullet in someone's head."

"Murder?" Simon spat out. He hitched his thumb at Alma. "You really believe she could do something like that? Look at her. She's not a killer."

"I won't know that until I've questioned her, now will I?" Egan met the lawyer's glare with one of his own, and Egan was good at it, too.

"Fine," Simon finally snapped. "You can question Alma…" Then he stopped, his attention going to the window.

Griff immediately turned in that direction, putting

Rachel behind him in case there was about to be another attack. But it wasn't a gun.

It was Sheriff Raleigh Lawton.

This was another first, for Rachel to see her half brother, but she didn't question who he was. Maybe because there was a strong resemblance between him and her other brothers.

She made a sound, a soft moan that came from deep in her throat, and she took hold of Griff's arm. Maybe because she was feeling dizzy, but it probably had more to do with seeing the proof of her father's infidelity.

"Sheriff McCord," Raleigh said in greeting when he came in. "Ranger Morris."

"Griff," he automatically corrected, though he figured Raleigh preferred to stick with the formal title. The man had certainly been keeping his distance from his half siblings.

And his father.

Raleigh nodded a silent greeting to Rachel, but his gaze did linger on her for several moments. It was as if he was studying her features, just as she was doing to him.

"I'm sorry about the trouble you had," Raleigh told her, before turning to his mother.

"Thank you for coming," Alma said. Obviously, she'd called Raleigh to tell him about the interview.

"Yes, thank you," Simon repeated. "You need to convince your fellow cop to back off."

Raleigh shrugged in that same lazy way that Egan had just moments earlier. "Actually, I'm not here just for my mother, Simon. I'm also here because of you."

And with that, Raleigh shifted his attention from

Simon to Egan. "I have some possible evidence that my mother's lawyer might have been the one who tried to kill Rachel."

Chapter Six

Rachel wasn't sure who was more stunned by Raleigh's accusation—Simon or everyone else in the squad room.

From the moment she'd seen her half brother come walking in, she'd thought he'd come to defend his mother and give them a good dressing down for "harassing" her. Instead, it was possible he was giving them their first real lead that could help them solve this case and put an end to the danger.

Well, Raleigh could be doing that *if* he actually had something.

"What the hell are you talking about?" Simon snarled. Obviously, there was no love lost between Raleigh and him because Simon gave him a look that could have frozen Texas in summer. "What possible evidence?"

The veins were suddenly bulging on Simon's neck. In contrast, though, Alma didn't seem angry. However, it appeared she was on the verge of crying. Her eyes watered.

"Sheriff Ryland in Silver Creek found a dead guy," Raleigh explained, "and when he sent out the picture, I immediately recognized him." He took out his phone, pulled up a photo of a man and turned the screen toward Simon for him to see. "I think you'll recognize him, too."

Simon took a quick intake of breath when he saw the picture. Raleigh then showed it to Griff, Egan and her. But not to his mother. Maybe because he didn't want her to see the man who was obviously dead from a gunshot wound.

"Who is he?" Griff asked.

"Dennis Gale," Raleigh and Simon answered in unison.

It was Raleigh who continued. "Dennis was a PI, and he worked for Simon."

Well, that was a connection that Simon obviously didn't want. Because it connected him not only to the dead guy but also to the car bomb.

"Dennis *used* to work for me," Simon corrected. "I fired him about a month ago."

"Why?" That question came from Griff, but Rachel figured any one of them could have asked it. Alma included, since her eyes widened a little in what appeared to be surprise.

Simon glanced around as if searching for the right way to explain this. Of course, the right way for him would be an explanation that would no longer make him a person of interest.

"Dennis was a drunk," Simon finally said. "He botched a case where I had him keeping surveillance on a client's wife. He tried to shake down the wife for money, and in exchange he wouldn't report to me that she'd been doing some illegal things. The wife came to me, and since she had a recording of Dennis trying to blackmail her, I fired him."

"And you didn't come to me with any of that?" Raleigh snarled.

"Attorney-client privilege," Simon snarled right back. "There were things on the recording that would have violated what my client told me in confidence." He paused, muttered some profanity. "Obviously Dennis got himself mixed up in something bad."

"Yeah," Griff agreed. "Something that implicates you. Where were you last night?"

Simon's eyes narrowed. He didn't like that question aimed at him any more than he had when Griff had asked it of Alma.

"I was at work in my office until around 10:00 p.m.," he snapped. "And yes, someone saw me there. I have a cleaning service that was in the building all the way up until the time I left."

"That doesn't mean you didn't hire someone to launch the attack in Silver Creek," Griff quickly pointed out. "Someone like your former PI. Then, you could have killed Dennis when he failed to kill Rachel."

Simon cursed, and it was so raw that it caused Alma to blush. "I think you'd better go ahead and start that interview with me," she said to Egan. "I'd like to get out of here as soon as possible."

Egan glanced at Raleigh, Simon and her before he shrugged again and started walking toward the interview room. "Don't think the questions for you are over," he warned Simon. "They're just beginning."

Good. Because if Simon knew anything, then maybe her brother could figure out a way to get him to talk.

"You really think Simon could have hired a killer?" Griff asked Raleigh after the others were in the interview room.

A muscle flickered in the man's jaw. "I don't know. He hates Warren, and he's in love with my mother. That's a bad combination."

Yes, it was. "You don't happen to have financials on Simon, do you?" Rachel pressed.

"No. But I might be able to get them because of Dennis's murder." Raleigh looked at her. "Are you okay? Were you hurt in the attack?"

She felt a tightness in her chest, and it took her a moment to realize why. Raleigh's tone sounded, well, brotherly. Part of her didn't like that. She didn't want to have this man feel any connection whatsoever to her. Ditto for her not wanting to feel anything for him. But simply put, none of this was Raleigh's fault. He hadn't asked his mother and her father to have an affair, and now they were all having to live with the consequences.

"You don't have to answer," Raleigh went on, "but how's your mother?"

Again, it sounded somewhat brotherly, and while she didn't want to talk about this with Raleigh, she didn't see any reason to be rude about it, either. "She's about the same, still in the hospital." No need for her to clarify that it was a mental hospital or that her mother had had a breakdown. Raleigh almost certainly knew all that.

So that she wouldn't have to continue this conversation, Rachel was about to remind Griff that she wanted to listen to Alma's interview, but Raleigh spoke again.

"I'll let Egan know this, too, but I got a threatening email this morning." He took a piece of paper from his pocket. "I printed it out after I forwarded it to the FBI so they can try to figure out who sent it."

They'd had no luck with that so far. Whoever was emailing them was bouncing the messages off foreign servers. Still, maybe the sender had made a mistake this time and not covered his or her tracks.

Griff took the paper from Raleigh, and Rachel moved closer to him so she could read it. The words seemed to jump right out at her: *"Sheriff Warren McCall will pay for what he's done, and that means you're going to die. I'll make sure all of his children die while he watches."*

Griff mumbled some profanity under his breath and handed the paper back to Raleigh. "That's similar to the ones we've all been getting." He turned to her then, and Rachel must have looked pretty bad because Griff cursed again and looped his arm around her waist. "I need to get her off her feet."

Raleigh nodded, and he looked as concerned as Griff did. Worse, Rachel thought there might be reason for concern because she was suddenly dizzy again. She'd never had two seizures in the same day, and if it happened, she'd almost certainly be hospitalized. No way did she want that, not with everything else going on, so she immediately tried to steady herself.

Griff led her up the hall, not to the observation room but rather to the break room, and he did just as he'd told Raleigh. He got her off her feet by having her sit on the sofa.

"You're shaking," he pointed out when he got her a bottle of water from the fridge.

She was, and it only added to her frustration. "I hate feeling weak," she mumbled. "And I hate people thinking I'm weak."

"Yeah, I know." Griff sat on the arm of the sofa next to her and brushed a kiss on the top of her head.

He did indeed know. In fact, Griff knew plenty about her since she'd poured out her heart to him over the years. And over those years, he'd actually listened.

"You just need to get some rest like the doctor said," he assured her. "And you probably need to eat something."

She did, but it wasn't her top priority. "I want to listen to what Alma is saying."

Griff no doubt wanted that, too, but he didn't budge. Probably because he knew if he got up, then so would she. "Egan will tell us if either Simon or Alma say anything we can use."

Egan would, but Rachel wanted to hear it for herself. However, she didn't want to risk wobbling again. There were already too many people worried about her, and that was only causing all of them more stress. But it was stress that she was certain Griff would understand.

"It's so hard for me to see Raleigh," she said. "Because he's proof of what my father did."

Griff nodded. "I can tell Raleigh to leave if that would help."

"No. He might have more pull with his mother than Egan does. He might get her to tell us things that she wouldn't otherwise say." Rachel paused. "But I can't stay at the house with my father. I thought I could, for another night, anyway, but seeing Raleigh…"

She didn't finish that, and judging from Griff's expression, there was no need. He knew what this was doing to her.

He dragged in a long, weary breath. The kind a person would take when he was about to say something he might regret. "It probably won't be as secure as the ranch, but I can take you to my place." He also paused. "Unless that'll just trigger more bad memories for you."

"Anyplace I go will trigger memories." Including those of the night she'd spent there with Griff.

Those memories came back now, too.

She'd spent so many years fantasizing about being with Griff that way, but Rachel certainly hadn't expected it to happen at such a low point in her life. Even then, it'd still lived up to her high expectations.

And the memories weren't going to let her forget that.

"I do have a guest room," he reminded her, probably because he wanted to assure her that a sleepover wouldn't lead to sex.

She nodded and made the mistake of looking up at him. Griff was certainly a cure for her bone-weary fatigue because all that vanished. Apparently, so did her common sense, because Rachel thought about kissing him. She thought about pulling him to her and just getting lost in his arms. It would no doubt feel good, and for a few moments she wouldn't have to think about this awful mess they were in.

However, there would be consequences.

A kiss would mean she had forgiven him, and she wasn't certain she could do that. Not today, anyway. Still, that didn't stop her from weaving another fantasy.

He dropped his gaze to her mouth, and when their eyes connected again, she saw the heat there. She figured there was no chance he'd be the one to initiate a kiss. Not after what had happened between them a month ago.

But he did.

Griff leaned down, barely touching her lips. Coming from any other man, it might have been chaste, but there was nothing chaste about Griff.

He paused, his mouth hovering over hers, and even though he didn't say anything, Rachel could feel the fierce battle he was having with himself. She was having that same battle, and was clearly losing because she didn't move away from him. She stayed put, waiting for him to continue with what would almost certainly be a huge mistake.

Griff cursed himself, and her, and got up from the sofa. "The timing isn't right for us to play with fire," he mumbled.

That was the truth. Heck, it might never be right. That didn't stop her from feeling the disappointment, though. And that made her stupid. Because the last thing she should be doing right now was thinking about kissing Griff, and she hoped if she repeated that often enough to herself that it would finally sink in.

There was a knock at the door before it opened, and Rachel quickly tried to prepare herself in case it was Raleigh. It wasn't. It was Thea. She glanced at both of them, maybe sensing that something had nearly gone on between them. But if she did pick up on the attraction, she didn't say anything about it. Instead, she hitched her thumb to the squad room.

"Marlon Stowe just arrived," Thea said. "And he's demanding to see you."

That got Rachel to her feet. "How did he know I was here?"

"He said he's been watching the sheriff's office from the diner across the street. Yeah," Thea added, when Rachel frowned. "I thought it was creepy, too. Anyway, he claims he has to see you because he's got something important to tell you."

"What?" Rachel pressed, when Thea hesitated.

Thea frowned, too. "Marlon claims he has proof that it was your father who tried to kill you."

Chapter Seven

Griff had to mentally replay what Thea had just said before it sank in. And when it finally did register in his head, it caused him to curse. He didn't know Marlon, but Rachel had already been through enough without having to deal with this clown's accusations.

"Proof?" Griff snapped.

Thea sighed, nodded and looked at Rachel. "Of course, he's saying he'll only give that proof to you and nobody else. If you don't want to deal with him, I can arrest him for obstruction of justice—"

"No," Rachel interrupted. "I'll see him. Or rather, I'll hear what he has to say. But if this is some kind of trick, then maybe you can charge him with something. *Anything.*"

She sounded more exhausted than she looked, and that made Griff realize just how wrong that near kiss had been. Rachel definitely didn't need him adding another layer of trouble to her life.

She took some sips of water before she headed back to the squad room. Thea stayed ahead of them, and Griff moved to Rachel's side. He also put his hand over the gun in his holster. He doubted that Marlon had come here to attack Rachel, but since the man had once had a restraining order against him, it likely meant he had a dangerous edge.

Since Marlon was also a person of interest in Rachel's attack, Griff had seen a picture of the guy, but seeing him in person was still a surprise. That's because he looked like a teenager. He wasn't. Griff knew the guy was twenty-six, but he could have passed for someone ten years younger.

"Rachel," Marlon said in greeting.

Because Griff's arm was touching Rachel's, he felt her tense. Obviously, this guy set off alarms for her, which meant he did the same for Griff.

Marlon flashed a wide smile, as if this was a social visit. However, he didn't extend that smile to Griff. "Ranger Morris. I was just doing a computer check on you while I was having coffee at the diner. Discovered some interesting things. You'd be surprised what you can learn on the internet." He motioned to the laptop bag he was carrying.

Maybe that comment was meant to intimidate Griff, because Marlon had almost certainly learned about Griff's criminal parents. But it didn't intimidate him in the least. Griff just stared him down. He also decided to hurry this conversation along.

"You have some kind of accusation you want to make against Rachel's father?" he asked.

Marlon turned back to Thea. "I said I would only talk to Rachel about this. I told you to make that clear to her."

"I didn't agree to that, and neither did Rachel," Thea

insisted. "And I can promise that Griff wouldn't have agreed to it."

The man huffed, his gaze slashing to Rachel. "So, do you want to know about your dad or not?" There was no trace of that friendly tone or smile left, and Griff figured this was more Marlon's usual personality.

Yeah, the guy was definitely wound tight.

Rachel folded her arms over her chest and stared at him. "Of course I want to know, but I don't understand why we should keep it just between us. If my father truly did try to murder me, and you can prove it, then he'll need to be arrested—immediately. That means you'd end up repeating whatever you have to say to Ranger Morris and the cops."

That *wound-tight* expression went up a notch. "I thought you and I could talk privately first," Marlon pressed.

Thea had been right. No way was that going to happen, but Griff didn't even have to say so because Rachel put down her foot first.

"There's no reason for us to talk privately," she insisted. "Is there?" She didn't wait for him to answer. "The only thing I want from you is this so-called proof that you have about my father."

There was a flash of anger in Marlon's eyes before he must have remembered that Griff was watching his every move—and ready to arrest his sorry butt if he did anything wrong.

"I was hoping you'd talk to Taryn," Marlon finally said. "I want you to tell her to come back to me. I figure that won't be hard for you to do since you're the one who talked her into leaving me." There was plenty of bitterness in his voice.

Rachel shook her head. "I didn't talk Taryn into anything. I just listened to her while she cried on my shoulder."

Marlon's suddenly narrowed eyes told Griff that the man didn't believe that. Well, tough. Even if Rachel had managed to sway Taryn, that was probably the best thing that could have happened, considering what had gone on in Marlon's other relationship.

Griff huffed, put his hands on his hips and glared at the man. "You'd better not have come here to coerce Rachel in exchange for possible evidence in a murder investigation. Because if so, you'll go to jail. I'll personally see to it."

And the stare-down started. It didn't last long, though, because Marlon must have seen that Griff wasn't bluffing. No way was he letting this clown out of here before he told them what he knew.

"Fine," Marlon finally said, "but I'll need a table for my laptop so I can show you the photos."

Photos. Well, hell.

That certainly sounded like some kind of legit evidence, so maybe this wasn't just a ploy for Marlon to get back at Rachel for "interfering" in his relationship with Taryn. Griff only hoped it wasn't evidence against Warren. Even though Rachel and her dad were on the outs, it wouldn't help her mental state if Egan had to arrest the man for attempted murder. Or worse—murder. After all, there was a dead man in this, Dennis, and even though he was connected to Simon, it didn't mean he didn't have a connection to Warren, too.

Since Egan was still in the interview room with Alma, Griff motioned for Marlon to follow Rachel and him to Egan's office. Griff knew that Egan wouldn't mind, but it did make him feel uneasy when Marlon took the time to study the family pictures Egan had on his desk, wall and filing cabinet. Some were of their parents, others of Rachel and Court. Another was of Egan's late fiancée.

"Shanna Sullivan," Marlon muttered, when his attention landed on the fiancée's picture.

Rachel had obviously already been creeped out by this guy, but that had her snapping back her shoulders. "How do you know Shanna?" she asked. Except it wasn't just a simple question. It was a demand.

"Her murder was all over the news." If Marlon was the least bit concerned with Rachel's sharp tone, he didn't show it. "I remember reading the stories of how upset your brother was."

Shanna's murder during a botched robbery attempt had indeed made the news for several days, but that had happened nearly two years ago. Griff figured that wasn't nearly recent enough to stick in Marlon's mind, especially since the murder hadn't taken place near Marlon's hometown of Silver Creek. No, it was more likely that he had done intensive computer searches on Rachel, as well, and that Shanna's name had come up.

Nearly everything that came out of this guy's mouth seemed to be some kind of red flag, and Griff hated that Rachel had been under the same roof with him for nearly a month. Because she'd run from her father, it might have put her in the path of a dangerous predator. Of course, this *predator* was now trying to point the finger at Warren.

"You can set up your laptop there." Griff pointed to the edge of Egan's desk. "And while you're doing that, you can explain to me why you have this fixation with Rachel."

Marlon took out his laptop and a large manila envelope, and Griff noticed that the man had a white-knuckle grip on his computer bag. "Is that what you told him?" Marlon asked Rachel.

"No," Griff said, before she could answer. "She said you blame her for Taryn breaking up with you. But the way you're acting seems more like a fixation to me."

"Well, it's not." Marlon shifted the tense grip to his laptop and envelope when he put them on the desk. "Despite what went on between Taryn and her, Rachel's been a good customer at my parents' inn, and I'm trying to do her a favor." He stared at Griff. "Or would you rather me not give you something that would cause you to have to arrest your mentor?"

Griff was certain that tightened his own jaw. "Just show us what you have."

His reaction seemed to amuse Marlon, and Griff instantly regretted that he'd shown any emotion about Warren. Now this clown knew it was a sore spot and might try to use it.

"You should know up front that I take pictures," Marlon continued, as he pulled up a file of photos. He motioned toward the envelope. "I also printed out copies of the ones I thought would *interest* you."

Griff glanced at the file and saw that there were hundreds of photos, and judging from the quick look that Griff got, some had been taken of the sheriff's office from the diner. Apparently, Marlon had been busy while he tried to spy on Rachel.

"I took these last night," he went on, and he clicked on the first photo. "Now, before you start accusing me of anything, I hadn't planned on taking pictures of Rachel. I was just going to take some sunset shots for the inn's webpage. But about the time I started, Rachel just happened to come outside."

Well, it was indeed Rachel, and she was coming out of the inn. It wasn't dark yet so Griff could easily see her and a couple who were on the sidewalk just a few yards from the front door. Rachel seemed to be searching through her purse, and she definitely didn't have her attention on Marlon.

"I was looking for my car keys," Rachel volunteered. "I didn't see Marlon." Her voice was tight and clipped, no doubt because she didn't like the idea that someone like Marlon had been photographing her.

The next shot had her just to the edge of the camera range. The inn was in the background, and Marlon was behind her and to her right. However, Griff saw something else.

A man.

He was on the left side of the inn, and definitely not in plain sight like the couple. He seemed to be lurking behind some shrubs.

Griff pointed to the murky image. "Zoom in on that," he told Marlon.

"I've already enlarged it. And printed out a copy for you to keep."

Marlon clicked on the enlarged picture on his laptop, and even though the light wasn't that good, Griff got a look at the man's face, and it was someone he recognized. Apparently, so did Rachel.

"That's Buddy Hoskins," she said, touching her fingers to her mouth.

Yep, it was, and Griff was instantly suspicious. For one thing, Buddy was from San Antonio, a good hour away from Silver Creek. But what was more concerning was that Buddy was the one who'd supposedly sent that text to Warren to meet him at the bar. The bar where someone had likely drugged Warren.

"I know him," Rachel said. Her forehead bunched, and Griff knew why. Apparently, so did Marlon.

"He was your father's criminal informant," Marlon supplied. "I know that because I talked to him. In fact, I stopped him from following you."

She shook her head. "When did this happen? And what did he say?"

Griff wanted to know the same thing, because he was having a hard time figuring out why Buddy would have admitted to Marlon that he was a CI.

"After you got in your car and drove off, Buddy started hurrying to the parking lot," Marlon explained. "That's when I saw he'd parked a truck there." He motioned toward the envelope again. "I got a picture of the truck, too, so you could match the license plate."

Smart thinking, but the truck might not even belong

to Buddy. If so, it could give them a lead as to who had sent him to Silver Creek.

"I ran to Buddy," Marlon went on, "and I demanded to know why he was there. I said if he didn't tell me, I'd call the cops, and that I wouldn't let him leave until they got there. Anyway, that's when he said he was there because Warren had hired him to find Rachel."

Rachel shook her head again. "That's not right. My father wouldn't have hired a man like Buddy, not when he has plenty of law enforcement connections."

"Maybe Warren didn't want to use those connections if he was going to do something illegal," Marlon quickly pointed out. "You know, like maybe blow up your car so you'd come running back here to McCall Canyon and to him. If so, it worked, because here you are."

Griff immediately saw a flaw with that theory. "Warren wouldn't have risked hurting Rachel just to bring her back home."

Marlon made a sound of disagreement. "She wasn't hurt. Didn't get a scratch on her from what I can see. Heck, for all I know, the shooter could have been firing blanks at her."

There weren't blanks. Griff had heard the bullets smacking into the buildings along that alley. But that led him to his next question. If Warren hadn't hired Buddy, then why had the CI been there?

"What else did Buddy say to you?" Griff pressed.

"Not much, but he didn't have to. I could see that he was fidgeting and in need of a fix." Marlon made eye contact with Griff. "I experimented with drugs when I was in college and got hooked. I've been clean for over two years now, but I know an addict when I see one, and Buddy's an addict. That's when I realized he had to be some kind of criminal informant." He paused. "Or else he was working for someone else who wanted to frame Warren."

Bingo. That was a theory that Griff had a much easier time believing. Hearing it even seemed to make Rachel relax a little.

"Still, I don't think you can rule out Warren putting all of this together," Marlon added, shifting his attention back to Rachel. "I'm sorry. That's probably not something you want to hear, but I want you to take it seriously. Despite what you think of me, I don't want you hurt."

The jury was still out on that because the third theory was that Marlon had orchestrated the attack and then arranged for Buddy, Dennis and Warren to be in Silver Creek. That way if the guilt didn't stick to Warren, Marlon could try to pin this on Simon. Either way, Griff needed to talk to Buddy.

He took out his phone and texted a fellow Ranger to put an APB out on the man. Maybe when they found him, he would have answers to help clear this up.

"What?" Marlon practically shouted. "I don't get some thanks for doing your job for you?"

There it was. The mean streak had returned. "Thanks," Griff grumbled, but he didn't bother to put any enthusiasm into his voice. Though he was grateful. Because this gave them a new lead to chase.

One they could hopefully chase from his place, so that he could get Rachel the rest she needed.

"Thank you," Rachel added to Marlon. She didn't gush, either.

Marlon glared at her and grabbed his laptop. Griff didn't want him taking the envelope, so he snatched it up and thumbed through the contents. There were three pictures, and even though he only glanced at them, they appeared to be the same shots taken outside the inn, along with the one of Buddy's truck.

"Maybe next time when I see or hear anything, I'll just keep it to myself," Marlon grumbled.

Griff doubted that. People with fixations preferred to have contact with their targets, and because of Marlon's anger, Rachel was indeed his target. "FYI, withholding evidence is a crime," Griff warned him.

That caused Marlon to curse and move even faster in shoving the computer back into his bag. He looked ready to storm out, but he stopped and stared at Rachel. "Be careful about trusting Ranger Morris. His loyalty is to your father, not you."

Marlon was wrong about that, but Griff didn't feel especially good about it. Warren had practically raised him, and now he was going to have to investigate the man for murder and attempted murder.

"Are you okay?" Griff asked Rachel the moment Marlon was gone.

She nodded, scrubbed her hands over her arms again. "Just go ahead and call my father."

Griff would, but first he wanted a closer look at the photos Marlon had left. He knew that Rachel would, too, so he had her sit behind Egan's desk, and he laid them out in front of her. Her attention went straight to the first shot, where she was riffling through her purse.

"I can't believe I wasn't aware of my surroundings," she said under her breath. "Two men were watching me, and I didn't even notice. I was just trying to make it to the pharmacy before it closed."

Yes, and Griff had been only a few miles away. If he'd made it to Silver Creek just minutes earlier, he could have questioned Buddy and might have been able to stop the attack.

Rachel pushed aside that photo and went to the next one—the zoomed-in picture of Buddy. Griff hadn't needed to see it again to know that Buddy had indeed been watching her. What he hadn't noticed before, though, was that the side of Buddy's shirt seemed to be bulky. That probably meant he'd been armed.

Griff silently cursed. He wished that Marlon had called the cops. As close as the inn was to the Silver Creek sheriff's office, they could have been there in minutes and maybe arrested the man.

"Buddy's truck," Rachel said, when she looked at the third and final picture.

This shot wasn't nearly as clear as the other two. Probably because Marlon had snapped it in a hurry while trying to get to Buddy. It was a late model blue Ford and, thankfully, the license plate was in view. Griff was about to phone the number in when he saw something else.

Or rather, *someone* else.

A figure just at the edge of the photo. Not in the actual parking lot, but next to a tree that appeared to be a good ten yards from Buddy's truck. It definitely wasn't War-ren, but it was someone both Rachel and he recognized.

Hell.

What was Brad doing there?

Chapter Eight

Brad.

The DA's name kept going through her head, and Rachel couldn't make it stop. First her father had been in Silver Creek. Then Dennis and Buddy. And now they could add Brad to the list. It was too bad Brad wasn't available to defend himself, but he hadn't answered his phone when Griff had tried to call him, and his assistant had said he was away on a business trip.

Rachel wanted to dismiss it as nothing, but she couldn't. After all, Brad hadn't mentioned that visit when he'd seen her yesterday at the sheriff's office. There was no good reason for him to hide something like that.

But there was a bad one.

If he'd been the one who'd attacked Griff and her, there's no way he would have volunteered that he had been in the area less than a half hour before someone had put a bomb on her car.

"Don't make yourself crazy over this," Griff said.

His voice was surprisingly calm, though she wasn't sure how he'd managed that. Since he could have been killed in Silver Creek, this had to be eating away at him.

Plus, she knew that Griff didn't like Brad, that there was this rivalry between them. And that rivalry was because of her.

"Am I Brad's motive for the attack?" She hadn't intended to ask the question aloud, but was glad she did.

"Probably," Griff readily answered, which meant he'd already considered it. "I don't think he's as unhinged as Marlon, but Brad's always had feelings for you. Maybe he got fed up with waiting for you to return those feelings again." But then he shook his head, groaned. "And it's also possible that Brad was set up, too."

True. He could have been lured there like her father. Maybe even Buddy was, as well, and that caused her to huff.

"We can't rule out any of our suspects," she said. "Not Marlon, Brad, Simon nor Alma."

Griff made a sound of agreement and took the turn to his ranch. As he'd done since they'd left the sheriff's office, he also kept watch around them and glanced back at Thea's cruiser to make sure she was staying close. She was. Because Rachel was watching her, too, in the side mirror, she had no trouble seeing Thea.

His sister had agreed to do protection detail with him, though Rachel hated to tie up one of Egan's deputies—especially since Egan had something else to investigate. Now that he'd finished his interviews with Alma and Simon—Marlon never returned to the sheriff's office for his interview—he would need to focus on finding a money trail that would link any of their suspects to the attack. Rachel wasn't sure how easy it'd be to get financials on a district attorney, but at least he wouldn't have to start that process until he'd interviewed Brad.

Griff turned onto the ranch road, and his house came into view. Rachel had tried to brace herself for the memories that would come with seeing the place. However, it wasn't exactly memories that she got. The heat came, and the old attraction slid right through her before she could stop it.

Great. This wasn't a good start to what would be at least one overnight stay. And it wouldn't matter that Thea would be in the house with them, because Griff and Rachel would still be sharing the same space.

The very space that had landed them in bed.

He pulled to a stop directly in front of the house and got her moving inside. His golden retriever, Scout, was right there in the foyer, waiting for them, but as soon as Griff gave the dog a few rubs on the head, Scout headed off to the back of the house. She knew there was a pet door off the kitchen and that the dog spent more time outside than he did in.

Griff had a security system, and he shut the door and armed it as soon as Thea was in the foyer. She was carrying a large pizza that she'd ordered from the diner, and had her laptop tucked under her arm.

"I'll be in the kitchen if you need me," Thea said. "Help yourself to pizza if you're hungry, because I doubt there's much more than beer and sandwich stuff in Griff's fridge." She glanced at them and then seemed to hesitate a little when her attention landed on Rachel.

Rachel hoped Thea hadn't picked up on the attraction

she was feeling for Griff. And while she was hoping, she didn't want Griff to pick up on it, either.

Too late.

One look at him, and she knew he was feeling things that he also shouldn't be feeling.

"Right," Thea mumbled. Her mouth quivered as if she might smile, but Griff's glare stopped that. "Don't forget about the pizza," she added, and headed to the kitchen.

"Feed Scout," Griff called out to her. "And make sure he has plenty of water."

Thea mumbled that she would and disappeared from sight. Griff's house wasn't huge, but there was a wall separating the kitchen from the foyer.

"You should eat something," Griff pointed out. Maybe because he didn't want to talk about these feelings simmering between them.

Rachel didn't want to talk about it, either, and thankfully, she didn't have to because her phone rang, and she saw her dad's name on the screen. She needed to talk to him, to tell him about Buddy being in Silver Creek, but Rachel dreaded this conversation. Everything she'd say would no doubt seem like an accusation.

And that's exactly what it might be.

She answered the call, put it on speaker and immediately heard her father's voice. "Rachel, I'm sorry. I just now saw the missed call. I guess I fell asleep."

That could be an effect of the drug he'd been given, and she hoped his head was clearer now than it had been during their previous conversation.

"Dad, when Buddy texted you, did he say anything about going to Silver Creek?" she asked.

"No." He didn't hesitate. "I kept the text, and he wanted to meet me in San Antonio. Did he go to Silver Creek?"

"Yes, he was at the inn where I was staying, and he told the owner's son that you'd hired him to find me."

Her father cursed, something he rarely did when she was around to hear it. "No way in hell would I have hired Buddy to do something like that. He's a good CI mainly because he's a druggie rat who can't keep a secret and always needs money. But I wouldn't have let him get anywhere near you."

Rachel believed him, and that meant someone else had sent Buddy there.

"Buddy didn't answer when I tried to call him," Griff said. "Any idea where I can find him?"

"His favorite bar is a seedy place called the Moonlight on the south side of San Antonio. But if you go there, don't take Rachel. It's not a safe place."

It tightened her stomach to hear her father being so protective of her when she was still furious with him. But she couldn't expect him to stop being a father simply because he'd screwed up.

"By any chance do you remember seeing Brad anytime in the past twenty-four hours?" Griff asked.

"Brad Gandy? Why? Does he have something to do with this?"

Rachel found it interesting that her father didn't jump to deny that Brad was involved.

"He was in Silver Creek, too, and in the same area as Buddy," Griff explained. "That means they were both there when the attack happened."

It sounded as if her father bit off more profanity before it could make its way out of his mouth. "How soon are you bringing in Brad?"

"As soon as he gets back from a business trip," Griff assured him. "By any chance do you remember anything else that happened last night?"

"No. I'm sorry about that."

So was Rachel, because if her father could remember who'd given him that drug, then they'd have the ringleader. Well, maybe. It was possible the ringleader had used another patsy so they wouldn't be able to ID him or her.

"I'll let you know if Brad or Buddy gives us anything," Griff added to her father.

"Good. Make sure Rachel gets some rest."

She didn't respond to that, but did give her father a quick "goodbye" before she ended the call. She looked up at Griff as she put her phone back in her pocket. "The person behind this could consider my father a loose end. One that needs to be eliminated."

"Yeah. That's why Egan has a deputy at the ranch, and the hands have been told to be on the lookout for anyone suspicious."

That was good, but it made her feel a pang of guilt. If she'd gone to the ranch with Griff, her father would have been better protected, and Egan wouldn't have needed two deputies standing guard, one at each house. It definitely had her rethinking her pressing Griff to bring her here.

"It'll all work out," Griff said, and he brushed a kiss on her forehead. The kind of kiss he'd given her in the break room at the sheriff's office. Coming from any other man, it wouldn't have been as hot as it was.

He looked down at her, their gazes connecting, and mercy, that sent the heat swirling again. For a moment she thought he might kiss her again. A real kiss this time. But he took hold of her arm to get her moving.

"You really should eat something," he said.

She silently cursed the disappointment she felt. Silently cursed what else she did, too. Rachel stopped and pulled him to her. She had to go on her tiptoes to kiss him, but she managed it. In fact, she managed it even better when Griff leaned down. He hooked his hand around her waist, dragging her even closer, and he deepened the kiss.

Just like that, things went from hot to scalding, and Rachel knew this had been a huge mistake. It would be hard to put up those barriers that she'd just knocked down.

Griff seemed to have some common sense left, though, because he let go of her and took a step back. His breathing was too fast. So was hers. In fact, hers was coming out in gusts, and she was light-headed. Obviously, she didn't think straight whenever she was around him.

"We can go two ways with this," Griff said. "We can forget it happened or talk about it."

She was leaning toward forgetting. If that was even possible. Still, she should try. But Rachel didn't get a chance to give him her answer because she heard the dog bark. From the sound of it, Scout was in the back-yard, and that wasn't an ordinary bark. The dog sounded frantic, as if he'd spotted something that shouldn't be near the house.

"He barks at deer sometimes," Griff said, but he drew his gun. "Thea, turn off the lights," he called out to his sister, and the rooms were close enough for Rachel to see that Thea did that.

Griff did the same to the foyer light and moved Rachel to the corner of the living room, putting himself in front of her. It put him in a good position to look out the front window, but the only view she had was of his back. Once again, Griff was protecting her.

Scout continued to bark, and Rachel didn't think it was her imagination that the dog was becoming even more agitated.

"Do you see anyone?" Thea asked. She was obviously still in the kitchen. Like Griff, she was probably at the window and had her gun drawn.

"No," Griff answered. "And no vehicles came up the road, because we would have heard them."

That didn't mean someone hadn't parked nearby, though, and gotten to his ranch on foot.

"Wait," Thea said a moment later. "I think someone's by your barn."

That put Rachel's heart right in her throat, and she was about to ask Griff for his backup weapon. But there wasn't time for her to do that.

Because a shot slammed into the house.

GRIFF DIDN'T TAKE the time to curse himself for bringing Rachel to his place, even though that bullet confirmed that he'd made a huge mistake and had put her life at risk again.

Another shot came, and this one blasted through the front window. It meant the gunman was on the move, since the second one was a good ten feet from the first one that'd been fired.

"Get down," Griff told Rachel, though it wouldn't be nearly enough to keep her safe. If the shooter was using cop-killer bullets, then the shots could easily get through the wall to her.

Griff tried to hear if there was any movement outside the house. He didn't want this guy trying to break in. But he didn't hear anything.

Not even Scout barking.

Hell, he hoped that didn't mean their attacker had done something to his dog. Since Scout wasn't much of a guard dog, he might not have actually attacked the gunman, but would have continued to bark to alert Griff that something wasn't right.

Since there could be more than one gunman out there, Griff fired off a quick text to Egan. It would take him at least fifteen minutes to get to the house—an eternity when someone was trying to kill you.

The gunman fired three more shots, one after another, and each one caused his heart to race even more. They were almost certainly doing the same thing to Rachel. Maybe even something worse, and he hoped like the devil that this didn't trigger another seizure, when she hadn't even had time to recover from the last one.

Griff made sure Rachel was as far down as she could get before he moved away from her and went back to the front window. Not directly in front of it, but rather to the side. He glanced out, but before he could try to spot the gunman, another shot slammed into the window right next to him.

The glass spewed across the room, probably some of it flying in Rachel's direction. He made a quick check on her, but couldn't tell if she'd been cut.

Another shot took out more of the glass, and Griff knew he had to do something to stop this. He couldn't just stand there and let this jerk continue to rip the house apart. Griff readied his gun, leaned out from cover and fired in the direction of the shooter. He had no idea if he'd hit the guy, but at least it stopped the shots, if only temporarily.

He heard the footsteps a split second before his sister said, "It's me." Thea was crouched down as she made her way from the kitchen to the living room. "Do you have eyes on him?" she asked.

"No."

She scrambled to the other side of the window and looked out, just as the gunman sent more bullets their way. Part of Griff wanted to tell his sister to get down. He wanted to protect her, too. But Thea was a cop, and not only would she not appreciate him playing big brother, Griff also needed her as backup.

"If you give me a gun, I can help," Rachel said.

Her voice was shaking. She probably was shaking, too, but he knew her offer was genuine. However, he would pass on her helping. She was already in a dangerous enough position without putting her closer to the line of fire.

"Scout is in the kitchen," Thea said, while she took another quick glimpse out the window. "I think the gunshots scared him, because he came in through the doggy door and ran into the pantry."

Good. Maybe he'd stay there, so that would be one less thing for Griff to worry about.

Especially since he had plenty to be concerned about right now.

The proof of that was more shots coming through the window. These next bullets took out what was left of the glass. In a way that was good, since they couldn't be hit with any other flying pieces, but the reflection off the glass had probably made it a little harder for the gunman to see them.

"If we fire at him together, it might cause him to back off," Griff said to Thea.

His sister didn't hesitate. She nodded and waited for his cue. Griff didn't have to warn her to make this fast. Thea would. And maybe, just maybe, it would work.

"Now," Griff said.

Thea and he leaned out together and started shooting. Griff emptied the clip and ducked back behind cover to reload. Thea did the same, and their joint gunfire worked. For a few seconds, anyway. But the gunman just started shooting again, and Griff could see the bullets tearing through the wall right next to where Rachel was crouching.

He cursed, hurried to her and moved her behind the sofa. It was still lousy cover, which meant he couldn't wait for Egan. He had to do something now.

"Wait here with Rachel," he told his sister, and he saw the flash of concern in Thea's eyes.

However, it was much more than just a flash in Rachel's. She took hold of his arm when he started to move away from her. "You can't be thinking about going out there."

That's exactly what he was thinking. "I'll go out back and duck behind the shrubs on the side of the house. I might be able to spot this guy and take him out."

Rachel shook her head. "And he might be able to spot you first."

That was true, but anything they did right now was a risk, including staying put.

He dropped a quick kiss on her mouth, knowing it wouldn't stop her protest or reassure her. Still, he couldn't take the time to try to make this better. The only thing that would help was to stop the guy from shooting.

Thea stayed by the window, but the shots forced her to drop down to the floor. Griff didn't tell her to be careful, but he hoped that she would be, and he raced out of the room to the kitchen. He had to take a moment to disarm the security system, since he didn't want it going off. The blare of the alarm would mask any sounds if the shooter tried to get into the house, and he definitely wanted to be able to hear something like that.

The shots continued as Griff went onto the back porch. He paused only long enough to look around and make sure no one was lurking out there, ready to gun him down. He didn't see anyone, so he hurried to the side of the porch and jumped down into the yard. Thankfully, there was a line of mountain laurels that would conceal him enough.

Well, hopefully they would.

He used the shrubs as cover as he made his way to the front of the house, then peered around the corner to the area across from his driveway. There were plenty of trees there, which made it an ideal place for a gunman to hide.

Still, there was something troubling about this attack. Thea had said she'd seen someone near the barn, and the shooter wasn't anywhere near there. Did that mean he'd run from the barn to the trees? If so, that would have been a risky move, since Thea could have spotted him. Just in case there was someone still near the barn, Griff continued to glance over his shoulder while he pinpointed the shooter's location.

Finally, he saw the gunman. Or rather, the rifle the guy was using. Griff took aim.

And fired.

He sent three bullets right at him, and just like that, the shots stopped. Maybe that meant he'd killed him, or the guy could just be on the run. Either way, at least he was no longer firing into the house.

Griff paused, listening, but kept his gun ready in case he had to fire again. He waited and watched for any signs of movement in those trees.

Nothing.

But he did hear a sound behind him, and pivoted in that direction, bracing himself for an incoming shot.

But that didn't happen.

"Don't shoot," someone said. Whoever it was had slurred his words and sounded drunk. "I'm comin' out now. And I got my hands in the air."

The man staggered out from the barn, and just as he'd said, he did have his hands raised.

It was Marlon.

Chapter Nine

Rachel forced herself to drink the tea that Ruby had fixed for her, but it tasted like dust. Probably because her stomach was still twisted in knots. In the past two days, someone had tried twice to murder her, and both times Griff had gotten caught up in the attack. This last time, so had his sister.

They could have all been killed the night before at Griff's house. And there was no guarantee someone might not try again. Because the person who'd shot at them with that rifle had managed to escape.

That certainly didn't help her stomach.

Neither did being back at the ranch with her father upstairs. But they hadn't exactly had a lot of options as to where they could stay.

Griff's house had been shot up, and there'd been no time to put together a safe house. So it had been either the ranch or sleeping at the sheriff's office. Egan had nixed the last idea because that was where they'd taken Marlon for questioning—after a trip to the hospital. The man had been either too high or too drunk to answer any questions, but Egan planned on doing that as soon as the doctor released him.

Truth was, Rachel hadn't especially wanted to be near Marlon, either. However, she had wanted answers from the man, and so far Marlon was plenty short on those. He hadn't managed to tell Griff or Egan a single thing of importance after he'd turned up by Griff's barn.

She heard footsteps coming toward the dining room, set down her teacup and automatically got to her feet. To put it mildly, she was on edge, and part of her expected the gunman to come walking in. But it was Griff. Judging from his creased forehead, he'd either gotten more bad news or else was worried about her. She probably looked as wound-up as she felt.

"Your dad seems better this morning," Griff said in greeting. "Still no memory of what happened, though."

That was too bad, but at least Griff and he were talking. Maybe Griff could spur him to recall something that would help them, especially since Marlon wasn't being any help.

"How's Scout?" she asked. It certainly wasn't the most pressing question she wanted an answer to, but it was important, since the dog had also been shaken up from the shooting.

"He's fine. I just got a text from Ian to let me know that Scout was having fun playing with his kids."

Deputy Ian Mead had taken the dog to his place for a day or two. Ian had a house in town with a big yard, and Griff had figured that would be a better place for him than the ranch, what with all the security they had in place. Plus, the hands still had to manage the daily operation of the ranch, so it was better not to put Scout in the middle of that.

"Marlon had the same drug in his system as your dad did," Griff continued a moment later. "And like your dad, he says he doesn't remember anything about the attack. He claims he doesn't even know how he got to my house."

Rachel wasn't sure she believed that. "He could have followed us from the sheriff's office, parked up the road and walked to your barn."

Griff nodded. "But he wasn't armed, and there was no gunshot residue on his clothes or hands when Egan tested him. There wasn't even a trace on Marlon."

She groaned, wishing all this could be tied up in a neat little package. One that would lead to Marlon's arrest. Apparently, that wasn't going to happen.

"Marlon could have hired the triggerman who was shooting at us from the trees," Rachel pointed out. "And the gunman could have been Buddy. Maybe he needed a fix badly enough that he was willing to kill for it."

Obviously, that wasn't news to Griff, and he quickly nodded again. "Buddy hasn't turned up yet. And the CSIs are combing that area across from my house now for anything that can give us an ID on the shooter." He paused. "It's possible, though, that he was just a hired thug, but it could have been one of our other suspects."

Yes. Either Simon, Brad or Alma. Though Rachel couldn't picture Alma traipsing around a wooded area with a rifle. As for Brad, he still hadn't contacted them so he could explain why he'd been at the inn in Silver Creek, but he wasn't the rifle-toting sort, either.

"Simon and Alma have alibis," Griff went on. "But

that's because they say they were together. Alma said that Simon spent the night at her place because she was so upset after yesterday's interrogation."

So they could be lying for each other. Or one of them could have slipped out without the other's knowledge and gone to Griff's. Even though Rachel and he hadn't exactly spread it around that they were going to his house, someone could have been watching them.

"Alma did give Egan complete access to her bank accounts," Griff went on. "And she did that without a court order. He'll have the Rangers go through everything to see if there's a money trail."

It didn't sound as if there would be. After all, Alma wouldn't have just given them her accounts to examine if she'd thought there was anything to find. "What about Simon? Did he give Egan access, too?"

"No." Griff's mouth tightened. "In fact, he tried to talk Alma out of it. He claims we're all on a witch hunt and that we'll manufacture evidence if necessary."

They wouldn't, but it had to look like it to Simon, since there was now plenty of bad blood between Alma and the McCalls.

"Egan said he didn't think Alma was holding any real grudges against your dad," Griff stated. "From what he gathered from the interview, she seems to be trying to move on with her life."

That could be all for show. Still, that theory didn't feel right. If Alma wanted to get back at her former lover, why not just go after him? Or Warren's wife, so Alma could get her out of the picture?

When that last question popped into Rachel's head, a bad thought followed.

"Is there still a guard with Mom?" she asked.

"Yes. A PI I trust, Kevin Teal. I called him about an hour ago just to make sure all was well. It is. Helen was still sleeping, but the nurse will tell her that I want to talk to her. Well, the nurse will do that if your mom's having a good enough day, and then maybe Helen will call me back."

Maybe. But Rachel knew from experience that her mother had more bad days than good. Plus, a conversation with Griff might be too much for her to handle.

"I can't go visit her," Rachel said. "Because I don't want to risk our attacker following me there. Plus, she'd see the worry on my face, and that would upset her even more."

Griff made a quick sound of agreement. "If she calls back, you can talk to her. That might help both of you."

It would. She was a grown woman, but it was still comforting to hear her mother's voice. Even if it was also a reminder that her mother was ill and might never be the same again.

Rachel hadn't really wanted to think beyond the present, but it was possible her mother would file for a divorce. And she certainly couldn't fault her for that. Still, it ate away at her to think that her mom might never come home.

Griff glanced around the room. "Where are Thea and Ruby?"

"Thea's at the back of the house, keeping watch. Two

hands are guarding the front, and Ruby's in the kitchen. She fixed breakfast, if you're hungry."

He eyed the table and her unfinished cup of tea. "You're not eating?"

Rachel shook her head. "I'm not hungry yet. Maybe later, once my nerves settle a bit." She hated that her voice cracked a little. Hated it because Griff already felt bad enough about the attack without thinking she was about to fall apart. "I'll be okay," she added.

He showed no sign whatsoever that he believed that, and with a heavy sigh he went to her and pulled her into his arms. She got another of those chaste kisses on her forehead, but just the simple hug helped. Of course, it would have been better if it hadn't helped, because then she would have moved away from him. It really wasn't a good idea for them to be touching like this.

Griff eased back enough that he could look down at her and make eye contact. "Your dad's worried about you. *I'm* worried about you."

She wanted to tell him there was no need for that, that she was fine, but the lie didn't make it past her throat.

"I know," he said, brushing her forehead with another kiss. "You hate us worrying about you."

She did, but maybe she could soon convince them that she was okay. It was just that she had been thrown off-kilter with the seizure and the two attempts to murder her. It was going to take a lifetime for her to forget the sound of that explosion and those bullets.

Rachel was about to step back, but Griff spoke before she could do that. "You kissed me," he said. "Right before all hell broke loose at my house."

He hadn't needed to add that last part. She was well aware of what kiss he was talking about. And yes, she had indeed done that.

"I'm trying very hard to remember why that kiss was such a bad idea," she replied. Though that was probably something she should have kept to herself, because it caused Griff to smile.

He had an amazing smile. One that reminded her of why she'd kissed him, and wanted him in the first place.

For a moment she thought he would back away and take that bedroom smile with him. After all, they were in the dining room, where anyone, including her father, could come walking in at any minute. But this time it was Griff who did something stupid, by leaning in and putting his mouth on hers.

Just like the other times they'd kissed, the heat came. Mercy, did it. Rachel could feel it make its way from her mouth to all parts of her body. And the heat just kept coming when he pulled her deeper into his arms.

He tasted good. A taste she had no trouble remembering. Of course, it helped that they were now pressed right against each other so she could feel the tight muscles in his chest. She also heard the deep groan that rumbled in his throat. Apparently, his brain was protesting this, but the rest of him continued with it.

Griff slipped his hand around the back of her neck, angling her head so he could deepen the kiss. It was too much, too soon, but Rachel did absolutely nothing to stop it. In fact, she made things worse by sliding her hands around his back and inching their bodies even closer.

Even though this was still just a kiss, it was beginning to feel a lot like foreplay.

He groaned again and muttered some profanity when he stepped back. She hated the feel of him moving away from her, and the kiss had so clouded her mind that it took her several moments to figure out why he had put an abrupt end to it. But even over the low roar of her pulse in her ears, she finally heard what Griff must have.

The sound of an approaching car engine.

Considering how recent the attacks had been, Rachel was stunned that she hadn't been more alert, but the vehicle had already come to a stop in front of the house.

"If there'd been a problem, the hands would have called us," Griff said, probably because he'd seen how tense she'd suddenly gotten.

That was true, but it still took a couple seconds for her to rein in her too-fast heartbeat.

Griff went to the foyer, and huffed when he looked out one of the side windows. "It's Brad."

Obviously, the hands hadn't known that Brad wasn't exactly a welcome visitor. Not anymore. But they probably hadn't heard about his change in status, since he often came to the ranch.

"Stay back until I find out if he's armed," Griff warned her.

She did. Rachel stepped into the adjacent family room while Griff disengaged the security system and opened the door.

"Where's Rachel?" Brad immediately snapped. "I need to see her."

Griff didn't budge, and in fact, he blocked Brad from

coming in. "We've been trying to get in touch with you for hours. Where have you been, and why didn't you return our calls?"

"I was away on business, but I came as soon as I heard what happened. Someone tried to kill Rachel again." Brad didn't pause long enough for Griff to respond to that. "What the hell were you thinking, taking her to your place? You knew how dangerous that could be for her."

No way could Rachel stand there and let Griff take the blame for that. "I insisted we go to his house." That was close to the truth, anyway. She just hadn't wanted to come back home.

Brad tried to barge in again, but Griff pushed him back on the porch. Rachel figured this could turn ugly fast, so she went closer. However, she still didn't get near the doorway, since there could be a sniper in the area.

"Could you go ahead and search Brad for a weapon so the three of us can talk?" she asked Griff.

"The three of us?" Brad snarled. He was snarling even more when Griff patted him down. "And now you're treating me like a criminal. I'm the DA and Rachel's a close friend, or did you forget?" He added a glare at Griff with that last question.

Griff ignored him, continued the search and came up with a gun. Probably one that he took from the concealed holster that Brad usually wore. Griff put the weapon on the foyer table. "You'll get that back when you leave."

When Griff finally allowed him to come in, Brad's gaze zoomed straight to her. "What the hell is going on?" But as soon as he'd growled out that question, his expression softened. He went to her as if he might pull her into his arms, but Rachel dropped back a step. She would have dropped back even farther if she had to, because she had no intention of letting him touch her.

Brad's soft expression vanished, and he aimed another glare at Griff. "What have you been telling Rachel to turn her against me?"

"I didn't tell her anything, but we did see a picture that made us think twice about trusting you," Griff answered. He shut the door.

"A picture?" Brad questioned. "What picture?"

"One that was taken outside the inn at Silver Creek where Rachel was staying. It was snapped the very night someone tried to kill her. Any reason you wouldn't tell us you were there?" Griff pressed. "And before you answer, remember that anything you say can and will be used against you if I decide to arrest you for withholding evidence."

Brad opened his mouth as if he might blast Griff for that, but just as quickly turned back to her. "This isn't how it looks."

Rachel folded her arms over her chest. "Then why don't you tell us what happened? Because it's looking pretty bad right now."

He nodded, but it took him several long moments and a couple deep breaths before he finally got started. "I didn't mention it because I didn't want you to think I was stalking you. I wasn't," he quickly added. "But I got an anonymous tip that you were staying there, and I wanted to see for myself."

"An anonymous tip?" Griff sounded as skeptical as

she felt. Although someone had lured her father there after he'd been drugged.

Brad took out his phone. "It was a text." He scrolled through and pulled up the message from an "unknown sender." "I thought it might have come from Warren. He's always wanted Rachel and me to get back together, and I figured he gave me her location so I'd go after her and bring her home."

She looked at Griff to see if he was buying this. He wasn't. But Rachel wasn't sure just yet what she believed. "Why would you think my father would send you a text from an unknown number?" she asked.

"I thought maybe he wouldn't want you to know that he was the one who'd tipped me off to your location. I figured he had a burner cell lying around and used it to cover his tracks."

That was a stretch, but it was possibly true. She wouldn't have wanted her father involved in any search to find her. Actually, she hadn't wanted anyone involved, because she'd wanted to stay hidden away. But at the time she would have been especially resistant to having her father, or Griff, find her. It was amazing how her perspective could change after such a short period of time.

"Why didn't you say something to me when you saw me at the inn?" Rachel pressed.

"Because I saw the other two men, and I wanted to make sure they weren't following you. I mean, your whole family was getting those threatening emails, and I didn't know if someone was stalking you."

"Apparently, a lot of people were doing just that. You, included."

Brad shook his head. "No. I just wanted to make sure you were safe. If one of those men had gone after you, I would have stopped him. But the two of them got in some kind of argument, so I left to try to see where you were going. My car was parked up the street, but by the time I got to it, you were already out of sight."

That meshed with what Marlon had told them, and Brad wouldn't have necessarily recognized either of the men. Well, he wouldn't have recognized them if he was innocent.

"What'd you do then?" Griff asked, using his lawman's tone.

Brad lifted his shoulder. "I left and came back home."

Now she was skeptical again. "You drove all the way to Silver Creek to see me and then just left?"

Brad huffed and looked away from her. "I realized how stupid it was to go there. You're a grown woman, and if you'd wanted me to know where you were, then you would have told me. It felt as if I'd violated your privacy." He glanced at Griff then. "And I figured you'd already had enough of that."

That was no doubt a dig at Griff, and it meant that Brad had perhaps heard about her going to him the night of her father's shooting. Griff ignored the dig and kept on questioning Brad.

"Did you see Warren when you were in Silver Creek?"

"No," Brad answered without hesitation. "And I saw nothing illegal going on."

Griff didn't exactly roll his eyes, but came close. "You didn't notice that one of the men was taking pictures?"

"Of course I did. He was taking pictures of the inn,

and that's when Rachel came out." Brad paused. "I don't remember him aiming the camera in my direction, though."

"He claims he was taking a picture of the parking lot and that you just happened to be in the shot," Griff explained.

Brad's eyes narrowed a little. "That guy was Marlon Stowe, the jerk who has it in for Rachel?"

Griff nodded. "That's the one. Now explain to me again why you wouldn't have told Egan or me about this little visit to Silver Creek."

"Because I knew it would look bad," Brad snapped. "There was no way I could explain it to Rachel where she wouldn't think bad of me." He turned to her again. "But I swear, I was just trying to make sure you were okay. You were so upset when you left town, and I was worried."

Brad reached for her, but as she'd done before, Rachel stepped back. He huffed and scrubbed his hand over his face. "I don't know why I bother. It's obvious that Griff's turned you against me."

"This has nothing to do with Griff." Again, that was mostly true. "And you did do something wrong. But you didn't tell the truth. This puts Egan in a very bad position, because now he's got to work with a district attorney he might not be able to trust."

"He can trust me!" His voice was practically a shout, but she could see him trying to push down his temper. "*You* can trust me. But can you say the same thing about Griff? Rachel, he nearly got you killed by taking you to his house. Please. Don't stay here with him. Let me protect you."

"No." She didn't have to think about that, either. And her response had nothing to do with that kiss. "I'm staying in Griff's protective custody."

That tightened every muscle in Brad's face. "Even after he lied to you?" He aimed an accusing finger at Griff. "I didn't tell you the truth about seeing you in Silver Creek, but Griff's lie was much, much bigger. He knew about Warren's affair and kept it secret. That's the kind of man he is."

And with that, Brad snatched up his gun and stormed out, slamming the front door behind him. Griff didn't say a word. He locked the door and went to the window, no doubt so he could make sure that Brad left.

"That's not the kind of man you are," Rachel argued. And, yes, the kiss probably was responsible for her saying that. Still, it was true. Griff wasn't a liar by nature, but she was beginning to wonder if Brad was.

Griff was still watching Brad drive away when his phone rang, and she saw the name on the screen. Kevin Teal. That was the bodyguard at the hospital where her mother was staying.

Griff answered on the first ring and put the call on speaker. "Is everything okay?" he immediately asked.

"Everything's fine with Mrs. McCall. She's still asleep. But she just got a visitor, and I thought I'd run it past you first because he's insisting that he talk to her. The guy says his name is Buddy Hoskins."

Oh, God. Buddy was there.

"Call the cops," Griff insisted. "And whatever you do, don't let Buddy anywhere near Helen."

Chapter Ten

"I should be there at the sheriff's office when the San Antonio cops bring in Buddy," Rachel said.

It wasn't the first time she'd mentioned that in the past half hour, since they'd gotten the call from the PI at the hospital, and Griff knew it was frustrating for Rachel to be tucked away at her family's ranch while not one but two of their suspects were being brought in for questioning. SAPD was on the way to McCall Canyon with Buddy, but at this very minute the doctors were also in the process of releasing Marlon, who would also be escorted to Egan's office.

And that was the reason neither Griff nor Egan wanted Rachel there.

Either Marlon or Buddy could be the person who'd tried to kill her, and while it might give her some satisfaction to face them down, it was way too dangerous. Griff doubted that either man would attack her at the sheriff's office, but a trip there would mean being out on the road. With the sniper still at large, it was a huge risk he didn't want to take.

Griff continued to set up his laptop while Rachel

paced across her office. "You'll be able to watch the interrogations," he reminded her. "Egan will text us when he's ready."

Griff was trying to link to the camera in the room where Egan would be conducting the interviews. She already knew all that, of course, but judging from the look she gave him, merely watching wouldn't be enough.

He considered playing the guilt card and mentioning that he didn't want to be shot at again today, but he didn't want to put that on Rachel. She already looked ready to drop, and that's why Griff stopped what he was doing. He took her by the hand and had her sit on the small sofa.

"Why would Buddy have even tried to see my mother?" she asked. Griff put a bottle of water in her hand, and she took a sip as if she were on autopilot.

It was a question he'd been giving a lot of thought to in the short time since they'd learned about it. Part of him wanted to dismiss it as the actions of a druggie who might not even know what he was doing. But that couldn't be right. Buddy would have had to remember Warren's wife, along with also knowing that she was in the hospital. According to Warren, the man had never met Helen, so what could he have wanted to say to her that he couldn't have said to Warren? In a simple phone call...

Yes, something about that definitely didn't make sense.

Griff was in such deep thought that it took him a moment to realize Rachel was staring at him. "Please don't keep anything from me. There have been too many secrets already."

Yes, there had been, and Griff didn't want any more.

He was just now starting to tear down the walls that Rachel had put up between them, and he didn't want to do anything to ruin that. Of course, even without the walls, she still might never fully trust him again.

The kisses might have been just that. Kisses. The attraction had always been strong between them, but that didn't mean things were going to change. And Griff wasn't even certain he wanted that, because in the back of his mind he would always wonder if he was good enough for her. Old baggage was a bear when it came to relationships.

"This isn't much of a secret because I told you I was going to let your father know about Buddy trying to see your mother, but Warren asked to watch Buddy's interview," Griff said. "That means he'd have to be in the office with us. He'll understand if you say no."

She stared at him, then gave a heavy sigh. "Let him know it's okay. He might see something in the interview that'll help with the investigation."

That was Griff's take on it, too, so he sent Warren a text to let the man know he could come to Rachel's office. She stood, looking as if she was trying to steel herself for this. What she didn't do was sit behind her desk, nor had she the entire time they'd been in the room. Instead, she went to the bookcase, which was chock-full of family photos.

There was a tap at the door. Warren, no doubt. But he didn't come in until Griff opened it for him.

"Thank you," Warren immediately said.

Rachel didn't look back at her father when he came in. She kept her attention on the photos. There were some old pictures of Egan, Court and her as children. Another of Griff and her after he'd just become a Ranger. There was also a picture of Rachel with some of her former coworkers at social services, where she'd once worked. That was four years ago, before she'd taken over as ranch manager.

"I'll probably go back to my job as a social worker," she said. She gave another sigh. "Well, I will when someone stops trying to kill me."

"If that's what you want," Griff settled for saying. He looked at Warren to see how he was handling this. Not well, but then her dad must have known it was a strong possibility that Rachel wouldn't want to keep working for him.

"I can't stay here. I can't do this." Rachel tipped her head toward the desk, then finally made eye contact with her father. "This isn't about punishing you. It's just what I need."

He nodded, ran his hand over his head and nodded again. "All right. I'll see about getting some help in here. Any objections to Rayna coming in?"

Rayna would almost certainly be Warren's daughter-in-law soon, since she was engaged to Court. She was also a good choice since she was in the process of moving her horse training operation to the ranch.

"I think Court and Rayna would like that," Rachel said, and there wasn't a trace of bitterness in her voice.

For Warren, that lack of bitterness was probably not a good thing. If Rachel had been speaking out of anger, he could hold out hope that one day she would get past what he'd done and come home. But whatever she was feeling was a few steps past the bitterness stage, and she was clearly making plans for the future.

Plans that might not include any of them.

Griff's phone dinged with a text message from Egan. "Buddy's in the interview room," he relayed, and that sent the three of them to his laptop. "Egan has Marlon in another room, and he'll question him when he's done with Buddy."

The moment Griff had the feed turned on, he saw Buddy already seated at the table. The man was hunched over, his elbows on the tabletop, his hands pressed to the sides of his head.

"Can Buddy hear us?" Rachel whispered.

Griff shook his head. "It's a one-way feed for both the camera and audio. Buddy knows he's being recorded, though." And Griff hoped that didn't cause the man to hold back any information that could incriminate him.

"You've agreed to talk to me without your attorney present," Egan reminded Buddy the moment he walked into the interview room.

"Yeah, yeah." The man wasn't slurring his words, but he did seem agitated and hungover. "Let's just finish this so I can get out of here. Last I heard it's not a crime for a man to go to the hospital to visit someone."

"That depends on what you planned to do if you got in to see my mother," Egan snapped. From the sound of it, he was agitated, too, but then he was probably working on caffeine and adrenaline.

"Well, I wasn't planning on hurtin' her if that's what you're thinking." He groaned, pressed his hands even harder to his head. Since Buddy was a junkie, he was likely in need of a fix. "I just wanted to ask her some questions, that's all."

"What questions?" Egan demanded.

"I just want to know what's going on."

Egan pulled back his shoulders. "That's exactly what I planned on asking you. Now start talking. And FYI, Helen McCall isn't the one with answers about any of this, so in the future, you stay away from her. Got that?"

"Yeah, I got it." Buddy mumbled something under his breath that Griff didn't catch. "But I don't have answers, either. I don't know what the hell's going on, but I figure it's something bad or I wouldn't have been dragged in here to the sheriff's office."

"You're right about it being bad," Egan confirmed. "And it's going to get a whole lot worse for you if you don't start talking. For starters, why did you text my father and ask him to meet you in San Antonio two nights ago when you were actually in Silver Creek? And before you say that you weren't there, we have this." Egan took out the photo of Buddy in the parking lot at the inn.

He picked up the picture, stared at it for a moment and shook his head. "Yeah, I was there. Warren sent me a text asking me to check out the place. He said his kid was staying there, and she might have crossed paths with somebody bad."

"I didn't do that," Warren insisted. "I wouldn't have done that. I didn't even know where Rachel was."

Griff believed him, and judging from the look Rachel gave him, she did, as well. "Is Buddy capable of setting up an attack and an explosion?" she asked her father.

"No." Warren seemed pretty certain about that. "The

bombing and the shooting were part of an organized plan, and Buddy's anything but organized."

Griff couldn't argue with that, and while they could possibly rule out Buddy, they still didn't know who was behind this. If Buddy couldn't tell them, then maybe Marlon could.

"Two nights ago, did you send Warren a text to have him meet you at a bar in San Antonio?" Egan asked, continuing with the interview.

"No," Buddy answered, but then he hesitated. "Maybe. I honestly don't remember. Sometimes I forget things."

Yeah, probably when he was wasted. Maybe that's what had happened. But Buddy could be concealing the truth because it would make him an accessory to attempted murder. Or even murder.

Buddy had another look at the picture, and his brows drew together. "Who took this?"

"You don't remember?" Egan asked.

Buddy kept studying it. "Was it that Marlon fella? The one who works there?" Then he cursed, and didn't wait for Egan to respond. "It was him, wasn't it? That little nitwit's trying to set me up."

That got Griff's attention. Apparently, it got Egan's, too, because he immediately fired off another question. "How exactly is Marlon trying to do that?"

Buddy cursed some more. "I don't know, but he's a meth head with a mean temper. He must have wanted me there in his town to set me up for something."

"You know Marlon well?" Egan said, taking the question right out of Griff's mouth. Considering the sounds of surprise Warren and Rachel made, this was news to them, too.

"I know him," Buddy spat out. "I used to help him get his stuff every now and then, but we had a parting of the ways when I quit doing that sort of thing. It was too risky, and I didn't want to go back to jail."

"Marlon never mentioned that he knew Buddy," Rachel said. "He told us that he guessed Buddy was a CI, and made it seem as if that night was the first time he'd ever seen Buddy."

Marlon had indeed said that, and now Griff tried to think of a reason why Buddy would lie. He couldn't think of one, but could certainly come up with a reason for Marlon lying. No way would he tell the truth if he was the one behind these attacks.

"Now I'm thinking that maybe Warren didn't send me that text to check on his kid," Buddy went on. "Maybe it was this idiot Marlon." He groaned. "He sent me a text to get me there so he could set me up, didn't he? He planned for me to take the fall for what nearly happened to Warren's kid and that Texas Ranger."

Rachel pulled in a breath and placed her palm on her chest as if to steady her heart. "Marlon is bad news," she whispered. "He wants to get back at me for what happened with his girlfriend, and what better way to do it than to set up his former drug supplier, who also happened to be my father's CI?"

Buddy would indeed make a good patsy, and Griff wasn't surprised when Egan excused himself from the interview and stepped out of the room. A moment later, Griff's phone rang with a call from him.

"You heard?" Egan asked.

"Every word. You believe him? Because I certainly do."

"Yeah, I believe him, and that's why I'm going across the hall now to talk to Marlon. I'd rather not wait until we can set up a feed from the camera to your laptop, so I'll just have to let you know what Marlon says."

Griff thanked him, ended the call and turned back to the screen. Buddy was on his feet now, shaking his head and mumbling under his breath. Obviously, he was becoming even more agitated. That went on for a couple of seconds before he threw open the interview room door and stormed out into the hall.

"I wanna talk to that meth head now!" he shouted. He added a lot of curse words. "You lied. You made the cops think I was in Silver Creek to kill somebody, and you know that wasn't true. I was set up."

The camera angle wasn't wide enough for Griff to see Egan or Buddy, but he had no trouble hearing them. Or Marlon.

"What's he doing here?" Marlon snarled. His voice wasn't as loud as Buddy's, but it was close.

"You set me up," Buddy repeated.

"You stay the hell there," Egan interrupted, and a moment later, Griff saw him putting Buddy back in the doorway of the interview room.

Now Griff could see not only Egan's face, but Marlon's, too, and Marlon was not a happy camper. His eyes were narrowed, and every muscle in his face was tight.

"I didn't do anything to you," Marlon insisted. "You just showed up in Silver Creek, where I happen to live."

"Buddy says you know him," Egan told Marlon. "It's true?"

Marlon took his time answering that. "Yeah. I met him

when I was using, but until the night before last, I hadn't seen or spoken to him in two years."

"You sent me a text to lure me to Silver Creek," Buddy snapped.

"No, I didn't." Marlon turned to Egan and repeated that. "And I didn't mention that I knew Buddy because I didn't think it was important. What was important was that he was there spying on Rachel and that he was up to no good."

The accusation caused Buddy to try to launch himself at Marlon, but Egan put a quick stop to it. He practically shoved the man back into the interview room.

"You need help?" someone asked. Court. He made his way up the hall toward them.

Egan gave a quick nod. "Make sure Buddy doesn't come out. I'll finish the interview with him when I'm done with Marlon."

Even though he wouldn't be able to see or hear Egan in the interview room with Marlon, Griff hoped that Buddy would say something else that would help them unravel what was happening. However, Rachel's phone rang before Court could get Buddy seated.

"It's Dr. Baldwin," she said, looking down at the screen.

Since he was the doctor who managed her seizures, Griff hoped nothing was wrong. Obviously, Rachel thought that was a possibility, because she stared at the screen a moment longer, as if dreading to hear what he might say.

"I'll be right back," she added to Griff and Warren, and went into the hall to take the call.

"Is she okay?" Warren asked, keeping his eyes on her until she closed the door behind her.

"I don't know," Griff answered honestly. It obviously wasn't what Warren wanted to hear. He had enough to worry about, but Griff could tell that he'd just added his daughter to his worry list.

Griff intended to stay put and respect her privacy, but when he heard Rachel gasp, he opened the door to check on her. Seeing her didn't help relieve any of his worries. That's because there wasn't a drop of color left on her face, and without saying a word, she handed him the phone.

"Dr. Baldwin? It's me, Griff. What's wrong?" He wasn't sure he was ready to hear what had caused Rachel to react that way, but since she looked ready to slip to the floor, he hooked his arm around her waist, and he put the call on speaker.

"I'm not sure I should be the one to tell you," the doctor said. "That should come from Rachel."

"Tell him," Rachel insisted.

Even with that order, Dr. Baldwin hesitated several moments. "When you brought Rachel to the hospital, I had some tests run. Well, I just got back the results." The doctor paused again. "Rachel's pregnant."

Chapter Eleven

Pregnant.

Rachel kept repeating the word to herself, but it didn't make sense. Apparently, Griff was having a similar reaction, because he looked as stunned as she felt. And she was confused, too. Because there was something about this that didn't make sense.

"The test results must be wrong," she told Dr. Baldwin. "I took a home pregnancy test two weeks ago, and it was negative."

Judging from the look of shock that went through Griff's eyes, he hadn't had a clue about the test. But then, they hadn't exactly had a chance to discuss something like that.

"Were you having symptoms?" the doctor asked her. "Is that why you took the test?"

"No. No symptoms. I just, uh, wanted to be sure."

"I would ask if you're having symptoms now, but with all the stress you've been under, you might not have even noticed if you were. Anyway," he continued, "home pregnancy tests are reliable, but not as reliable as the test I had done. I can repeat it, of course, but with everything that's going on in your life, I didn't think you'd want to leave the ranch."

Dr. Baldwin didn't seem especially hopeful that there'd be a different outcome if she took a second test, but Rachel had to know for sure. "Is there any way you can have someone bring a test kit here?"

"Of course. But if it's positive, I'll need to examine you again, because we might need to adjust your seizure meds."

Oh, mercy. She hadn't even thought of that. The possibility of a pregnancy didn't seem real, but if it was, there was no way she would want the meds to affect the baby.

"What should I do?" she asked, and tried not to sound as if she was about to cry. That's because Griff had his attention pinned to her, and she could see both the worry and the guilt written all over him.

He was blaming himself for this.

"Just stay put. I'll have a medic bring you another kit," the doctor stated. "It'll probably be similar to the one you took two weeks ago. You'll get a quick result. I'll also have the medic get a blood sample from you, and I can have that tested in the lab."

He ended the call, and Rachel just stood there for several long moments, staring at her phone after she took it from Griff. She was too stunned to think of anything beyond redoing the test, but reality soon started to sink in. It was obviously doing the same for Griff, because she heard him groan. Then, she saw the apologetic look in his eyes.

"Don't," she warned him. "I'm not going to let you

put the blame for all of this on your shoulders. No one forced me to get in bed with you."

"No, but you weren't thinking straight."

That was the truth, but it also stung. Because it made it seem as if she'd been with him only because she'd been out of her mind. But the truth was she'd always been attracted to Griff, and that night had been no different.

"Let's just wait until I repeat the test," she said. Rachel also glanced over Griff's shoulder to see if her father had heard any of this. His back was to them, his attention still focused on the computer screen. If he'd heard anything, he wasn't showing any sign of it.

Good.

She needed to process this before she had a conversation about it.

A baby.

That sent emotions slamming through her. She'd always wanted children, but the timing couldn't be worse. Even though things were improving between them, Griff and she were still at odds. And that wasn't the biggest problem. There was someone trying to kill them, and if she got hurt in an attack now, a baby she carried could be hurt, as well.

"You need to sit down," Griff whispered to her.

He put his arm around her and started walking. Not toward the office, but rather to the family room. He had her sit on the sofa, and she didn't stop him from giving her the kid-glove treatment, because her nerves were tangled and raw.

His phone dinged with a text message, and even though Rachel knew it could be important, she didn't move so she could see the screen. In fact, she wasn't sure she could move, and the bad thoughts came. Not just of their attacker, but also her seizure meds. She wasn't sure they should be taken during pregnancy. And then there was the seizure itself. That couldn't have helped, either. Sweet heaven. She needed to ask Dr. Baldwin about that, too.

Griff disappeared for a couple seconds, then came back with a glass of water. "That was a text from Egan," he said. "He's going to have to let both Marlon and Buddy leave."

Since Egan didn't have enough concrete evidence against either of the men, she'd expected that, but the news still twisted away at her. Buddy and Marlon were suspects, possibly both very dangerous, and as long as they were at the sheriff's office they weren't a threat. But now they'd be back on the street, where they could plan another attack. Of course, they might not have to do any planning if Simon was the one behind this.

She had a long drink of water and looked at Griff from over the rim of the glass. "You could fix yourself something stronger." Rachel tipped her head to the bar in the corner of the room.

He shook his head. "I'm okay."

"Liar." Nothing about his expression or body language indicated that he was okay. In fact, Griff possibly looked worse than she did, and Rachel passed him the glass of water. "Don't worry. If I really am pregnant, just know you don't have to do anything."

A new emotion went through his eyes. Anger. "Yes, I do." He gulped some of the water as if he'd declared war on it. "You think I'd let you go through something like this on your own?" He didn't wait for her to answer. "Because I would never abandon my child. *Never.*"

Only then did she realize she'd hit a nerve. His own parents had basically abandoned Thea and him, and even though Griff rarely spoke about it, that abandonment had cut him to the core. It had also left him struggling to try to fit in. Warren had helped with that. Some. But there was probably nothing that would make Griff forget the feelings of being unwanted by his own father.

"I'm sorry," she said. "I just didn't want you to feel trapped or anything."

Anger flashed through his eyes again, but he didn't get a chance to respond to that because his phone rang. It wasn't Egan. This time it was her mother's bodyguard, Kevin Teal, and it gave Rachel a new jolt of concern that something else might have happened at the hospital.

Griff answered right away, and even though he hesitated, he put the call on speaker. He was probably debating if he wanted her to hear this. She did. But if it turned out to be more bad news, Griff no doubt would have preferred to give her a toned-down version.

"Griff, I thought you'd want to know that Mrs. McCall just called Alma Lawton and asked to meet with her. Alma agreed. Neither her doctor nor I could talk her out of it. Her doctor definitely doesn't think this is a good idea."

Rachel didn't think so, either. She groaned and took out her phone so she could call her mother, but stopped when the bodyguard continued.

"Alma's on her way here now," Kevin said. "And she's

not alone. She said she'd be bringing her lawyer, Simon, with her. Griff, I think it'd be a really good idea if you got here right away."

GRIFF TRIED TO FOCUS. Hard to do, though, with all the thoughts flying through his head. Well, one specific thought, anyway.

The baby.

Rachel could be pregnant. He kept emphasizing the *could be* part of that, but the doctor hadn't seemed to think this was a false alarm. Still, Rachel and he needed to wait for the test to be repeated. Of course, there'd be a delay with that, since they were on their way to the hospital in San Antonio.

It was this trip that Griff knew should have his full attention, and that's why he kept trying to shove the idea of a baby to the back of his mind. He needed to keep watch to make sure someone wasn't following them to launch another attack. Besides, it wasn't as if Rachel and he could discuss the pregnancy, anyway, while Thea drove them in the cruiser. Since Rachel hadn't volunteered anything about this to her father or his sister, Griff would keep it to himself, too.

But he wasn't having much luck keeping it out of his thoughts.

A baby. He wondered just how long something like that would take to sink in. And just how hard this would be on Rachel. She was already dealing with too much right now, and this certainly wouldn't help. The pregnancy alone would have been enough pressure, but the fact that it was his child would only add to it.

And if there was a baby, it was his. Griff had no doubt about that.

And that would give Rachel some new baggage. After all, the child would have been conceived while he was still keeping her father's secret. That was the same as lying, and he was still trying to rebuild her trust after he'd done something like that. The distrust wouldn't help right now, because she might not want him to be part of her or the child's lives.

That wouldn't stop him from being a father, though. A real father.

Griff continued to keep watch. Rachel was doing the same. Both were making sweeping glances all around them, and at the end of one of the glances, their gazes connected. Even though she didn't say anything, Griff recognized the shell-shocked expression. Probably he looked the same.

"It'll be okay," he said. He'd been repeating that a lot lately, and Rachel didn't seem to believe it any more now than she had the other times.

The corner of her mouth lifted in a smile. Definitely not from humor, though. She started to say something, but then shook her head. "You're sure Kevin will call you if Alma and Simon try to get into Mom's room before we arrive?"

She already knew the answer to that was yes. Griff had spelled out to Kevin that no matter how much Helen insisted, Alma and Simon would not be allowed into her room. The reason for that was simple. Simon was a suspect, and Griff didn't want him anywhere near Rachel's mom unless he was there with her. And as for Alma, well, Griff couldn't see anything good coming out of a conversation between Warren's wife and his mistress.

"They'd better not upset my mother," Rachel added in a mumble.

That could very well happen. If Rachel couldn't talk Helen out of seeing Alma, then the visit might happen no matter how much everyone protested.

Rachel glanced behind them again, and while Griff knew she was looking for an attacker, she was also no doubt making sure her father wasn't following them. From the moment Warren had heard that Alma was going to the hospital, he'd wanted to be there, as well. But since Helen had repeatedly refused to see him, that wasn't a good idea, so Rachel had nixed it.

That didn't mean Warren would stay put at the ranch.

Griff only hoped if the man did leave, he would at least take a couple of the ranch hands with him. After all, threatening letters and emails had been sent to Warren, too, and he could possibly become the target for the attackers.

But that didn't feel right.

This felt more personal. Of course, both Brad and Marlon had personal connections to Rachel. Simon was a different story, and maybe Griff would get a chance to talk to the lawyer when they were at the hospital. Which shouldn't be long at all now, because Thea took the final turn into the parking lot and pulled to a stop directly in front of the hospital doors.

"Stay here with the cruiser," Griff told his sister. He didn't want anyone tampering with it.

Court was already there by the door, waiting for them,

since he'd had a shorter distance to drive. He came out to stand guard while Griff hurried Rachel inside.

"Are Alma and Simon here?" Rachel immediately asked her brother.

Court tipped his head to the waiting room, and Griff spotted them. Simon was pacing while talking on the phone, and Alma was seated with her hands in her lap. They weren't alone. There were six other people in the area, and Griff gave each one an uneasy glance. None of them looked like would-be killers, but anyone could be carrying a concealed weapon.

Hell. He hated bringing Rachel here.

"Mom's still insisting on seeing them," Court explained, "and Alma's still insisting on seeing her."

Rachel sighed. "Let me talk to Mom."

She started walking toward the elevator, and Griff and Court stayed right with her. But they'd gone only a couple yards before Alma got to her feet and headed in their direction. Griff had hoped Rachel could avoid a confrontation with the woman, but they seemed to be on a collision course.

"Rachel," Alma said to her.

"Mrs. Lawton." Rachel dragged in a deep breath. "You shouldn't be here. My mother is not mentally strong right now, and seeing you could set back her recovery."

Alma nodded without hesitation. "That's why I was surprised when she called and asked me to come."

Griff looked at Court to see if that was true, and he nodded. What the heck had Helen been thinking?

"I don't especially want to see Helen," Alma went on.

"I mean, she's the wronged woman in all of this. I had an affair with her husband."

"Why did my mother want to talk to you?" Rachel pressed.

"She said she wanted my side of the story." Alma paused. "If she'd sounded bitter or angry, I would have said no. But she sounded broken." She glanced away, her mouth quivering a little. "I understand a lot about that. When Warren and I parted ways, I was not in a good place. If someone could have given me answers, I would have wanted to hear what they had to say."

"There's no answer you can give Helen that will help," Griff assured the woman. He braced himself in case Rachel objected to his interference, but she kept her attention on Alma. "However, just about anything you say to her will hurt."

"I'm asking you to tell my mother that you've changed your mind, that you can't see her," Rachel said to Alma, and there was just as much emotion in her voice as there had been in the other woman's.

And speaking of emotion, Simon ended his call and practically stormed toward them. "I hope you're not harassing my client," he snarled.

"No, they're not," Alma said, before any of them could answer.

The lawyer flinched and narrowed his eyes at Griff. "What did you say to her?"

"The truth, that she should go home," Griff answered, but he also kept watch around the waiting room.

"That's not for you to say. For any of you to say,"

Simon insisted, sparing Court and Rachel a glare. "If Mrs. McCall wants to see Alma, then she will."

Griff was instantly suspicious. "Why would it matter to you whether or not Alma sees Helen?" And he hoped like the devil that it wasn't so Simon could get into Helen's room and carry out some kind of sick revenge against Warren and his family. If that was the case, the lawyer would never admit to it.

Simon hiked up his chin. "I think a good air-clearing is exactly what we need. What Alma needs," he amended. "Warren pursued her in their relationship, and Helen should know that."

Alma took hold of his arm. "No. She shouldn't." She looked at Rachel. "I'm sorry about coming here. I thought it would be a good thing if your mother talked to me, but I can see I was wrong." With her grip still on Simon, Alma started to walk away.

The lawyer immediately started to protest, but Alma kept moving. Because Griff had his attention on the doors, he saw the man walk in.

Brad.

"What the heck is he doing here?" Rachel asked, taking the question right out of Griff's mouth.

Griff didn't know the answer to that, but he stepped in front of Rachel. Brad noticed the move, and he frowned.

"Relax," the DA growled, and he looked past Griff at Rachel. "I got here as soon as I could." He tipped his head toward Alma and Simon, who were leaving through the hospital doors. "I see you told them to get lost. Good. I came here to do that for you."

Rachel moved to Griff's side and stared at Brad. "How did you know they were coming to see my mother?"

"I have a friend who works here," Brad readily admitted. "I asked her to keep an eye on Helen for me."

Rachel huffed. Griff did more than that. He cursed. Because it wasn't Brad's place to do something like that without telling the McCalls.

"Why would you do that?" Rachel demanded.

He looked at her as if the answer was obvious. "You've had so much trouble lately that I thought you'd want an extra pair of eyes on your mother. Especially since someone's doing their damnedest to try to kill you." He shot Griff a glance to let him know he blamed him for that.

"I don't want your friend watching my mother. We have a bodyguard to do that," Rachel said, and she turned to Griff. "Could we leave now?"

That surprised him, because Griff had been certain that Rachel would want to see her mother. And that meant something was wrong. He slipped his arm around her waist, and that's when he felt her trembling.

"I'm dizzy," she whispered to him.

Well, hell. At first he thought she might be on the verge of another seizure, but if she was, she wouldn't be asking to leave the hospital. No. This might be pregnancy related.

"You'll explain to your mother that Alma can't see her?" Griff asked Court.

Her brother nodded. "Just go ahead and get Rachel back home. She looks like she's about ready to keel over. Should I call Dr. Baldwin and tell him you need another exam or something?" he added to Rachel.

"No." She answered too fast. So fast that it caused Brad's attention to snap toward her. The DA studied her. Not just her face, either. He glanced at her stomach.

Great. Now Brad was suspicious. Griff didn't mind him knowing that Rachel might be pregnant. It could get the man to back off from trying to have a relationship with her. But Rachel wasn't ready for anyone to know just yet.

"Be careful," Brad said to her, and it sounded a little like a warning. Probably a warning for her to be wary of Griff.

Ignoring Brad and his comment, Rachel kissed her brother goodbye, and Court followed them back to the entrance. As he'd done when they'd arrived, he stood guard while Griff and she got into the rear seat of the cruiser. Brad stayed back, but he continued to stare, or rather, glare, as Thea drove away.

"Brad is in love with Rachel," Thea mumbled under her breath as she glanced back at the man.

Yes, he was. Or maybe it was more like an obsession. For years, Warren and Brad had pressed the notion of Rachel marrying the DA, and now that it was pretty clear that wasn't going to happen, maybe Brad just couldn't accept it.

"Uh, is something else going on that I don't know about?" Thea asked. His sister was looking at him in the rearview mirror.

"No."

Griff said it at the same moment that Rachel answered, "I'm just worried about my mom."

Thea shrugged and made a *suit-yourself* sound, and

got onto the road that would eventually take them back to the interstate. It had two lanes, with traffic going in both directions. That meant he needed to keep watch not only behind them, but ahead, as well.

As Griff had done on the drive down, he glanced around and immediately spotted something he didn't like.

A dark-colored truck that pulled out of the hospital parking lot behind them.

It was probably nothing, he told himself. After all, this was a busy area, since it was the route to the hospital and other businesses, but there was something about the vehicle that put a knot in his stomach. In part it was because the driver was speeding. This was only a thirty-mile-per-hour zone, and the truck was doing more than that, catching up with them.

Rachel must have picked up on his sudden concern because she turned in the seat, looking to see what had captured his attention. "Is something wrong?" she asked.

He wanted to say no, to assure her that everything would be okay, but he couldn't do that. The truck sped up even more, closing the already short distance between them, and it quickly became apparent that the driver wasn't going to stop.

"Watch out!" he told Thea.

But his warning was already too late. The truck slammed into the back of the cruiser, and the jolt sent them into the other lane. From the corner of his eye, Griff got just a glimpse of the oncoming SUV before it slammed into them.

Chapter Twelve

Rachel had no idea what had happened, but she certainly felt it. One second she was on the seat, and the next she was slung forward. The seat belt stopped her from slamming into the back of the driver's seat, but the tight snap of the strap also knocked the breath out of her.

And that's when she saw the SUV.

Or rather, what was left of it. The front end was now crumpled onto the cruiser.

Almost immediately steam started to spew from the busted radiators, making it nearly impossible to see in front of them. Behind them, though, was the truck that had caused the collision, ramming into them. Rachel prayed that had been an accident, but judging from the way Griff drew his gun, she doubted it.

No. This couldn't be happening again. This couldn't be the start of another attack. The two others had been terrifying, but this one was even worse.

Because the danger could now extend to her baby.

If she was indeed pregnant, her child could be hurt. Or worse. And that might happen when she still didn't know who was trying to kill them.

"Are you okay?" Griff asked her.

Other than fighting to catch her breath, Rachel thought she was all right, and thankfully, Griff didn't seem to be hurt, either. But she couldn't say the same for Thea. Griff's sister was moaning, maybe in pain, or maybe, like Rachel, she was having trouble breathing.

Rachel unhooked her seat belt so she could lean forward and check on Thea, but Griff pushed her right back down. And not just in a sitting position. He made sure her torso was flat on the seat.

"There could be a gunman in the truck," he warned her.

Rachel was in shock, but also filled with adrenaline. Mercy. If there was a gunman, they were trapped. Worse, the person or persons in the SUV could be in on it. Or maybe they were innocent bystanders about to be caught in the middle of a gunfight.

"Call Court and get him out here," Griff told Rachel.

Even though her hands were shaking hard, she managed to get out her phone and press her brother's number. "It went straight to voice mail," she relayed to Griff.

He cursed, but she held out hope that Court hadn't been attacked, too. She knew from experience that there were plenty of dead zones for cell service in the hospital, and that might be why he hadn't answered. She sent him a text, praying that he would get the message and respond. Fast.

From the front seat, Thea groaned again, and Rachel saw the woman lift her head. She looked back at them, the realization of what had happened registering in her eyes. Like Griff, she drew her gun. Thea also called San Antonio PD for backup.

Good.

Rachel prayed that it wouldn't take them long to arrive. This could have been just an accident, but with everything else that had gone on, she had trouble holding on to that hope.

"Can you see who's in the truck or SUV?" she asked.

"No," Griff answered. "Just outlines behind the tinted windows, but it looks like there's just one person in the SUV. Can't tell about the truck, but I think there are two of them." He paused. "I doubt it's a good sign that no one's gotten out."

No. That meant they were either hurt or else waiting to open fire on them while they were basically trapped there.

Rachel lifted her head just a fraction so she could see out the side mirror. There were already other sounds of chaos. People hitting their brakes, probably to avoid crashing into the smashed vehicles. Someone yelled out that he was calling an ambulance. The person who did so likely thought the officers inside the cruiser had been badly hurt, since Thea and Griff were staying put inside.

Praying, Rachel continued to watch, and saw the driver of the truck lower the window. So whoever it was, he was at least alive.

And then she saw the gun.

Griff pushed her flat on the seat again, and she braced herself for the shot to come. And it did.

But not at them.

One bullet, then another, slammed into the windshield of the SUV.

Sweet heaven, what was going on? Was it possible that Griff and she hadn't been the target, after all?

"Put down your weapon now," Griff shouted to the truck driver.

Whoever it was didn't listen. He fired two more shots, both of them into the SUV.

"I can't shoot back," Griff mumbled, making that sound like profanity. "There are too many people around."

There were no more shots, but Rachel heard something else. The squeal of tires on the asphalt.

"Hell, he's getting away," Griff snarled.

Thea shook her head. "I can't go after him. The cruiser engine is busted."

Rachel lifted herself up again to have another look. Yes, the truck was indeed leaving the scene. The driver had turned around in the middle of the road and was heading back in the direction of the hospital. That gave her a new jolt of fear. What if the shooter went after her mother? Just in case that was the plan, she sent off a warning text to Court.

There was the howl of police sirens, and Rachel knew it wouldn't be long before the San Antonio cops arrived. An ambulance, too, because Thea would need to be checked out, and so would whoever was in the SUV.

"The driver of the SUV's getting out," Thea said.

Griff was still keeping watch around them, but that caused him to turn toward the front. Rachel looked, too, and she saw the SUV door open on the driver's side. However, she didn't see the person. Whoever it was stayed hunched behind the door. At first, anyway. But then he staggered out into the open.

Oh, mercy.

It was Buddy.

"Does he have a gun?" Rachel blurted out.

Neither Griff nor Thea answered. And it probably didn't matter, anyway. Because that's when Rachel saw the blood all over the front of Buddy's shirt. He clutched his hand to his chest, his gaze connecting with theirs.

Before he collapsed.

"ARE YOU OKAY?" Griff asked Rachel. He figured she was tired of that question. Griff certainly was. But so far, he hadn't been able to do the necessary things to keep her from nearly being killed.

"I'm okay," Rachel lied.

She glanced at him and then at the road, when the San Antonio cop took the turn toward the ranch. Thankfully, they hadn't had to wait for someone in McCall Canyon to show up and drive them back. No way had Griff wanted to wait around near the hospital with the gunmen possibly still in the area.

"I'm worried about Thea, though," Rachel added.

Yeah, so was he. Unlike Rachel and him, Thea had been taken to the hospital for a possible cracked rib that she'd gotten in the collision. Soon, he'd need to call and check on her, though Egan had assured Griff that he would make sure Thea got back to the ranch safely once the doctor had given her the all clear.

Buddy might not get an all clear, though. He was alive. For now. But Griff wasn't holding out hope that the man

would make it. Still, if Buddy could just regain conscious-
ness long enough to tell them who was behind this, then
Griff could arrest the person and stop another attack.

That might get that stark, troubled look off Rachel's
face.

Of course, they would have to wait awhile to see if
Buddy could give them that information. The man was
currently in surgery to remove the bullets from his chest,
and even if he made it through that, it might be hours
before Egan or someone else could get in there to talk
to him.

One thing was for certain—Griff wouldn't be doing
the interrogation. For that to happen, he'd have to take
Rachel away from the ranch again, and he wasn't going
to do that.

The San Antonio officer, Detective Wade Martinez,
pulled to a stop in front of the ranch house. The door
opened, and both Warren and Ruby looked out at them
as they hurried in. Martinez waited until they were inside before he drove away.

"We heard what happened," Warren immediately said,
checking Rachel as much as she would let him. She gave
Ruby a hug and started for the stairs, no doubt so she
could go to bed, but stopped when she saw the bag on
the table in the foyer.

"It's from Dr. Baldwin," Ruby said. "Lucy Martin's
boy, Dave, who's a medic, brought it by for you. He said
he was supposed to draw blood, too, but he said he could
come back. All you have to do is call him."

Rachel eyed the bag as if she was hesitant about touching it. No doubt because it contained the pregnancy test.

After everything that had just happened, she probably wasn't feeling steady enough to do the test, no matter what the results.

"I'll call Dave after I've rested a bit." She took the bag and went up the stairs toward her room.

Griff considered following her, but decided to give her some time. He doubted that she'd be doing much resting, though.

"You need me to fix you a drink?" Ruby asked Griff.

It was tempting, but he didn't need alcohol clouding his head. The fatigue and spent adrenaline were already doing enough of that. He thanked her, though, and Ruby excused herself to go to the kitchen.

"Does Rachel blame me for this?" Warren asked.

Because of his fuzzy head it took Griff a moment to realize what Warren meant. "You mean because Buddy was your CI?" He didn't wait for Warren to confirm that. "No. She doesn't blame you. You had no way of knowing that Buddy would do something like this."

Warren shook his head. "I'm the one who invited him into my life."

"Nearly everyone who's been in law enforcement has dealt with a CI," Griff argued. "Plus Buddy could have been just a patsy. He could have been lured to this crime scene the way someone lured you to Silver Creek."

Warren stared at him, nodded and then patted his arm. "Thanks."

"For what? Believing you?"

"For believing *in* me. But then, you always have."

That seemed like some kind of apology for something. Maybe because Warren had always thought Griff wasn't good enough for Rachel. But there was no apology needed. If their situations had been reversed, Griff might have felt the same way.

"Go ahead," Warren prompted. "Make sure Rachel's okay." He gave him a pat on the back and walked away.

Griff went up the stairs, but he didn't intend to see Rachel. Instead, he was going to the guest room that was next to hers. Or at least that was the plan. But it got derailed when he found her door open, and saw her standing in the doorway of her bathroom, holding one of the pregnancy test sticks in her hand.

She looked up and their gazes connected. "The package said to wait three minutes. It'll be a plus sign if it's positive and a minus sign if it's negative."

All right. Griff wasn't sure if those three minutes were up or not, because Rachel didn't add anything else. She went to the foot of her bed and sat down. No way did he want her to be alone for this, so Griff went in, shutting the door behind him. He walked over and eased down next to her, but she was holding her thumb over the little screen on the test.

"It's terrifying," she added. "And exciting." She had that same apologetic look in her eyes as Warren had earlier.

"It's the same for me," Griff admitted, though right now the terror was winning out.

Since Rachel looked as if she could use it, he brushed a kiss on her cheek. What he hadn't expected her to do was lean against him. She dropped her head onto his shoulder.

"I thought maybe you'd want to punch me or something right about now," Griff said.

Rachel lifted her head, met his gaze. "You mean because of the attack or the possible pregnancy?"

"Either. Both."

Now she brushed a kiss on his cheek. "We've both been through the wringer. I think it's best if we declare a truce."

Considering that just hours ago he'd kissed her, it felt as if they were well past the truce stage.

Well past three minutes, too, for the test.

Griff was about to move her thumb so they could see the results, but his phone rang before he could do that. When he saw Egan's name on the screen, he knew it was a call he had to take.

"Is Thea okay?" Griff asked the moment he answered. He put the call on speaker so that Rachel could hear.

"She's fine. No cracked or broken ribs. Just a deep bruise. Egan said Ian will take her to the ranch so she can spend the night there, but I'll need him back here once he's dropped her off."

Yes, probably because Egan was neck-deep in this investigation. Griff would help with it in any way he could, but his top priority was keeping Rachel safe.

"Buddy didn't make it through surgery," Egan added a moment later. "And he didn't say anything to the medical staff."

Griff tried not to feel the punch of dread that came along with that, since he'd been expecting it. Still, it stung. Apparently it did for Rachel, too, because she groaned softly.

"What about the San Antonio PD?" Griff asked. "Do they have anything on the shooter who killed Buddy?"

"Not so far, but there were several traffic cameras in the area. They'll access the footage and go from there. This is their jurisdiction, but they'll keep us in the loop since the attack's probably tied to the ones on Rachel and you."

The chances were indeed high that it was tied to them, but Buddy was a CI, which meant he could have had someone who wanted him dead. There was some support for that theory, as well, since the shooter hadn't attempted to gun down Rachel and him. Of course, the killer could have made Buddy a priority if the man had intended to rat out the person who'd hired him.

"I'll bring in Marlon again to see if he knows anything about Buddy," Egan added. "Who knows, he might surprise me and tell me the truth."

That would indeed be a surprise, but there was another possible player in this, too. "What about Brad?"

Egan's heavy sigh let Griff know that getting the DA in was a little trickier than questioning Marlon. "I'll see what I can do."

"If you think he's innocent—" Griff started to say, but Egan interrupted him.

"I don't. I mean, I don't know if he's innocent or not. I don't like the way he keeps pushing Rachel. It's obvious he's jealous of you and her. I just don't know if he'd be willing to take jealousy as far as murder."

That was the big question, and maybe Egan would be able to get the answer. Answers about Alma and Simon, too, since they were still on the suspect list.

"How's Rachel?" Egan asked.

Griff looked at her, but didn't have a clue about that.

"I'm just tired," she answered. "Let us know if you get anything from Marlon or Brad."

Egan assured her that he would, and ended the call. Rachel didn't move. She just sat there, her attention now on the pregnancy test. She pulled back her thumb, and that's when Griff saw it.

The plus sign.

Rachel was pregnant.

Chapter Thirteen

Rachel forced herself out of the shower. She'd already been in there way too long, and it wasn't helping her relax as it usually did. But then, there was probably nothing that would take away the tension she was feeling.

Griff likely wasn't faring much better. After she'd seen that plus sign on the pregnancy test, Rachel had practically kicked him out of her bedroom, using the excuse that she needed to rest. She had. She was exhausted. But after two hours of trying to take a nap, she'd finally given up on it and tried the shower. Since this hadn't worked, she would just have to face the problem head-on and go and talk to Griff.

The problem was she didn't know what to say.

Yes, Griff had been nothing but supportive and would continue to be, but never once had she heard him talk about having children. And now that was being forced on him.

Rachel certainly didn't feel that way. With each passing minute her mind was moving from the problems this pregnancy would create to the fact that in about eight months she would be a mother. A thought that no longer terrified her. In fact, she was starting to imagine herself holding her baby. Raising it. Loving it.

So maybe the shower had helped, after all.

She dried off and got dressed, since she would need to go downstairs and make an appearance. It was 9:00 p.m., but Griff, Ruby, Thea and her father would no doubt be waiting to see if she was okay. She'd have to put on a front for them so they wouldn't worry more than they already were.

Rachel glanced at her phone and groaned when she saw the missed call from Egan. Since it could be important, she called him back right away, and he immediately picked up.

"What's wrong?" she asked.

Egan didn't jump to say anything, which probably wasn't a good sign. "I got worried when you didn't answer."

"Sorry. I was in the shower. Did something happen?" And she tried to prepare herself for the worst. "Is Mom okay?"

"Mom's fine, but Marlon's missing. I already let Griff know this, but I called Marlon to come in for questioning, and when he didn't answer, I had a Silver Creek deputy go check on him. His folks said he packed a bag, took the spare cash they keep in the inn's safe and left."

That didn't sound like something an innocent man would do. "Can you put out an APB on him?"

"Already done that. If and when he turns up, I'll let you know. I've also told the hands to be on the lookout in case he goes to the ranch."

That caused her chest to feel tight. No way did she

want Marlon anywhere near here. "What about Alma and Simon? Will you be questioning them again, too?"

"Oh, yeah. First thing in the morning. Alma's at home. Raleigh called to tell me that. I don't know about Simon. Like Marlon, he didn't answer, but there's no sign he's on the run or anything."

No, but that didn't mean he wasn't responsible for what was going on. Rachel had ruled out Alma as being behind this, but she certainly hadn't ruled out Simon.

And that left her with one other suspect she wanted to ask about. "Any idea where Brad is?"

"Not missing, that's for sure. He just stormed out of here." Egan paused. "I'm beginning to think Brad has spies everywhere."

Rachel made a sound of agreement. "He said he's got someone keeping an eye on Mom."

"Yeah, I'm fixing that. It's a nurse, and I got her name from Brad." He paused again. "I also got something else from Brad. He said you had a pregnancy test delivered to the ranch. Is it true?"

She could have sworn her heart skipped a beat. "How did Brad know that?"

Egan groaned. "So it's true. And as for how he knows, my guess is he's got a spy or two here in town, as well. Are you pregnant?" He came right out and asked the question.

Rachel considered dodging it, but her brother wasn't a fool, so he probably already knew the answer. "I don't have test results yet, but I'm sure I am."

He didn't groan again, but Rachel could practically feel him scowling. "It's Griff's baby," he stated. "And no, you don't have to confirm it. Griff didn't, by the way, when I asked him about it."

"You what?" she snapped. "Why would you ask Griff something like that?"

"Because I told him that Brad knew about a pregnancy test being delivered to you at the ranch, and I figured Griff's several moments of stunned silence said everything I needed to know. Do you need me to kick his butt for you?"

It was such a big-brother thing to say. "No." But she apparently did need to talk to Griff. He was probably beating himself up right about now. "Just keep this to yourself," she added. "Because I don't want it getting back to Mom until I've had a chance to tell her."

She ended the call with Egan and went out into the hall. She could hear her father and Ruby chatting about some food deliveries they needed to postpone because of security reasons. Since Griff didn't seem to be in on that conversation, she went to his room, and when she knocked, it was only a few seconds before the door flew open.

And she saw Griff naked.

Well, almost naked, anyway. He wasn't wearing a shirt, and even though he was wearing jeans, they weren't zipped all the way. Judging from his damp hair and soap scent, he'd just gotten out of the shower. Rachel hoped it'd done him more good than it had her, but his expression said otherwise.

He still had a towel in his hand, but he stepped back so she could come inside. "You talked to Egan," he said, shutting the door.

She nodded. "He knows I'm pregnant."

Griff's eyebrows lifted. "Is he on his way over here to beat me to a pulp?"

Rachel couldn't help it; she smiled. Though this definitely wasn't a smiling situation. "Egan will accept this." Only because he didn't have another choice. "He just wants to make sure I'm okay."

Griff stared at her. "Are you?"

She stared back. Which probably wasn't a good idea because of his lack of clothes. She had some incredible memories of touching and kissing his bare chest, and seeing him like this brought all that back. Not just the memories but also the heat that went along with them.

"Are *you* okay?" she asked, turning the tables on him.

He gave one of those half smiles, put the towel aside and reached for his shirt, which he'd draped over the back of a chair. Part of her hated that he was covering up, but Griff must have known it wasn't a good idea for them to be behind closed doors while one of them was half-naked.

He walked closer to her while he was still buttoning his shirt, and she took in more of his scent. The soap, yes, but Griff's own scent was beneath that, and it gave her body another of those heated tugs that she didn't need.

"Since Brad knows about the pregnancy test," Griff said, "I'm sure he can guess what went on between us."

That didn't erase the heat she was feeling for Griff, but it did cool her down some. That's because she followed it to an easy-to-see conclusion. Brad was already upset with her, and this definitely wouldn't help. But would he do something stupid?

Maybe use his spies to spill the news to her mother?

"Yeah," Griff mumbled, when she groaned. "You definitely need to keep your distance from him. And Court will make sure Brad doesn't have any contact with your mom."

"That's a good start. But I should tell my mother."

"After what happened earlier, you're not going to the hospital." He sounded like a lawman with that order.

"No," she agreed. She could still hear the sound of those gunshots. "I can call her in the morning."

Though she hated to give her mom that kind of news over the phone. At least she'd be able to tell her father and Ruby in person, and Rachel turned to go downstairs to do that. But that meant walking past Griff.

He was clothed now. For the most part, anyway. His jeans were still unzipped, and he'd missed the bottom buttons on his shirt. The opening created enough of a gap for her to see some of his stomach. And just like that, more memories came. She hadn't been sure anything could stop the sounds of the attack in her head, but she'd been wrong. That stopped it.

Worse, Griff had followed her gaze and knew what had caught her attention.

Their eyes met, connected, and he seemed to be waiting for her to do something. Maybe for her to make the first move. Or to come to her senses and leave. He had no doubt figured that he shouldn't be the one to start something that shouldn't happen in the first place.

At least that's what she thought.

But she was wrong.

Griff cursed, the profanity aimed at himself, and he

reached out, sliding his hand around the back of her neck. Still cursing, he pulled her to him and kissed her.

FROM THE MOMENT that Rachel had come into his room, Griff had told himself to keep his distance from her. That hadn't worked right from the start, because he'd seen the heated look in her eyes.

A look that he was certain was in his own eyes, too.

But with some willpower, he could have kept it at just a look. Apparently, though, he was fresh out of any shred of willpower tonight.

The kiss sure didn't help, either. Because there was plenty of fire when he touched his mouth to hers.

Still, he could have forced himself to back away *if* Rachel hadn't made that silky sound of pleasure. Along with that, she moved her body right against his. Griff knew that no amount of willpower was going to stand a chance about that.

It was Rachel who deepened the kiss, and she slipped right into his arms as if she belonged there. Certain parts of his body believed that she *did* belong there. But Griff tried to hang on to what little common sense he had left.

"You're pregnant," he reminded her, though it apparently was a dumb thing to do.

She pulled back, blinked, and even though she didn't come out and voice it, her expression said, *"So?"*

She was right, of course. Pregnant women kissed and had sex. Still, most women probably didn't do that when they were still coming to terms with their condition.

"This could be a reaction to the spent adrenaline," he murmured, trying again.

It wasn't any stronger an argument than the pregnancy one—even if it was a possibility. Obviously, though, Rachel wasn't going to let that get in the way, because she came right back to him for another kiss.

The first kiss was tame compared to this one. This was foreplay, plain and simple. And Griff knew if he was going to put a stop to this, then it had to be now. His mistake was savoring the kiss and the feel of her a little bit longer. It was just enough time for him to pass the point of no return.

Cursing himself again, he hooked his arm around her waist, snapped her to him and did his own share of deepening the kiss. Once he'd done that, he knew this would lead to only one place.

The bed.

Thankfully, they weren't that far away from it. Judging from the sudden urgency of Rachel's kisses, the foreplay wasn't going to last that long. It hadn't the other time they'd been together, either, but he intended to savor this no matter how soon it ended.

Rachel slid her hand in the opening of his shirt, her palm landing on his stomach. And she touched him. Along with that kiss, it packed a punch, and the punch got stronger when she pulled him against her so that their bodies were aligned in a perfect way. Well, it would have been perfect if she hadn't had on so many clothes.

Griff did something about that.

Rachel was wearing a loose cotton dress, and he caught the bottom of it, pulling it off over her head. Of course, that meant breaking the kiss for a couple seconds, but they went right back to it as soon as he tossed the dress aside.

He wasn't the only one with the notion of getting naked, because Rachel rid him of his shirt. Or rather, she did after torturing him while she unfastened the rest of his buttons. The process involved a lot of touching, and by the time she'd gotten it off him, Griff was burning for her.

The burn went up a huge notch when he unclipped her bra and her breasts spilled out into his hands. No way could he miss not kissing her there, so he lowered his head, took her nipple into his mouth and got rewarded with another of those silky sounds of pleasure.

Even though she was clearly enjoying it, Rachel didn't let the breast kisses go on much longer. She went after his jeans, unzipping him, and slid her hand down into his boxers. That did it for foreplay, and Griff hoisted her up and carried her to the bed.

He kept kissing her when he put her on the mattress, but hadn't planned on landing on top of her. He'd intended to drop down by her side. Rachel, however, pulled him down so they were face-to-face. There weren't many things that could have gotten Griff to slow down, but seeing her did it.

Man, she was beautiful.

She always had been, but she seemed even more so now. Maybe because of the fire that was in her eyes. Or maybe because of the way she was looking at him. Griff reminded himself that this was about lust, but at the moment it seemed like a whole lot more.

She held the eye contact while she shoved off his boxers. Griff did the same when he rid her of her panties. He wanted to hold on to this for a long time, but that wasn't possible. Rachel lifted her hips, taking him inside her, and Griff knew it would be over much too soon.

Because his body gave him no choice, he moved, pushing into all that tight heat. And Rachel moved, too. There was definitely no hesitation as she took everything he was giving her and gave just as much right back.

Soon, very soon, Griff's mind went to a place where reason didn't exist. He had to finish this. Had to finish her so they could find some kind of release.

He adjusted her enough to give her the pressure she needed. It didn't matter that they had been together only one other time. Griff just seemed to know the rhythm of her body. And he carried her right over the edge.

Rachel made another sound. It was more of that silky pleasure mixed with relief. That was his cue to let himself go. Griff gathered her into his arms, kissed her and gave in to the fire.

Chapter Fourteen

Griff's kiss felt a little bittersweet to Rachel. She'd known that the sex wouldn't last, but the kiss—and his climax—were a reminder that it might be a while before this could happen again.

If ever.

Now that some of the fire had been sated, Griff might remember that this was the last thing they should be doing. After all, there was a would-be killer still out there somewhere, and Griff, she and her entire family were in danger. His sister, too, since she was in the house. Sex shouldn't have been on the agenda, and yet it'd seemed as necessary to Rachel as taking her next breath.

When Griff lifted his head, she saw the regret that was already starting to show in his eyes. Rachel huffed and kissed him again. He tasted just as good as he looked, and at first she thought she could keep him in the moment if the kisses continued. But Griff grumbled something and rolled off her, landing on his back.

"The baby," he said. "I don't want to hurt you."

Oh.

Rachel certainly hadn't forgotten about being pregnant, but she'd become so lost in the pleasure that she hadn't considered it might not be a good idea for Griff's weight to be on her like that. Still, she hated the fact that he was no longer inside her.

Griff helped, though, with that loss she felt. He pulled her into the crook of his arm so that their bodies were touching. It wasn't anywhere near as intimate as sex, but it was still nice. Plus she had a great view of his naked body. There was something to be said for that.

"I'm not going to say I'm sorry for this," he told her.

Good. That was a start. Rachel had been afraid he was going to put all the blame for this on his shoulders. If there was any blame, that is.

"There's no reason for you to apologize. I started it," she reminded him. "I kissed you first."

She considered adding more to that, but it probably wasn't a smart idea to admit to Griff that she'd been thinking about getting him naked. Not just tonight, either. She'd been thinking about it for weeks.

Heck, for years.

He leaned over, kissed her. "This should make us even then." And he let the kiss linger for a few steamy moments.

No, it only made her want him all over again, but when Griff sat up, she figured that wasn't going to happen. "I need to check on Thea," he stated.

"Thea?" Rachel hadn't expected him to bring up his sister at a time like this. "Is she okay?"

"She's fine. When I checked on her about an hour ago, she was keeping watch over the backyard," Griff explained while he put on his shoulder holster. "I just need to make sure she doesn't need a break, because she probably won't ask for one. And then I need to see if the San Antonio PD found anything on those traffic cameras on the street where Buddy was murdered. Plus you need to eat something, so you should come downstairs with me."

She wasn't the least bit hungry, but when he glanced at her stomach, she realized he was probably concerned about the baby. Or so she thought. But then he ducked his head, his mouth lingering a moment over her abdomen. He waited until he had eye contact with her before he planted a scorching kiss just below her navel.

It was a nice moment, but it didn't last, of course. He groaned again, got up and started dressing. Rachel watched for a moment, just enjoying the view, but then got up, as well. She'd barely managed to put on her clothes when her phone rang, and when she fished it out of her pocket, she saw her mother's name on the screen.

Her heart dropped.

It was past regular visiting hours, which meant it was too late for her mother to be making a routine call. So Rachel immediately answered.

"Mom, are you okay?" she blurted out.

That got Griff's attention, and he hurried to her. Rachel put the call on speaker so he could hear.

"People have been keeping things from me so that it won't upset me. I don't like that," her mother said.

That certainly didn't sound like the threat Rachel had thought she might hear her say. "What kind of things?" And while she had her on the phone, Rachel tacked on another question. "And why did want to see Alma Lawton?"

"I, uh, just wanted to meet Alma face-to-face, to ask

her…why she'd had an affair and a son with my husband. I needed to know why Warren was with her and if he loved her."

Rachel sighed. "Mom, I understand why you'd want to talk to her about that, but I'm not sure knowing will help."

Great. She heard her mother start to sob, and more than anything Rachel wanted to be there with her. To assure her that things were going to get better. At least she hoped they would.

"Are you in love with Griff?" Helen asked.

Rachel was certain that put a shocked look on her face, and it did the same to Griff. "Who told you that?" she pressed. "Was it Brad?"

"Brad? No, I haven't seen or heard from him in a while now. No, this came from that other man who called me. He said his name was Marlon Stowe."

Everything inside Rachel went still. "When did you talk to Marlon?"

"I just got off the phone with him."

"I'll make sure Marlon's not at the hospital," Griff said, taking out his phone. He moved away from her to make the call.

"Mom, what else did Marlon say?" Rachel continued.

"That you've been staying at the ranch with Griff. That you've been sleeping with him."

Rachel couldn't deny any of that, but she wondered if it was a guess on Marlon's part or if he had the ranch under surveillance. If he was watching them with infrared binoculars, Marlon might be able to tell that she'd been with Griff in his guest room. The thought of him spying on them turned her stomach.

"Marlon was upset with you," her mother went on, "because he said you lied to his girlfriend and that now she's very angry with him. I told him you weren't a liar, but he insisted that you were, that you'd ruined his life. He wanted me to talk to you, to convince you to go to his girlfriend and tell her that you'd made a mistake."

Hearing each word caused Rachel's muscles to tighten. "I didn't make a mistake. Marlon isn't a nice man, and if he ever calls you again or tries to visit you, you're to let the staff know immediately."

Her mother sobbed again. "You're scaring me, Rachel."

"I'm sorry. I don't want to say these things to you, but it's important that you understand."

"I do understand. But please don't tell my doctor that Marlon's call upset me. He might take my phone away."

That might not be such a bad idea. But Rachel didn't want to do that just yet since it might make her mother feel even worse not to be able to call her kids whenever she wanted. However, Rachel did need to have a conversation with the staff about at least monitoring the incoming calls. Especially calls from Marlon, Alma or Simon.

"You didn't answer my question about you being in love with Griff," her mother said several moments later.

No, she hadn't answered, and Rachel didn't intend to do that. Not in front of Griff, anyway. Her feelings for him were, well, complicated, and she needed to work them out for herself before she started sharing that with others.

Besides, Rachel doubted Griff wanted to hear the *l*

word from her since he no doubt was having to deal with his own feelings. Not just about the pregnancy and her but also the threats to their lives. Those threats were much worse and the stakes much higher now that there was a baby involved.

Rachel told her mother good-night and then looked up at Griff. He was by the door, but maybe he was waiting to see if she was going to bring up any part of the conversation she'd just had. She wasn't.

"Why don't you go ahead and check on Thea," she settled for saying.

Griff opened his mouth, then closed it as if he'd changed his mind about what to say. "Come with me and get something to eat."

Since she should have at least a snack, Rachel got up to follow him. However, they'd made it only a few steps before there was a slight crackling sound.

And the room was suddenly plunged into darkness.

GRIFF AUTOMATICALLY PUT his hand over his gun.

He assured himself that this could be nothing, but after everything else that had been going on for the past two days, he didn't want to take a chance.

"The generator should kick in soon," Rachel said. "It won't be full power, but at least we'll have the security system and the lights."

The security system was a must. No way did he want someone breaking in without them knowing.

Griff waited for the generator. And waited. But nothing happened. It was too much to hope that it was simply malfunctioning.

He went to the window and looked out. There were no signs of an intruder. No signs of ranch hands, either, but the last time he'd checked on them, two were on the front porch. With Thea keeping watch at the back of the house, the three should have been able to see anyone approaching from the sides or the road.

"Are the lights out in Court's place, too?" Rachel asked.

Griff looked in that direction, but didn't see anything. That could be because Court had turned off the lights when he went to the hospital to be with his mother. And Court's fiancée, Rayna, wasn't there because last Griff had heard, Court had her staying with friends in a nearby town, instead of coming back to McCall Canyon after the horse show. With Buddy's killer still on the loose, Court hadn't wanted her there alone, and Rayna hadn't wanted to stay at the main house.

"You think something's wrong," Rachel said. Her voice was a little shaky, probably because she already knew the answer to that question.

Yeah, he thought something was wrong, but Griff hoped this was all just a bad coincidence.

"Don't go near the window just in case," he warned her, and he went to the door. He didn't open it yet, but instead put his ear to it and listened for any unusual sounds.

Nothing.

And there should have been *something*. By now, Warren or Thea should have been checking on them to make sure they were all right. But the house was quiet. Too quiet.

"Call your father or Ruby to make sure they're okay," Griff instructed.

Behind him, he could hear Rachel taking out her phone. A moment later, he also heard the curse word that she mumbled under her breath. "My screen says there's no service."

Griff took out his own phone and saw the same thing. Hell.

There were dead zones for cell reception all over the ranch, but Griff had made at least a dozen calls from this room without any problem. And since the electricity being off wouldn't have affected the service, then it likely meant someone had managed to jam the signal. To do that, the person would have had to be darn close to the house.

"Is the security system on battery backup?" Griff asked.

"I'm not sure."

Since the house belonged to a former sheriff, it probably was on backup. If so, that meant the alarm would still go off if they had an intruder.

"Stay back," he warned Rachel as he reached for the doorknob.

He heard her slight gasp and knew she was afraid, but he didn't want to go to her just yet. Not until he'd made sure that everything was okay.

Griff opened the door just a fraction and peered out. Nothing. Well, nothing considering that the hall was even darker than the guest room. Just in case someone was hiding in the shadows, he used the flashlight on his phone to look around, but he still didn't see anything.

Didn't hear anything, either.

"Warren?" he called out.

"I'm here in the foyer," the older man answered.

Relief swept through him. Through Rachel, too, because she released the breath she'd been holding. "Are you okay?" Griff asked.

"Fine. But my phone's messed up. The security system, too, because the lights are all flashing on the monitor by the door."

That definitely wasn't a good sign. "Have you seen anyone?" By anyone, Griff meant an intruder.

"No. But I was about to go to the kitchen to check on Thea. Ruby's in her room, so I'd better make sure she's okay."

Ruby's room was at the end of the hall, and the door was closed. It was possible that the woman had already gone to bed and was asleep. That would explain why she hadn't come out into the hall when the power went off. Still, Griff needed to make sure all was well.

"Let me know if Thea's all right," Griff told Warren, and he glanced back at Rachel. "Wait right here."

Even with just the light from his cell phone, he could see that she looked shaken up. He hated leaving her alone, so Griff took out his backup weapon and handed it to her. That didn't do much to ease the fear in her eyes, but she took the gun, holding it in a death grip.

"Hurry," she said. "And be careful."

He would do both, and because he thought they both needed it, Griff went back and gave her a quick kiss before he stepped out into the hall.

Ruby's room was only four doors down, probably about twenty yards, but it suddenly felt as if it were miles away. Griff made his way along the hall, keeping watch over his shoulder. He thought he might be able to hear someone walking up the stairs, but he didn't want to take any chances, since an intruder coming up that way would get to Rachel before him.

There was a large floor-to-ceiling window at the end of the hall right next to Ruby's room, and Griff had a quick glance outside. And he saw something he darn sure didn't want to see.

Thea.

She was in the backyard and had her gun drawn. Her gaze was darting all around her, the kind of looks a lawman would make who'd heard or spotted something. Definitely not good, because he didn't want his sister or anyone else out there without backup.

There was also another problem.

Thea wouldn't have deliberately disarmed the security system when she went outside, so that confirmed that it wasn't working. Not a good time for that. Now, he only hoped the would-be killer didn't sneak into the back of the house while Thea was outside.

Griff considered opening the window and calling out to his sister, but decided he should go to her instead. So that she'd have backup. That meant first checking on Ruby and then having Warren stay with Rachel.

"Ruby?" Griff knocked on her door, and when she didn't immediately answer, he tried the knob.

Unlocked. But when he opened the door, he saw no signs of the woman. She could be in the bathroom, but going in there meant he wouldn't have line of sight of the guest room, and he didn't want to risk someone getting to Rachel. Or her taking it upon herself to come out into the hall to try to help him.

Griff heard a sound. Not coming from the guest room. This seemed to have come from the foyer. It wasn't footsteps but more like a heavy thud. As if someone had run into something or fallen.

Rachel must have heard it, too, because she hurried to the doorway of the guest room. That sent Griff hurrying to her. Because if there was an intruder in the house, whoever it was might rush up the stairs and try to shoot her.

"You need to stay back," Griff insisted when he reached her, positioning himself at the door.

She shook her head. "But I think something happened to my father."

So did Griff, but he didn't want that *something* to happen to her, as well.

"Warren?" he called out again.

Griff didn't shout because he didn't want his voice to mask the sound of footsteps. But he didn't hear anything. He especially didn't hear Warren's assurance that he was okay.

He didn't get that.

But he did hear something else.

It hadn't come from the foyer, but rather from outside in the backyard.

"Watch out!" someone shouted.

Thea.

And it was followed by another sound that Griff definitely didn't want to hear. His sister screamed.

Chapter Fifteen

Rachel's breath froze. Oh, God. What was happening?

Despite Griff's warning for her to stay away from the guest room window, she ran there, hoping to get a glimpse of Thea. It would give her partial views of the back and side yards. But his sister wasn't visible. No one was.

Griff looked, too, though he volleyed glances between the window and the guest room doorway. Rachel knew the last thing Griff wanted was to take her down those stairs. But that scream changed everything.

"We have to check on her," Rachel insisted.

Griff seemed to have a debate with himself. One that didn't last but a few seconds and ended with him cursing. "I might be able to see Thea from the window at the end of the hall. Stay right next to me."

The moment she nodded, Griff got them moving. He didn't run, exactly, but it was close to that pace as he hurried out of the guest room. He also kept firing glances over his shoulder. And she knew why. If someone had attacked Thea, then he or she could be coming after Griff and her.

But there was another problem.

The scream hadn't been the only thing Rachel had heard. Just moments before that there'd been another sound near the front door. She prayed that no one had managed to break in, because if so that meant the intruder had gotten past the two hands who were on the front porch. She hadn't heard the sound of gunshots, but that didn't mean the men hadn't been harmed in some way.

When they made it to the large hall window, Griff moved her so that her back was against the wall and their sides were to the stairs. He glanced out. So did Rachel. But there was still no sign of Thea.

"My sister was there just a few minutes ago," he mumbled. He tipped his head toward the center of the backyard.

There were no hiding places in that spot, but there was a detached garage about twenty feet away. It was possible Thea had seen something that spooked her and had run there.

"She's a cop," Rachel reminded Griff. "She knows how to take care of herself." And she prayed that Thea had done whatever was necessary to be safe.

Even though they were a good distance from the stairs now, Rachel heard something that she thought was coming from the foyer. It sounded as if someone was moaning in pain. Griff must have thought so, too, because they started moving again—this time with him in front of her.

"Keep watch on the bedrooms in case someone comes out of one," he whispered.

That definitely caused her heartbeat to rev up even

more. She hadn't considered that they could be ambushed, but she did now.

If someone was indeed on the second floor of the house, it meant the person had maybe broken in without anyone seeing him or her. Possibly while Griff and she had been making love. No way would she have heard something, and that was the very reason she should have never gone to his bed. In hindsight, that could have been a fatal mistake.

Griff slowed the pace considerably as they started down the stairs. The staircase was curved, and that wasn't an advantage right now because it meant they couldn't see into the foyer until they were halfway down. That's probably why Griff kept pausing and lifting his head. He was listening for any indication that an attacker was nearby.

Each step seemed to take hours, and with each one, her pulse drummed in her ears. The fear came, too, washing over her and making her unsteady. Rachel forced herself to take several long breaths. It didn't help much, but the only thing that would help right now was for her to discover everyone was safe and that this had been a false alarm.

Griff didn't call out to her father or Thea as he crept down the steps. Rachel followed, dismayed when she learned the foyer was pitch-dark. Not good; they couldn't tell if anyone was there or not.

There was another of those moaning sounds, and this time she was able to pinpoint it. It was coming from the family room just off the foyer.

"Make sure no one comes at us from behind." Griff

whispered that reminder, and they continued down the steps.

Again her heart started to race, but Rachel kept up, staying close to Griff but also keeping watch. Not just behind but all around them.

When they reached the foyer, Griff went to the front door and tested the knob. It was still locked. But he mumbled some profanity when he looked out the side window to the porch.

"The ranch hands aren't there," he said.

It felt as if her stomach went to her knees. There was no way the men would voluntarily leave their posts. Not when they knew that a killer was after Griff and her. And that meant someone had either lured them away...

Or killed them.

She didn't want to ask if there was any blood on the porch, but prayed there wasn't. Enough people had already been hurt or killed because of her, and she didn't want to add the ranch hands to the growing list.

The sound of another moan grabbed her attention, and Rachel frantically looked around until she finally spotted someone on the floor.

"Don't," Griff said, when she started to run in that direction.

She knew he was right, that this could be some kind of trap, but everything inside her was screaming for her to get to the person to make sure he or she was all right. "It could be Thea," she reminded him.

Of course, she hadn't needed to tell him that, and thankfully, Griff didn't act out of emotion. He took slow, cautious steps toward the prone figure while he continued to keep watch. Rachel did the same, and she was holding herself together until she saw who it was.

Her father.

He lay in a crumpled heap on the floor. Just like that all the anger she had for him vanished, and Rachel knew she would do anything to save him.

"Check and see if he's hurt," Griff instructed.

While Rachel went to Warren, Griff's gaze slashed from one area of the house to another. Rachel stooped down, putting her fingers to her father's neck. "He's got a pulse."

Thank God. But she didn't have time to savor the relief, because he moaned again, and his eyes fluttered open for a few seconds. He was barely conscious and obviously in pain, or something, but she couldn't see any blood or any sign of an injury. At least she didn't until she held the light from her phone to his neck, and saw the puncture wound there.

"I think someone drugged him," she managed to say. At least she hoped it was just a drug like the one he'd been given the night before last, and not something lethal.

Griff pivoted toward the other side of the family room, taking aim. Rachel hadn't heard anything in that direction, but soon saw someone.

Ruby.

The woman was cowering in the corner next to an armchair. "Warren told me to run and hide," she said. Her voice was shaking so much it was hard to understand her.

With Griff still standing guard, Rachel hurried to her, and as she'd done with her father, she checked Ruby to make sure she hadn't been hurt. There were no signs of injury, and unlike Warren, it didn't seem as if she'd been drugged.

"A man's in the house," Ruby said, her words rushing out with her breath.

Rachel's breath did some rushing, too. Oh, God. Someone *had* broken in.

She looked around. So did Griff. But Rachel didn't see anyone. Whoever it was, though, had probably drugged her father. He was also likely responsible for the missing ranch hands.

And for Thea's scream.

But what Rachel still didn't know—was the intruder one of their suspects? Was it Marlon, Simon or Brad? Or maybe it was just a hired gun who'd been sent there to kill them.

"Did you recognize the man?" Rachel asked in a low voice.

Ruby shook her head. "He was wearing a mask so I didn't get a look at his face. Warren told me to hide," the woman repeated.

That was a good thing or else Ruby would have ended up on that floor. Or she could have ended up dead if she'd fought back.

Griff glanced around again, and Rachel could tell he was trying to figure out what to do. He didn't want to leave them there while he went to find Thea, but he couldn't exactly take them with him, either.

"See if your father's gun is still on him," Griff told Rachel. "If it is, give it to Ruby."

Rachel scrambled back to her dad so she could check, and found the small gun he carried in a boot holster. He'd probably had his primary weapon in his hand when he'd been attacked, which meant the intruder had taken it. Not exactly a comforting thought, though the snake had almost certainly brought his own weapons with him.

But why hadn't he just come in with guns blazing?

And why hadn't he killed Warren?

Maybe this was some kind of sick cat-and-mouse game as he tried to get to Griff and her. If so, it could be working. Because they couldn't just stay put, not with Thea in possible danger. Heck, they couldn't even call for backup.

She brought the gun to Ruby, and even though the woman was shaking badly, Rachel knew she could shoot. It came with the territory of working on a ranch, since snakes often came into the yard.

"Keep watch," Griff instructed Rachel, and while she did that, he helped her father to his feet and moved him to the corner with Ruby. It wasn't ideal cover, but it'd been an effective hiding place for her, and at least they weren't out in the open.

Once Griff had finished, he turned back to Rachel. "You can stay here with them while I look for Thea."

She was shaking her head before he even finished. "You need someone to watch your back." Rachel paused and wished there was a better way to put this. There wasn't. "This person is after us. If we're apart, it'll only make it easier for him."

She could tell that Griff wanted to come up with a good argument for her to stay put. But he couldn't. The safest place for her to be was with him, and yet it might not be safe at all.

Griff must have realized there was no time to debate

this, so he nodded. Other than their cell phones, there wasn't any other light in the room, but it was enough for her to see his worried expression. Still, he motioned for her to follow him.

"Stay close and watch our backs. I'm sorry it has to be this way," he added. "And if something goes wrong, just get down as fast as you can. Don't try to return fire or fight this guy."

"All right," she agreed, but it wasn't something she could promise. No way would she just stand by if someone was trying to kill Griff.

With her breath stalled in her throat, Rachel followed him out of the family room. As he'd done on the stairs, he kept his footsteps slow while he gazed around him. Rachel watched, too, and listened, but didn't hear anything. She wasn't sure if that was a good sign or not.

They made their way through the dining room. The windows were all shut in there, but when they got to the kitchen, Rachel immediately spotted the open door.

A new jolt of fear came because Griff had said he'd seen Thea in the backyard. If the intruder had gotten into the house this way, he would have gone right past her, and that might have been about the time she'd screamed.

Griff's steps slowed even more as he scanned the kitchen island and the breakfast nook. No one was there. But a passageway to their left led to an eat-in kitchen. It was too dark to see much of anything there. However, Rachel did see something on the other side of the room.

Another partially open door. This one to the pantry.

It wasn't an ideal hiding place, since there was only one entrance. If the intruder was in there, then he was trapped.

Or waiting for them to come closer.

Griff motioned for her to get lower. Rachel did, so did he, and while they crouched down, they started for the pantry. But they'd made it only a few steps when he stopped.

"Use your phone to light up that area on the floor," he whispered, motioning to a spot several feet from the pantry door.

Rachel did. She reached around him, shining the light on the tile, and that's when she saw what had captured his attention. The dark colored drops and spatters. And she had no doubts as to what it was.

Blood.

Griff prayed that the blood belonged to the intruder and not Thea or one of the now missing ranch hands.

Of course, if it wasn't his sister's or that of someone else helping them, it meant Rachel and he were possibly about to have a showdown with the snake who'd orchestrated all this, since the blood drops led right to the pantry. Griff would have welcomed that if Rachel hadn't been right behind him.

He considered taking her back into the family room to wait with Ruby and Warren, but if the intruder was in the pantry and Rachel was truly his target, he'd probably just try to gun them down if they ran. Well, he would try that if he was capable of shooting. Maybe he was too injured to do so.

Better yet, maybe he was dead.

A dead man wouldn't be able to give them answers about the previous attacks, but he wouldn't be able to harm Rachel, either. Griff would give up those answers about why this was happening if it meant keeping her safe. Heck, he'd give up anything to make sure that happened. Because it wasn't just Rachel's life that was at stake now. So was their child's.

Griff dragged in a deep breath and started inching toward the pantry door. He kept his gun ready while he continued to glance around them. After all, the blood and the open pantry door could be a trick so the guy could sneak up on them. When he reached the door, Griff looked inside.

And he came face-to-face with a gun.

"Don't shoot," someone mumbled.

It was Thea. She was sprawled out on the floor, her back against the wall and her gun aimed right at him. Griff also saw the source of the blood. It was coming from the left side of her head.

Griff glanced around the pantry. Like the rest of the house, it was large, with rows of shelves and stacked boxes of supplies. Still, he could take it all in with a sweeping glance, and when he didn't see anyone with Thea, he pulled Rachel inside, then stepped behind her, staying close to the door in case he had to return fire or get them out of there fast.

"A man sneaked up on me and clubbed me," Thea whispered, her words slurred. "I tried to shout a warning to all of you, but he hit me on the head and took my gun. I had a backup weapon on me, though." She rubbed her neck and winced. "He gave me some kind of shot, too, but I don't think I got the full dose. That's because I pushed the needle away and ran."

It was probably a drug to knock her out, as the intruder had done to Warren, and judging from the way she was talking and her unfocused eyes, the drug was working. That wasn't good, but Griff reminded himself that it could have been a lot worse. If Thea's attacker had gotten close enough to hit her, then he could have easily shot and killed her.

So why hadn't he?

The answer to that twisted him up inside. Because this snake wanted Rachel. It had been that way right from the start of the attacks, and unfortunately, it didn't rule out any of their suspects.

"Did you recognize the man who did this to you?" Griff asked his sister.

Thea shook her head and winced again. She was obviously in pain, but Griff had no way to call for an ambulance. He only hoped the injury wasn't serious.

Rachel grabbed some paper napkins from one of the shelves and pressed them to Thea's head, obviously trying to stop the bleeding.

"He's wearing a mask," she explained a moment later. "But whoever it was, he must have come from the front on foot because I didn't hear a car engine. I was watching the back and the sides of the house, so I know he didn't come from anywhere in my direction."

Yes, unless he'd managed to sneak past Thea. But that didn't seem likely. That meant the guy had probably gone after the ranch hands first. But it was darn bold of him to attack two armed men with just a club.

"The back door's open," Rachel said. She was whispering, too. "Did you do that or did your attacker?"

"I don't know. Maybe I left it open when I ran in. Everything's getting fuzzy. I tried to run to the stairs so I could get to Griff and you, but then I got woozy, so I ducked in here. If the guy came in this way, I didn't hear him."

So how had he gotten in? Griff knew for a fact that he was inside because he'd attacked Warren. That meant he was likely hiding somewhere, waiting to strike. Too bad the house was huge, because all the rooms would give this clown lots of places to lie in wait.

"Do you think you can move?" he asked his sister.

Thea nodded and took the paper napkins from Rachel. "But I can't see straight enough to shoot."

"I don't want you for backup." Rachel and he helped Thea to her feet. "I'll leave you both with Warren and Ruby in the family room so I can find this guy."

They looked at him. "You shouldn't do that alone," Rachel whispered.

No, he shouldn't. But he didn't have a lot of options here. He had a cop and former cop, both drugged, which meant it would fall to Rachel and Ruby to protect them.

Definitely not ideal circumstances.

But it wasn't wise to go searching through the house with them in tow while he was looking for a killer. Maybe this guy would just come after him so Griff could put a fast end to it.

He didn't remind Rachel to keep watch—she was already doing that. She also clutched the backup gun he'd given her. With his arm hooked around Thea's waist, he leaned out from the pantry to make sure someone hadn't sneaked into the kitchen. If the intruder had managed to do that, Griff didn't see any signs of him.

Before he moved Thea and Rachel out of the pantry, he went over and shut the outer door. It wouldn't keep someone out, but at least he'd be able to hear if it opened. After all, the intruder who'd entered might not have come alone. He could have hired thugs waiting outside to finish them off if he didn't succeed.

Griff had a quick debate with himself about where to position Rachel, and he finally decided to place her on the other side of Thea. It took him a couple seconds to get them lined up in a way that they'd all be able to use their guns if necessary.

Griff prayed that it wouldn't come down to that.

Because if it did, that meant Rachel and the baby would be in the line of fire.

He moved as fast as he could, which wasn't very fast considering that Thea kept stumbling. Plus he had to keep watch. Not easy as they made their way through the massive house.

They'd just made it back to the dining room when he heard something. Footsteps, maybe. And they weren't coming from the family room just ahead. No, these were coming from behind them.

He pivoted, putting himself in front of Thea and Rachel. Griff brought up his gun. But he didn't see anything so he waited and listened.

Thankfully, he'd been to the McCall home so many times that he knew the layout like the back of his hand. With the kitchen door closed, that meant the person hadn't come in from outside. So, he was probably coming from the direction of the living room. Unfortunately, he could cut through the family room to make it back to the foyer. If that happened, Ruby and Warren could be sitting ducks.

So could Thea, Rachel and Griff.

Because the intruder could come at them from the side. With where they were standing, they'd be easy targets.

"Get all the way down on the floor by the hutch," Griff whispered to Rachel and Thea. It wasn't much cover, but it was the only solid piece of furniture in the room.

Rachel nodded and took hold of Thea to do that. While the movement was necessary, the rustling it made could be masking the sound of other footsteps. Not good. Because Griff needed to be able to pinpoint the location of the goon if he got any closer.

The moment Rachel and Thea quit moving, he heard what he'd been listening for: another footstep. And it seemed to be coming from the foyer. The intruder was probably heading toward them. Griff turned in that direction, but it was already too late.

The shot came right at him.

Chapter Sixteen

Rachel could have sworn the sound of that shot stopped her heart for several seconds. Oh, God. Griff could have been hit.

She frantically looked up, checking for signs of an injury. She didn't see any; thankfully, the bullet had smacked into the wall right next to where Griff was standing.

Rachel reached out, catching his arm and pulling him to the floor. He'd already started to crouch down, and landed right next to Thea and her. However, he didn't stay down. He jumped up, ready to fire, but when he cursed, Rachel guessed the shooter wasn't in sight.

"Keep watch toward the kitchen," Griff whispered to her. "He could circle back around and come at us from that angle."

Rachel hadn't needed anything else to make her more alert, but that did cause her stomach to knot. This stress couldn't be good for the baby.

It also couldn't be good for Thea.

Griff's sister was obviously trying to fight off the effects of whatever drug she'd been given, but she was also in pain. She groaned or winced every time she moved. That didn't make her a good candidate for backing up Griff if she had to return fire. Rachel wasn't exactly a good one, either, because there was no way Griff was going to let her put herself in danger. That meant staying on the floor while he came out from cover to try to put a stop to this.

There was one hope in all of this. Maybe by now Court or Egan had tried calling the ranch, and would have known something was wrong when no one answered. If so, they could be on their way here right now. Maybe they would get to them before someone else got hurt.

Despite her heartbeat crashing in her ears, Rachel forced herself to try to listen for any sounds of the intruder, and she definitely kept her eye on the kitchen area. Unfortunately, there were spots she couldn't see, and if the shooter wanted to sneak up on them, he could duck behind the large kitchen island and make his way closer. If he did that, he'd have a clean shot of Thea and her.

Thea was trembling all over now, but was obviously still trying to fight off the effects of the drug. It was a battle she seemed to be losing, so Rachel moved in front of her, sandwiching her against the wall and the china hutch.

The new position put Rachel at a better angle if she had to shoot into the kitchen. She wasn't an expert shot by any means, but if the intruder showed himself, she would fire at him. Even if she didn't hit him, it might give Griff enough time to adjust his aim and take out the guy.

Rachel heard some movement straight ahead. Someone was on the other side of the wall, which meant he could be going either to the kitchen or back to the family room. She prayed it would be the kitchen, since that would keep this monster away from her father and Ruby.

Because she was so focused on watching the kitchen, the sound of the shot stunned her. It hadn't come from the sides at all. The gunman had fired through the wall directly in front of them. This bullet tore through the window to her right, shattering glass everywhere. Even though they could have easily been cut by the flying shards, the shot hadn't come close to hitting them. That meant the shooter had fired a blind shot with the hopes that he'd get lucky.

"I can't just shoot into the wall," Griff whispered. "This idiot might have one of the ranch hands with him."

Mercy, she hadn't thought of that, and it was a good thing she hadn't sent a bullet or two his way. It could have maybe been a deadly mistake—and exactly what the gunman had wanted them to do.

There were more sounds. Footsteps. At first they were headed toward the kitchen, then the opposite direction. Either this idiot was playing games with them or else there were two of them. That reminder certainly didn't help tamp down the fear and adrenaline.

Rachel wanted to call out to her father, to make sure he was okay, but there was a chance their attacker didn't know Warren's and Ruby's exact location. He could use any response they might make to hone in on them and start firing. Even if the guy didn't go into the room, he could still manage to kill them with more of those blind shots.

She looked up at Griff just as he was making one of those sweeping glances around them. He was all lawman now, primed and ready for the fight. But she also saw something else in his body language.

The worry.

He was afraid for her, for their baby, and that wasn't a good thing to be feeling right now. It could cause him to lose focus.

The loss of focus didn't last long, thank goodness. That's because another shot tore through the wall, heading their way. Again, it didn't come close to hitting them, but the noise was deafening, and made it nearly impossible to tell if the shooter was on the move.

Another shot quickly followed, and this bullet took out the rest of the window. Rachel had to duck down and put her body over Thea's when the glass spewed at them.

"Are you hurt?" Griff whispered.

"No." Rachel wasn't sure that was true, but she didn't want him worrying about them right now.

That's because she heard another sound. Not footsteps this time. But she thought maybe it was a gasp, and it'd come from the family room, where Ruby and her father were. Rachel scooted up a little so she could try to see them, but the wall of the arched opening between the two rooms prevented her from doing that. It also didn't help that there was a lot of furniture in the way.

Mercy. Their attacker could use that to hide from view.

The gasping sound caught Griff's attention, too, because he pivoted in that direction. Rachel couldn't tell if he saw anything because she had to keep her focus on the kitchen in case the shooter came that way, but there was certainly some movement now in the family room.

Everything inside her was screaming for her to go

help her father and Ruby, but that could be exactly what the gunman wanted her to do. Because there was no way Griff would let her go in there alone. The shooter could use that as an opportunity to kill them both.

There was more movement. Louder this time, and it sounded as if some kind of struggle was going on. Rachel couldn't tell what, but she knew it had to be bad when Griff cursed and dropped down, pushing Thea and her closer against the hutch and the wall.

"Griff," someone said.

Her father.

His voice was weak and shaky. He definitely sounded as if he was still fighting the effects of the drug he'd been given.

"I'm sorry," Warren added a moment later.

That caused her breath to stall in her throat. Rachel glanced out, afraid of what she might see, and what she saw was her father being pushed into the dining room. There was someone behind him.

And that person had a gun to her father's head.

GRIFF HATED THAT it'd come to this. Hated that some thug was now holding Warren at gunpoint.

And he especially hated that he hadn't been able to stop it.

He'd seen the movement in the living room, but because of the darkness, he hadn't been able to make out who had Warren, and that's why Griff hadn't fired. When Griff had spotted the gun, he knew he had no choice but to get down or the intruder would have shot him. Then there would have been no one to protect Rachel and Thea.

"I'm sorry," Warren repeated. "I couldn't stop him."

Rachel's father could barely speak. Could barely stand, even. He was wobbling, but his attacker had his arm slung around Warren's waist and was holding him in place like a human shield.

Griff waited for the intruder to say something. He didn't; he just kept inching Warren closer. Probably so as to be in a better position to shoot them. Hell. And now they were trapped.

"What do you want?" Griff demanded. "And where's Ruby? Is she all right?"

The man didn't jump to answer, and Griff couldn't get a good look at his face. It also appeared the guy was hunching down a little. Probably to make certain that Griff wouldn't have a clean shot. If so, it was working. Worse, Griff couldn't tell if this was one of their suspects or another hired thug.

"He hit Ruby with a stun gun," Warren said. "She fell."

Which meant the woman could have hit her head or something. That was yet another reason to put an end to this, so that Griff could get Warren, Thea and Ruby to the hospital. Of course, the number one priority right now was making sure they were safe.

And they weren't.

None of them were as long as that guy had a gun pointed at Warren.

"Well?" Griff snapped. "Are you ready to tell me why the hell you're doing this?"

Griff probably should have reined in his temper to keep the anger out of that demand, but it was hard to do when this idiot was putting so many people in danger.

The man groaned, and it seemed to be from frustration. *Welcome to the club.* Griff was frustrated and furious that he had allowed Rachel and the others to be in the middle of this mess.

"I didn't mean for it to come to this," their assailant finally said. And Griff had no trouble recognizing the voice.

Brad.

The shock hit Griff hard. Even though Brad was on their suspect list, it was difficult to believe that a man he had known most of his life was now holding Warren at gunpoint. But Griff didn't have to guess why Brad was doing this. The man had clearly gone off the deep end.

Because of Rachel and him.

Rachel gasped, too, and shook her head. "Brad, you have to let my father go right now."

"I can't." The DA didn't hesitate. "Now, all of you throw down your guns. All three of you," Brad emphasized. "And you've probably already figured out that you can't call for help. I've planted some signal jammers all around the house, and I've got one on me."

Brad took out the small device from his pocket and tossed it onto the table. That explained why they couldn't get out a call. Brad had obviously planned this attack for him, to bring those. But maybe something had gone wrong for it to come down to this. Griff was betting Brad had planned on getting a clean shot at Rachel and him before now. But time was running out, since Egan or Court had probably sent someone out to check on them.

"If you argue with me about it or try to do something

stupid," Brad warned, "I'll start shooting Warren. I won't kill him, but I'll hurt him."

Griff saw Rachel tense. She didn't argue, though. She tossed her gun. Thea's, too. Griff wasn't so quick to move, but he wasn't in a position to bargain. He didn't want to be unarmed, but this wasn't a bluff. Brad would indeed shoot Warren.

Griff tossed his gun onto the floor in front of them. Hopefully, though, it was still close enough for him to get to it if Brad started shooting.

"I didn't think it would come to this," Brad repeated. "I thought by now that Rachel would have seen that Griff wasn't right for her, and would have come back to me."

"That isn't going to happen. Not ever." Even though she practically whispered that, it was obviously loud enough for Brad to hear, because he groaned again. "Do you think I could be with you after this?" she added. "You didn't only attack me. You attacked *us*. Griff, my father, Thea, Ruby and the ranch hands."

"Ruby and the ranch hands are fine," Brad snapped. "I used a stun gun on them and tied up the ranch hands. They never even saw my face."

But everyone in this room had seen it. And that meant he couldn't leave them alive. Brad was planning on killing them all.

Maybe.

"If you want to win Rachel back," Griff said, forcing himself to keep his voice calm, "then you should start by letting Warren go. Then we can sit down and talk about this."

"I'm not stupid." That was practically a shout. "I know it's too late."

"Maybe not." Even though it was a lie, Rachel also tried to sound a whole lot calmer than Griff knew she was.

"It is too late." Brad cursed her, calling her a vile name. "I saw you with Griff, you know. A month ago, when Warren got shot, I was going to check on you, to make sure you were okay. But I saw you leaving the hospital with Griff. I followed you, and you went to his place." His anger increased with every word he said. "You stayed the night with him. You slept with him."

Griff was about to lie and say that Rachel and he hadn't done that. It might save her. But then he got a glimpse of Brad's face, and knew that he must have seen Rachel and him in bed that night.

"What did you do?" Griff pressed. "Did you look through the window? Did you spy on us?"

"From a distance. I couldn't get too close to the house because I didn't want your dog barking. I knew then that I had to take a step back and figure out what to do. I had to figure out how to get Rachel back."

"And you did that by blowing up my car, by trying to kill me?" Rachel snapped.

She definitely wasn't trying to calm him down now. Instead, she was dealing with her own anger, something that Griff understood, since he wanted to rip this idiot limb from limb for what he'd put Rachel through.

This time Brad didn't jump to answer, but Griff could practically feel the man's ire turning to rage. "You let him get you pregnant." Brad's voice was low and dangerous now. "Don't bother to deny it. I know about the pregnancy test."

Griff figured that was because of Brad's spies, which were seemingly everywhere. Of course, it wasn't something Rachel and he could have kept secret for long, but Griff would have preferred a gentler way of telling his sister and Warren. Both were too drugged up to react now, but he was certain he'd get an earful from Rachel's dad.

If they made it out of this, that is.

Griff had hoped he would be able to reason with Brad, but they were well past that now. Especially since Brad had probably killed Dennis and Buddy. Well, maybe he had. There was another player in this.

"What happened to the gunman you hired?" Griff asked. "The one who shot at Rachel and me in Silver Creek? Or was that you?"

"No." Brad cursed again. "It was Dennis and Buddy who did that. I told them to set someone up, and they chose Warren. The idiots. Marlon would have been a much better choice. And no, I didn't murder Dennis. Buddy did when Dennis turned on us and tried to extort money from us."

"Buddy only did that because you gave the order to do it," Griff said.

"No!" Brad repeated. "Buddy did that all on his own, and then he tried to get me to pay up. That's when I knew I had to put a stop to him. I put a tracker on his truck, and I followed him to the hospital in San Antonio. I think he was on his way there to tell Helen and anyone else who'd listen what I had done. I knew then I had to finish this myself."

Griff shook his head. "You could have just finished it by walking away, by accepting that it wasn't going to work out with Rachel and you."

Brad groaned, the sound of a man who was in a lot of mental pain. "I could never accept that. Never. And I'm tired of talking about all of this."

Griff was tired of it, too, especially since he was never going to convince Brad that he was doing the wrong thing. Still, there were a few more questions that needed answers.

"Are Simon, Alma or Marlon helping you?" Griff asked. He didn't expect Brad to respond and was surprised when he did.

"Of course not," the DA spat. "I wouldn't trust any of them with this. But Marlon will get what's due him. He'll be the one arrested for this."

Yes, but something about that didn't make sense. "Why drug Warren and take him to Silver Creek if you weren't going to make us think he was behind this?"

"That was all Dennis and Buddy's doing. Marlon's the one they should have focused on. Never trust idiots," Brad snapped. "Now, I'm playing cleanup. At least if the CSIs find my prints here in the house, they won't think anything about it because I've come here a lot. I'm a close family friend. *Was* a close family friend," he corrected, but his voice cracked on the words.

Obviously, Brad was going to set up Marlon in some way. For multiple counts of murder. And because of Marlon's past behavior, he would indeed be a suspect. Griff disliked Marlon, but the man didn't deserve this. Especially since Marlon's arrest would mean that Brad would go free.

If Griff didn't' do something, and fast, Brad might get away with it, too. He was the district attorney, and knew all the inner workings of the sheriff's office. He might even be able to manipulate the investigation.

But Griff wasn't going to let that happen.

No way would he let this lunatic kill Rachel and the rest of them.

Behind him, Griff felt Rachel move, and he hoped like the devil that she wasn't going to try to stand up. "So, the only person you've killed was a druggie CI who'd gone rogue," she said. "That's good. That means we can try to fix this."

Brad leaned out even farther, maybe to try to see her expression. It must not have been one he liked because he made a feral sound of outrage. "How could you have chosen Griff over me? He comes from nothing, and you let him touch you like that."

Hell. That wasn't the right thing for Brad to say to her. Griff was used to such talk, but it must have hit a nerve with Rachel because she cursed Brad.

Not good.

Because it apparently was more than the man could take. He aimed his gun at Rachel. Griff could have sworn his life passed before his eyes when he thought Brad might kill her.

But he didn't.

Brad didn't pull the trigger. He shoved Warren to the side and, yelling like a crazy man, charged right at them.

FROM THE MOMENT that Rachel had seen Brad holding her father at gunpoint, she had known it would come down to this.

This had become a fight for their lives.

She hadn't expected Brad to get rid of his human shield so that he could go after her, but the rage must have gotten the better of him. Griff apparently hadn't thought he would do that, either. Griff was already in the process of reaching for his gun on the floor, but had to stop when Brad plowed right into them and smacked them against the wall.

The DA was heavily muscled and outsized Griff by a good forty pounds, so the hit felt as if a Mack truck had come at them. The jolt from the impact shot through Rachel when her head collided with Thea's, and Griff's sister cried out in pain. Rachel hoped the woman wasn't hurt even worse than she already was. She also hoped that they could put a stop to Brad before he tried to kill them.

After all, Brad still had hold of his gun.

As close as he was, if he pulled the trigger now he could easily hit one of them. But why hadn't he just shot them when he was holding her father? Maybe Brad had figured that would have given Griff enough time to grab the gun and return fire. Then he would have been an easier target, since her father would have likely slumped down, leaving Brad's body exposed.

The impact of Brad slamming into him caused Griff to move farther away from his own weapon, and Rachel couldn't get to it, either. That's because Brad was now in the way. Even though he was right against them, he still managed to bring up his gun, and he bashed it against Griff's head.

The blood splattered across her face.

Griff's blood.

Sweet heaven. Now Griff was hurt. If Brad managed to knock him unconscious, he could try to beat him to death. Of course, she would do whatever it took to stop that, but she had to be careful not to get punched in the stomach. A blow like that could cause her to miscarry, and that was a risk Griff definitely wouldn't want her to take. Still, she couldn't just let him die. Not after…well, not after everything they'd been through.

Brad tried to take aim at her with the gun, but Griff latched onto his wrist, holding it with both hands. Brad could no longer shoot her, but he used his left fist to hit Griff anywhere he could reach.

Rachel glanced at her father to see if he was in any position to get one of the guns from the floor.

He wasn't.

Her dad was obviously still woozy, and was now groaning, maybe in pain. He'd taken a hard fall when Brad had pushed him, so he could perhaps be injured. After all, he was still recovering from the gunshot wound that he'd gotten just a month ago.

She couldn't think about that now, though. Not when Brad hit Griff again. Even though the blow was harder than the first one, Griff still managed to push Brad away, shoving him backward and then lunging at him. The impact sent them both sprawling into the middle of the floor.

Right on top of those guns.

Brad somehow managed to keep hold of his own

weapon, and even got in another hit to Griff's head. Not good. She wasn't sure how much more of this Griff could take.

Rachel had to figure out some way to stop this.

But how?

She stood up to try to get closer to the fight so she could help. Brad must have seen her out of the corner of his eye because he quit punching Griff and turned in her direction. He brought up his gun.

Big mistake.

Rachel saw rage fire through Griff's eyes, and he rammed his elbow, hard, into Brad's shooting hand. The DA's aim shifted to the right, but he still managed to pull the trigger.

The sound of the bullet blasted through the room. And through her. For several heart-stopping moments she thought she'd been hit, but she hadn't been. The shot tore into the china hutch right next to where she was standing.

Griff was still on the floor, but he grabbed Brad, trying to pull him back down. Cursing him, and her, Brad fought back. He was swinging his arms and fists wildly, obviously fighting for his life now. But then so were they.

Thea caught Rachel's arm, yanking her back down next to her. Just in time, because Brad fired again. He probably would have gotten off a third shot if Griff hadn't tackled him. This time, Brad didn't get the upper hand. Despite his size, Griff landed a punch on the man's jaw.

Brad's head snapped back, and he looked dazed. But that lasted only for a moment. The rage returned, and he probably would have tried to shoot her again if Griff hadn't continued to punch him.

Since Brad still wasn't giving up, Rachel scrambled across the floor to snatch up one of the guns that Griff, Thea and she had tossed there. She tried to take aim, but it would be too big of a risk for her to fire because she could hit Griff. She didn't pull the trigger.

But someone did.

Brad.

Unlike the other shots, this one was muffled. That's because the gun was between Brad and Griff.

Oh, God.

And that's when Rachel saw the blood.

Chapter Seventeen

Griff heard the sharp gasp that Rachel made, and even though he didn't want her anywhere near Brad, she came rushing toward them. He figured she was doing that because she thought he'd been shot.

And maybe he had.

It took Griff several long moments to realize that he wasn't in pain. Well, not in pain from a gunshot wound, anyway. He was hurting from where Brad had managed to punch him in the face too many times. However, the person who was in pain right now was Brad.

Groaning and cursing, Brad moved off Griff and looked down at the front of his shirt. There was blood and lots of it. In the heat of the fight, Brad had shot himself. But he was still very much alive.

Brad still had the gun, too.

And that made him even more dangerous than before. The sound that tore from his mouth didn't even seem human, and there was a wild, insane look in his eyes when his attention landed on Griff. Griff expected the man to try again to shoot him. He didn't, though.

Brad turned the gun on Rachel.

Griff's heart went to his throat, and he lunged at Brad as fast as he could move. This time he managed to wrench the gun from his hand. But it was too late. Griff heard Rachel make another sound. This time, it was a shout.

"No," she yelled. "Please, no."

It seemed like a prayer to him, and Griff was doing his own share of praying. He pinned Brad to the floor and looked at Rachel, hoping that he wouldn't see her wounded.

Or worse—dying from a lethal shot.

But he couldn't tell if she'd been hit because she turned and ran to her father. That's when Griff realized that Rachel was okay, but that Warren had been injured.

Griff couldn't go to her because he didn't want to risk letting go of Brad. The man was still very much alive, and Griff couldn't let him get away and try to go after the guns that were scattered around the room.

Thea was moaning, too, as she fought to get to her feet. Griff didn't know what she was going to do at first, but she kicked the guns away from Brad's reach and then took the jammer from the table. She bashed it against the china hutch.

Good.

Maybe now they'd be able to make a phone call.

"You'll need these," Thea said, taking a pair of plastic cuffs from her jeans pocket.

"Check on Rachel and Warren," Griff said, after he mumbled a thanks. "And try to call for an ambulance."

His sister practically stumbled across the room, a reminder that Warren wasn't the only one who needed medical attention. So did Thea. Probably Rachel, too. And

Brad, of course. But at the moment Griff didn't care if the man lived or died. In fact, it took everything inside him not to kill the DA on the spot.

Brad smiled, making Griff's rage go up a notch. "Rachel will never really be yours." He kept smiling while Griff got the cuffs on him. "No way will Warren McCall let trailer trash like you be with his daughter."

Griff hadn't even been sure that Rachel was listening, but she made a sound of outrage and came back toward them. Thea was on the phone, probably with the hospital, and had her hand pressed to Warren's shoulder. The older man was definitely bleeding, but not as much as Brad.

"Brad's dying," Griff told Rachel, because she looked ready to launch herself at the man.

She stopped, dropped down to her knees beside Griff and kissed him. "I just wanted you to know that I'm in love with you."

Maybe she'd said that as a dig to Brad, or Rachel could have just gotten caught up in the heat of the moment. Either way, Griff found himself wishing that the words were real, that she truly did feel that way.

Brad cursed them both, but they ignored him as they gazed at each other. There was plenty Griff wanted to tell her. Not in front of Brad, though. And definitely not while so many things were unsure.

"Egan and the ambulance are on the way," Thea relayed. "Someone needs to check on Ruby and the hands."

Griff certainly hadn't forgotten about them, but for a moment he'd been wrapped up in what Rachel said.

"I can go see about Ruby," Rachel volunteered, and

she was already turning to go there when Griff caught her hand.

"Wait here with Thea and your dad. Warren needs you right now." Yeah, that was playing dirty pool, to use her father, but Griff didn't want her straying off in case Brad had a hired gun somewhere in the house.

Griff dragged the DA to the corner and used his belt to tie up the man's feet. Even though Brad was cuffed and injured, he was desperate enough to try to make an escape.

After all, he would be facing multiple counts of attempted murder and at least one count of murder for killing Buddy. Being a DA wouldn't help him, and in fact might work against him. Brad had to know that he could get the death penalty for his crimes.

Once Griff was sure the man was secured, he picked up his gun and made certain Rachel was across the room with Thea and her father. She was, and was currently applying pressure to Warren's bleeding shoulder.

"Keep watch," Griff told his sister. He hated to put this on her right now, but there wasn't a choice.

Griff waited until Thea nodded before he hurried into the living room. It was still dark, since the power was off, but he spotted the woman right where he'd left Warren and her earlier. She was unconscious, though, which meant Brad had maybe drugged her after he'd used a stun gun on her.

Griff lifted her to a sitting position, propping her against the wall. It was all he could do for her now, so he went to check on the ranch hands. Brad had said he'd only tied up the men, but he could have hurt them, too.

Griff hadn't taken more than a step or two before he saw movement in the foyer. Someone was by the now-opened front door. Griff took aim but didn't fire, because it could be Egan or someone who worked at the ranch.

It wasn't.

It was Marlon.

The man stayed back, peering at Griff from around the edge of the door.

"What the heck are you doing here?" Griff demanded.

"Brad." And that was all Marlon said for several moments. "He brought me here. He said you were going to kill him and then set me up to take the fall. I can't let you do that."

Hell.

That's when Griff saw the gun that Marlon was holding by the side of his leg.

Even though the man didn't have it aimed at Griff, that could change in the blink of an eye. And worse, Rachel, Thea and Warren were all still in the dining room and could be hit if shots went through the walls. However, Griff figured he was Marlon's target now.

"Put down that gun," Griff warned him. "Brad lied to you," he added, though he doubted that Marlon was going to believe it. Especially since Marlon thought the worst about Rachel and him.

He shook his head, and he didn't put down the gun.

"Griff's the one lying," Brad shouted out. "He shot me. He tried to kill me."

Until then, Griff hadn't known that the others could hear Marlon and him. But they didn't just hear them,

Rachel peered out from the dining room, and she, too, had a gun.

"Get back!" Griff ordered.

But Rachel didn't move. "I'm not just going to stand here and let Marlon shoot you."

Griff was about to play dirty again and remind her of the baby, that this was too big of a risk to take, but he didn't get the chance. Marlon was lifting his weapon toward Rachel, but Griff didn't give him a chance to take aim.

He fired, sending two shots right into Marlon's chest.

The man looked down at the front of his shirt and his eyes widened. But only for a second before he dropped to the floor.

Griff cursed. Not just because Marlon had wasted his life, but also because Rachel had had to see another man die. Right in front of her. Heaven knew how long the sight of this would haunt her dreams. It would certainly haunt Griff's.

Outside, he heard the sound of a siren. Egan. It wouldn't be long now before he got there. Only a few minutes. But Griff didn't want him to walk in on another shooting, so he went to Marlon, kicked away the gun and checked to make sure the man was truly dead.

He was.

Griff shifted his attention back to Brad then. He was still alive, but was bleeding out fast. Warren was faring slightly better, thanks to Thea helping him. Rachel, however, didn't have a drop of color in her face.

She started toward Griff just as he went toward her,

and when she reached him, she practically fell into his arms. "I was scared," she whispered.

Yeah, he'd been terrified. Not for himself. But because he could have easily lost her to a gunman.

Griff couldn't help himself. He kissed her. And while it wasn't one of those heated kisses that had landed them in bed before, it was a reminder that even now the attraction between them was still strong.

A reminder, too, that it might be a whole lot more than just attraction.

Griff would have asked her about her "I'm in love with you" comment, but the cruiser pulled to a stop in front of the house, and Egan came barreling out. Not one but two ambulances pulled up right behind him. Griff let go of Rachel so he could head to the front door.

Egan's face was a mask of worry and concern. "Thea said Brad tried to kill you," he began. He glanced at Marlon on the floor, but his attention zoomed to his sister.

"I'm okay," Rachel insisted.

"You've got blood on your face," he quickly pointed out.

She wiped it away, looking at her fingers when she was finished. "Griff's blood. I'm the only one who wasn't hurt. Dad, Thea and Ruby all need to go to the hospital."

"So do you," Egan insisted. "I don't care if it's your blood or not. You're getting checked out by a doctor." He gave her hand a gentle squeeze before he went to check on Warren.

"I will, but only after everyone else," she argued as

her brother walked away. "There are two hands outside, tied up. They'll need to be checked, too."

"Court and Ian are circling the house now to make sure no one else is out there," Egan assured her. "They'll find the hands."

Two medics came rushing in, and Griff directed them to the corner where Ruby was still unconscious, and to the dining room. One went to Ruby, the other to Thea and Warren. Since this was going to quickly become a busy path, he took Rachel to one side of the living room.

Another medic came in and Griff pointed him in Brad's direction. That left Rachel and him standing there, and since she no longer looked steady on her feet, Griff slipped his arm around her.

"This one's dead," the medic called out, when he got to Brad.

Since Griff had known the man most of his life, he probably should have felt some sadness. He didn't. After what Brad had tried to do to Rachel, Griff was finding it hard to forgive him.

"He's dead," Rachel said, her voice a little shaky. He thought she might cry. She didn't. "At least we won't have to worry about him coming after us again. Marlon, either."

Yes, that was a big plus. No way did Griff want to go through anything like this again. There'd been enough danger for a couple lifetimes.

He glanced into the dining room, to see the medic moving from Brad to attend to Thea. The other one was still with Warren, and Egan was right by his father's side. In fact, Egan was now having a whispered conversation with him.

A conversation that caused Egan to glance back at Griff.

Hell. Warren had probably told him that Rachel was pregnant. Warren wouldn't have done that to rile Egan; he'd probably only told him so he'd make sure Rachel got some medical attention. But Egan wouldn't be pleased about it.

And that meant Griff had a decision to make.

The timing couldn't have been worse. Both Rachel and he had blood on them, and there was a dead guy just a few yards away. The law enforcement chaos was about to set in, because this was now a crime scene. Still, Griff didn't want to keep this inside him for another minute.

"You said you were in love with me," he stated, putting it out there. He only wished he'd softened his tone a little. It came out like an accusation.

Rachel stared at him. Then nodded. "And you're thinking I said that to get back at Brad."

Bingo.

"I didn't," she quickly added, before he could speak. "I wasn't talking to him when I spoke, but to you. That's because I *am* in love with you."

She paused, maybe waiting for him to respond. But Griff was going to have to gather his breath before he could do that. She had stunned him with those words.

"I know this doesn't make things perfect," she went on. Her tone wasn't soft, either. She sounded like she was in the middle of an argument. "Maybe my family will never want us to be together, but I don't care. And you shouldn't, either. You're a good man, Griff."

Again, no breath. Mercy. He'd always wanted to hear Rachel say those things, and now that he was hearing them, it felt like a miracle.

She frowned. "Now would be a good time for you to tell me how you feel about me."

Since Griff didn't trust his voice, he pulled her to him and kissed her. It was way too long and hot, considering that Egan was probably still aiming daggers at him. But Griff didn't care. He had exactly what he wanted in his arms.

He had Rachel and their baby.

Griff eased back, looked down at her, and was pleased to see that he'd left her a little breathless, as well. "I love you," he said.

Despite everything, that caused her to smile. "Took you long enough."

"We found the hands," someone called out. It was Ian. "They're okay."

Good. That was one less thing to worry about. That worry list was way too long, and it was nice to scratch something off it.

The news must have pleased Rachel, too, because she pulled Griff back for another kiss. This one wasn't nearly as long or hot, because Egan cleared his throat and walked closer to them.

He dropped his narrowed eyes from their faces to Rachel's stomach. "It's true?" he said. "Did the test confirm you're pregnant?"

"Yes," Rachel answered. Kissed her brother on the cheek. "You'll be an uncle, and even though you're scowling right now, I predict you'll be happy about this one day. Almost as happy as I am."

Egan glanced around the crime scene and huffed. "Well, I suppose if you can be happy in the middle of all this, then I won't punch Griff for getting you pregnant."

"No, you won't punch him," Rachel agreed. "Because Griff just told me he's in love with me. That's good, since I told him I was in love with him, too."

Egan didn't exactly jump for joy, but Griff took it as a good sign that the man didn't curse. "Fine. Because I was about to tell him that I expect him to marry you. Not immediately," Egan snarled, when Rachel made a sound of outrage. "Catch your breaths first. Get cleaned up. Kiss some more. And then you can talk about getting married."

That sounded a little like a brotherly decree.

One that Griff liked. A lot.

"Well?" he asked Rachel. "What do you think?"

She leaned in for another kiss. "Yes, to catching our breaths, getting cleaned up and kissing some more. Especially kissing."

And that's what Griff did. He kissed her, pulling her so close that her body was pressed against his.

"When we talk marriage, what do you think your answer will be?" he asked, with his mouth still against hers.

She smiled again. "Yes, of course. Always yes." She took hold of his shirt and pulled him even closer.

That robbed him of the breath he'd finally managed to regain, but Griff didn't care. He wanted Rachel far more than his breath, anyway, and he let her know that with his next kiss.

* * * * *

COMING SOON!

We really hope you enjoyed reading this book. If you're looking for more romance, be sure to head to the shops when new books are available on

Thursday
6th September

To see which titles are coming soon, please visit
millsandboon.co.uk